Praise

EVERY[...]
IN TH[...]
GROUP CHAT
DIES

'With biting, mordant humor, Chilton sends readers
on a serial killer hunt for our disassociated, true-crime-obsessed
social media age. I laughed out loud, I gasped at twists,
and I thoroughly enjoyed every minute of this ride. Highly
recommend!' **Ashley Winstead**

'This novel does exactly what it says on the tin! A funny, twisty,
bloodthirsty murder mystery. Great fun!'
Julie Mae Cohen

'A darkly humorous and suspenseful tale that masterfully
intertwines modern technology with classic thriller elements.
L.M. Chilton delivers a compelling narrative that kept me
turning the pages late into the night. Fabulous!'
Joanna Wallace

'A funny, inventive murder mystery that is a real
page turner. Fabulous!' **Victoria Dowd**

'A lovely escape... Features a twist that I never saw coming.'
Tasha Coryell

'*Everyone in the Group Chat Dies* starts with the brilliant
premise of receiving WhatsApp messages from a corpse.
It's twisty, pacy and devilishly funny. I loved it.'
Katie Marsh

'An absolute joy of a thriller: fast paced, full of suspense, and
laugh out loud funny. L.M. Chilton provides a deft skewering of
flatmate culture and revels in the true horror of the group chat.'
Sarah Bonner

ALSO BY L.M. CHILTON

Don't Swipe Right

EVERYONE IN THE GROUP CHAT DIES

L.M. CHILTON

HEAD of ZEUS

An Aries Book

First published in the UK in 2025 by Head of Zeus,
part of Bloomsbury Publishing Plc

9 7 5 3 1 2 4 6 8

A catalogue record for this book is available from the British Library.

ISBN (PB): 9781837930319
ISBN (E): 9781837930272

Cover design: Gemma Gorton

Printed and bound in Great Britain by
CPI Group (UK) Ltd, Croydon CR0 4YY

MIX
Paper | Supporting
responsible forestry
FSC® C171272

Bloomsbury Publishing Plc
50 Bedford Square, London, WC1B 3DP, UK
Bloomsbury Publishing Ireland Limited,
29 Earlsfort Terrace, Dublin 2, D02 AY28, Ireland

HEAD OF ZEUS LTD
5–8 Hardwick Street
London EC1R 4RG

To find out more about our authors and books
visit www.headofzeus.com

For product safety related questions contact productsafety@bloomsbury.com

EVERYONE IN THE GROUP CHAT DIES

ONE

They say there are three sides to every story: mine, yours and the truth.

So, which one do you want?

Most of you will plump for the truth, right? That's the obvious choice. But before you make your final decision, hear me out. Because I'm telling you, my version is pretty damn hard to beat.

I mean, maybe not this bit, obviously. Because right now, I'm fishing half-empty beer cans out of an over-chlorinated hotel swimming pool, wearing a bright orange baseball cap with 'Hot Mess And Doin' My Best' emblazoned across the front.

Casual observers might tell you that slogan is fairly accurate, and my boss would probably say it's something I should be aiming for. But, from my point of view, while 'hot mess' is arguable, I can assure you, I am resolutely *not* doing my best.

The baseball cap is part of the standard-issue 'SUNKISSED & SINGLE' uniform and, contrary to the label's wild claims that it's 100 per cent polyester, on a day like this, it feels more like wool. Despite the early hour, the sun has very much got

1

his hat on too, and is already beating down relentlessly on the white plastic sun loungers dotted around the pool.

SUNKISSED & SINGLE HOLIDAYS (yes, the capitalisation is mandatory) is the number one Magaluf travel company for singles. At least, that's what they told me – repeatedly – during the two-week intensive training boot camp in Bolton (aka the second worst fortnight of my life). I shouldn't whinge though. I mean, where else could one learn both the full dance routine to Beyoncé's 'Texas Hold 'Em' and the most effective way to remove sun-baked vomit from under a sun lounger?

My task this morning is getting the area ready for tonight's 'Tidal Rave' pool party. Thankfully, it'll be a good couple of hours before any of last night's revellers emerge from their rooms, meaning at least I can get on with it in peace. Galling as it is to be cleaning up after them, what makes it worse is that, at almost thirty-one myself, I was just over the age threshold for a 'SUNKISSED & SINGLE UNDER THIRTIES VAY-CAY PAR-TAY'. Those mere months of difference meant that while the guests partied, I polished; while they drank, I daydreamed; and while they slept off their hangovers, I searched the deepest depths of my black-hearted soul. But hey, with free board and unlimited access to the hotel continental breakfast buffet, things could be worse. And, crucially, I'm a thousand miles away from anyone who knows who I am.

Or what I did.

As I attempt to net the final elusive beer can, an inflatable unicorn floats across the pool, cutting a lonely figure in the morning sunshine. He seems to be giving me the eye, as if to say 'come, weary Cinderella, let me carry you for a while'. And frankly it would be rude to turn such a generous offer down, right? So, slipping off my plimsolls, I pop my phone and hotel key card in the heel and clamber onto Mr Sparklefarts* (*name of unicorn subject to workshopping).

Pulling the brim of the cap over my eyes, I lie back and try to block out everything but the soft lapping of the water against the tiles. In the distance, I can hear the faint beat of dubstep drifting over from The Strip as the bars prepare for the lunchtime crowds.

I know I can't lie out here forever. For one, I think Horny McPointyface* (*hmm, we can do better, people) might be slowly deflating, and two, I can feel my pale, English skin beginning to fry under the boiling Mediterranean sun. But I reckon I have at least two more blissful minutes before my overly officious team leader emerges from the hotel, yelling his favourite catchphrase: 'Kirby Cornell, this isn't a holiday, this is an opportunity!'

And then, because the universe hates me, I hear my phone buzz from the side of the pool, lighting up the inside of my shoe like a shit disco.

I paddle Princess Glitterhoof* (*ladies and gentlemen, I think we have a winner) over to see what world-shattering news requires my immediate attention. Turns out it's just a WhatsApp notification from an ancient group chat that I could've sworn I'd muted a long, long time ago. I swipe the notification to open the chat and read the message.

Despite the heat, the words send a shiver through me. I stare at the screen, rub the chlorine out of my eyes, then read it again.

> Esme
> miss me?

It's the first message anyone has written in this group chat for ages, but that's not the really weird thing.

The *really* weird thing is, Esme died twelve months ago.

TWO

As I watched the Victoria sponge slowly deflate, I was overcome by a deep sense of affinity for the sad, soggy cake on screen.

'Rubbish!' Dave yawned. 'They should get me on this show. I would absolutely ace the technical round.'

Dave – aka Dave 'The Legend' (more on that later) – had commandeered the big beanbag in front of the TV, which, under strict Flat Four rules, granted him dominion over that most powerful of devices: the TV remote.

'Unless the technical round now consists of reheating a Greggs sausage roll in the microwave,' Dylan said, stretching out a leg from the sofa to give Dave a friendly toe poke, 'I don't fancy your chances of a Hollywood Handshake, mate.'

'Can't we watch that new documentary? You know, the one about the woman who strangled all her Tinder dates?' Seema asked, not looking up from her phone. 'If I see one more Victoria sponge, I think I'm going to kill somebody.'

'Oooh, now there's a true crime doc I would actually watch,' I said. 'A bloody massacre in the *Bake Off* tent.'

Welcome to a standard Thursday night in Flat Four,

Stewart Heights, 106 Courtney Road. We were squeezed into our classic formation: me, Dylan and Seema next to each other on our tatty sofa with Dave nestled on the beanbag, all half-watching yet another amateur baker spectacularly fail to make a sponge rise.

Currently, we were four shows deep into what I called the Netflix Paradox: despite an almost infinite number of shows, there was absolutely nothing to watch. Or at least, nothing we could agree on. I dreamed of a day when the world would only have two buttons on the remote – murders and cakes – and everyone's lives would be a lot easier.

As Dave began another epic scroll through the gazillion thumbnails on the TV menu, I reached for another slice of pizza.

'New season of *Ghost Detectives UK*, get in!' Dave cried with glee.

Dylan rolled his eyes. 'Please God, man, not that load of bollocks. Those guys have never even detected so much as a bent spoon.'

'Uh, not true,' Dave said. 'Remember all those floating orbs in the last episode?'

'They see those things every bloody week!' Dylan groaned. 'How many times do I have to tell you! It. Is. Just. Dust! The Ghost Detectives should come to your bedroom sometime, they'd have a field day.'

Dave shook his head. 'You need to open your mind, mate. Science can't explain everything, you know. There are mysterious forces in this world that none of us truly understand.'

I flicked a pizza crust at his head.

'Hey!' He turned around and scowled at me.

'It was the mysterious forces!' I protested, holding my hands up in mock innocence.

When I'd moved into this place a year ago, the hotchpotch of randoms that lived here were, well, just that – randoms, thrown together by a shared inability to afford anywhere nicer. And, if I'm being honest, to a certain extent, they still were. Random, that is.

Dylan, a trainee chef at the local pub, came as a two-for-one with his best-mate-slash-sidekick Dave 'The Legend' Watkins, while Seema was a true-crime-obsessed dental nurse who only really graced us with her presence when she wanted to watch something on the 'big TV'.

And lastly, there was me, Clare 'Kirby' Cornell, hot-shot local journalist. Maybe you've read a few of my greatest hits, such as 'Lost glove found in tree' or 'Man freed after getting head stuck in bin'? No? Well, just you wait for the upcoming $200m Hollywood adaptation starring Tom Cruise as Man With Just One Glove and Jack Black as the voice of the CGI glove, which I am sure will hit multiplexes ANY DAY NOW.

Unless you are the aforementioned Tom Cruise, or your parents are minted, you've probably experienced the joys of a flatshare at some point in your life. For most people, they're a minefield of passive-aggressive notes on the fridge door and actively aggressive cleaning rotas, but not for Flat Four. No way. Here, we were all about endless Netflix marathons paired with a slice of cold pizza and washed down with a makeshift 'whatever's left at the back of the cupboard' cocktail.

On the whole, we were a pretty solid unit – more than could be said for the flat itself, which was barely functional most days. Complete with dodgy boiler and at least six mysterious cracks in the ceiling (that our landlord claimed were 'part of the ambience'), it was a cosy little four-bed on the top floor of an ex-council building. Oh, and by the way, when I say cosy, I mean shit.

In an attempt to squeeze out every last penny from the flat, our landlord was even threatening to rent out the tiny box room next to mine that had been empty all summer (and currently used as a dumping ground for dirty laundry and Dave's never-used pandemic-era exercise bike). Luckily for us, there wasn't exactly a rabid mob desperately refreshing Spareroom.com for a place to live in Crowhurst.

While Dave was distracted by my flying pizza crust, Dylan pinched the remote and flicked back to the *Bake Off*.

'We almost missed the vicar with the nose ring dropping his flan,' he said.

'God forbid!' Seema cried, snatching the remote off him. 'Why do you guys always get to pick anyway?'

'Because whatever we choose, you'll just spend the whole time texting Hot Dentist anyway,' Dave said.

Seema folded her arms and huffed. 'Literally no one calls him Hot Dentist.'

'*We* all call him Hot Dentist,' I said.

'Yes, you lot all call him Hot Dentist, but the rest of the world, the solar system, the universe, have never once called him Hot Dentist. For a start, he's not even a dentist.'

'Ah ha! So he *is* hot!' I cackled.

Seema bristled with frustration. 'I've told you a million times, he's a dental *therapist*, and technically he's my boss. So actually, it's against the law to refer to him as hot.'

'Okay,' Dave said. 'So why don't you go and text Not Hot Dental Therapist while you watch your gruesome murder shows in the privacy of your bedroom?'

'Well, then I'd miss all your insightful comments about my love life, wouldn't I, David?' she shot back.

While they argued, I turned away from the TV and gazed out the living room window behind us. It was a warm mid-August evening, still light, and the sky was turning a pleasing shade of orange. Across the rows of terraced houses opposite our building, I could see the flickers of television sets in every window and wondered how many were entangled in the same tedious negotiations. I exhaled, leaving a cloudy patch of condensation on the glass, onto which I drew a little sad smiley with my finger.

'Revolutionary idea,' I said, 'but maybe we just turn this thing off and do something else?'

None of them replied, too engrossed in the television.

'Guys!' I yelled. 'I said, let's turn the flipping TV off for once! Come on, look at us slobbing around the lounge. We're still in our twenties, for God's sake!'

'Late twenties,' Dylan added.

I shot him a look. 'I'm just saying, Reverend Patrick dropping his flan is the most interesting thing that's happened in this flat for months.'

'Hey, now come on, that's unfair,' Dave said.

'Is it?' I asked.

'Yeah, that dude from Solihull made a sourdough in the shape of Queen Elizabeth last week.' Dave bowed his head, made the sign of the cross across his chest and mouthed 'RIP Your Majesty' very quietly.

'That's not what I mean!' I cried. 'I'm saying surely there's something more exciting we could be doing with our Thursday evenings.'

Dylan patted me on the shoulder. 'We could watch *CSI* after this if you like?'

I launched a well-aimed cushion at his head.

'What's got into you?' Seema tutted, picking up the cushion and placing it back neatly. 'Normally you're the first one in your pyjamas.'

Thanks to her amazingly lush jet-black hair, Seema always managed to look glamorous, even when she was curled up on the sofa in a long cardigan and boyfriend jeans.

'These are *not* pyjamas,' I said, looking down at my Taylor Swift 2018 tour T-shirt and jogging bottoms. 'This is my post-work loungewear.'

(Reader, they were 100 per cent my pyjamas.)

'Remember when we used to go to the pub on a Thursday night?' I continued. 'Now we watch repeats of baking shows and eat pizza.'

'Well, that's when Thursdays were the new Fridays,' Seema said.

'Yeah, now Thursdays are the new *Sundays*,' Dave explained.

'Every day is the new Sunday around here!' I cried. 'Look at us, Dave's drinking a hot chocolate for goodness sake!'

'It's actually an Options,' he corrected me. 'Mint flavour. Only ninety-nine calories per cup.'

I pointed to his face. 'Are we just going to accept that? Dave "The Legend" is drinking a cup of mint-fricking-Options. Remember when he ate two entire rotisserie chickens in one sitting for a bet?'

There's a moment of silence. Unfortunately, we do all remember that, and it did not end well.

'We could get the bong out?' Dave suggested.

I glared at him. 'No, we are not getting the bong out, thank you, Legend.'

'Please don't use my nickname ironically.'

'We are literally drinking hot chocolate and watching *The Great British Bake Off* at seven p.m. on a Thursday night. I'm not sure the nickname still applies, Dave,' I said.

Dave was the kind of man who thought nothing of wearing a complete replica football kit indoors, shorts and all, but looked like he hadn't actually kicked a ball since 2014. I'd given him the nickname Dave 'The Legend' myself, and as much as he might deny it, it was an entirely ironic moniker.

'Alright, what do you want to do then?' Dave asked.

'I dunno. We could have a house party or something?' I suggested meekly.

'Seriously?' Dylan said. 'The last party we had ended with a game of Cluedo and you fell asleep on the sofa before midnight.'

'To be fair to me for a change,' I said, 'it was Strip Cluedo. And I only fell asleep because my hay fever medicine made me drowsy.'

'You know Creepy Frank's rule about parties, guys,' Seema said. 'And besides, aren't we getting a bit, you know, old for that sort of thing?'

Creepy Frank was our aforementioned landlord, who lived in the ground floor flat of the building, and I can assure you that *his* nickname was not ironic.

'What about a dinner party?' Dylan suggested. 'There's a show on here about how to roast the perfect parsnip...'

The three of us groaned at him in unison. The moment I agreed to a dinner party, I knew my thirties had officially arrived, and the slow, inevitable countdown to death had begun. So obviously, I was keen to delay that particular soirée until the last possible minute.

'Alright, that's it, no more TV. Gimme me that!' I cried, and launched myself at the beanbag, making a grab for the remote.

Dave tried to wrestle it out of my hand while Dylan whacked him with the empty pizza box and Seema stood there yelling at us to stop messing around before we broke something. Suddenly, we were interrupted by the ring of the door buzzer.

We froze and looked at each other in confusion.

'Who on earth is that?' I said. 'Everyone we know is here.'

Sticking the remote in the back pocket of my jeans, I headed into the hallway. But before I could look through the peephole, there was the clank of a key in the lock, and the door swung open.

'Hi,' said the young woman standing in our doorway. 'I'm Esme. Your new flatmate.'

THREE

'I'm sorry, what did you say?' I asked.

'The box room,' she announced, like it was the most obvious thing in the world. 'I'm renting it for the summer.'

Esme waved her door key at me before depositing it into the salmon-pink baguette bag hanging daintily over her forearm.

The box room's previous occupant, Max, was currently on a secondment in Birmingham. Much like the rest of the flat, it was freezing in the winter, stuffy in the summer and entrenched with the faint stench of damp pretty much all year through. But apparently our money-grabbing landlord must have found someone desperate enough to rent it until Max returned in the autumn. Although this Esme person did not, at first glance, appear to meet the classic definition of desperate. With heart-shaped lips and a black bob that fell effortlessly into a neat fringe just above her perfectly shaped eyebrows, she was quite striking.

Esme stepped into the hallway without invitation and peered into the lounge. Her presence had an immediate effect, like we'd been graced with a surprise visit from a minor royal. Dave's face lit up like a Christmas tree, while Dylan

13

started combing his hair back with his fingers. Seema began frantically tidying up the sofa cushions.

'Sorry the place is an absolute mess,' she said. 'Creepy Frank didn't tell us you were coming.'

'Creepy who?' Esme asked.

We looked at each other in confusion.

'Oh, wait, don't tell me Max sub-let you the room?' Dylan said with a groan of realisation.

'Is there a problem?' Esme asked. 'I'm just here for a couple of months, until he gets back from, um, Birmingham, isn't it?'

'That *wanker*.' Dave shook his head. 'Frank will kill us if he finds out.'

Esme's face fell.

'Oh,' she said, 'does that mean the room isn't available anymore?'

'No, no, it's totally available!' I said. 'In fact, it's never been more available! We were just saying things were getting boring round here. I mean, things are pretty much *always* boring around here. Don't let that put you off though!'

I took her hand and dragged her into the lounge.

'Welcome to Flat Four. Let me give you the tour. If you have a spare three minutes, that is. It's not exactly The Ritz, but we love it. Well, love is a very strong word. But we like it. Okay, maybe "like" is also a little excessive. Anyway, this is the living room. Obviously. All your usual amenities: beanbag, settee, coffee table. We hang out here a lot.'

I quickly kicked the pizza box under the sofa.

'And when it comes to Dave, hanging out is the operative phrase,' Seema said.

Dave glared at her. But it was true, when you lived in such close quarters, things like privacy and me-time were virtually non-existent. Since I'd moved in, pretty much nothing about my flatmates had been left uncovered, up to and including Dave's balls.

'Oh, and our pride and joy: the big TV, of course,' I went on.

The forty-two-inch mega-beast was the true centrepiece of our crumbling little flat. It boasted both Netflix *and* Amazon Prime (although, admittedly both passwords were stolen from ex-boyfriends, who so far hadn't noticed I was completely destroying their algorithms with multiple viewings of *The Holiday*, even in the middle of summer).

'But hey, you know, we were actually just about to go to the pub,' I said, pressing the off switch on the remote.

'Nice,' Esme said, but in a tone that was more neutral than Switzerland on a cloudy day.

'And at the end of the hallway are the bedrooms,' I pointed down the corridor. 'Oh, and, you'll love this. The best thing about having the top floor flat is, we can go up on the roof and sunbathe. Providing the good weather lasts, of course.'

'You have a roof terrace?' Esme asked.

'Actually, no,' Seema said. 'It's literally just a roof. But you can get up there from the box-room window. You can see the whole town from there.'

'Yeah, that's actually the best way to experience Crowhurst,' Dylan said. 'About a thousand yards away from any of the locals.'

'Dave goes up there with his bong when he gets stressed,' Seema added. 'He takes the inflatable mattress and gets stoned looking up at the stars.'

Esme raised one of her perfect eyebrows.

'Don't listen to her,' Dave said. 'I don't get stressed. If

anything, I'm the stress relief around here. I'm like one of those balls you squish when you're having a panic attack.'

'Everything is balls with you, Dave,' Seema muttered. 'And Creepy Frank will be the one having a panic attack if he ever finds out you go up there. It probably breaks every health and safety regulation going.'

'Frank's the landlord,' I explained to Esme. 'Max probably warned you, he loves sticking his nose in our business. Well, technically it's his business, I guess, cos he owns the place. Doesn't help that he lives in the ground floor flat, which is super inconvenient, especially when we have one of our infamous house parties!'

Dylan suppressed a laugh, but I ignored him and walked Esme down the hallway to the box room.

'And this is you,' I said, as I swung open the door. 'Excuse the exercise bike. And I'm sure Dave can blow up this mattress in no time.' I could feel my face flush with embarrassment.

'I'm sure I can manage,' Esme smiled, stepping inside. 'Excuse me while I unpack.'

I looked at her tiny bag and wondered what she could possibly be unpacking. But before I could ask, she'd closed the door. I turned around to face the others, who were crammed into the hallway behind me, watching everything.

'Flat meeting, now,' I hissed, marching them into the lounge.

'What is someone like her doing here?' Dylan asked.

He had a point. Crowhurst wasn't anyone's first choice for a summer holiday. The French Riviera it was not. Nestled in the foothills of the Bragland Fells, Crowhurst was a small countryside town with above-average views and a below-average attitude to newcomers. In short, it was dull. With a capital D. Maybe not quite the dullest town in the UK, but definitely up there alongside Longton and Reading. (And, yes, that was hypocritical coming from me, as I'd left a pretty cushy job writing for a trendy website in London to come here. But then again, I didn't have much of a choice – *The Crowhurst Gazette* was the only place in the country that had even considered giving me a job, after everything that went down at NewsBites.)

'I think she seems nice,' Seema said.

'You can say that again,' Dave grinned enthusiastically, shooting Dylan a conspiratorial look, like he was trying to mentally high-five him.

I rolled my eyes. 'Do me a favour, boys, and hold off trying to sleep with the new flatmate on night one, okay?'

Dave arched an eyebrow. 'You're the one who said we should make her feel welcome.'

'Not *that* welcome,' I said. 'How old do you reckon she is, anyway? She looks about twenty?'

'Who cares anyway?' Dave interrupted. 'An extra flatmate means cheaper bills for all of us, right?'

I had to admit the fact that my bank balance was currently pirouetting ungracefully around my overdraft limit did give the idea of a new roomie a certain appeal.

'Plus, she *is* pretty fit,' he added.

'Keep it in your pants, Dave,' Dylan sighed.

'Don't tell me you hadn't noticed, mate,' Dave said.

I wasn't going to mention it to Dave, but even I had noticed. I know, I know, we shouldn't compare ourselves to other women, but it's hard not to sometimes. It's not that I didn't like how I looked, but I did tend to shy away from a selfie these days. Kind people say I look a tiny bit like Emma Stone, but the less charitable ones go for Jessie, the cowgirl from *Toy Story*. Anyway, if you need a point of reference, imagine someone somewhere in between those two, on a bad hair day, and minus the cow-print chaps.

'Why any normal person would want that room is beyond me,' Seema said. 'Surely Max can't be charging her much for it? It doesn't even have a proper bed. And I still think it's totally off that he didn't tell us she was coming, by the way.'

'He's still on the flat group chat, but I think he's muted us,' Dylan said.

Seema looked worried. 'Frank will evict the lot of us if he finds out.'

'Simples. We just don't tell him.' Dave shrugged.

'David, please tell me you did not just use the Meerkat catchphrase,' Seema groaned.

'Lying to Frank is a bad idea,' Dylan said. 'What if he pulls one of his surprise inspections?'

'He can't just barge in here,' Dave said. 'He has to be invited in.'

'He's the landlord, not a vampire, hun,' Seema said.

I wasn't 100 per cent convinced by that. When it came to Creepy Frank, the line between landlord and Lord of the Undead was a little blurry. One of the big problems with living in the same building was that Frank was prone to 'popping round' when you least wanted him to. Which was pretty much anytime of the day, to be honest.

'Okay, well we can just pretend she's one of Dylan's one night stands,' Dave grinned.

Dylan gritted his teeth. 'I do not have one night stands.'

'We prefer the term TRLs,' Seema said. 'Temporary Romantic Liaisons.'

'I don't have TRLs either, thank you very much,' Dylan said. 'So we'll have to think of something else to tell Frank.'

'Don't worry,' Dave said. 'He'll be far too distracted with the fayre to even notice.'

Frank owned a lot of property in town, and took an unhealthy interest in local matters. He was on the Parish Council, the planning committee, the residents' association and probably ran the book club too. One of his many duties was overseeing the annual village fete aka the Crawe Fayre, the one day in Crowhurst's calendar when the whole town invited tourists to marvel at its overgrown marrows and risk their lives on the dilapidated bouncy castle.

'Why did you tell Esme we were going to the pub? It's my one night off!' Dylan said. 'The Lion is full of old men still arguing about Brexit and VAR. If you really want a drink, we have plenty of alcohol here. And a sofa that doesn't stink of stale beer and sweat.'

'Um, have you smelt our sofa lately?' I asked him. 'And this alcohol you refer to, do you in fact mean the three-year-old half-finished bottle of vodka in the back of the cupboard?'

'We have vodka?' Dave's eyes lit up.

'Come on,' I said. 'I'm sure we can drag our arses to the pub and pretend we're cool, fun young people for one night?'

'Hey, who's pretending?' Dave said. 'I can press The Fun Button any time you like.'

Word of warning, if you want to survive a night out in Crowhurst, don't ever let Dave The Legend push his so-called 'Fun Button'. Unless your definition of 'fun' is downing three pints and trying to flash the statue of the town founder on the high street.

'Tell you what,' said Dave, 'let's bet on why Esme has come

to the arse end of nowhere to spend the summer. Worst guess buys the first round.'

'Alright,' I said. 'You're on. I reckon her grandmother lives here or something, and she's come to look after her for the summer.'

'Nah, she doesn't exactly look like the caring type.' Dave screwed his face up. 'Maybe she's the secret love child of that retired footballer who lives down Weston Avenue? Apparently he's got about twelve illegitimate kids.'

'Does he even still live here? I thought he went to jail for tax evasion?' Dylan asked.

'What about an actor?' Seema suggested. 'Oh, you don't think she's making a podcast do you?'

'In Crowhurst? Come off it,' Dylan said. 'That would be the world's most boring show. There is absolutely nothing to get excited about here.'

'Hey, that's unfair,' Dave said. 'Crowhurst has its very own bogeyman, remember?'

Dylan glared at him. 'All that stuff happened thirty years ago. The last thing this town needs is a podcast, especially about *that*.'

'Reality TV star then,' Seema said. 'Final answer.'

'Dutiful granddaughter,' I said.

'Foreign exchange student,' Dave suggested, hopefully.

I rolled my eyes.

'Fine, undercover spy then.' Dave shrugged.

'Aren't all spies undercover?' I asked. 'That's sort of their "thing", isn't it?'

Before anyone could guess again, we heard the box-room door open, and Esme emerged, looking identical to how she had when she walked in. We all turned to face her expectantly.

'Hey, so we were wondering…' I started.

She held out her hand up to stop me.

'These walls are wafer thin.' She rapped her knuckles on one of them to prove her point. 'And sorry, but you're all wrong.'

'Oh,' I said. 'So why are you here then?'

A faint smile crossed Esme's lips.

'I've come here to catch a serial killer,' she said, matter-of-factly.

We stood there, mouths open, staring at her.

'So, what do I win?' she asked.

FOUR

If you didn't live there, you might expect a leafy suburban town like Crowhurst would be an idyllic pocket of Englishness, tucked away in the countryside, where children are constantly having *Famous Five*-style adventures in rowing boats. But the truth is, absolutely sod all happens here. In fact, it's so deeply embedded in the home counties that most people would have forgotten it even existed, if it weren't for three things:

A retired Burnley FC goalkeeper (that I can never remember the name of) lives here.

King Harold allegedly marched through what is now the ASDA car park, on the way to the Battle of Hastings.

And, oh yeah, thirty years ago, Crowhurst was home to the UK's seventeenth worst serial killer.

Waaay back in the Nineties, some guy called Peter Doyle murdered five teenagers, then promptly threw himself off Staker Point cliff. He wasn't even a very famous serial killer, I mean, relative to the other sixteen. Occasionally he'd pop up on a BuzzFeed list of the top-twenty underrated murderers, but compared to the rest of them, Peter Doyle looked like a

22

forgotten *X Factor* contestant who was booted out at Judges' Houses.

Melton Mowbray got pork pies. Crowhurst got an insane, bloodthirsty serial killer. Those are the breaks, I guess.

So, unless you happened to be a huge fan of either Burnley FC or murderous psychopaths, there really wasn't much reason to visit.

Take The Red Lion, our de-facto local, for instance. I'd love to tell you that it was one of those charming countryside pubs you might see in a British rom-com circa 2003, full of cosy fireplaces and floppy-haired posh boys in polo-neck jumpers. But I'd be lying. Instead, it had a stack of falling-apart board games in one corner and some absolutely rank-looking homemade scotch eggs in the other. Honestly, Jude Law would take one look at the place and get the first Uber Exec back to Chelsea. That is, if you could even get an Uber around here.

Luckily (or unluckily) for us, it was right at the end of our street.

It's fair to say Esme, who was wearing a crop top and Adidas Gazelle trainers with white socks pulled up over the ends of her jet-black leggings, looked a little out of place.

'Here we are! Crowhurst's premier night spot,' I said, ushering her in through the door.

Her face remained utterly expressionless as she surveyed the smattering of locals, quietly sipping their pints of pale ale while staring at the packets of nuts hanging behind the bar.

While Dave immediately bought a round of dubious-looking shots, we sat down at the table at the back (I should say *our* table, because when we used to come here every week, we always bagsied the big one at the back with the comfy armchairs).

'Wow, really buzzing in here tonight,' Dylan said, looking around.

'Hey, this actually counts as busy for a Thursday in Crowhurst,' I said, elbowing him in the ribs. 'And it's either this or another episode of bloody *Ghost Detectives*, okay?'

Dylan sighed and reached for a shot glass. He downed the murky brown liquid and immediately gagged.

'Sweet Jesus, what was in that, Dave? It tastes like something the devil threw up.'

'Tonight's special. Barman called it "Black Death": vodka with a dash of soy sauce.'

He passed a shot to Esme and she recoiled like he'd handed her a hand grenade with the pin out.

'Can't be worse than the Eggermeister,' Seema said, tipping it down her throat.

I grimaced at the memory. Last time we were here, the 'special' was a pickled egg doused with a shot of Jägermeister. Unsurprisingly, Dave The Legend was the only one 'special' enough to try it.

'Sorry, it's bit of an old man's pub,' I said, motioning to the regulars propping up the bar, whose eyes were following Esme's every step. 'They're not used to anyone under thirty in here.'

'It's cool,' Esme nodded, sipping her soda.

I had to wonder if cool meant something different to Gen Z, because this place definitely did *not* fit any definition of the word that I knew.

'Dylan will be thrilled to hear that. He works here,' I told Esme.

'In the kitchen,' Dylan quickly clarified. 'I'm not a barman, I'm the chef.'

Dylan secretly aspired to be one of those intense chefs you see on American TV shows. You know, the type you'd see hanging out the back of the kitchens after a tough shift making a particularly tricky soufflé, smoking a cigarette and looking like they haven't slept in a week. But in reality, he was less 'The Bear' and more 'The Badger'.

'Yeah, he's normally tied to the microwave out back,' Dave said. 'Little bit of advice: never order the shepherd's pie, it's straight out of the ASDA freezer.'

'Ignore him,' Dylan said. 'Dave's been hit in the head with one too many golf balls.'

'I happen to give golf lessons at a very exclusive Country Club down the road,' Dave explained to Esme.

'Is that what they're calling Crowhurst Pitch and Putt these days?' Seema asked, while tapping away on her phone.

'Guys, guys, let's not argue in front of the children,' I said. 'We get it. Dylan's going to open a Michelin Star restaurant on Crowhurst high street. One day Dave will caddy for Tiger Woods. A glittering showbiz career whitening Love Islanders' teeth awaits Seema. And I'm going to be the first person to win a Pulitzer prize and an Olympic gymnastics gold medal in the same year.'

'So *that*'s why they call us the Deadbeats,' Dylan said dryly.

'So now that everyone is suitably impressed, how about we get to know our new flatmate?' I said. 'You were joking about coming here to catch a serial killer, right?'

'Oh God, unless… don't tell me you mean Peter Doyle?' Seema asked.

'Good luck with that one,' Dave laughed. 'You'll need a shovel. That prick's been dead for thirty years.'

When he said that, the pub seemed to go strangely quiet. I glanced round at the group of older men at the next table, who seemed to be staring at us now.

'Are you a journalist too?' I asked.

Esme looked at me somewhat blankly. She was at that age where you don't even have to be pretty to be pretty, all dewy skin and high cheekbones, a smattering of freckles decorating her petite nose. I noticed she was wearing a cute, gold necklace with a lowercase 'e' hanging from it.

She picked up her phone, poked the screen a few times then turned it towards us. A video of Esme, fully made-up and animatedly talking to the camera, was playing.

'Oh, so you're a TikToker?' I said.

She smiled at me and shook her head, like I was a grandmother confused by a TV remote with too many buttons. 'It's called ShowMe. TikTok is so last year.'

Dylan nudged me with his elbow. 'Yeah, come on, Kirby, TikTok is *sooo* last year.'

'Hey, I know what ShowMe is!' I protested.

Truth was, while I had seen the new video-sharing app on my fourteen-year-old cousin's phone, I'd assumed it was 99 per cent make-up tutorials and dance routines. Neither of which would require moving to the back end of nowhere.

'ShowMe is a little bit wilder than TikTok, a little bit edgier,' Esme explained.

'You mean less regulated?' Dylan raised an eyebrow.

Esme narrowed her eyes at him. 'No, I mean it's uncensored.'

She handed me her phone, and I looked at her profile. Her username was @ShowMeSherlock and she had a lot of followers. And by a lot, I mean nearly half a million. I scrolled through a couple of her videos. In the first one, I could see Esme walking around a field, before focusing the camera on a set of footprints in the mud. In the second video, it was just her face talking to the camera while she occasionally pointed to a montage of screenshotted news headlines and photos behind her. The videos had a disorientating effect, making me feel confused and exhilarated in equal measure.

'I investigate cold cases, unsolved murders, missing people, things like that,' Esme said.

'Oh, right, you're one of *those*,' Dylan said.

'One of what?' She turned her cold, green gaze on him again, like a beam of Kryptonite.

'One of those armchair detectives.'

'Armchair?' Esme looked slightly offended.

'Actually, they don't really like that label,' Seema interjected. 'Some of them find it a bit disrespectful.'

Seema, having exhausted every true-crime documentary/ podcast/based-on-a-true-story drama known to humankind, knew her stuff.

'Disrespectful? Isn't what they do a bit disrespectful to the victims and their families?' Dylan asked. 'I wonder how they feel, seeing this plastered all over social media?'

'I'll show you exactly how they feel,' Esme said. Taking her phone back, she flipped through her videos until she found the one she wanted, and turned the screen to us.

It showed Esme, approaching a red-brick terraced house. She knocked on the door until an older woman appeared, and then handed her a plastic bag. The woman delved inside, pulled out a tatty blue jumper, and then immediately started crying. I felt a sharp pang of sympathy for her, and I couldn't help but think about my mum, who, full confession, I hadn't called since I left London, and how she'd feel if anything ever happened to me.

'That was her son's sweater,' Esme said, closing the app and putting her phone down. 'I found it discarded about two hundred yards from where he went missing. The police missed it, but I didn't.'

'Isn't that, like, evidence?' Seema asked.

'Maybe, but you saw how much it meant for his mother to have it,' Esme shrugged.

'She'd rather have her son back, I reckon,' Dylan shrugged.

Esme's expression stiffened for a second. 'I'm all about helping people.'

'All about increasing your follower count, more like,' Dylan said, barely under his breath.

'Shouldn't you let the police deal with all that stuff?' I asked. 'I mean, that's their job, after all, that's what they're trained for.'

'The police?' For the first time, I saw Esme drop the ice-cool act for a split second, and her voice sharpened. 'Don't make me laugh. You really trust the police? They're the ones committing the crimes half the time. And if they're not committing them, they're covering them up or taking bribes or—' She stopped, composed herself and reached for her vape pen.

'I don't think you can smoke that in here...' Seema started.

Esme ignored her and sent a plume of strawberry-scented smoke across the table. 'Anyway, there are things that the police can't do, legally anyway. But I can. And that means I actually get shit done.'

I wondered what she meant by 'shit done'. There was no

mystery to solve here, no miscarriage of justice or dangling threads.

'The Crowhurst murders aren't a cold case,' I said. 'They don't need investigating. Everyone knows what happened. Peter Doyle killed those people. The case is well and truly closed.'

'That's just it,' she said, her pale green eyes resting on mine. 'I'm not so sure it is.'

FIVE

Dylan folded his arms and leant back in his chair. I could tell he was not on board with any of this.

'People around here aren't going to like it if you go around digging up all that stuff,' he said. 'Crowhurst has moved on.'

Dylan and his mum had lived here their entire lives, and even though he liked to pretend he was far too cool for this arse-end-of-nowhere town, I was sure it was a case of 'the chef doth protest too much'.

'Okay, chill,' Esme's face softened, 'I only plan on being here for a month or two, max. I just want to make a few videos, talk to some of the locals, follow up a couple of leads, then I'll be out of your hair. But if you're really not comfortable with this sort of thing, I suppose I can go and find a hotel or something.'

'Good luck with that,' Seema said. 'There's a Travelodge about 30 miles up the A24, but that's about it.'

'Tell you what, let's vote on it,' Dave said. 'On the count of three.'

Esme looked puzzled as we all put our fists behind our backs.

'This is how we decide things in Flat Four,' I explained. 'Watch.'

'One, two... three!' Dave cried, whipping out his fist and proudly waving his thumb in the air.

I looked over at Seema, who was grinning at me with her thumb up too. Dylan's hand was still behind his back.

I stuck up my own thumb, and a faint smile spread across Esme's face. Then, in unison, we turned to look at Dylan expectantly. Dave drummed his fingers on the table to build up tension as Dylan held his fist out, wobbling it like a Roman emperor about to decide the fate of a brave gladiator.

'Fine,' Dylan sighed, shaking his head as he flicked his thumb upwards.

We all whooped in approval.

'Four out of four!' Dave grinned, looking and sounding like an excited puppy. 'You're officially one of us now. Welcome to the Deadbeats!'

'Uh, cool, I guess,' Esme said, picking up the final shot of Black Death and tipping it into her mouth. She grimaced, then slammed the glass down on the table, much to Dave's delight.

'That's more like it! We need to toast this momentous occasion properly!' he said. 'Another round?'

'Stay there, Legend,' I said, getting up. 'This one's on me.'

I made my way to the bar, dodging a few more unsavoury glances from the locals. As I attempted (and failed pathetically) to catch the eye of the barman, I felt a tap on my shoulder. I turned around to see Esme.

'Thought you might need a hand,' she smiled.

'Thanks, maybe you can get this guy's attention.' I nodded in the direction of the barman. 'I mean, I know I'm not as young as I used to be, but there was a time when I was good at this.'

Esme raised a hand, and the guy came to her immediately. I tried not to be offended and placed our order. While the barman poured the drinks, we stood in awkward silence as I pretended to find the coasters on the bar incredibly fascinating.

'So, um, are you single?' I asked, unable to think of anything better to say.

'Depends who's asking,' she replied.

'How about nobody?' I laughed. 'Cos there is literally no one to date here. Honestly, it's like the Pied Piper came through Crowhurst and lured all the eligible men under forty away. Probably by playing "Wonderwall" on acoustic guitar.'

'What about Dylan?' she asked.

'Dylan? Please,' I scoffed. 'I said eligible.'

'Well, he totally likes you,' Esme said.

I almost snorted with laughter.

'Hasn't taken his eyes off you all night,' she added.

'Are you kidding? Dylan wouldn't go for someone like me,' I said, glancing back round to look at our table. Dylan and Seema were laughing at Dave as he tried to balance a shot glass on his chin. I guessed the 'Fun Button' had been well and truly pressed.

I mean, some people might say Dylan was good-looking, in a conventional way. If you liked the brooding, cynical type, that is. He's got *conventional* thick, wavy dark brown hair that is always falling over his deep, soulful – but extremely *conventional* blue eyes. Sometimes, if you were very lucky, you might get a flash of his wide, dumb – but utterly *conventional* – grin that, sure, has probably melted a couple of hearts.

But I'd lived with Dylan for nearly a year, and he'd seen me in my jogging pants, no make-up, eating Honey Loops on the sofa at eight p.m. more times than I like to mention. And that's an image that's hard to get out of your head. Even so, I guess we've sort of flirted, a bit. And it's not like I didn't find Dylan attractive *per se*. Like I said, he was handsome, if you liked that sort of thing. But dating a flatmate would just be asking for trouble, right?

'Well, if you're not interested, do you mind if I...' Esme began.

'Oh yeah, you should totally go for it! He's one of the good ones. I think. If there even is such a thing these days. I mean, maybe he's a bit old for you? And he works a lot of late shifts. Oh, and you'll probably be fighting off most of Crowhurst's divorcees. But, yes, in conclusion, yep. One hundred per cent. Do not let me stop you. Not a problem with me, by any means.' I looked back at Esme, who couldn't hide the smirk on her face.

'Chill,' she laughed. 'I'm not even into guys at the moment.'

'I hear you, sis. Going boy sober for the summer, good plan,' I nodded.

'Um, yeah, something like that.' Esme smiled ambiguously.

Just then, the barman placed three freshly drawn pints and a glass of soda water on the bar, saving me from shovelling myself into an even bigger hole.

'Oh, hey, now you're officially a Deadbeat, you know what this means?' I said, desperate to change the subject. 'We can add you to the flatmates group chat!'

I whipped out my phone. I absolutely *loved* a group chat, probably because, as you might have noticed, when I engaged in actual face-to-face conversations with humans, they tended to quickly head southwards. Maybe that's why I'd ended up writing for a living, because if I had time to think about each word before I committed to it, I usually made a lot more sense.

If you're anything like me, you'll have at least eight or nine group chats on the go. I was constantly flicking through them, just to see if anyone was doing anything exciting and/or sharing a half-decent cat meme.

Not that any of them were very active these days. No one had posted in the Cornell Family Chat for months (last post: Dad whining about the price of petrol these days). And the most chat we'd had on Tortellini Gang (old school friends I hadn't seen for a decade) was when Gillian questioned whether it's okay to ghost a paramedic, or if key workers deserve an exemption. SurreyWideBoys was mostly my work buddies wildly speculating if the paper would survive until Christmas.

But the Deadbeats group chat was my absolute fave, mostly because, since leaving London, I'd lost touch with a lot of my old mates. Moving to Crowhurst was supposed to be a fresh start, and the Flat Four crew had no pre-conceptions of me, which was the way I liked it.

'I mean, it's mostly updates about the broken toilet flush three times a day and photos of my lunch,' I told Esme. 'But there's some good bants on there too. Shit, I shouldn't say bants, should I? I sound like a middle-aged man on a stag do.'

'It's all good,' she said, picking up the water and taking a delicate sip. 'Here's my number.' She held up her phone so I could copy it down.

'You're in!' I smiled, as a little notification popped up on her screen. 'Trust me, you're gonna love it so much you'll never want to leave.'

SIX

PRESENT DAY

Max Robertson has left the chat.

I'm lying in the hammock after my shift, soaking up the dregs of Magaluf sunshine, when this notification pops up on the Deadbeats group chat.

I've ignored the weird messages from 'Esme', figuring it was someone's idea of a stupid prank, and instead, I'm busy dousing myself with a generous helping of factor 30. I debate snapping a quick 'legs or hot dogs' pic, but ultimately decide it's far too 2018. And also, I try really, really hard to avoid social media these days.

It's not like I've had a lot worth posting over the past year. Ever since Esme died, I've been drifting. Some might even go so far as to say I was hiding. The truth? Well, we'll get to that.

A potted history of my employment over the last year: three months sofa-crashing, some disastrous bar shifts, a spell teaching English to some very confused Japanese mature students, all followed by my current stint at SUNKISSED & SINGLE. My chances of another glittering job in journalism were about the same as me getting a decent tan, so what was the point in even trying?

No one has replied to this morning's message from 'Esme' on the Deadbeats group chat, so when my phone dings with another notification, Max's name is the last one I expect to see. To be honest with you, I'm kind of amazed he was still in the chat at all. I'd assumed he'd quietly snuck out ages ago. It's not like he ever posted in it, even when he lived with us.

I haven't seen Max since he moved out of Flat Four, a few months before Esme moved in. Frank re-let the flat after we all left town, and as far as I know, Max never came back to Crowhurst after his secondment. I have no idea if he knew about what happened to Esme, or if he even cared.

I tap 'Max Robertson' into Google, half out of curiosity, half out of the desire to think about something other than Esme. Shielding my eyes from the sun, I scroll through the first few results, until I see a headline that makes me freeze.

COMMUTER HIT BY RUSH-HOUR TRAIN

I can't click on the link fast enough, but unfortunately the reception here is even weaker than my work ethic. The page only half-loads, showing me just a black-and-white photo of a grinning man at the top of the page under the headline. But I recognise him instantly, the hair is a little bit thinner, and his teeth are straighter – but that's Max alright.

'Your network connection is unstable' my phone kindly informs me.

Yeah, well, so am I, pal, but hey, like my hat says, I'm trying my best.

When the rest of the page finally loads, I quickly scan the article.

Thirty-two-year-old marketing consultant Max Robertson was waiting for the train at Birmingham Moor Street during rush hour yesterday morning. Witnesses reported that the platform was extremely crowded, and Max lost his footing while jostling for a better position. He was carried by the train some distance down the platform, and an ambulance declared him dead at the scene.

I almost fall out of the hammock.
Max is dead.
I stare at the screen, my jaw hanging open. I admit I never really knew him that well, but still, *dead*. And in the most horrible way possible. Max and I hadn't been flatmates for very long, but to be honest, not to speak ill of the dead or anything, he'd always been a little bit of an arsehole. Not that all arseholes deserve to be hit by speeding trains, of course.

I check the date on the article and see that it is two days old. But that doesn't make any sense, because Max only left the group chat just minutes ago...

Quickly, I copy the link and paste it on the Deadbeats chat.

> have you guys seen this? It's so awful

I wait a few seconds for a reply, but when it looks like none of them will, I push my phone away from me in frustration. Just as I do, it pings with a new message alert.

'Finally,' I say under my breath. 'One of them actually cares.'

But then I see the message, and the whole world seems to stop turning for a second.

Esme
Everyone in the group chat dies.

SEVEN

TWELVE MONTHS AGO

Group Chat: The Deadbeats

> Kirby
> getting kebabs, see you back at the flat

> Seema
> pls don't go to the Grillennium Falcon, u know what happened to Dave last time

> yeah I think that's when the toilet flush got broken

> Dave The Legend
> UNDER NO CIRCUMSTANCES GET THE PRAWN DONER

After we were kicked out of The Red Lion at closing time, we stumbled back through the town centre. Even though it was nearly midnight, the August evening was warm, muggy almost. We were in the middle of a mini-heatwave, and it had been pushing 27 degrees for nearly a week, but it felt like a storm might be finally coming.

The others had gone on ahead, but Esme and I were hanging

back, partly because, thanks to the delightful mixture of Pinot and Black Death, I was having to take each step quite, quite carefully.

Inspired by the Christmas gift of a Fitbit watch from my father (arrived in the post, a week late, from Amazon, with no card), my new year's resolution had been to walk 10,000 steps a day. I had decided that, in my thirtieth year on earth, it was time to finally live up to my potential. Eat better. Drink less. And try to manage slightly more exercise than just my daily trek from the fridge to the sofa. I'd even fiddled with the settings so that the watch would play the loudest, most annoying beepy song of congratulations when you reached the magic 10,000 steps, because I wanted the whole world to know when I reached that glorious milestone. Yes, I was well aware it was the middle of summer, and so far, I had spectacularly failed to ever reach that target. The closest I'd come was a hungover afternoon in the big ASDA, where I'd spent three hours wandering the aisles staring at food like I'd never been in a supermarket before.

So far today, I'd reached a whopping 620 steps.

'Want a puff?' Esme asked, holding out her vape pen.

'Oh, um, okay, go on then,' I said tentatively.

I'd smoked for all of about three weeks when I was fifteen, desperately trying to impress a floppy-fringed boy from my English class who worshipped Hemingway (hey, what can I tell you, I was in my shy-boy era). But Dad found my pack of Gauloises in my PE bag and promptly sat me down for a very long (and to be fair, quite interesting) lecture on the increasing rates of lung disease across the UK. And that was that. But a little toke on a vape couldn't hurt, right? Besides,

Dad hadn't taken much interest in anything I'd done for the last ten years, so I figured what the hell.

I sucked in a mouthful of Strawberry Ice. It was a bit like eating candy floss, but without getting sticky pink sugar all around your mouth. I was actually enjoying it, until the sweet smell of the fumes was usurped by the even more alluring vinegary whiff of chips.

'Shall we?' I asked, pointing to the burger van that was parked on the high street. 'Unless I eat something, I'll be hanging at work tomorrow.'

Esme shrugged her approval, and I steered us towards the Grillennium Falcon, Crowhurst's best (and only) food truck. I leant on the counter, letting the hot, greasy steam billowing from the fryer hit my face.

'Chicken kebab and fries for me, please,' I said, giving the guy a cheery smile. 'And…'

But when I looked over at Esme, she was eyeing the van like it had just taken a giant dump on her doorstep.

'Um, do they have anything that's not made from dead animals?' she said, mouthing 'vegan' when she saw my bemused expression.

I gave her an enthusiastic thumbs up and turned back to the van window.

'Uh, actually make that two bean burgers, please,' I said in a low voice. 'And, um, maybe hold the fries, thank you.'

He grunted an acknowledgement and flipped a couple of patties onto the hot plate.

'Cows don't grow on trees, right?' I said, turning back to Esme. *God, why did I say that? What does that even mean? I was such a grade-A doofus sometimes.*

Esme was looking at her phone, and either didn't hear me

or had nothing to add to that incredibly deep piece of wisdom. Eventually the guy plonked our burgers unceremoniously on the counter, neatly wrapped in greaseproof paper. I took one, handed it to Esme. She tossed her hair back and took the daintiest of bites, while I side-eyed the other. I'd been promising myself since my birthday that I'd go veggie at least two days a week, but now, drunk at midnight on a school night with a hangover already peeping over the horizon, really wasn't the time to start.

We turned onto our street and Esme immediately started filming on her phone. I couldn't think why, as Courtney Road was hardly one of Crowhurst's top sightseeing spots (unless you had a desperate urge to read the spurious claims about Colin McAdam's penis that are daubed all over the bus stop). It was dark and the street was empty. The only movement was the plastic tape around the roadworks, fluttering in the breeze, occasionally catching the glare of the flashing orange lights around the large hole in the road.

'Looks so eerie, doesn't it? Good to get a bit of B-roll footage to set the scene,' she said.

I nodded, my mouth full of burger. It didn't look that eerie to me, to be honest. Just like every other street in every other town with a stretched local council budget in the middle of a cost of living crisis. When Esme pointed her camera at a telephone pole, I thought she must be taking the piss, until I saw that it wasn't the pole she was interested in. Clumsily stapled to it was a badly photocopied poster for the village fayre.

'ANNUAL CRAWE FAYRE! Celebrate the harvest this weekend at the Crowhurst Recreational Ground!' it announced proudly in size eighteen papyrus font. 'Raffles, rides and tarot readings. Stoning of the crow begins at 7.30 p.m.'

Underneath, there was a black-and-white photo of someone wearing a cheap-looking crow costume, holding its wings aloft, like it either wanted a cuddle or was going to peck your eyes out. Either way, I think I'll pass.

'This was where Peter Doyle murdered those teenagers in 1996,' Esme said.

'Kind of gross, isn't it?' I said. 'You'd think being the scene of a bunch of gruesome murders would put off the tourists. But the fayre has been going for hundreds of years apparently. Back then, the town elders probably used to perform some sort of satanic ritual while sacrificing the local virgin. Now it's just a bunch of rigged coconut shies and a bouncy castle.'

Esme frowned, like she'd actually been hoping some poor sod would be burnt at the stake.

'At least the papers didn't give Peter Doyle some cheesy name like "The Crowhurst Killer",' I went on.

'Ooh, Crowhurst Killer,' she said, her eyes widening. 'Sick, I'll use that.'

'Oh, no, please don't. The guy was a psychopath. He doesn't need a cute alliterative nickname.'

'It'll make a great hashtag though,' Esme said, brightly.

She lowered her phone and stared at the poster for a second before tapping a perfectly manicured fingernail on the photo of the crow.

'He was dressed like this when he killed them, wasn't he?' she said quietly. 'Wild.'

'Yeah, that's Jack Daw,' I explained. 'He's like the town's weird mascot-slash-bogeyman. Someone dresses up as him for the parade every year. I guess in 1996 they picked Peter Doyle. Big mistake, huh?'

I sensed this might be my moment to ask her what she'd meant in the pub about her so-called investigation.

'So, is that why you've come to Crowhurst?' I asked. 'For the fayre? Do you think something is going to happen there? Something to do with the murders?'

Esme smiled at me enigmatically. 'You'll just have to follow me to find out.'

'Hmm, well, that's gonna be tricky, because I'm not on ShowMe.'

'Shame,' she said. 'You'd be good on it.'

'Really? You think I could be a ShowMeSherlock?' I laughed.

I couldn't imagine anyone would be interested in anything I had to say. My social media output was limited to the odd sunset or, if pushed, hot-dog legs on holiday (although with my legs, saveloys would be more accurate). After what happened in London, I could do without the endless trolling and misogynistic comments.

'Anyone can do it, if they put the time in,' Esme said. 'People don't see the hours I spend on re-takes and editing. Honestly, it's a full-time job.'

That made me wonder if it actually *was* her job. I couldn't imagine she was getting many product placement deals on her bloodthirsty serial killer content. Maybe she was sponsored by Strawberry Ice vapes?

'Oh yeah, of course, I didn't mean...' I buried my face in my bean burger. 'I wouldn't know where to start.'

'Comes naturally to me, I think. Maybe in another life I might have been a forensic scientist or a criminal psychologist, or something,' she said. 'But you have to study for years to do that. You're a journalist though, right? You must do investigations like this all the time.'

'Are you kidding?' I replied. 'I'm not sure "Whatever Trevor" is ever going to let me write about anything other than the council's inability to finish any of these roadworks.'

So far, everything I'd written for *The Gazette* had been mind-numbingly dull. To be fair, there wasn't exactly a lot going on *to* write about. If New York is the city that never sleeps, then Crowhurst was the town with chronic narcolepsy.

'What's a "Whatever Trevor"?' Esme asked.

'Oh, right, sorry, that's just what I call my boss, Trevor, *The Gazette* editor,' I said. 'Nice guy. Looks a bit like an angry peach. Makes me sit through endless town-planning meetings. He took a real chance on me, but I wish he'd let me loose on the fun stuff occasionally.'

Esme eyed me suspiciously. 'You think serial killers are *fun*?'

'No, of course not. I just mean they're a bit more exciting than writing about those.' I pointed to the large hole in the road, right outside Stewart Heights. 'I feel like I've been reporting on the unfinished roadworks since I got here. Trevor says I'm not ready for anything else yet.'

'So why are you doing what this Whatever Trevor guy says? You don't need some boomer telling you what to report on.'

Leaning against the lamppost, I stared into the depths of my stupid bean burger, hoping it might suddenly decide to tell me all the answers.

'Well, mainly cos "try not to get fired" is top of my to-do list this month, I guess. And Trevor is probably right, you know? I'd just make a mess of it. Do you have a job? Or can you make money out of… this.' I waved my hand at her phone.

'Rich parents,' Esme explained.

'Oh,' I said, surprised at her bluntness.

'I mean, would I prefer it if they were penniless and gave a shit about me? Of course. My mother has virtually disowned me. Emotionally, anyway. She still pays my credit card bill every month, obviously. But I'm hardly going to turn that down, am I?'

I nodded, thinking about how the bean burgers had probably pushed me into my overdraft again this month.

'You wouldn't know it to look at her, but underneath all the designer clothes, she's a sadistic POS,' Esme continued.

'The devil wears Prada, right?'

Esme looked at me blankly. 'She's more into Gucci, actually.'

'No, I mean,' I started, 'uh, never mind.'

'I won't need her hand-outs anymore soon, anyway,' Esme said. 'My ShowMe account is about to *majorly* take off. And when it does, I'll be pulling in sponsored content, ad partnerships, collabs, all that good stuff. Totally about to girl boss it.'

Suddenly I felt the need to justify my somewhat unimpressive role as a middle-of-nowhere small town reporter (aka Whatever Trevor's tea girl).

'*The Gazette* is just a stepping stone to other, bigger things for me,' I said, trotting out the well-worn excuse that I used whenever the subject of my career cropped up. The truth was, my job felt less like a stepping stone and more like, I dunno, one solitary pebble in the middle of a puddle.

'Mmm.' Esme clearly didn't believe me or she just found

me incredibly uninteresting. Or both. 'I didn't realise anyone bought actual newspapers anymore.'

'Well, we do have a website, if you can call it that. It's completely unreadable unless you can navigate past the seventy-two pop-ups trying to sell you Viagra and garden gnomes. It's like an endless game of whack-a-mole. No one reads it, but there's not much I can do about that. Nothing interesting has happened here for thirty years!'

'Then you have to make something happen,' she said.

'Um, well, that's not really how journalism works…' I started.

'You need to get on ShowMe,' Esme said, turning around and pointing her phone directly at me. 'No pitches, no deadlines and definitely no Trevors. Just press record and off you go. See?'

'Oh no, turn it off!' I said, putting my hand up to shield myself from the camera. 'I look terrible.'

'Alright, suit yourself,' she shrugged, lowering her phone.

When Esme's attention shifted, it was like a spotlight had been shut off, leaving me with a weird sensation of loneliness. I don't know why I craved this woman's approval, after knowing her for about five minutes, but I did.

'Uh, hey, wait a sec,' I squeaked. 'Maybe it's just the Black Death talking, but perhaps it is time I put myself out there.'

Esme looked up and smiled. I pulled my phone out of my bag and scrolled through the app store until I found ShowMe's little waving hand logo. In a matter of seconds, it was downloaded. But my drunken brain couldn't quite make sense of the chaotic stream of videos. As I poked aimlessly at the screen, trying to make it stop, I could hear Esme laughing.

'Here, let me show you, grandma,' she said, gently taking my phone out of my hand.

I watched her navigate the app like a pro while I polished off the last of my burger, and by the time I'd finished, Esme had set me up with my very own ShowMe account.

'Why don't you show the world how dangerous these big holes in the ground are,' she said, handing me the phone back.

I pressed record and started filming myself.

'Hi!' I said. 'Here we are in Courtney Road, and just look at these roadworks behind me. The council says they've run out of budget for this quarter, but they've been like this for months!'

I pointed the camera down the big hole in the road, and the screen was filled with murky pipes and dirt.

'How was that?' I asked Esme.

'Uh, well…'

'Oh.' I laughed. 'That bad?'

'Little tip. It's not really about the story, it's about who's telling it,' she said. 'You have to sex it up a bit, you know?'

'Er, you want me to make a hole in the ground sexy?'

'Let's go again. I'll film you, and this time be yourself, but dial it up by five. Actually, make it ten,' Esme said, pointing her phone at me. 'Ready… I'm recording… *now*. So, I'm here in Crowhurst, talking to one of the town's top investigative reporters.'

I stared at her gormlessly for a second, and she mouthed 'go on' at me, whirling a finger in the air to indicate that I should get a bloody move on.

'Uh, yep, that's me, Kirby Cornell,' I said, posing under the spotlight of the lamppost. 'World's greatest journalist!'

'Is this a ten?' I mouthed at her, and she smiled.

'So, how many people have been almost fatally injured here this week, Kirby?' Esme said from behind the camera.

'Ummm? What?'

'There are reports that a small child very nearly fell into these roadworks last Tuesday, is that correct?'

'Oh, right, yes,' I said, getting into character. I mean, God knows what character I thought I was playing, but I went with it. 'Literally, uh, *tons* of people have almost fallen down this very hole. And it's been here for absolutely *ages*. Like, years. In fact, I think a cat might have died down there.'

'Get a bit closer,' she mouths.

I stepped back and pointed behind me at the hole. Esme nodded in encouragement, so I took another step back. For a second, her eyes met mine, glinting jade in the street lights, and the faintest smile crossed her coral-pink lips.

'Trust me,' she said.

And with that, she placed her hand on my shoulder and gave a firm push.

EIGHT

Airports have always ranked pretty high on my 'least favourite places on earth' list, just behind The Red Lion toilets and very slightly ahead of a McDonald's at quarter-past-fucked-up on a Saturday night. And so far, Palma de Mallorca departure lounge is doing nothing to change my mind.

At least when you're flying off somewhere sunny, airports are filled with promise, excitement and giant Toblerones. One hut for pizza, another for sunglasses. But when the holiday is over, and you're queuing up behind fifty-seven other disgruntled, sunburnt Brits at the passport check, every step is like walking in shoes half a size too small.

And this time, I don't even get to go home. Not really, anyway. I don't know if I even have a home anymore, to be honest. Flat Four, Stewart Heights hasn't been home for a long time.

I'm currently trapped in the no man's land after you pass through the duty-free. You know, that bit when you've gone to your gate, but you still have ages 'til take-off and you're stuck there, crammed into an uncomfortable plastic chair with nothing to look at besides acres of tarmac or your own sad reflection in a solitary out-of-order vending machine.

Why am I here? Well, check this little beauty out:

> **Esme**
> I know your secret. If you want it to stay hidden, then meet me at The Red Lion pub, at 5pm this Saturday.

As group chat messages go, that one is a doozy.

I'd managed to ignore 'Esme''s threats up to this point, but I could hardly focus on work after that, could I? Not that I'd been concentrating particularly hard on upselling tickets to Elbows Deep, Magaluf's second most popular male strip troupe. But when my manager caught me staring gormlessly at my phone instead of the strippers that night, he told me I might want to reconsider my priorities. I told him he was right, and immediately started packing.

The Deadbeats might have disbanded a long time ago, but if they were in any sort of danger, I didn't have a choice. I had to go back. So now here I am, counting down the minutes until my flight departs, taking me back to dear old England, and eventually Crowhurst.

I plonk myself down and idly flick through the photos on my phone, watching as it slowly ticks down to zero per cent battery. Scrolling back through my camera roll tells a tragedy in reverse chronological order. Generic beach sunsets and cocktails shots are eventually followed by the only photo I have of me and Esme, taken that night in The Red Lion, the day she arrived. A drunken group shot that Dave insisted on that I'd forgotten all about, but now can't bring myself to delete.

I read her message on the group chat like I've done about ten thousand times over the past twenty-four hours. It had to be someone's idea of a joke, right? Maybe it was Dylan, trying desperately to get me to come back? Or one of the other flatmates attempting to get my attention, maybe. Whoever sent it, it definitely wasn't Esme.

I don't believe in ghosts.

I left town right after she died. I had to endure Crowhurst's finest's 'good cop, bad cop' routine first, of course, which was more like 'bad cop, even worse cop'. But I kept my nerve, stuck to my story, and got the hell out of there as soon as they let me.

I guess the others did the same. I'd barely heard from them since. Seema had texted me a couple of times, and Dave occasionally liked a couple of my rare Instagram posts, all of which I ignored. Dylan had seemingly disappeared from the face of the earth, and I couldn't blame him.

I kept flicking back through the photos, and soon my screen filled with images of the Deadbeats, stuffing our faces with whatever the Booze and Biscuits shop on the corner had on two-for-one offer.

Dave The Legend, tummy poking out of his ill-fitting football shirt as he held a can of Heineken aloft.

Seema demurely picking the pepperoni slices off her pizza.

And of course, that selfie of Dylan and me, huddled under his jacket in the back seat of my old Mini. A photo that still makes me feel simultaneously sick and exhilarated every time I have the misfortune to catch sight of it.

Those days slobbing around the flat seem like a million years ago. What happened with Esme, though, that feels like it was yesterday. Especially those nights when I'd wake up at three in the morning, my heart pounding my ribcage like a pneumatic drill after yet another panic attack. For months after she died, every time I closed my eyes, I'd see Esme's broken body, crooked limbs stuck out at unnatural angles, blood seeping out of a crack in her head.

My thoughts are interrupted when the final boarding announcement for my flight booms across the airport, first in Spanish, then again in stilted English.

I stand up, sling my backpack onto my shoulders, and make my way onto the plane. By the time we touch down in London Luton a couple of hours later, I've sunk one of those mini bottles of Pinot Grigio and devoured six packets of peanuts. As Frida Kahlo once said, 'I tried to drown my sorrows, but the bastards learned how to swim'. So now I just feed my demons instead, and get them nice and chunky.

As I walk through customs, I start to feel nauseous, the cocktail of salty snacks and airplane wine curdling in my belly. I have a really bad feeling about this. But I know I have to see it through. Whoever sent that message on the group chat somehow has Esme's phone, and if they have that, God knows what else they know…

So I'm going to work out who the hell is pretending to be Esme, and then I'm going to find out exactly what they want from me.

'Anything to declare?' the sign above the door asks me.

Hell yeah, I do.

NINE

Suddenly, I felt the loose tarmac giving way under my feet, and before I could react, I was falling backwards.

'You cow!' I yelled.

Snatching at the air, I tried desperately to grab anything that might break my fall. My hand hit Esme's necklace, snapping the chain and sending it flying above me, its gold letter 'e' glinting in the light of the street lamp.

With a scream, I clattered against the plastic tape, tumbling through it down into the hole. Luckily, I landed on something soft (my arse), right in a muddy puddle of rainwater. The hole was actually deeper than I thought, full of rocks, dirt and gross old pipes. I looked up to see Esme's face, gaping at me with a mixture of pity and revulsion.

'Sorry. I didn't think it was that deep.' Esme bent down, grabbed my arm and heaved me up onto the pavement.

My hair was full of crud and my elbow was scraped to shit. There was a bit of blood, but other than a possibly incurable case of extreme humiliation, I was physically fine. Esme took a bunch of tissues from the zip-pocket of her bag and handed them to me.

'What was that about?' I cried, steadying myself on the barrier while I wiped the dirt off my face. 'You pushed me!'

'Yeah, and now everyone will see how dangerous these holes are. Trust me, it's worth getting your hands a little bit dirty if it gets results.'

'Isn't that, like, fake news?' I stuffed the muddy tissues in my jacket pocket.

'You fell in the hole, didn't you? Nothing fake about that.'

'Well, yeah, because you pushed me,' I muttered.

Esme smiled and shook her head, like she was watching a little lamb stumbling over its first steps, not a fully grown professional woman. But, to be fair, standing in the middle of the road in my soggy Converse, I didn't exactly look super professional right now.

'Maybe that's just what you needed, mmm? A little push? The holes *are* dangerous, you said so yourself, right? All we've done is prove that's true. You have to be part of the story, Kirby. It's the only way to make people listen.'

A warm wind blew across the street, and I nodded. What she was saying made sense, I suppose, but I sure didn't remember seeing Esme fall in any filthy holes in her videos.

'Uh, I guess so,' I mumbled, brushing the gravel off my jeans. 'Well, sorry I called you a cow then, I guess. And, crap, your necklace!'

I peered down into the hole, but it was pitch black down there.

'Oh forget it, it's a dupe,' she said. 'You okay? Anything broken?'

'Just my pride,' I exhaled, flicking mud off my denim jacket.

'Occupational hazard, right? All part of the job.'

Somehow, looking at Esme, I doubted that she had ever ended an evening with mud caked in her hair, a bloody elbow and a wet arse.

'Listen, I do shit like that all the time. I just don't put those bits online,' she smiled. 'If you want to be popular on ShowMe, it's all about curation.'

As I stood there, soaked in lukewarm, muddy ditch water, I couldn't help but wonder if there was any way to curate my actual life.

TEN

TWELVE MONTHS AGO

Group Chat: The Deadbeats

> **Dylan**
> @kirby I left a glass of water on the coffee table for you

> **Dave The Legend**
> hope u left a bucket too

> **Seema**
> @kirby pls, pls don't throw up on the rug, Frank will murder us if he has to get that dry cleaned

> **Dylan**
> again

The sound of drilling turned out, in fact, not to be coming from inside my skull.

After the best part of two bottles of cheap white wine, plus Dave's dubious shots, I was sure that the insane hammering reverberating through my brain was the result of a classic Deadbeats hangover.

But when I craned my neck to peek out the window,

I discovered it was actually coming from the roadworks outside, where two men with gigantic pneumatic drills were happily going about their business, seemingly unaware it was FRICKING SEVEN A.M. ON A FRIDAY.

At least, I thought it was seven a.m., anyway. My phone was nowhere in sight so I couldn't check. I had that horrible momentary panic that you get after a night out drinking:

Shit. Had I dropped it in the roadworks?

After Esme had gone to the 24-hour corner shop to buy a vape refill, I vaguely remembered coming in and thinking that I'd 'just sit down for a bit and rest my eyes before bed'. After that, things were kinda fuzzy, but evidently, I'd fallen asleep on the sofa. One of the others had kindly placed one of the old throws over me and left a glass of water on the coffee table.

My back was stiff from the weird lump in the middle of the settee and my eyeballs were gently pulsating (I could probably thank the final, completely unnecessary Eggermeister we snuck in before the last orders bell for that).

Back in my early twenties, I could drink the best part of a bottle of gin, stay out 'til daybreak and wake up feeling fresh. Well, maybe not *fresh* exactly, but not like I needed to be rushed to A&E for an emergency liver transplant. Nowadays, any more than a medium glass of red and I'm gasping for a gallon of water and an aspirin at three a.m.

I slumped back on the cushion, and my face pressed up against something hard. I peeled it off and it took my hungover brain a moment to work out what it was.

My phone.

I must have been sleeping on it all night, because it had left a depression in my cheek. I tapped on the screen a few times and it didn't light up. *Dead.*

I hid under the throw for a while, before eventually rolling off the sofa and stumbling into the kitchen. The bedroom doors were all shut, so I assumed I was first up, which – result – meant I at least got the bathroom to myself for once.

But first, coffee. I swung open the fridge to see – surprise, surprise – there was no milk left, which probably had something to do with the soggy Coco Pops littered around the kitchen table. Dave's choice of after-pub snack left a lot to be desired.

I closed the fridge door and came face to face with the Polaroid we'd stuck there. It was of all of us, messing around, gurning for the camera (well, except Dylan, who was posing and trying to look like a moody Eighties popstar). Even Max had managed to squeeze himself in. I'd just moved in when it was taken, and I loved that photo. Like Spider-Man always said: if you have no power, that must mean you have no responsibilities either. And this photo sort of summed that up for me.

I dumped three heaped spoonfuls of Nescafé into Dave's Tottenham Hotspur mug (the biggest we had) and resigned myself to a cup of coffee that would closely resemble my mood this morning. Black as hell.

In approximately one hour and twenty-two minutes, I would be sitting in our daily conference meeting, where I'd be expected to come up with three pitches for the paper. And, as usual, I had absolutely nothing. The chances of my hungover brain coming up with a scintillating new angle on the latest round of funding cuts for the Crowhurst mobile library by nine a.m. were about as high as... well, a very low thing indeed (see, I told you my brain was not exactly firing on all cylinders this morning. Or whatever brains fire on. Synapses?).

As the kettle boiled, I stuck my phone in the charger Dylan kept in the kitchen and waited for it to wake up. When it did, it started buzzing like crazy. A shot of ice-cold adrenaline ricocheted around my poor, hungover body, and suddenly I was 110 per cent awake.

My brand-new shiny ShowMe app had 94 notifications.

Oh God, she didn't...

My thumb couldn't move quick enough. I whacked the ShowMe icon like it was a greedy mosquito and it opened to confirm my worst fears. Not only had Esme posted the video, it already had *3,017 views*.

Unhelpfully, she'd also tagged me in. I forced myself to watch it back, squinting through one eye. Sure enough, there I was, Crowhurst's newest roving reporter, chatting shit about a dead cat, randomly yelling 'cow!' and then going ass-backwards into a ditch, breaking Esme's necklace in the process.

Of course, you can't see Esme push me, so it just looks like I've forgotten how to walk. Thankfully, most of it looks quite dark, oh, except for the bit when I stand under the lamppost and announce that I'm the *'world's greatest journalist'*. Ffs.

I could die. Three thousand people had now seen me pratfall into a massive hole. Some of them had even chosen to follow me on ShowMe too, presumably because they couldn't wait for more exclusive footage of me being a total idiot.

Esme had even commented underneath the video.

ShowMeSherlock:

girlbossing too close to the sun! Seriously tho, these roadworks are v v dangerous, someone shld really do something about them *@crowhurstparishcouncil*

Succumbing to the strong urge to pour my now lukewarm coffee directly over her head, I marched down the hallway to the box room and rapped loudly on the door. When there was no answer, I opened it very slightly and peeked in.

But weirdly, Esme wasn't there. And even stranger, the blow-up mattress was completely deflated, and hung over the exercise bike, as if no one had slept in the room at all.

Where the hell was she?

I went to WhatsApp to fire her a text, but before I could, I saw that she'd messaged the group chat. *Good*, I thought, hoping that she was apologising for posting that ridiculous video. But when I swiped the text, my heart skipped a beat.

Sent at ten past one in the morning.

I'd been in such a daze this morning, I hadn't seen her message. But boy, was I seeing it now.

> Esme
> if anything happens to me u need to know

> crowhurst killer is a lie

ELEVEN

TWELVE MONTHS AGO

Group Chat: The Deadbeats

Kirby

@esme hey just saw your message. What does that mean? r u okay?

ps guess who's gone viral! thank u soooo much for that @esme

@esme if ur reading this, pls pick up your phone

and could you delete that video when you get a mo

I look like a ducking idiota

ducking

ducking

DUCKING!

for duck's sake, ducking autocorrecta mo

Normally I'd have driven my crappy little Mini to *The Gazette* office, but the construction van had blocked our road, and I had this hangover from hell, so I didn't want to risk reversing out and into another hole.

Esme wasn't answering her phone, or replying to my numerous group chat messages, but I figured she must have got up early and sneaked out of the flat before I'd woken up. I hadn't heard the front door close, but then again, I was pretty comatose.

After a much-needed shower, I checked myself in the full-length mirror we had leant up against the wall at the end of the hallway. Denim jacket, skinny jeans and a white T-shirt. One of the benefits of living in a town that still hadn't emerged from the twentieth century, was that at least I always looked vaguely fashionable. Until Esme came along, that is.

I loved this blue denim jacket. It had belonged to my mum, who'd had it since she was a teenager in the early Eighties. By the time I was sixteen, they'd kind of come back into fashion, and I'd dug it out of her wardrobe. It was covered in patches of punk bands I'd barely heard of, like The Slits and The Cramps. And even though it wasn't exactly stylish these days, something about it made me feel connected to her. I liked to imagine her strutting around Camden wearing it, listening to her Walkman. If they even had those back then.

I left the flat and walked up the high street to Fast Forward, formerly Crowhurst's only coffee shop (until the Greggs opened three doors down on the high street). The number nine bus went from just outside, and I could pick up a pastry to sweeten up Whatever Trevor before my pitch. And yes, I would also be having a very necessary second coffee – with milk this time.

'Morning, love,' Betty said from behind the counter as I walked in. 'The usual?'

'Yes please, and a sausage roll to go, thanks, Betty.'

Dylan's mum worked part-time at Fast Forward, so it was usually where we ended up if a) we were hungover or b) we'd run out of food at home. Back in the day (by which I mean around circa 2002), Fast Forward had been Crowhurst's video rental shop. But when the town finally moved on, Betty's husband Vinnie had repurposed it as a café. He'd kept the name, left all the old DVD and VHS cases on the shelves and even saved the life-size cardboard cut-out of Vin Diesel. Betty kept saying she would get around to chucking everything out someday, but I hoped she wouldn't. I loved the nostalgia of rifling through the chunky plastic cases, giggling at the photos of Bruce Willis with hair, and feigning shock that Tom Hanks had existed before 1990.

It was Dylan's dream to turn the place into a cute little bistro one day (my words, he actually preferred to call it a modern suburban brasserie with a seasonal menu), providing he could persuade Vinnie to let him, that is.

Betty poured me a cappuccino, and I sat at the counter scrolling through Esme's ShowMe videos, hoping one of them would have some clue to what she meant by 'Crowhurst Killer is a lie'.

Her last three ShowMes were about the Crowhurst murders, and featured Esme gesticulating at the camera, making everything sound very dramatic. In all her videos, she wore her signature 'e' necklace and carried her pink baguette-style bag. The most recent one was posted yesterday morning.

It began with a shot of the Crowhurst Station sign as her train pulled into the platform.

'*Hey, Watsons!*' she said, turning the camera on herself as she left the station. '*So, you wouldn't know it by looking at it, but this,*' she spun around to show the rows of red-brick houses behind her, '*is the location of one of the most obscure, but bloodthirsty, murder sprees in British history. Can't believe no one talks more about this one. Now, Crowhurst looks like a pretty cute little town, right? Well, it wasn't so cute back in 1996 when Peter Doyle decided to stab five teenagers to death, then kill himself before he could stand trial. Or did he? Well, hold tight, cos thanks to a tip-off from one of my loyal Watsons, I've uncovered something that will change everything you think you know about the Crowhurst murders...*'

Annoyingly, she'd ended on this cliffhanger, and none of her other videos seemed to provide any clues to what this mystery revelation might be. 'The Watsons' she mentioned appeared to be Esme's army of followers, who meticulously studied every piece of footage they could find on the web, often discovering vital details that they claimed the police had missed.

I could see the appeal of hundreds of people validating your every move with little red hearts and supportive comments. The most feedback I'd ever had from one of my *Gazette* stories was a disgruntled email questioning if I was dyslexic after I'd misspelt the name of the sports centre.

Sipping the foam off my cappuccino, I switched to Google to do some fact checking. As the murders all happened pretty much pre-internet, I couldn't find many reports from the time. There was a very unreliable-looking Wikipedia page and a

MailOnline article from about ten years ago, the twentieth anniversary of the murders.

Five teenagers were murdered over one August weekend in 1996 during the town of Crowhurst's harvest celebrations. The killer, local man Peter Doyle, was still dressed in the 'Jack Daw' crow costume that he'd been wearing during the annual 'Crawe Fayre' earlier that day. The youths had allegedly aimed fireworks at Doyle's caravan, carrying on a tradition of scaring the crow character to avoid a bad harvest. Doyle avoided arrest when he jumped off the cliffs at nearby Staker Point. After searching his mobile home, police acquired enough evidence to satisfy their enquiries, including the costume and the murder weapon: a ceremonial trowel used as part of the harvest festival. A partially decomposed body, presumed to be Doyle, was recovered from the River Muse shortly afterwards.

I had to admit, it did all sound a bit suss. Judging from the rest of the article, the police had faced a lot of criticism from the papers at the time, as Peter Doyle had continually avoided arrest for minor crimes committed over the previous years.

'Betty, you grew up here, right?' I asked. 'Do you remember much about the murders?'

She paused, the steam from the milk foamer momentarily obscuring her face, but I could swear I saw her wince. In a second, it's cleared, but by then, she's regained her cheery persona.

'I was only a teenager at the time,' she said. 'I was on holiday with my parents when it all happened, thank the Crow. But I remember when we got back, it was like a different town. Journalists and TV crews everywhere. Crowhurst was infamous for years after that. Rubber-neckers driving through just to have a gawp. And the fayre was more popular than ever, I can tell you that much. Some people round here seem to think the murders were actually good for the town! Can you imagine that? I think they wanted Jack Daw to be our very own Freddy Krueger or Michael Myers.'

'Who?' I asked.

'Video nasties.' Betty nodded towards the old horror VHS tapes in the corner.

'Right,' I said, looking at the gruesome, blood-spattered covers. 'Except he was real, though. Peter Doyle, I mean.'

'Yes, love, he was very real.'

'They found his body at the bottom of Staker Point after the murders, right?' I asked.

'So they say.' Betty busied herself by wiping down the counter.

'So they say?' I repeated. 'What do you mean?'

'Best not to go digging around in that business, I reckon,' she replied, ignoring my question and turning back to the coffee machine. 'Leave the past behind you, that's what they say, don't they?'

I glanced at my phone again. If Esme really had discovered any new evidence in the Crowhurst murders case, that would be a *huge* story. The biggest thing that had happened to this town in decades. Definitely a lot bigger than the potholes on Courtney Road. But it was a massive *if*. I mean, it was definitely possible that she was just hyping the whole thing up for likes and follows. That's what these ShowMe kids do, right? What was it that Esme said? Sex it up a bit?

I went back through her feed and watched some of her earlier videos. She did her fair share of poking around abandoned office blocks and trespassing through farmers' fields. Her previous posts seemed to follow a pretty standard formula – a brief recap of a cold case to camera, then travelling to the location of the crime to do some hands-on investigating (which usually involves digging for clues in someone's bins, or banging on some poor pensioner's door until she agreed to answer Esme's questions). Occasionally she'd analyse some CCTV, zooming in on the grainy footage, or attempt to interpret a suspect's body language.

'The internet is the new crime scene' was one of her many catchphrases, along with 'the truth is in the details'.

Although Esme didn't seem to have actually solved any of the cases she had investigated so far, she was good at tracking down people and hounding them until they either cried or confessed just to get rid of her.

I was interrupted by Betty tapping me on the shoulder.

'That's your bus, isn't it, love?' she said, pointing out the window. I'd been so engrossed in Esme's videos, I'd almost missed it. I looked down to see the counter covered with crumbs, and realised I'd absent-mindedly eaten Trevor's sausage roll.

'Here.' Betty handed me another. 'On the house. Say hello to Trevor for me.'

I thanked her and rushed outside, clutching my paper bag, just in time to jump on the number nine bus. Ensconced in the back seat, I pulled up WhatsApp and scrolled through the group chat again.

There was just that one text from Esme, late last night (followed by a lot of me panicking and writing 'ducking' over and over). Her message didn't even make sense. I mean, I know Gen Z don't give a toss about grammar on text messages, hell, they don't even use capital letters half the time. But what did 'a lie' mean? Maybe it was Gen Z slang that I was just too old and uncool to understand.

Then it hit me: *ducking autocorrect*.

Heart racing, I quickly tried typing out the same phrase into WhatsApp. The autocorrect function kicked in, automatically changing it before my eyes.

From 'Crowhurst Killer is a lie' to 'Crowhurst Killer is alive'.

'Alive,' I said out loud. 'She meant to write *alive*. The Crowhurst Killer is alive!'

The two old ladies sitting in front of me turned around and scowled.

'Sorry,' I mouthed, standing up and ringing the bell.

Holy crap. I grabbed onto the pole next to me to steady myself. Peter Doyle was alive? That would be crazy. But so far everything about today had been a bit crazy. I jumped off the bus, my mind spinning.

If Esme was right, then I sure as hell had something to pitch to Trevor now.

TWELVE

TWELVE MONTHS AGO

Group Chat: The Deadbeats

> Kirby
> @esme does that mean what I think it means?

> @esme meet for a coffee later?

> @esme or not, no worries

> @esme its totally chill

If you thought Crowhurst itself was quiet, try venturing past the town centre to the part some of the locals liked to humorously refer to as Greater Crowhurst. While the town itself still maintained an aura of countryside quaintness, once you got past the big ASDA, it was a no man's land of miscellaneous silos and scrubland. And if you stayed on the bus too long, you might be lucky enough to discover the dubious delights of Crowhurst Business Park.

Despite the incredibly sexy name, CBP (as absolutely no one called it) was as soulless a place as any you'd find on earth. It consisted of three concrete monoliths, calling themselves flexioffices, surrounding a roundabout. The Parish Council had given the go-ahead to renovate the area just before the pandemic, but since then two of the buildings had remained virtually empty. In fact, the only signs of life I'd seen here were the sporadic daffodils sprouting from the muddy patches of grass dotted around the car park. But, luckily for me, this oasis had been the proud home of *The Crowhurst Gazette* since 1962.

In our building's basement was the huge old printing press that had once been used to print every local paper in the county, but, as most of them had folded or gone online, now it was just *The Gazette*, once a week.

I looked up at the bland office block and checked the step count on my watch.

A pathetic 1,012 steps. That had to be a malfunction. I aggressively tapped the face of the watch, as if the number would magically double if I pressed it hard enough. But it didn't budge. There was nothing else for it, I was gonna have to take the stairs to the third floor. It was worth it; every step I took was one step closer to being a proper adult.

As I beeped my pass on the door, I should have been coming up with more ideas for tomorrow's paper, but I couldn't stop thinking about Esme's message.

Crowhurst Killer is alive...

If that's what she even meant. But I needed a pitch for that morning's conference meeting, and in lieu of any movement on the roadworks story, that was gonna have to be it.

The moment I stepped into the office, a defeated sigh echoed across the floor, like I'd set off the world's least frightening burglar alarm.

'Cornell.' Trevor looked visibly disappointed that his little news sanctuary had been disturbed. 'What are you doing here?'

I resisted the temptation to tell him that, according to the pathetic payslip that I received every month, I was under the impression I worked here.

'Oh, sorry, Trevor, but I need to tell you—'

He held up a finger to indicate to me that I should wait, then retrieved a small piece of yellow foam from each ear.

'Can't hear a thing with these in. The roadworks outside my house finally started up again first thing this morning. Absolute bloody racket. Doesn't help that my hyperacusis has been flaring up.'

'Hyper what?' I ask.

'Sensitive hearing,' he said. 'Very sensitive. So if you wouldn't mind keeping the noise...' He motions downwards with the palms of his hands.

'Oh yeah, sorry, forgot,' I mumbled.

'You are aware you can work from home now, aren't you? There are no rules about coming into the newsroom anymore.'

I looked around at what Trevor was generously calling 'the newsroom' – a couple of desks, two ancient-looking computers and, unbelievably, a fax machine.

To be fair, since the Surreywide takeover, we had been doing most of our meetings over Zoom, which thanks to the combination of my verbal diarrhoea and the flat's terminally slow Wi-Fi, was an excruciatingly painful experience for all involved.

'Well, actually, I'm glad I did come in,' I said. 'Because I think I might have a major story that I really think could be something—'

'That's what the morning Zoom conference is for.' Trevor took a long, slow sip of his tea.

Now don't get me wrong, I really liked Trevor. He had taught me a lot (including how to use the Oxford comma correctly and the precise moment to take the tea bag out for his perfect cuppa) but he wasn't exactly a risk taker. The kind of man who would never, ever run with a pair of scissors. No, Trevor was all corduroy trousers, un-ironed shirt and eight cups of *very* weak PG Tips a day. And having worked his way up from tea boy to chief reporter and finally editor, he was as much part of the furniture at *The Gazette* as the desk he was seemingly superglued to. But, when it came to hard-hitting journalism, Trev liked the news like he liked his tea: lukewarm and slightly stewed.

'But since you're here,' he continued obliviously. 'There is actually something I wanted to speak to you about.'

I flinched as my momentum screeched to a halt. *This didn't sound good…*

'I saw your video.'

Shit. I felt my cheeks blush. How the hell had he seen that? Trevor wasn't exactly in the ShowMe demographic.

'Oh,' I mumbled. 'Well, it wasn't really *my* video as such. Actually, what happened was my friend—'

'Aren't you a little old for TikTok?' Trevor asked.

'ShowMe,' I said, shaking my head. 'It's called ShowMe. TikTok is *so* last year.'

Trevor stared at me like I just attempted to communicate with him via the means of performative dance. 'Whatever it's called, it's not really something we encourage here,' he said.

'What you do in your spare time is up to you, but all I ask is that my reporters maintain a certain level of...'

'Dignity?' I asked.

He paused.

'Professionalism,' he finished.

'Right, but, Trevor, last year you made me dress up as a chicken and chase that local councillor down the street when he refused an interview, so I hardly think—'

Trevor held up a hand, indicating that perhaps now would be a good time for me to stop talking.

'I'm sorry,' I said. 'I'll get her to delete it. But, listen, I—'

Trevor silenced me with a raise of a single eyebrow. He reached for a Tupperware box of party-sized sausage rolls next to his keyboard and fished one out between his finger and thumb.

'I think that would be for the best. Your generation needs to be careful. These things are on the internet forever, you know,' Trevor said, adopting a kinder tone.

'How did you even see it anyway?' I asked. 'I wouldn't have picked you for a ShowMe fan.'

'I have three daughters, Kirby.'

'Oh, right, yes,' I nodded. 'Forgot about that.'

'Well, it just so happens I had a call from Crowhurst Council this morning, and it seems one of the chief councillors has teenage children too. And...'

'Oh God,' I muttered. This is it, I was going to get fired.

'And, well, work on the roadworks has resumed immediately.'

My jaw dropped. 'Wait, what? So the video actually worked?' *Esme was right.*

'Terrible news for my ears, but a good result for Crowhurst,

I suppose. It was clear from your video that the holes are a, um, significant risk to the public,' he said. 'Apparently, it has stirred up quite a bit of interest already and the council would prefer to avoid any further negative publicity.'

I couldn't believe it. Maybe I was cut out for this journalism lark after all. I held my palm up ready to receive a thoroughly deserved high-five. Inevitably, Trevor left me hanging.

'I shouldn't need to ask you this,' he said softly, 'but did you really fall in that hole?'

I felt the enthusiasm slowly drain from my body, like air seeping from a day-old party balloon. 'Uh, well, my friend sort of pushed me. A bit. But that doesn't change the fact that the roadworks are dangerous. The end justifies the means, right?'

'The truth is what's important, Cornell, not the end result,' Trevor said, dipping the eraser end of his pencil into his mug to retrieve the tea bag. 'And whether you're writing an article for the paper, or presenting the news on TV, a story is only ever as trustworthy as the person reporting it.'

I'd heard this speech approximately twenty-two times before, and bitten my tongue so hard that it felt like it's done ten rounds with The Meg.

'What do I always tell you?' he asked, depositing the soggy tea bag on a saucer next to him.

This was actually a tough question. The man repeated so many of his personal idioms, I could get a full house at Whatever Trevor Bingo every time I came to work.

'Umm,' I hesitated. 'Live, laugh, love?'

'There are no shortcuts to the truth,' he said, as though that was the obvious answer.

'Yes, you're right, I remember. And a good journalist always backs up their instincts with proper research. You've told me a thousand times. I really am sorry about the video. But listen, the friend who made it, she's like a sort of internet sleuth, and she's found out something about Peter Doyle. I think this might be the big story we've been looking for. It could get a *lot* of hits on the website.'

I saw his face contort, the same way it does every time I mention things like 'SEO' or 'page retention rate'.

'And sell a lot of newspapers,' I added quickly.

Trevor adjusted the collar of his shirt, and I could see a smattering of eczema where he'd been nervously scratching his neck.

'I'm afraid we may not even have an actual newspaper for much longer. Sales are well and truly in the toilet, advertising revenue has halved in the past six months, and the sad reality is, the bigwigs at Surreywide don't expect *The Gazette* to last the rest of the year.'

My heart sank. Surreywide was the neighbouring county's biggest news organisation, a conglomerate blob that collated all the news for the south-west of England, and spewed it out in manageable bite-sized online chunks.

'Oh,' I said. 'What does that mean for us?'

I knew the Surreywide board dreamed of the day when they could replace all five of *The Gazette*'s staff with AI chatbots who didn't require holidays or salaries. Or any sort of human interaction, for that matter.

'Out on our ear, I'm afraid. They'll fold *The Gazette* into Surreywide.com. All the Crowhurst news will just have to fit onto one webpage alongside the thirty-two other towns in the county.'

Trevor gazed into the depths of his milky tea, and for a

moment, I was worried he was going to start weeping into it (which might actually improve the flavour, to be fair). *The Gazette* was everything to him. And, right now, to me too. Without it, I'd be spending the last of my savings on a one-way ticket back to London to face the music. And that was not an option.

'The ShowMe video worked for the roadworks, didn't it? Maybe we could do something similar for this Peter Doyle story to boost sales? If you can't beat 'em, join 'em, right? It might be a good way to reach a younger audience?'

I could barely finish my sentence before I was hit by Trevor's biggest sigh of the day so far.

'This is Crowhurst, Cornell. Look around you. There is no "younger audience" here.'

He had a point.

'I'm just saying, my friend has loads of followers and—'

'It is the role of *The Gazette* to celebrate, to champion and, yes, sometimes, criticise,' Trevor went on. 'But always with the town's best interests at heart. We serve the town; it doesn't serve us.'

'What's that supposed to mean?' I asked.

'It means, we don't do this for personal gain. Likes and followers, and such. We do it for Crowhurst. All these ShowMes, YouTubers and podcasters care about are views and hits and goodness knows what else,' he said. 'That's not news, that's a popularity contest. It's exactly this sort of thing that's destroying local newspapers.'

'But *this* story is all about the community!' I pleaded.

Trevor sipped his tea and considered this for a moment. 'What sort of lead does this friend of yours have exactly?'

I hesitated. After that monologue of doom, I'd suddenly lost my nerve. I couldn't just come out and say it, could I?

You know that dead serial killer that the whole town despises? Well, this girl I met ten minutes ago says he's actually alive. Or at least that's what I think she meant. I could be totally wrong. But let's go with it on page one.

Trevor would laugh me out of the office and back to Fast Forward for extra pastries like I was the work-experience girl.

'Well,' I paused and took a breath, 'nothing yet. But there's a rumour—'

Trevor let out another of his trademark Big Sighs, one of his many signals that I should stop talking.

'I grew up here, you know. I lived through that nightmare, as did many of the relatives of the victims, who still live in Crowhurst, I might add. When the murders happened, the town really pulled together, with the help of *The Gazette*. The rubbish the tabloids were printing made our tragedy sound like a horror movie. They called Doyle a serial killer, but of course, he was a spree killer. But that doesn't sound quite so...'

Please don't say sexy. Please don't say sexy...

'Sensational,' he finished. 'The people he killed were our friends, our neighbours. They'd studied at our schools, shopped in our shops, read our newspaper. They deserved respect, and that's what *The Gazette* gave them, because we knew them better than anyone. So, while I am still the editor, we will not be giving the paper over to rumours and conspiracy theories. We stick to the facts. Especially after your escapades in the roadworks last night. You're not "Lois Lane", fighting corruption and catching criminals. Your sole job is to inform and educate the community. That is the duty of a local journalist.'

It totally figured that the only female journalist Trevor could think of was a fictional comic book character from the 1930s. But he was right. Maybe I should just stick to potholes and local politics and leave the investigative stuff to Esme. While she was out there finding missing people – or at least their sweaters – and investigating murder cases, here I was, trying to find new adjectives to describe Farmer Jacobs' prize marrow. And I couldn't even do that right.

Trevor must have still had some journalistic nous left, though, because he rolled his ancient wheelie chair over to my desk, and placed a fatherly hand on my shoulder.

'I've no doubt that you'll be sitting in my chair one day, Cornell. But you'll have to earn it first. Just like I did. There are no shortcuts, remember? So promise me you won't go around town stirring everyone up about Peter Doyle. We all need to move on from that man.'

I looked at his squeaky old chair, with one wheel hanging off and a strip of thick black tape covering a tear in the fabric, and nodded meekly.

'And if you wouldn't mind filing six hundred words on the roadworks story by the end of the day, that would be marvellous. And, Cornell?' he said, reaching for his earplugs.

'Yes?'

'No more videos, please. We'll have another chat next week, okay?'

'Great, I'll put a meeting in—'

'Over email.' Trevor turned back to his computer screen and slowly inserted another sausage roll into his mouth, a clear indication that this conversation was officially over.

THIRTEEN

I have to change trains three times and then get a rail replacement bus to get to Crowhurst from the airport, and by the time I finally arrive, it's fair to say I'm not in the greatest of moods.

But as the bus pulls into the high street, a surprising wave of nostalgia washes over me, before it's quickly engulfed by the PTSD tsunami that follows.

Someone has graffitied 'Twinned with Packington Landfill' underneath the Welcome to Crowhurst sign, which, while technically inaccurate, feels about right.

I walk the short distance to The Red Lion and notice half the shops are closed. I'd planned to stop by Fast Forward, but when I pass, it's all boarded up, which makes me wonder what happened to Betty. And Dylan, of course. By the time I've reached The Lion, I've counted at least six more empty shops, and there were only about ten open to begin with.

As I step inside, it's like I've been sucked out of an airless vacuum and re-entered the atmosphere. I'm immediately hit by that sticky, almost vinegary warmth that only a post-smoking-ban English pub can provide. But where there used to be a wave of noise – laughter, glasses clinking, the histrionic beeping from the ancient quiz machine in the corner – now it's strangely quiet.

No scotch eggs. No board games. The only noise is coming from the new addition of two gigantic plasma TV screens behind the bar, showing what appears to be the South Korean table tennis championships.

I check the time on my Fitbit. It's almost five, but there is no sign of the Deadbeats. I go to the bar, order a glass of wine and glance furtively around the pub. Maybe I'm just being paranoid, but the handful of locals seem to be staring at me like I've waltzed in here in a tutu. For a moment, a cold, sick feeling builds in the pit of my stomach, and I wonder again if coming back to Crowhurst is a terrible mistake.

'Lovely tan,' the woman behind the bar says as she pours my wine. 'Been anywhere nice?'

Heavily freckled would be a more accurate description than tanned, but I'll take it.

'Nice might be pushing it,' I reply, thinking back to Elbows Deep and the congealed vomit.

'Here for the fayre?' she asks.

'That's this weekend?'

I hadn't even thought of that. The Crawe Fayre is literally the last place on earth I want to be. Surely they wouldn't still be running it, not after what happened last year.

'That's right. Not had many out-of-towners in this year. Can't blame them, I suppose…' she trails off.

I feel nauseous. That means it's the anniversary of Esme's death. I quickly change the subject.

'I was wondering, does Dylan still work here?' I ask.

'Who?'

'The chef? Dylan Barnes. About six foot, good hair? Permanent bags under his eyes.'

She crinkles up her face. 'Alesky is the chef here. Started three months ago. Was there a problem with your meal?'

She turns back towards the kitchen before I can answer.

'Alesky! Did you use the bad meat again? I told you, one more time and you're fired.'

'Uh, no, I didn't order anything...' I start. But it's pointless, she's not listening.

I take my glass over to the table at the back, where we always used to sit, and slip my tattered backpack off my shoulders. I've carried this thing around for so long, it feels like it's part of me. I've grown so accustomed to its weight on my back, it's almost comforting. In fact, knowing everything I care about was safely strapped to my person was pretty much the only comforting part of my life for the last twelve months. (Okay, I admit it, Elbows Deep were actually pretty entertaining, but other than that dubious highlight, the past year has been an A-grade shit show.)

I check the time again – five past five. I sip my wine and wonder if anyone's going to show. I called them all from the bus, but, predictably, not one of them picked up. In fact, Dylan's number didn't even connect. A quick Google easily located Seema on LinkedIn, and weirdly she seems to be working as a receptionist in a spa over in Norbridge. As for Dave, it looks like he's finally found his true calling – working as a part-time zombie impersonator at a paintball centre just outside Guildford. There are about twenty photos of him on their website, posing slack-jawed with winning teams, holding guns aloft, throwing their paint-splattered goggles in the air. But nothing comes up at all for 'Dylan Barnes'. It's like he's been scrubbed from the internet.

The flatmates of Flat Four, Stewart Heights, didn't have that much in common to begin with. We were just four randoms who happened to find themselves in need of a cheap room. But a year ago, something happened that tied us together and tore us apart in equal measure. And now that something – or someone – was seemingly back.

It had to be a prank, right? Esme is dead. I saw her body, smashed into pieces. The police had to winch her body up. Her funeral was on the news. There is no way she is alive and even less chance that she's WhatsApping us. A sick joke makes a lot more sense than a ghost. Phone companies re-use numbers, so my best theory was that someone got Esme's number once her contract ran out. Probably some bored teenager somewhere who's written the same thing in all Esme's old group chats, just to see who bites. And so far, it looks like I'm the only idiot who took a mouthful.

I get out my phone and, after dismissing the six missed calls from my mum, find the number on the spa's website. If Seema won't pick up her mobile, maybe I can go straight to the source.

'Hi!' I say, in my cheeriest voice. 'I'd like to make an appointment for a detoxifying eucalyptus and seaweed body wrap, please.'

'Um, okay,' I hear Seema's familiar voice on the line. 'Let me just see if we have any space today. What was the name?'

'Clare Cornell,' I say.

There's a pause before she speaks again.

'Kirby! Is that really you?' For a moment, she sounds just

like the old Seema I remembered, and all the memories come flooding back.

'Well, I just go by Clare now, but yeah, it's me. And guess where I am?' I clink my nail on my wine glass.

'The Lion?'

'Right. The Lion. So where are you?'

There's another pause.

'Uh, yeah, sorry, Kirby. I'm stuck at work. I saw the messages. And your missed calls. But, well, it's just really busy right now. We're not really allowed on our mobiles at reception.'

'What are you doing working in a spa anyway?' I ask. 'You should be digging out someone's root canal, not booking in facials.'

I hear her fiddling with her earrings on the end of the line.

'Things didn't really work out at the surgery. After everything that happened, I just wanted a new start.'

When she says that, a little part of me dies inside. God knows I knew how she felt, but she'd studied so hard for those exams. The fact that she'd never seen it through makes me want to cry.

'How'd your parents take that?' I ask.

'Not so well, as you can imagine. But, Kirby, I really can't talk now, I—'

'We can't just ignore this. Did you see what happened to Max?'

'Oh come on, that was horrible,' she says. 'But you can't seriously think it might really be Esme?'

'No, of course not, Esme is dead. But someone has her phone. Someone *knows*, Seema.'

'Knows what?'

'You know what. The truth about what happened to her,' I say.

The line goes quiet for a moment.

'You think it's blackmail?' she asks.

'Don't you only get blackmailed if you have money? I don't know about you, but I'm broke.'

I glance at my rucksack beside me. All my earthly belongings are in there, and every single item needs to be either washed at 90 degrees or ceremonially cremated. I changed into my last fresh clothes in the airport bathroom – skinny black jeans, hooded cardigan and a white V-neck.

'Okay, so why don't you just chuck this imposter out of the group chat?' Seema asks.

'I can't, Dylan's the group admin. And he's seemingly disappeared off the face of the earth. Besides, whoever this is, we need to find out exactly what they want from us.'

'But we all swore that we'd never tell anyone what really happened,' Seema says. 'You didn't tell anyone, did you?'

'No,' I say, defensively. 'Of course not.'

'You don't think Dave could have…' Seema trails off.

'He hasn't shown up either,' I say. 'We need to find him and Dylan, then figure out what we're going to do about this phoney Esme. We need to know what she knows, because if she knows too much, then we are fucked, you know?'

'Uh, yeah, I, um, know.'

'Do you still speak to Dylan?' I ask her. 'What happened to Fast Forward, it's all boarded up?'

Seema doesn't speak for a moment.

'I don't…' She pauses. 'We all moved away from Crowhurst after… after it happened. Look, Kirby, I honestly can't talk right now, this is a luxury spa, people want to relax, not listen to us chat about death threats. This would be better face to face anyway, right? Let's meet somewhere a bit more private when I've finished my shift. I still have Hot Dentist's key for the surgery in Crowhurst. Meet you there after closing time?'

I agree, hang up, down the rest of my wine and side-eye my rucksack, which, now it's off, I am not looking forward to putting back on. I scan the smattering of regulars at the bar. Is 'Esme' one of them? Is she here watching me, waiting to see what I'll do next?

I figure sitting here and getting drunk all afternoon isn't going to solve anything. It's quarter to six now, and it doesn't look like anyone is going to turn up.

But just as I'm getting up to leave, I feel a heavy hand on my shoulder. I turn around to see a large tattooed man with a shaved head, wearing whites.

'You no like my goulash?' he says in a thick Polish accent.

'Um, yeah, loved it,' I say. 'Best. Goulash. Ever.'

He stares at me silently, the veins in his temples gently pulsating, and I wonder for a second if he's going to kiss my forehead or headbutt me.

'So why do you complain?' he asks gruffly.

'Uh, well…' I start, before giving up. 'Here.'

I reach into the top of my backpack and pull out my SUNKISSED & SINGLE baseball cap. 'Brought you a present.'

I stick the hat on his head.

'Suits you.'

'Uh, thanks,' he says, peering upwards.

And with that, I escape out into the street. Before I meet Seema, there's another old friend I need to check in on first.

FOURTEEN

TWELVE MONTHS AGO

Group Chat: The Deadbeats

> **Dylan**
> @kirby you're late, dinner's almost ready

> **Kirby**
> pls u would not believe the day i've had, i don't know what i want to take off first, my bra or my shoes

> **Seema**
> i feel u hun

> **Dave The Legend**
> oi oi

> **Seema**
> shut up dave

> **Dave The Legend**
> why is it everyone moans when i want to take off my pants, but kirby is applauded for removing her bra

> **Seema**
> cos she can do it with one hand

The first thing that hit me when I flopped through the front door of Flat Four was a waft of aromatic spices and freshly warmed naan bread. I followed my nose into the kitchen to see three big pans of curry, bubbling away on the stove.

The kitchen table was set with plates and cutlery, and there were even a couple of old candles jammed into the necks of empty wine bottles in the centre. Dave and Seema, clearly hungry and impatient to start devouring everything, stared at me.

'Hey,' I said. 'Sorry I'm late. Today has been mad. First that crazy message from Esme, then it turns out the chief councillor saw me in her terrible ShowMe video, then Trevor says the board are going to shut the paper down and – oh my God, this smells amazing! Who are you trying to impress?'

'Have you forgotten your big "let's stop slobbing around in front of the TV" speech already?' Dylan said, head bent over a pan of steaming rice. 'We're having a dinner party.'

'Dinner party? I thought we all agreed we were far too young for that sort of thing?'

'We pitched the idea to Esme last night at the pub,' Dave said. 'She was bang up for it.'

'Really?' I asked. I didn't remember that conversation. 'Where is Esme anyway? I've been calling her all day, but she never picks up.'

'No one her age actually answers the phone,' Seema said. 'Wish I could get away with that. God, if I didn't pick up when my mother called, she'd march over here and barge the door down.'

I took the wooden spoon from the sideboard and started stirring one of the pots.

'Oh no no no,' Dylan cried. 'Do not touch that, Kirby! You know what happened last time!'

Full confession: Last time I'd tried to make us dinner, I'd almost burnt the flat down. And considering I was making a salad, I thought that was impressive in itself. Anyway, as a result, I was now banned from going within three feet of the hob.

'I'm just testing the thickness!' I said, pulling out the spoon and tasting the delicious red sauce.

'And?' he asked. Despite his too-cool-for-school attitude, Dylan was still a little insecure about his cooking.

I prodded his stomach with the spoon. 'Perfect level of thickness.'

'Very funny,' he said, and tried to wrestle the spoon back off me. I retreated, waving it at him like a lightsaber. He tilted his head at me, clearly doubting my Jedi skills.

'What's that?' he said, pointing behind me. When I turned to look, he grabbed the spoon off me in one swift movement.

'Hey! No fair!' I cried. 'And you got sauce on me!'

I looked at the flick of red splashes on my white T-shirt and groaned. This was never going to come out.

Ever since I'd moved into Flat Four last year, Dylan and I had vibed. Not in a romantic way. I don't think Dylan really 'did' romantic. Don't get me wrong, it wasn't like he was a player – he just made it very obvious that he didn't have time for a relationship. He'd claim it was because he always had to work late at the pub, but that sounded like a convenient excuse to me.

'Did you see Esme's message on the group chat?' I asked.

'Oooh yes, a real mystery, isn't it?' Seema said. 'It's sooo exciting. Reminds me of this podcast I heard where—'

Dylan interrupted her by placing the bowl of steaming rice in the middle of the table.

'I think Esme is on to something,' Dave said. 'There's more to this town than meets the eye, you know. I've always said Crowhurst has a seedy underbelly.'

'You're the only one around here with a seedy underbelly, mate,' Dylan said. 'I'm sure Esme will be here in a minute, then you can ask her all about the shadowy dark forces yourself.'

'We've waited ages already,' Dave whined. 'Can't we start eating now?'

'We said seven p.m.,' Dylan said, checking the time display on the oven. 'Give her another five minutes. Have another poppadom if you have to. Kirby, take a seat and relax, why don't you?'

Dave karate chopped through the pile of poppadoms and started picking through the shards with his fingers.

'Oh Dave, don't do that, your fingernails are disgusting!' Seema made a faux-retching face.

Pulling up a chair, I sat down and grabbed a wine glass. 'This all looks delicious, Dyl, thank you.'

'To be fair, it wasn't just me, I had a couple of great sous chefs.'

'I put the nuts into bowls,' Dave said, proudly.

'And I poured the wine, natch,' Seema said.

'You should've told me earlier, I could have helped too,' I said.

They all looked at each other before finding their cutlery very interesting indeed.

'Oh right, I see. *That's* why you kept this quiet,' I said.

'Well, let's not forget the burnt salad incident...' Dylan started.

'No, please, can we all forget the burnt salad incident? Everyone deserves a second chance!' I protested. 'I could've prepared my famous cheese course?'

'Buying half the cheese counter from Sainsbury's doesn't really count as cooking, Kirby. And Esme is vegan anyway.'

I flinched. Part of me couldn't help but wonder where he'd picked up that little detail.

'So, I've done chickpea masala, a cauliflower jalfrezi and a sweet potato dahl,' Dylan went on. 'And we've got rice, homemade bhajis and naan.'

'Sounds lush, mate, nice one,' Dave said, then leant over and whispered loudly in my ear. 'Just don't tell Esme that we usually just eat off our laps in front of the telly.'

I had to admit, it did feel nice to eat a proper meal, all together like a family. It had never felt that way at home. I was what you called a marriage-saving baby. Mum and Dad had me eight years after my twin brothers Ethan and Nathan. I think they thought it would bring them closer together. It didn't work. My parents divorced when I was seven, and my then-teenage brothers went to live with Dad in his huge house with a swimming pool and satellite TV. He was a successful actor, and Mum was an English teacher, so our worlds were very different. I always felt like I was a disappointment to Dad, like he'd gone away to this big magical place, and left me behind. After that, it was just Mum, me and whatever leftovers were in the freezer.

'No laps tonight. This is supposed to be a sophisticated dinner party,' Dylan said.

'Oh God, by sophisticated, you don't mean there's going to be jazz, do you?' I groaned. 'Please, please tell me you don't mean jazz.'

He rolled his eyes and fiddled with his phone. Dylan was one of those guys who refused to listen to anything recorded after about 1968. I think he liked the idea that drinking whiskey and listening to some old timer strangle the life out of a trombone counted as a hobby. But to my pleasant surprise, the kitchen filled with the soulful voice of Nina Simone, which Dave took as his cue to start ladling spoons of each dish onto his plate.

'Not yet!' Dylan scolded. 'Wait for Esme, this is for her benefit after all.'

That smarted a little. Since when did Dylan care so much about Esme, anyway? Last night he seemed pretty unimpressed by her. I didn't remember him ever making this level of effort for anyone else.

Dave groaned, placing the spoon back and reaching for a conciliatory peanut.

'So, speaking of Esme, did anyone even hear her leave this morning?' I asked. 'I think she must have got up before me. Her mattress wasn't even blown up.'

Seema shook her head, but Dave's eyes darted towards Dylan.

'You saw her, didn't you, Dyl?' he asked, innocently.

'Uh, I heard the front door go, I think,' Dylan said. 'That ancient mattress probably deflated overnight. I reckon Frank bought it in the Eighties. And even then it was second-hand.'

'But where would she even be going that early?' I asked, checking my phone again. 'And why isn't she back yet?'

Dylan topped up my wine.

'We're not her parents, Kirbs. Maybe she met up with some mates or something,' he said, a little defensively. 'Come on, let's all put our phones away and have a drink. I'm sure Esme is fine.'

'Yeah, I mean, how much trouble can she possibly be in? It's Crowhurst, duh,' Seema said. 'I don't think anyone's died here of anything except old age since… well, you know.'

'Yes, I do know. The Crowhurst Killer,' I said. 'That's what worries me.'

'Peter Doyle? You don't have to worry about that old psycho, he's looong gone,' Dave said, drawing a finger across his neck and rolling his eyes back.

Or was he? I wondered. Should I tell the others that Esme thought differently, or would they think I was an idiot?

'Aren't any of you a little bit freaked out by the whole "if anything happens to me" bit of her message? What if, I dunno, Peter Doyle survived somehow?'

'Come off it,' Dylan laughed. 'Don't be ridiculous.'

'You mean he didn't break his neck when he jumped off Staker Point?' Dave said, the cogs in his dense brain clearly turning. 'And now he's back to his old tricks? Cool!'

'Cool?' I said. 'I don't think those poor teens thought it was very cool in 1996.'

'Well, they made the classic mistake of getting themselves killed. Wouldn't happen to me,' Dave said.

'Um, how do you work that one out, Legend?' I asked.

'You've seen scary movies. They never kill off the main character, right?'

'And what makes you think you're the main character?' Seema scoffed.

'Pretty obvious, isn't it?' Dave pointed to his chest. 'I exude main character energy.'

Seema almost spat out her wine. 'Honey, you're the comic relief who gets killed off first.'

'Nah, that would be Kirby, she's the goofy one,' Dave said.

'Wait, are you saying I'm the Phoebe of the group?' I asked.

'Well, I'm Rachel,' Seema said. 'And, sorry, babe, I love you, but you're nowhere near tidy enough to be Monica.'

I folded my arms and pouted.

'Who am I then?' Dylan asked.

'You?' Dave said. 'You're Gunther.'

'This is ridiculous,' Dylan sighed.

'You're right, it is ridiculous. There's no "The One Where They All Get Butchered by a Psychopath" episode—' Seema started.

'No, not that, although that is ridiculous,' Dylan said. 'I mean all this Peter Doyle crap. It's ancient history.'

'Not that ancient,' I said. 'It was only thirty years ago. Your parents probably hung out with him.'

'I hope not, he was just some drunk who lived in the woods,' Dave said, dipping a naan into the pot of curry. 'Dylan, didn't your stepdad used to go fishing with him?'

'No!' Dylan said, then paused for a moment. 'At least, not that I know about. And ease up on the dipping, will you?'

'I heard he had a terrible upbringing,' Seema said. 'Grew up in an orphanage in Krakow.'

'No, it was Moscow,' Dave said, matter-of-factly chewing on his naan. 'Born in a Russian gulag. Dad was in the Bratva, mum was a cleaner. Killed his first man before he was ten.'

Dylan blew out his cheeks. 'You've all watched too many true-crime documentaries,' he said. 'Peter Doyle was just a sick bastard, pure and simple.'

Dave wiped the curry sauce off from around his mouth and reached for a bhaji. 'The older kids at school used to scare the crap out of us, chanting "Peter Doyle's gonna chop you up" and chasing us round the playground,' he went on. 'And my mum used to drag me to that crappy exhibit they used to have at the fayre. Oh, do you guys remember the waxwork?'

'Oh God, that thing!' Seema groaned. 'I was sooo desperate to go and see it, but Mum and Dad wouldn't let me. They told us Peter Doyle would eat us for dinner if we didn't do our homework.'

Seema liked to make out that her parents were super strict. The opposite was true, in fact. I'd met them a few times, and they were lovely. I think they just had high standards. Both doctors, they'd emigrated here from Pakistan in the Eighties. They didn't mind so much that Seema wasn't particularly religious, or that she drank and dated. But they weren't exactly thrilled that she was nearly thirty, unmarried and still hadn't passed her final dental exams.

'Hang on, Peter Doyle ate someone?' I asked, looking at the curries and suddenly feeling a bit queasy.

'Yeah, it was like the Crowhurst Chainsaw Massacre,' Dave says, and I swore I caught a glint of glee in his eyes.

'That's bollocks, he never ate anyone,' Dylan said. 'I don't think, anyway.'

'They had an actual exhibit here about the murders?' I asked. 'Like a serial-killer museum?'

'Well, museum is generous,' Dave said. 'But yeah, back in the day, there was this display in a tent at the fayre every year. They stuck a crummy waxwork and some old front pages of *The Gazette* in there. The Peter Doyle waxwork looked more like Michael McIntyre after a rough night than a bloodthirsty serial killer though. We used to stick chewing gum on him.'

'It was really inappropriate, if you ask me,' Dylan added. 'They called it a "tribute to the victims", but it felt more like a celebration of Doyle. My mum wouldn't let me anywhere near it either.'

'And people really came all the way here just to see a waxwork of a serial killer?' I asked.

'Well, all the way from Norbridge, at least. It was hardly LEGOLAND. But the fayre did get really popular for a few years. Same bunch of saddos who watch all those true-crime documentaries.' Dylan tilted his head at Seema.

'Excuse me.' Seema waved her fork at him. 'They're educational!'

'Yeah, educational if you want to decapitate a bunch of people.'

'Seema doesn't need any lessons in that, she could bore anyone to death talking about Hot Dentist,' Dave sniggered.

Seema, being used to this sort of comment, rolled her eyes, deeply. 'This, coming from a man who had a crush on the sexy M&M for three years.'

'You don't know everything about me, you know. I've got chicks sliding into my DMs 24/7,' Dave said, grabbing another bhaji. 'It's Kirby who'll probably die waiting for Dylan to ask her out.'

I bit my poor, long-suffering tongue – hard. But I could tell Dylan was beginning to lose his patience.

'Dave, if you keep eating *all* the bhajis, then you're gonna find out in a minute *exactly* how I'd murder someone,' Dylan said.

Dave threw the bhaji into the air defiantly and caught it

in his mouth. 'Go on then, tell me, how are you going to do me in?'

'Dunno, maybe smash you over the head repeatedly with a pot of curry?' Dylan suggested.

While they bickered, I took my chance to sneak another look at my phone under the table. *Still nothing.* I was starting to get seriously worried.

'Shouldn't Esme be here by now?'

'Yes, she should, because I would really, really like to start eating this,' Dave said, swivelling his eyes towards the dahl.

'Am I the only one who cares more about their flatmates than their food?' I huffed. 'What happened to "Deadbeats Forever"?'

'You didn't seem to care that much about your flatmates when you used up all the hot water in your hour-long shower this morning,' Dave shot back.

'I didn't realise my showers were being timed, David. But fine, if you're all so desperate to eat, then let's eat.'

I grabbed the ladle and began angrily splashing servings of dahl on everyone's plates.

'Kirby,' Dylan started. 'Er, we're meant to be waiting for Esme—'

I glared at him and spooned another dollop onto his plate.

'Wait, I don't want any—'

I ignored him and carried on ladling the curry until it was spilling onto the table.

'Hate to agree with Dave, but I think we're all getting a little hangry,' Seema said. 'I only had a Kinder Bueno for lunch. Hot Dentist gave me the snack out of his Tesco Meal Deal. So maybe we should make a start before all this gets cold?'

'What, like my shower this morning?' Dave interjected.

'Dave!' Dylan snapped. 'Give it a rest.'

For what seemed like the length of one of my showers, everybody silently shovelled spoonfuls of curry into their mouths. The only sound came from Dave aggressively chewing on a naan. I looked over at Seema who was concentrating very hard on her fork, and then to Dylan, who was intent on rearranging the napkin tucked into his shirt. I shuffled a bhaji around my plate for a bit.

'An hour? Really?' Dylan whispered to me.

'No! He's exaggerating,' I hissed back. 'Forty-five minutes, tops. But I really needed it this morning, okay?'

'Don't worry, Kirby,' Seema said gently. 'Esme's clearly got better things to do tonight. She'll turn up when she turns up. There's no point fretting about it.'

Dave snorted out loud. 'That's not your usual policy, is it, Seema? I've seen you waste a whole weekend staring at your phone trying to manifest a text from Hot Dentist.'

Seema's brown eyes narrowed, and she looked like she was about to slap Dave with a naan bread.

'Take that back,' she said. 'Otherwise...'

'Otherwise what? You're going to get your dentist pal round to check my fillings? Cos last time I had to wait three months for an appointment, so I won't hold my breath.'

'Drop it, Dave,' Dylan snapped. 'I know your love life stinks, but there's no need to take it out on all of us.'

'Alright, let's talk about you then, mate,' Dave turned his attention to Dylan. 'Seems like you're done mooning over Kirby now the ever-so-lovely Esme has arrived. Maybe you'll have more luck with her? Or have you already?'

I felt my face flush.

'You really are pushing your luck now, mate,' Dylan pushed his chair back aggressively and stood up. I was beginning to worry that one of them might really murder someone in a minute. Dave got up too, and now all three of them were leaning over the table yelling.

I'd had enough of this. I held up my phone and waved it at them.

'Aren't any of you worried?' I cried. 'What if Esme never came home last night? She could be lying in a ditch somewhere, and we're all here arguing about who uses the most hot water!'

They stopped shouting and all turned to look at me.

'Esme could be dead!' I said. 'Dead!'

The silence was suddenly broken by the ping of a ShowMe alert from my phone.

'Esme is LIVE!' it said.

FIFTEEN

PRESENT DAY

Stewart Heights towers above me, a giant concrete reminder of my past. When I crane my neck to look up at the building, the sun peaks out from behind it, blinding me for a second. I shield my eyes and find the windows of Flat Four. The lights are on in the lounge, and I can't help but wonder what poor sods are living there now, squeezed on the same battered sofa. I'd bet my life that Frank's still not fixed the boiler.

I walk to the parking bay and spot my car immediately. Her paintwork isn't quite as gleaming as before, but at least my little Mini is still there, right where I left her, sloppily parked as usual (what can I tell you, I was in a hurry) but intact.

I pat the bonnet lovingly, then immediately regret it, as it's absolutely filthy. I'm slightly surprised she's still here, to be honest. I mean, I'd paid the permit for the entire year, so I'd be pretty pissed off if she'd been towed. But mostly I'm pleased to see all four tyres are present and the windows haven't been smashed in. Maybe I should be offended that no one wanted to nick her.

Emblazoned on the side, in garish yellow and a green that was somewhere between vomit and mulch, is the logo for

Foxtons, the ubiquitous high street estate agent. My cousin had sold me the car third (or possibly fourth) hand when I got my job in London, and whoever owned it before him must have worked there. Or stolen it. Sure, it did not scream 'hip, young professional journalist', but it was cheap and (semi) reliable. Sadly, it had proved impossible to remove the large FOXTONS letters and paintwork, which meant everywhere I went, people assumed I was going to try and sell them a vastly overvalued two-bed semi in Kettering.

I chuck my rucksack in the back, and sit in the driver's seat for a minute, not moving. It's a weird sensation, being here again, like putting on an old dress that you used to love, but now doesn't quite fit like you remember. When I catch a glance of the back seat in the rear-view mirror, my mind involuntarily flashes back to the rainy night that I spent there. I can almost feel the cold clasp of the seat belt digging into my back as I—

Stop.

I'm not here to reminisce about old times. I need to find the others and figure out who's really behind these messages, before someone else gets hurt. Whoever it was, they didn't show at The Lion. Unless they'd been waiting and watching, seeing who would actually turn up.

So, here's the plan: first, I'll convince Seema to help me. Then, we'll go find Dave, who is sure to know where the hell Dylan is. Together, we can work out what to do about this mysterious 'Esme'.

It's one of my Top-Five Best Plans, and I have total confidence in it.

Unfortunately, it can only work if the damn car starts. If not, I'm going to have to wait thirty-five minutes for the number fifty-nine bus, which is going to throw the whole 'getting the band back together' thing way out of whack. I stick my key in the ignition and pray to the car gods for the best. But before I can even turn it, there's a loud ding from my phone.

A new notification alert on the Deadbeats group flashes on the screen.

Seema has left the chat.

Now why the hell would she do that?

SIXTEEN

TWELVE MONTHS AGO

I almost dropped my phone in my cauliflower jalfrezi.

'It's Esme!' I pointed to my phone screen. 'I set the app up to alert me when she posted a new video. And she's doing a ShowMe live, right now. Look!'

I propped my phone up on the wine bottle so we could all see, and everyone gathered round my chair. On the screen, we could see Esme chatting to the camera as she walked along a dark street. It was kind of grainy, and her face was only illuminated by her phone and the occasional headlights of a passing car.

'What's she saying?' Seema asked. 'I can't hear.'

I whacked the volume up and we leant in.

'—gonna have to really speak quietly, cos I'm doing this live, and I have zero idea what's about to go down, so let me know in the comments if you can't hear or see properly. It's pretty dark round here... So, yeah, basically, I'm about to confront the person I think really knows what happened thirty years ago up on Staker Point.'

We watched as Esme turned into a side street, and then

into what looked like a park. There were a few trees behind her, but other than that, it was pitch black.

'*And yes, sorry, Watsons, I am being deliberately vague! But, right here, in black and white,*' she waved what looked like a page of a newspaper that she was clutching in her free hand, '*is the person who knows everything about the Crowhurst Killer. I was sent this in the post – old school, right? – by an anonymous source. If you've been following my videos, you'll know that I think there's something pretty suss about the whole Peter Doyle thing. It's all a bit too convenient, don't you think? But I reckon I've worked out who might have some answers, and it's gonna blow your mind when you find out who! So just... bear with me a sec...*'

Her expression suddenly shifted from her usual ShowMe smile to a look of mild confusion. She quickly stuck the paper in her handbag.

'*Oh wait, hush up a minute, guys, someone is coming. What, no way! Is that...? It is you, isn't it? Hey, I didn't... what are you—*'

Suddenly, the camera blurred, like someone had knocked her phone out of her hand. For a very, very brief second, I could've sworn I saw another figure appear, but the camera moved too quickly for me to make out any features. Then the screen went deathly black.

I wasn't prepared for what happened next – a scream. A sharp, blood-curdling scream. And then, a horrible silence.

A second later, the words '*live stream has ended*' popped up on the screen.

We sat there, staring at the phone, dumbfounded, not really knowing what to say.

'Is that it?' Seema asked eventually. 'It's over?'

I grabbed my phone and refreshed the app, hoping the stream would restart, or Esme would post a new video, explaining that she just dropped her phone or something. Anything that would prove she was okay. But nope, there was nothing.

'What happened?' I cried.

'Maybe she just tripped over?' Seema suggested.

'No.' I shook my head. 'There was someone else there, didn't you see them? I'm calling her.'

I rang Esme's number, but it went straight to voicemail, so I bashed out a couple of messages on the group chat.

'You all heard that scream, right?' I asked the others. 'We should tell someone, shouldn't we?'

'Oh my God, we should totally call the police!' Seema said, almost too excitedly. 'They say the first twenty-four hours after someone goes missing are the most important!'

I'd completely lost my appetite, but somehow Dave was still managing to chomp on poppadoms.

'And say what?' he asked. 'That our flatmate who we've known for all of two seconds dropped her phone?'

'Come on, guys, it's obviously a set-up.' Dylan started clearing away the plates. 'This is what these ShowMe kids do. Create a bit of drama to grow their follower count. She'll wait until everyone's really worried, then pop up in a new video like nothing ever happened. I guarantee it.'

'Hold up a sec,' Seema said. 'Did anyone recognise anything in the background that might tell us where she was walking? Can you replay the video, Kirbs?'

'No,' I said, tapping frantically on my screen. 'Once a live ShowMe finishes, that's it, you can't view it again.'

It had been too dark and too close up to tell which part of town Esme was in.

'Maybe she told someone where she was going?' I said. 'We could try her friends and family?'

With a cold shudder, I realised we didn't know anything about Esme. Not even her last name. I racked my brains. She mentioned her rich parents, and I was pretty sure she came from London. But that was it. Suddenly, I had an idea.

'What about Max?' I said. 'She sub-letted the room off him, right? He must have some sort of contact details for her. Maybe a next of kin or something?'

'Ugh, Max,' Dave groaned. 'That tosser. He's still on the group chat but he never replies. He thinks he's too good for us, but I bet he still likes to keep an eye on what we're up to.'

Max had pretty much despised every second he'd lived in Stewart Heights, and hadn't looked back since he left for his secondment in Birmingham, but he was due back in the autumn.

'Oh, he's definitely muted us,' Seema said. 'We'll have to video call him.'

When he eventually picked up, Max looked annoyed before we'd even said hello. He was sitting on what looked like a posh hotel bed, his hair wet and slicked back, as if he'd just got out of the shower.

'Well, well, well. A Friday evening call from my old flatmates,' he sighed, with little to no enthusiasm. 'To what do I owe this enormous pleasure?'

'Max! What's going on with you, babe?' Seema asked. 'You never reply on the group chat anymore!'

'Uh, well, things are really full on at work,' he glanced over his shoulder. 'This secondment has really been a step up for me.'

'We need to ask you something about—' I started.

'Oh, I haven't missed that disgusting kitchen,' Max winced, his face filling the screen as he leant closer to his phone to look behind me. 'I'm actually surprised that whole building hasn't been demolished.'

I noticed Dylan's fists tightening. There was no love lost between Max and the others. Let's just say he didn't share their passion for all-night reality-TV marathons and getting stoned on the roof.

'Wanker,' Dave whispered, too loudly, while shaking his wrist to make the internationally recognised hand gesture.

I glared at him. 'Dave! If you're doing that, you don't need to say the word out loud!' I hissed.

Max coughed loudly.

'If you haven't noticed, I have company right now.' He motioned behind him as a half-naked figure disappeared into the bathroom. 'So, if you're quite done insulting me, maybe we could hurry this delightful exchange up a little?'

'Okay, it's about Esme.' I took a deep breath and attempted to summarise the situation quickly and succinctly. 'So, she arrived yesterday, and everything was cool, until we went to the pub and she pushed me in a hole. But actually, that all turned out pretty well to be honest. Anyway, that's not really important. The important thing is, she's just posted this weird video online and now we're freaking out because she's not picking up her phone. And, well, we realised we don't really know anything about her. Did Esme leave any next of kin information with you? Or even a surname?'

'Sorry, who?'

'Esme,' I said. 'The girl you sub-let the box room to.'

There was a pause. Max looked confused.

'I'm afraid I have absolutely no clue what you're talking about. I never rented out my room,' he said.

A cold tingle trickled through me. I leant closer to the phone.

'Um, say that again, Max.'

'I did not rent the room,' he repeated. 'Do you think I'm completely insane? Frank would throttle me if I tried to pull something like that.'

'Wait,' I said. 'This girl just turned up here yesterday. Petite, dark hair. Intense green eyes.'

There was another pause.

'Really hot?' Dave offered.

'No, sorry. And I'd really prefer it if you didn't let any old stranger sleep in my room, thank you very much. I'm still paying my share of the rent, you know. This Esme character sounds awfully rude. I expect everything to be exactly as I left it when I get back.'

'Alright mate,' Dylan sighed. 'Calm down, it's literally a blow-up mattress in a box room.'

'Well, if there's nothing else I can help you with, I really must go,' Max said, as a hand curled around his shoulder. 'Like I said, I'm kind of in the middle of something here. But I'll, um, see you in September, God willing.'

He hung up and I looked round at the others. Seema's mouth was hanging open and Dave looked like he was going to wet himself with excitement. Dylan just shrugged. But we were all thinking the same thing.

If Max didn't rent his room to Esme, then how the hell did she get a key?

SEVENTEEN

TWELVE MONTHS AGO

I lay on the sofa, refreshing ShowMe and worrying. It was almost midnight, and there was still no sign of Esme.

Her phone was going straight to voicemail and she wasn't replying to texts. As for the police, they'd been beyond useless. Without a surname, or any actual proof Esme was missing, they said there wasn't much they could do except take my details.

So, at this point, I didn't know what else to do, other than sit here and hope she waltzed back in the front door, sucking on her vape like nothing had happened.

I leant over the back of the sofa and lifted up one of the blind slats with my finger to peek outside.

Are you out there somewhere, Esme? I wondered.

The construction workers had long since gone home, and Courtney Road was motionless, save for an empty crisp packet blowing in the wind. I slumped back onto the settee. Some hot-shot journalist I turned out to be. Trevor was right, I was no Lois Lane. Esme had warned me that she was in danger. 'If anything happens to me…', she'd written on the group chat. And now something *had* happened to her. And here I was, staring out the window.

If this had been the other way around, she would have found me by now, and she'd be basking in adoration from the townsfolk and her legion of followers, or the Watsons as they liked to call themselves. But as it was, come Monday, she'd probably be lying in a ditch somewhere and I'd be writing six hundred words about Crowhurst Library's new colour photocopier.

My thoughts were interrupted when Dylan popped his head round the living room door.

'No word?' he mumbled, his toothbrush hanging out of his mouth, like he was James Dean posing with a cigarette.

'Nope.' I sat up and showed him my phone. 'Nothing on ShowMe either. Are the others still up?'

'Dave's up on the roof, I think—' He mimed taking a toke on a joint. 'Seema's on the phone to Hot Dentist, obviously.'

'Alright, I'm gonna chill here for a bit, just in case, you know?'

'We can watch some TV if you want? It'll really wind Dave up if we watched *Ghost Detectives* without him.'

'Nah,' I smiled. 'It's cool, I'm just gonna lie here and doom-scroll.'

'Wait, gimme a sec.' He waved his toothbrush at me before disappearing down the hallway and into the bathroom. I heard him spit out the toothpaste in his mouth before he reappeared.

He came back clutching a soft toy – a bright yellow Pikachu Pokémon.

'Thought you might like some company.' He threw the toy

to me, and I caught it. 'Have you met this guy? I won him last summer in the claw machine at the fayre.'

'You managed to grab this with the wobbly claw? I didn't think it was possible to win anything in those machines,' I said.

'Well, yeah, with composure, patience and a little bit of luck, you can do it,' he said. 'And ten quid's worth of pound coins also helps. Apparently they're programmed to give you a prize one in every ten goes.'

I examined the toy with a mixture of admiration and derision. He had a wonky eye and a protruding pink felt tongue that gave the impression he'd gone feral.

'He's a knock-off, isn't he? Probably full of nails and sawdust. I can't believe you kept this thing.'

'I was going to give it to Lily, but I wasn't convinced it would pass EU safety regulations.'

'Highly flammable?'

'Yep,' he nodded. 'So I had absolutely no choice but to keep it.'

Lily was Dylan's super-cute little sister. Half-sister, to be accurate. Dylan loved her more than anything. She had cerebral palsy, which meant that her parents could only work part-time, and they needed Dylan to chip in with bills and stuff. I think that's why he took his work so seriously. Shifts at The Red Lion didn't pay much, but he worked really hard so he could help them out more. At the same time, he'd been saving up every spare penny to convert Fast Forward into a small restaurant, serving traditional British fare with a modern twist.

'I bet you sleep with this thing, don't you? Who'd've

thought it? The brooding, cynical chef cuddles up to a fluffy Pokémon every night.'

'Yeah, yeah, whatever,' he smiled. 'Maybe I'm just more sensitive than you think, huh?'

'Well, you're more sensitive than the police, that's for sure. They couldn't care less about Esme. Why am I the only person who seems worried about her?'

'Did you tell them about her weird message on the group chat?' he asked.

'No,' I said, slapping my forehead. 'Why? Do you think I should have? Damn. I really should have, shouldn't I? What good am I if I can't even report a missing person right? I should call them back. What if Peter Doyle—'

Dylan came over to the sofa, knelt down and placed a hand on each of my shoulders, close enough that I could smell the minty Colgate on his cool breath.

'Kirby Cornell, I've lived here a lot longer than you, and trust me, people in Crowhurst don't really give a shit about anyone.' He pushed a rogue curl of auburn hair behind my ear. 'But believe me, Peter Doyle is ancient history. This town already slayed their bogeyman.'

I nodded. When he came that close to me, I kind of froze up a bit. Which was totally stupid – I was a grown woman. And it's not like I'd never had a boyfriend before. In fact, I'd had a very steady, very safe and yes, very boring boyfriend in London. My mates there always used to tell me I could do loads better, but I wasn't convinced. Anyway, Dylan was out of my league – all the women who came in the pub fancied him (granted, most of them were over fifty, but that didn't stop him flirting with them).

'Alright, I'm going to bed.' Dylan stood up and headed towards the hallway, but something made him stop at the lounge door. He looked back at me, his brow furrowed. 'Unless… are you sure you don't want some company?'

'Ah, this is awkward, but I already have a date.' I picked up the Pikachu and waved it at him.

As much as I would've enjoyed his company, I didn't want to be like those women in the pub. His head was big enough already.

'Alright, well, don't let him try anything,' Dylan said. 'I know what that guy is like. Total pervert.'

'Wandering paws, right?' I smiled.

Once Dylan had slipped off to bed, I spent an hour trying to distract myself by discovering which *Gilmore Girls* character I was (Rory, which is waaay off), which Taylor Swift Era best suited my mood (Reputation, okay, fair), as well as which Disney Prince I was most compatible with (the fox from Robin Hood, bizarrely, who is a) not a prince and b) a fox, so not sure that really counts, but I'll take it).

But whatever I did, I couldn't stop thinking about Esme.

The internet didn't reveal much more about her. I'd even tried a few reverse image searches using her profile pic, but the closest Google could come up with was a home-shopping host in Alabama that barely looked like her. For a so-called influencer, she didn't have much of an online presence. No LinkedIn, no Facebook, no YouTube. She had an Instagram and a TikTok with the same ShowMeSherlock handle, but it was just reposts of her ShowMe videos. And her profile simply said: 'Esme. Online investigations. Greater London. DM for collabs.'

I wondered what sort of collaborations people would

want to do with Esme. As photogenic as she was, her chosen subject matter was pretty grim – missing people, kidnaps and serial killers.

So, what was I supposed to do now? If it had been me that was missing, I knew what Esme would do. She wouldn't be moping about on the couch doing online quizzes, that's for sure. If nothing is happening, then you have to make it happen – that's what she'd said, right?

The police didn't care. My flatmates didn't care. But I knew some people who would.

The Watsons.

They could help me find her, but I how was I supposed to enlist them? If something had happened to Esme, she wasn't going to be able to make any new videos for them to analyse.

But I could.

If I was really going to galvanise them, I'd have to – what did Esme say – sex it up a bit?

So, pushing my hair back behind my ears, I wiped the sleep out of my eyes and opened ShowMe. Trevor had told me 'no more videos', but Whatever Trevor and his newspaper were about to be relegated to the past. ShowMe was the future. ShowMe could help me find Esme. And with ShowMe, no one could stop me. Okay, I was wearing my curry-stained T-shirt and pyjama shorts, so I wasn't exactly up to Esme's levels of professionalism, but it would have to do.

With a deep breath, I turned the camera on myself and started filming.

'*Um, so hey, er, everyone. If you've been watching ShowMeSherlock's videos, you'll know that Esme was looking into a cold case here in Crowhurst, the serial killer Peter Doyle. Well, I say serial killer, technically he's actually a "spree killer". Is that right? I'll have to google it. Anyway, he jumped off a cliff thirty years ago after murdering five people. Or so we all thought. Now Esme has gone missing. And I think she found out something about Peter Doyle. And I have a horrible feeling that whatever she discovered has put her in grave danger. My name is Kirby Cornell, and this is the search for ShowMeSherlock. I'm going to find out what happened to her and finish what she started. But I am going to need your help. Because I think I know what she found out...'*

I paused to compose myself, just like Esme did on her videos when she had a vital clue to deliver, and looked straight at the lens.

'Peter Doyle is alive.'

I stopped recording and hesitated for a second, but just a second. Something told me that if I uploaded this, then there was no going back.

So, with a simple touch of a button, I released the video into the wild.

EIGHTEEN

I sit in the Mini staring at Seema's message.

Sure, the group chat was getting a little creepy, but I can't understand why Seema would leave, just before we're due to meet. A chill runs through me when I think back to how Max had left the chat, and well, then look how that turned out...

Seema seemed fine on the phone. Well, maybe 'fine' is a little generous, but she at least sounded like she was up for talking. All I can do now is drive over to the dentist surgery, and hope that she turns up. Otherwise, I'm going to have to track down Dave by myself, and I'm not sure I can face that yet, unless I absolutely have to.

Driving through town is depressing. I'd love to tell you that the hazy late summer days turn Crowhurst into a picturesque cinnamon dreamscape, but that would be a massive lie. It's actually pretty much the same as Crowhurst at any other time of year, but at least the coating of crispy orange leaves covers up some of the fried chicken boxes and empty vapes. The few remaining familiar sights stir something in me, if not exactly fond memories, more a sense of a shared trauma.

When I pull up outside the dentist surgery, the door is unlocked, and inside, the waiting room is empty. It closes at half five, so it makes sense that no one is here, but it still feels eerie. I call out for Seema, but there's no answer.

Surely she didn't leave already?

I stick my head in the office behind the reception desk.

'Seema?' I call out again.

No answer.

The only thing I can hear is the faint, consistent drip of a leaky tap, like a single drop of water splashing into a porcelain sink.

I notice the surgery-room door is ajar, and I push it open with my foot. I'm instantly hit by the slightly sickly smell of that weird pink mouthwash that dentists use to wash your mouth out.

The next thing I realise is that someone is lying on the dentist's chair. There's a dental mask over their face, and their limp arms drape over the edge.

A drip of bright red blood splashes from their fingers onto the otherwise pristine white floor.

That's when I see it: a single black feather, lying in the pool of blood.

No... no way...

I can feel my whole body start to shake, but I take another step inside. Now the only noise I can hear is my heartbeat reverberating through my body. The chair's lamp is on, shining a crazy bright light over whoever it is, meaning I can't see shit. Shielding my eyes with my hand, I walk over and push the lamp away.

I don't want to look at their face, but I know I have to. Shaking, I reach over and pull the mask down, millimetre by millimetre.

I start to scream and then clamp my hand over my mouth, taking several steps backwards. Steadying myself against the door for a second, I try to regulate my breathing.

It's Seema, her eyes wide and her mouth agape. There's a wide, bloody gash in her neck. It looks like someone has taken a blunt instrument to it. Multiple times.

I stare at the body, and now I don't stop myself screaming. My hands still shaking, I reach for her lifeless arm that's flopped by the side of the chair and feel for her pulse.

Nothing.

I know I need to call the police, but I'm paralysed.

What the hell am I going to tell them? '*Erm, remember the girl who said Peter Doyle was back from the dead last year? Well, guess who's back again? You can trust me this time, honest.*'

And what if they discover the truth about what really happened a year ago? If they find out what we did that night, I'll end up stuck in a cold police-station interrogation room all night, waiting for a lawyer I can't afford.

Besides, there's no saving Seema now. Whatever this is, this is no prank. She has been distinctly unalived.

Quickly, I pull on a surgical glove from the box beside the chair and dial 999 from the landline phone on the reception desk. I don't tell them my name, just the address, then I hang up in a daze.

I figure I only have minutes before the ambulance arrives, so try to snap myself out of it and get the hell out of there. But just as I'm stepping out the door, my phone beeps, alerting me to a new message.

My heart sinks as I reach into my jacket pocket, knowing I have to read it, but wishing I didn't have to, and open WhatsApp.

Oh, you have to be kidding.

Of course, it's on the *fricking* group chat.

If my heart was beating fast before, it feels like it's about to burst out of my chest now. I just keep staring at the message, my phone stuck in my hand like it's superglued to my fingers.

> Esme
> You leave the group, you die.

NINETEEN

'Kirby, darling, your sausages are on fire,' Seema said matter-of-factly, not looking up from her phone.

For a second, my brain struggled to compute this sentence. To my knowledge, I, Clare 'Kirby' Cornell, did not own any sausages, alight or otherwise.

Then I remembered that, yes, I had actually started cooking breakfast about ten minutes ago.

In my defence, I hadn't slept much. I'd spent half the night just staring at my phone, rewatching my ShowMe video over and over. Just as I'd hoped, a lot of Esme's followers had been watching it too. I had added the hashtag *FindEsme*, and tagged in @ShowMeSherlock, and it had racked up over 10,000 views already. The comments were wild.

TheLeftyWanker:
this is massive

Drakesboy:
massively fake more like

Catsaremylovelanguage_12:
lol peter doyle is dead. someone else snatched her.

TopG4eva:
nice tits

Doom_Bot:
wait does this mean no more ShowMeSherlock videos

Shellfish_diet:
A spree killer is someone who kills a number of random people at one particular time and location in a frenzied and unpremeditated way, for your information.

TayTayLover:
so was Doyle's body ever found?

Doom_Bot:
yeah the police found a body, but it was too messed up to know if it was Doyle for sure

Shellfish_diet:
The police cannot be trusted. You should look for her yourself. I zoomed in on Esme's live video, and if you lighten the footage by 80 per cent, you can see the top of a helter-skelter in the background.

Part of me was excited by all the attention, but another, much bigger, part felt horribly exposed. What if I'd made a mistake? What if I'd been so desperate for a story that I'd convinced myself that a dead serial killer had risen from a watery grave, ready to wreak revenge on any Gen Z ShowMe sleuth that just happened to be hanging around?

Maybe Esme had simply realised there was no sensational secret to uncover here, and hopped on the train back to her minimalist Knightsbridge apartment to find some other, more interesting murderers to investigate. Looking at the tar-black sausages and mountain of soggy egg in front of me, I couldn't really blame her.

'Kirby! Sausages!' I heard Seema say again, more loudly this time, and I snapped out of my daze, grabbing the frying pan just before the sausages completely disintegrated.

'This is exactly why we banned you from cooking, sweetie,' she said. 'Put the pan down, and come and have some nice, safe cereal.'

'Um, yeah, sorry,' I mumbled.

Seema nodded and went back to her phone, texting furiously. I wondered what could have possibly happened during the past ten hours that she desperately needed to update Hot Dentist about.

Suddenly, Dave burst into the kitchen, wearing just a pair of loose boxer shorts. The grin on his face was as wide as the fly in his underwear. Standing in the doorway of the kitchen, he put his hands on his hips, like a triumphant superhero (albeit a superhero who forgot to get dressed properly that morning).

'Gordon Dillberry has got the shits!' he announced proudly.

We stared at him blankly.

'Did you hear what I said?' he asked.

'Er, yes?' I said. 'Should I call Trevor and ask him to hold the front page?'

'You don't understand! Everybody knows Gordon Dillberry was going to be the Thorny Crow this year! But he went and had a dodgy kebab from the Grillennium Falcon, didn't he! And now he's MIA. I warned him not to get the fish doner, you know what happened last time I—'

'Yeah, we all know, babes,' Seema sighed. 'There's actually

no need to recount the entire story every single time it comes up.'

'Anyway, now he can't do it, so I'm stepping up. This has been a lifelong dream.'

Every year the town picked one resident to cover in twigs and feathers, and parade around the fayre as Jack Daw, the Thorny Crow. The custom dated back to the 1700s, I think, when they apparently dressed the poor bugger in real feathers, but these days it was a much softer polyester number, stitched together by the Crowhurst Knitting Society.

'Wait, they have a substitute crow?' I asked. I shouldn't have been surprised that the Parish Council had a backup. It seemed like the whole year had been building up to this fayre, and nothing could be allowed to go wrong.

'Yep, and it's yours truly,' Dave grinned, eyeing my pan of scrambled eggs. 'What's with the cooked breakfast?'

'I woke up early, so I thought I'd do a fry up, make up for last night's disaster,' I said.

'Result!' Dave licked his lips and pulled out a chair. 'Load me up! This crow needs fattening!'

Seema visibly gagged.

'Could you please put some more clothes on before you sit next to me? The world does not need to see your balls, ever again.' Seema looked up from her phone and glanced at me knowingly. 'Believe me, those things are all kinds of problematic.'

'For the last time, my balls are *not* problematic,' Dave said. 'They are *legendary*.'

Dylan emerged from the shower with a damp towel wrapped around his waist. I found my eyes drifting to his surprisingly toned torso, which was covered in little tattoos. He caught my gaze and I quickly looked away.

'What's going on?' he yawned. 'Who let Kirby near the oven?'

'What is it with you boys and clothes?' Seema asked. 'Honestly, you treat this place like a locker room.'

'Look, now we're all up,' I announced. 'I need to tell you something. Last night I went on ShowMe and—'

Before I could finish my sentence, there was a knock on the door, very quickly followed by the sound of a key in the lock.

'Esme!' I cried, rushing into the hallway.

But as soon as I saw the figure pushing open the front door, my heart dropped to my stomach.

It wasn't her. It wasn't Esme. It was someone far, far worse.

TWENTY

The man at the door was wearing a heavy donkey jacket and jeans that were at least a size too big. Tall, and probably at least three stone overweight, he carried that extra heft like a wrestler, or those big guys you see lifting tree trunks over their heads on *World's Strongest Man*. I could imagine that as a younger man, he might have been quite intimidating. But now, with a receding hairline and deep frown lines across his forehead, he looked like he'd spent one too many winters in Marbella.

He didn't say anything, just stood there, taking up the whole doorway, a bulky brown package tucked under his arm.

'Good morning, Frank,' I said, trying to sound breezy, but my voice came out cracked. 'That's a lovely, um, jacket.'

He stepped into the flat with all the energy of a tired circus tiger, exhausted by years of fading applause and cheap beef.

'This place is a tip,' he grunted, kneeling down and running a finger along the hallway skirting board.

He peered at the absolutely miniscule amount of dust he'd

collected on his fingertip and sucked on his teeth. Behind me, Seema barely managed to hide her disdain.

'Can we help you with anything, Frank?' she asked. 'We were actually just having breakfast.'

'Am I not allowed to inspect my own property?' he asked. His eyes dropped to my chest, and I immediately felt like I wanted to throw up.

'You can't just walk in here anytime you like. Legally you're supposed to inform us before an inspection,' Seema said.

'"Can't" is a word I hear a lot from people your age,' Frank tutted.

'Are you sure they're saying "can't"?' Seema asked, innocently.

Frank's nostrils flared, and he craned his neck inside the kitchen. 'You should speak a little more respectfully to your elders,' he muttered. 'What's going on in here anyway? Why are you all half naked?'

'We're just having breakfast, Frank,' Dylan said. 'I think that's allowed under the terms of the lease.'

'Yes…' Frank sniffed. 'Well, something certainly smells… um, interesting.'

He pushed past us and began poking at the eggs, before dipping a fat finger into the pot of pesto on the sideboard. He pulled it out and licked it.

'Mmm, bit exotic for me,' he said.

'Might be that pesto and dust isn't the best combo,' I suggested.

'Dust might actually improve the taste of your cooking, to be honest,' Seema said under her breath.

Frank put the package he was carrying on the kitchen table.

'This is for young David,' he said. 'I hope you're all going to watch him at the fayre this weekend? Quite a moment for a young lad. I'll never forget my first time as the Thorny Crow.'

'Actually, since you mention it, Frank, I need to ask you something,' I said.

When he heard me say that, Dave placed a firm hand on my shoulder.

'No you don't, Kirby,' he said, beaming a big smile at Frank. 'Remember what we spoke about earlier? How we agreed not to bother Frank with all that stuff?'

He turned to me and mouthed the word 'eviction' very obviously.

'Don't tell me you've broken the toilet flush again,' Frank sighed.

'No,' I said. 'Well, yes, we have. But this isn't actually about that. This is about Esme.'

Dave groaned loudly and slumped against the wall, defeated.

'Esme?' Frank asked. 'Who is Esme?'

'The girl who's renting the box room,' I said.

There was an awkward pause.

'I don't know what you're talking about. I haven't rented the box room,' he said. 'Believe me, I wish I could. I'm haemorrhaging money on this place.'

An ice-cold tingle wriggled up my spine.

'Esme,' I repeated. 'She arrived yesterday. She had a key.'

There was another pause, longer this time.

'Are you sub-letting?' Frank said eventually. 'I could have all of you evicted for that.'

Dave gives me a 'told you so' look, and I was tempted to throw a burnt sausage at him. Instead, I took a deep breath and tried to keep my voice calm and reasonable.

'No, we're not sub-letting, Frank. We're just looking for Esme. This could be serious. She's been missing since yesterday and we're worried she might be hurt, or someone might have—'

'Might have what? Sacrificed her to Jack Daw, the Thorny Crow?'

'No,' I stuttered. 'Of course not. All I'm saying is, she arrived here yesterday, and we don't know her surname. Or anything about her really. And she didn't come home last night. Not that this is technically her home or anything, but you know what I mean, right? So we just want to make sure she's okay, but, we actually don't know where she is or where she went or what she's even really doing here. And, well, you're the landlord after all, so we just wondered if—'

Seema coughed loudly, a signal for me to get to the point.

'We wondered if you might know something about it,' I concluded.

Frank stared at us for a second, like a cow staring at traffic.

'What are you suggesting? That I've got her tied up in my basement? Now, now. You ought to be very careful about what you go around accusing people of. Besides, if you think I'm capable of doing that to one of my tenants,' he leant closer towards me and lowered his voice, 'then what makes you think I won't do the same to you?'

There was a sudden change in the atmosphere. Seema looked up sharply and even Dave looked appalled.

'I'm joking!' Frank roared after a painful moment of silence. 'For Crow's sake, your generation can't take a joke about anything, can you? Honestly, back in my day, we could say whatever we liked, without a snowflake bursting into tears because we hurt their feelings. I don't know anything about this Esme person. But, under the terms of your lease, you're not allowed to have guests stay for more than one week. And they are not, under any circumstances, permitted to have a key. So maybe it's better if she doesn't come back, hmm? There's plenty of people lining up to rent a highly desirable property like this, you know.'

Dylan pulled his towel tighter around his waist. 'Is there anything else we can help you with, Frank?' he asked. 'Only, if I don't put some clothes on soon, we're going to have to turn the thermostat up.'

'Just try and keep the place from turning into a pigsty, will you?' Frank muttered, heading back into the hallway. 'I hope to see you all at the fayre this weekend.' He stopped at the doorway and looked back at us with a smirk. 'Bring your friend Esme. If she ever turns up, that is. We're always looking for a handy sacrifice.'

TWENTY-ONE

As soon as Frank was gone, Dave gleefully peered inside the package.

'The Thorny Crow costume! What an honour!' he cried.

'It's not an honour,' Dylan said. 'Jack Daw isn't a hero, he's a symbol of a bad harvest. That's why we throw stones at him. The council always pick the village idiot to wear the costume.'

'Hey!' Dave scowled at him. 'That's not true.'

'Come on,' Dylan went on. 'Why do you think they offered it to Gordon Dillberry?'

'Fair point,' Dave agreed, begrudgingly, and started helping himself to the breakfast I'd prepared.

'Is that true?' I asked. 'Jack Daw is a bad guy?'

'Crows are an ancient symbol of bad luck,' Dylan said. 'So, back in the day, the villagers would chuck stones at Jack Daw, and make him "fly" away. "Then thar harvest that year be plentiful,"' he added in a mock West Country accent.

'Don't tell me cynical Dylan believes in all that "curse of the crow" stuff, does he?' Dave cried.

131

'Hold up, the curse of the crow?' I said. 'That doesn't sound good.'

'Don't listen to him,' Dylan said. 'There's no curse of the crow.'

'Something bad happens to anyone who plays Jack Daw,' Dave explained. 'Peter Doyle jumped off a cliff. This other guy who was Jack Daw in 1952 got run over by a tractor. And then Gordon got the shits, of course. Call that nothing?'

'Wow, that is quite the curse,' Seema said. 'You must be terrified, Dave.'

'Don't worry,' he said. 'Not even the squits can stop me fulfilling my destiny as the 409th Jack Daw in Crowhurst's long and storied history.'

'So Jack Daw just walks around the fayre while people throw stones at him?' I asked.

'Not anymore,' Dave said. 'Thanks to the woke police, we're only allowed to throw grapes these days.'

'This whole fayre is so fricking weird,' I said, shaking my head.

'Is it any stranger than pretending to drink the blood of Christ? Or fasting for a month?' Dylan asked.

'Or dressing up like a slutty cat on Halloween?' Seema added.

'Hey, that costume was supposed to be PG rated,' I said, blushing. 'It wasn't my fault the zipper broke.'

I flopped a mass of congealed eggs onto Seema's plate, and she inspected them with a mixture of disdain and genuine curiosity.

'What on earth did you do to these?' Seema asked, poking the little eggy mountain with her fork, like it had landed there from another planet.

'They look good to me,' Dave said, attempting to cram a forkful into his mouth.

'These are my famous scrambled eggs! They're meant to look like that,' I said.

'Oh, wait, these are *eggs*?' Dave said, taking another mouthful.

'They do look a little shambolic, to be fair, Kirbs,' said Dylan.

'Of course they're shambolic,' I said, plonking a spoonful on a plate for him. 'Scrambled eggs are shambolic by *definition*. They're not called "organised eggs", are they? Do you want some or not?'

'Er, yeah, I get that, but why are they green?'

'The pesto!' I cried. 'You people. Have you never been to Italy?' (Reader, *I* have never been to Italy.)

Dylan considered this for a moment, nodded, and pulled up a chair next to Seema, who was now scraping a heavy layer of Flora over a charred piece of toast.

'Maybe I'll just have cereal,' Dylan said, looking at his plate.

'Don't eat all the Coco Pops. They're my favourite. Number one, no question. They turn. The. Milk. Chocolatey,' Dave said, waving his fork in the air to accentuate his point. 'I'm not sure you understand quite how revolutionary that was.'

'It's the chocolate from the Coco Pops,' Dylan sighed. 'What you're gaining in the milk, you're losing from the pop. It's a marketing scam.'

Dave paused to consider this, and before he could respond, I whacked the kettle on, and any further ruminations were drowned out by the sound of the water coming to the boil.

'Okay, thank you, everyone, message received. I get it, I'm a terrible cook,' I said. 'Massive apologies. I'm just a little bit distracted this morning, you know, on account of a serial killer running around town.'

'Come on, Kirbs, not this again,' Dylan groaned. 'Could we please try and elevate the chat above serial killers and Dave's testicles?'

'Shame, those are my two favourite subjects,' Dave grinned.

'For the last time, there is no serial killer,' Dylan said. 'Not anymore, anyway.'

I took a breath. 'Are you sure about that?' I asked.

I brought ShowMe up on my phone, and played them my video from last night. The views were going mad. Every time I checked, they'd gone up by another couple of thousand. Dylan stared at the screen for a second, taking it in before he said anything.

'You put this online?' he asked.

'Yeah,' I mumbled.

Dylan had the same look on his face that my dad did when I told him I'd failed my maths A-level.

'Was that a good idea, Kirbs?'

'Uh, well, I had to do *something*. And look at what Esme's followers are saying. They all agree with me.'

'Her followers are a load of incels sat in their parents' basements, obsessively editing Wikipedia,' he said.

'At least they're doing *something*. Crowhurst's finest aren't lifting a finger. You heard what Esme said about the police. Turns out she was spot on. And listen to this, apparently, the body they found at the bottom of Staker Point was too damaged to properly identify. So it could have been anyone. What if Doyle got away, and now he's back?'

'Or, what if it's his ghost?' Dave offered, using his last bite of toast to scoop up the remains of his scrambled egg.

Dave was a big fan of conspiracy theories, the supernatural, chemtrails, alien abductions – you name it. If there was a twenty-minute YouTube video featuring a neck-bearded American waffling about it, he believed it. Once, last summer, he'd thrown out a Nutribullet because he was convinced it had been hacked by the Chinese government. (I'd failed to convince him that no one in Beijing was interested in how many tablespoons of peanut butter he put in his bespoke protein shake recipe.)

'Oh,' Seema piped up, 'my cousin told me about this guy who sank his yacht, drowned his entire family then faked his death. But he got caught when he tried to cash in his own life insurance.'

'Makes sense,' Dave nodded. 'So, Peter faked his death and hid out in a cave somewhere until he was ready to kill again.'

'Please,' Dylan sighed. 'This is ridiculous. Peter Doyle is dead. He's not a ghost, and he hasn't climbed back up a five-hundred-foot cliff thirty years later. Kirby, you're a journalist, you know better than this. It's bullshit, and we should not be entertaining it.'

'Hey, did you finish all the Coco Pops?' Dave asked, peering inside the empty box.

'Here, have these.'

Dylan slid his plate of uneaten eggs over to Dave, who dug in hungrily. I slumped against the fridge, defeated, and drained my coffee mug.

'I should never have let Esme wander around on her own,' I said. 'Us lot need to be looking out for each other.'

'Who, flatmates?' Dave asked.

'Women,' I replied.

Seema held up a spoon in silent solidarity.

'Seriously, guys, where is she?' I asked. 'None of us have any idea. One of the Watsons says he could see a helter-skelter in the background of Esme's live video. But there's no helter-skelter in Crowhurst.'

'There is when the fayre is in town,' Dave said, digging in to his second breakfast. 'Frank's setting up at the recreational ground this weekend, remember? The helter-skelter probably went up yesterday.'

I perked up. 'See? It's working. The Watsons are helping already. Let's go down the Rec and check it out. I can make another ShowMe.'

Dylan shook his head. 'It's videos like this that got Esme into trouble in the first place – if she actually *is* in trouble, that is. And if she is, we need to let the police handle it, not a bunch of armchair detectives.'

'The Watsons are good at what they do. They've helped Esme with cases in the past by sifting through a suspect's social media, tracking down their previous addresses, that sort of thing.'

'Wow, that sounds completely ethical,' he scoffed.

'Come on, like you've never scrutinised someone's Instagram stories to analyse their break-up?' I asked.

'Actually, no,' Dylan said.

'Guilty.' Seema held up her spoon again.

'Ooh, I had an Amazon package that was due three days ago,' Dave interjects. 'Maybe the Watsons could help track that down?'

'No, Dave, they cannot,' I said. 'But they can help us find Esme.'

Dylan scrolled through the comments on my video and grimaced.

'"Nice tits"?' he read aloud. 'Really, Kirbs? How is *that* helpful?'

If Dylan thought that was bad, he should have seen the comments on my website articles. I'd had to learn early on that, as a woman, any article I wrote would be either instantly dismissed on account of my gender, age, class, nationality, haircut, choice of nail varnish – you name it. Most of the time my editors had to turn the comments off. Sadly, I'd grown used to it. Or I thought I had.

'We have no idea who these "Watsons" really are,' Dylan went on. 'Look at these usernames. Shellfish diet? Cats are my love language? They're probably a bunch of twelve-year-olds in Ohio.'

'Even if they are, at least they're trying to help! You all seem to be completely cool with the fact that Esme has been gone all night,' I cried. 'But, fine. We'll all just stay here and do nothing. I've got plenty more pesto eggs for everyone.'

The room went silent for a moment. Dave concentrated very hard on his toast, and Dylan suddenly found a loose thread of cotton in his towel incredibly fascinating. It seemed like, in this flat, and in fact, the entirety of my life, no one really listened to anything I said, until I lost my patience.

I spooned another heaped portion of eggs onto Dylan's plate, and he stared down at it with a mixture of bafflement and dread.

'Okay, okay, back up a sec.' He stood up, placed a hand on my shoulder and gave it a little squeeze. 'I do care, Kirbs, I promise you. If you're really worried, let me get dressed and we'll go down to the Rec and have a look around. Maybe someone saw her.'

I put my hand over his, appreciating the gesture. 'Okay, thank you,' I said, calming down a bit. 'You can finish your eggs first if you want though.'

Dylan winced.

'I'll, um, save them for later. This is far more important.'

TWENTY-TWO

TWELVE MONTHS AGO

Dylan clambered into my Mini beside me as I tried for the ninety-ninth time to get the stupid thing to start.

Back in London, working for NewsBites, I'd spent half my life in this rust bucket, even sleeping in it some nights when I was doing two graveyard shifts back-to-back (or one of the many times it broke down halfway down the M25). Still, I had fond memories of the late-night car picnics on the back seat, usually consisting of a Tesco Meal Deal and a flask of lukewarm tea.

I turned the key in the ignition, only for the motor to sputter hopefully for a second, then die. Dylan raised an eyebrow. (Did I mention his very conventional eyebrows?)

'Just checking, are you planning on getting there tonight or next week?' he said.

I tried the engine again.

'You don't have to chaperone me, you know?'

'No, but I might need to give you a piggy back at this rate.'

I patted the dashboard. 'He doesn't mean it, girl. Come on, let's show him what you can do.'

I tried again, and this time, Foxy purred into life.

'See? She's like me, she just needs a bit of encouragement,' I said, as we trundled off down the high street, past The Red Lion and the Grillennium Falcon, towards the park.

A group of teenagers in hoodies were hanging around outside the newsagents, hoping someone would take pity on them and buy them a four-pack. Sure, Crowhurst was sort of pretty, but there was sod all for young people to do here, and even less if you weren't fortunate enough to legally buy alcohol.

That was the problem with small rural towns like this. Everyone left as soon as they could, running off to college or the nearest big city, which meant there was barely anyone left here between the ages of twenty and fifty. Apart from the residents of Flat Four, of course.

There wasn't much point in opening a cool cocktail bar or a swanky gym when most people were perfectly happy with a takeaway coffee and a brisk walk around the park. It was a vicious circle: the bored teenagers acted up so the older people ended up hating on them, then the teens started resenting the older people and leaving. Or vandalising the bus stops. Meanwhile, the population of the town just got older and grumpier.

The high street led down to the recreational ground, consisting of a couple of football pitches and a run-down playground. And if you fancied the twenty-minute hike through the surrounding Beacon Woods, you could admire the view from Staker Point, a five-hundred-foot cliff that looked down on the River Muse. But since everyone in town was all too aware what happened up there, most didn't bother.

Dylan was complaining that, due to pesto-eggs-gate, he didn't get a proper breakfast, so we stopped off at Fast

Forward for coffees and pastries, and by the time we got to the Rec, some hard-looking men in dirty jeans were hoisting a rickety metal wheel into the air. The Crawe Fayre wasn't much more than a zhuzhed-up village fete really: a bunch of bric-a-brac stalls and death-trap fairground rides.

An unseasonably cold breeze blew through the park, and Dylan pulled the collar of his old shearling jacket up (I think he thought he looked a bit like Bob Dylan or some old singer from the cover of his dusty vinyl records). We walked around for a bit, not really sure what we were even looking for. I glanced at my watch. It was getting close to midday, and I'd only done a few hundred steps. Not that my pitiful step count was the most important thing right now. We stopped when the helter-skelter was directly behind us.

'She must have been somewhere around here, I'm sure,' I said, kneeling down and running my hand through the grass.

'What are you doing?' Dylan asked.

'Looking for clues,' I replied. I got my phone out and started recording. 'This is what Esme does. This is where the Watsons think she was last night.'

I pointed the camera at the ground.

'Kirby, you're literally filming grass.'

I didn't want to admit it, but he was right. There was nothing here, and not even the Watsons were going to be able to find a clue in a video of some shrubbery. It looked like my glittering ShowMe career was going to be short-lived. We walked on to the playground, but with still no evidence in sight, I sat down on the swings.

'You know, me and Dave used to come down here after school with a four-pack of Desperados,' Dylan said.

'And now look at you, flat white and a croissant. You're getting old, Dyl.'

'Don't worry, I'm not quite middle-aged yet,' he smiled.

'Really? You do have a favourite spatula, remember.'

'I'll tell you something though,' he said, looking out across the Rec. 'This town isn't the same as it was when I was growing up. Tourism has dried up, and since they built the new motorway, we don't exactly get much passing traffic.'

'Are you worried about The Rookery?' I asked.

Dylan had shown me the plans for his restaurant, and it looked super cute. His mum and stepdad were considering loaning him the rest of the money he needed to take over Fast Forward. He was going to call it The Rookery, and he'd worked out the menu and everything. I just hoped the people of Crowhurst, who weren't exactly famous for embracing new ideas, would support it.

'Of course,' he said. 'But what's the other option? Reheat pies at The Lion for the rest of my life? I have to give it a shot.'

'What if you lose all the money?'

He put his empty cup down and stuck his hands in his pockets, rocking his swing gently back and forth with his feet. 'You only really lose when you stop trying, Kirbs.'

'I might not have a choice,' I said. 'Trevor told me *The Gazette* is probably going to fold. Half the readers are in the retirement home and the other half are in the cemetery. If I lose my job, I'll have to go back to London.'

I noticed Dylan's jaw clench as he stared off into the distance.

'I can't let that happen, Dylan,' I said. 'I can't go back there with my tail between my legs. I'm about to turn thirty, and I'm still in a flatshare, getting drunk and eating takeaways.

And now the next generation has arrived – literally on my doorstep – ready to take over with new technology that I have no idea how to use properly. I'm being overtaken before I've even had a chance to get started.'

We swung in silence for a bit, until Dylan let his swing gradually come to a stop and sat there watching me. I dragged my legs on the rubber matting until we were level with each other.

'You never told me why you left London for this little town in the middle of nowhere,' he said.

I kept my eyes trained on my feet. I hadn't told any of the Crowhurst lot why I really left my job at NewsBites. The 'London Question' was one I usually avoided, preferring to fob people off with phrases like 'I wanted to make my mark' or 'big fish in a small pond'. But that wasn't quite true. Things had ended badly in London, and *The Gazette* was supposed to be a fresh start, somewhere so remote, no one would know anything about me. Trevor was the only editor, out of the hundreds I'd applied to, to give me a chance. Of course, the fact that I'd skimmed over a few key details of my previous employment probably helped. But everyone lies on their CV, right?

'Nothing I wrote at NewsBites mattered,' I said. 'They wanted endless "millennial" hot takes, but I could never think of an opinion worth writing about.'

'You shouldn't have to think up an opinion, you just have them, don't you?'

'Yeah, well, I didn't have any interesting ones. But I thought *The Gazette* was somewhere I could make a difference, actually help people, you know? But so far, the only difference I've made was thanks to Esme. She's here five minutes, and she's already achieved more than I have in nearly a year.'

Dylan stared at me curiously, narrowing his eyes as if he was trying to look through me rather than at me.

'She's at least ten years younger than me,' I said. 'But she's so confident and, well, cool, and I still feel like I have no idea what I'm doing. I mean, I'm an actual fully grown human now. But I keep waiting for everyone to realise that I'm really just three golden retrievers stacked up in a trench coat.'

'I think they call that imposter syndrome,' Dylan said.

'Don't you actually have to be successful to have imposter syndrome?' I asked. 'More people have read the back of Dave's box of Coco Pops than my last three stories for *The Gazette*.'

Everyone I knew my age seemed to be doing something important with their lives. My mate Fiona from school was getting married next year. My cousin Louise had made junior partner in a big city law firm. And my old besties back in London, Hannah and Jules, just had a baby (who's totally gorgeous, of course).

'I promise you,' Dylan said, 'you're not the only one who feels this way. Look at Dave "The Legend" Watkins, for Christ's sake. He doesn't even put trousers on most days. The man is still excited when the toast pops out of the toaster. And Seema thinks she's going to run away to Paris with her boss, despite the fact that he's been married for ten years. You're only twenty-nine, Kirbs. You still have a lot of time left to figure this all out.'

'Yeah, well, this whole—' I gestured at my face with a swirling finger '—personality doesn't work as an adult! I'm called Kirby, for God's sake! No one finds the clumsy goofball thing cute once you're past thirty.'

'You sure about that?' he asked, a hint of a grin on his face.

I looked down at my Converse again, avoiding his gaze.

'Kirby, Kirby, Kirby.' Dylan rolled the name around his tongue. 'So, why does everyone call you that, anyway?'

I felt my cheeks flush.

'Um… well, do you remember the little pink guy from the Nintendo game?'

'I wasn't really into video games,' he said, getting his phone. He tapped away on Google and brought up an image of a little round pink blob with arms and legs. 'What, this thing?'

'Yeah! That's Kirby! I used to love watching my brothers play it on their Game Boy when I was little. They would let me play sometimes, but I was so rubbish. I was too young to understand the controls and I just pressed all the buttons at the same time. I guess back then I was all pink and squashed looking, like Kirby.'

'And you still are,' Dylan laughed.

'Hey,' I punched his arm, but I felt a flutter of butterflies in my stomach. 'Anyway, the nickname stuck. Kinda wish it hadn't sometimes. It hardly screams "serious news journalist", does it?'

'I kinda like it,' he said. 'So, your boss has a nickname, Dave's got a nickname, your death trap of a car has a nickname. Hell, you even gave the damn serial killer a nickname. How come I don't get one?'

'I promise to give it some serious thought,' I said. 'Let's just try and find Esme first.'

Dylan's eyes narrowed. 'Do you seriously think Peter Doyle is actually alive, after all this time? Or are you just trying to compete with the Esmes of this world?'

I clutched on to the cold metal chains of my swing and watched the sun sneak behind a grey cloud. 'All I know is that something happened to Esme last night, and we owe it to her to try.'

'I see,' he said, leaning just a tiny bit closer to me.

I did the same, and before I knew it, our faces were almost touching. Just then, a plump raindrop slashed on the tip of my nose, but I didn't flinch. Dylan reached out his hand and gently brushed my cheek. My eyes widened, and I swear my heart stopped beating for a millisecond.

'Bit of croissant,' he said.

'Oh,' I blushed, and suddenly the intensity of the moment became too much. I kicked myself into the air again.

Then, at the apex of my swing, I caught a glimpse of something pink in the undergrowth.

'What is that?' I yelled.

I jumped off the swing, landing with a thump on the rubber matting, and ran over to the bushes.

'Oh God,' I gasped. 'That's not what I think it is, is it?'

'I can't see anything,' Dylan said, following close behind.

I reached for my phone and zoomed in with the camera. It focused on a salmon-pink baguette bag nestled among the shrubs and a few old Coke cans.

But that wasn't just any pink bag.

It was Esme's.

TWENTY-THREE

TWELVE MONTHS AGO

Group Chat: The Deadbeats

Kirby
looky what we found

Dave The Legend
oh boy is that what i think it is

Seema
where?

at the Rec, in the exact place where Esme was filming

Dave The Legend
so... what's in it

Dylan
we are not opening the bag

Seema
you are so opening the bag

Dave The Legend
OPEN THE BAG

Dylan and I got back into the car, and I stared at the bag on my lap.

'Esme never went anywhere without this. Her baguette bag was like her "thing", she has it in all her videos. There's no way she would've just dropped it by accident.'

'So, what are we going to do with it?' Dylan asked.

'I guess we should take it to the police,' I said. 'But remember what Esme said about them? She didn't trust them. And neither do the Watsons. So, we should probably have a look first, just in case.'

I went to unzip the bag, but Dylan placed his hand on mine.

'Just in case what?' he asked. 'We shouldn't be going through her personal stuff.'

'The police don't even believe Esme is missing. If we just dump this at the station, it'll go straight in Crowhurst Lost Property, and that'll be the end of it. They probably won't even open it. We need to prove it actually belongs to her.'

Dylan went to say something, but thought better of it, so I opened the bag. Inside, there were some Sweaty Betty athleisure socks, a wrapper from a Pret olive and avocado sandwich and an eyeline pencil. I tipped up the bag and gave it a little shake and out dropped a folded newspaper page. I opened it up and saw that it was a front page of *The Crowhurst Gazette*. I checked the date on the top of the page.

'15 August 1996. This must be the newspaper she had in her video.'

I laid out the yellowing page from *The Gazette* on the dashboard in front of us. There was a large black-and-white photo of what must have been the Crawe Fayre. The photo showed a group of people, dancing and enjoying themselves. In the centre of the picture was a man dressed in a tatty crow costume. But the page must have got damp overnight, because the old news ink had smudged, obscuring half the faces. The headline read 'Exclusive! Witness saw Peter Doyle jump'.

The word 'LIAR' was scrawled underneath in what looked like eyebrow pencil.

'Esme must have been looking for this witness. She thought they were lying about what they claimed they saw,' I said. 'That has to be who she went to meet with last night. Remember what she said in the live video? She said the person on this bit of paper knows the truth about the Crowhurst Killer.'

Quickly, I scanned what was still readable in the article. 'Whoever it was, they're not named, it's just a bunch of quotes from a "police source". Someone claimed they saw Peter Doyle throw himself off Staker Point, and that seemed to be enough to convince the police that he was dead.'

I flattened out the old *Gazette* front page on my knees and looked at the people in the photo. Could one of them be the witness? Is that what Esme meant? I wondered how many of them still lived here. A decent journalist would track them all down, knock on their doors and find out what really happened that night up on Staker Point. That's what Esme would do.

That's what Esme had been doing.

I pulled out my phone, loaded up ShowMe and started recording.

'*Hey, Watsons, found this old front page of* The Crowhurst Gazette *in Esme's bag*,' I said, scanning the camera across the photo. '*Anyone know who any of these people are? They'd probably be in their fifties and sixties now, I reckon. One of them must know something.*'

'Another video?' Dylan sighed. 'Come on, we need to take

the bag to the police. What if there's fingerprints on it or something?'

I ignored him and uploaded the video, noticing that my previous one had just passed 22,000 views. I'd also gained hundreds of new followers.

'The police don't have the resources to find Esme, but we do. Half a million "armchair" detectives, at the touch of our fingertips. Just give the Watsons a chance, will you?' I said. 'They're the ones that helped us find the bag in the first place.'

Sure enough, moments later, my phone started buzzing with notifications. I scrolled through the comments.

TayTayLover:
ShowMeSherlock said the person she was looking for was on that bit of newspaper

Girdlelocks:
but which one of them is it? Can't see half of them.

Poirotsmustache:
any1 looked into this curse of the crow thing? There's a reddit forum that lists everyone who has been Jack Daw and most of them are unalive. Coincidence?

Cracker_fan:
google reverse image search brings up nothing

Magaman2016:
guy in the right-hand corner hugging a pumpkin looks like a right paedo

Shellfish_diet:
That's Robert Morris. I found his graduation photo online and double-checked it on his Facebook page.

'Bob Morris?' Dylan said, glancing over my shoulder. 'Do they mean Superintendent Morris?'

'Superintendent?' I asked. 'You mean, like, a police officer?'

I didn't wait for him to answer. I turned the key in the ignition and Foxy started first time.

Dylan looked at me and shook his head.

'Oh, so *now* you want to go to the police station?'

TWENTY-FOUR

TWELVE MONTHS AGO

Ten minutes later, we pushed through the revolving doors of Crowhurst Police Station and into a sparse reception area.

The station was tiny, with a single blue plastic chair in the corner, next to a mop and bucket on wheels. Its plain white walls were unadorned, except for an old-fashioned clock with hands, which filled the room with an ominous ticking. A woman in uniform sat at a desk behind a glass partition, looking like she very much wanted to be anywhere else.

Suddenly I felt a bit nervous. The police had already told me on the phone that they were doing everything they could – which, sure, didn't seem to amount to more than telling me to calm down and wait – but would a half-empty pink bag change anything? Maybe they could give me an update on the search, presuming they had actually started one.

Trevor always told me you can get anyone to tell you anything with a smile and a clipboard. Well, I didn't have a clipboard, but I approached the constable at the desk wearing my best grin. Sadly, she was too busy flipping through paperwork to notice. Either that, or she was secretly hoping I'd give up and walk straight out again.

To be fair, I expected the most she had to deal with on an average Saturday afternoon were angry shopkeepers complaining about the kids from the Dawkson Estate shoplifting Peperamis again.

'Hi,' I said. 'I called last night. I really need to speak to someone about a missing person. Is, um, Superintendent Morris here?'

'Missing person?' she repeated, without looking up. She had short, mousey-brown hair and thin eyebrows, and I reckoned she was probably in her mid-fifties.

'That's right, our friend, Esme, she didn't come home last night, so—'

'Under eighteen?'

'Oh, sorry, I already answered these questions on the phone last night. I really just want to speak to Superintendent—'

The constable glanced up from her paperwork and looked at me somewhat pitifully over her half-moon glasses. 'Under eighteen?' she repeated.

'Er, no,' I said. 'Well, I don't think so.'

She nodded. 'Any serious mental or physical health issues?'

'Um, not sure,' I replied.

She exhaled loudly, just to make it especially clear I knew how exasperating I was being. 'Are they in immediate danger or likely to come to immediate harm?'

I paused and thought for a second. 'Yes,' I said firmly.

The constable stared at me for a moment too long. 'Well, yes then, you will need to speak to Superintendent Morris.'

'Er, okay, great. Is he here?'

'Superintendent Morris will be back after lunch,' she said matter-of-factly.

I looked at the clock hanging on the wall. It was only a quarter past eleven.

'Lunch or brunch?' I asked.

'What?'

'You know, brunch. A meal eaten between lunch and breakfast. It's a portmanteau word. Like, um, a spork. Or Bromance. Or…' I couldn't think of another one.

'I know what brunch is,' she sighed. 'Superintendent Morris doesn't eat *brunch*, he is currently having *lunch*, and he will be back when he has finished.'

'Right, and if you had to hazard a guess – just like a ballpark figure – roughly how long will that be, do you think?'

She scratched her head with her pencil and pursed her lips. 'Well, that all depends whether he went to The Red Lion for a ploughman's – in which case, it'll be at least another hour – or popped to Betty's for a steak slice. If it's the latter, we're looking at, oooh, a good twenty minutes, I reckon. There's a seat over there, if you really want to wait.'

She motioned to the very uncomfortable-looking plastic seat in the corner. I looked back at Dylan, and he motioned for me to keep going.

'I will definitely take a seat,' I said, turning back to the constable. 'The seat looks really great, and I am looking forward to sitting on it. As seats go, it is banging. But, well, thing is, this might be just a little bit urgent. We found her bag, see? It was just lying in the Rec, which is where we think she was last night. And I've heard that the first twenty-four hours are the most important in a missing person case so…'

She put down her pencil and glared at me. 'Well, as you're

obviously the expert in missing people, maybe you don't *need* to wait for Superintendent Morris?'

I was out of my depth. I thought the council were obtuse, but they had nothing on these guys. I mean, sometimes I had to call the police to confirm certain specifics for a story, like whether it was a tabby or a tortoiseshell cat that got stuck up the tree in Winborne Park. But this was a little bit different. I raised my hands in a gesture of surrender and slumped down in the chair.

Dylan leant against the wall next to me. 'That went well,' he said.

'Don't.' I glared at him. 'Trevor normally handles this sort of thing. He thinks I'm not ready for this Lois Lane shit.'

'Whatever Trevor said that?'

'Well, not those exact words, no,' I said. 'But along those lines.'

Just then, a uniformed man pushed through the glass doors, holding a paper bag from Fast Forward in one hand and clutching a cardboard coffee cup in the other. His wispy hair had been blown back by the draught coming off the revolving door, and he was trying to comb it back without spilling his drink.

'That's gotta be him,' Dylan said.

I examined the newspaper again, and my heart leapt. Shellfish_diet was right. In the far-right corner, the man clutching a large marrow looked a hell of a lot like a younger version of the guy who just walked in the door. I quickly stuffed the front page back in my jacket pocket.

'Superintendent Morris?' I called out.

He didn't react, so I stood up and walked straight up to

him. He looked at me, then guiltily wiped the pastry crumbs from around his patchy grey stubble.

'Yes? How can I help you?' he asked, a little defensively. He had the gruff, slightly West Country accent that many of the older people in Crowhurst spoke with.

'So sorry, did not mean to disturb your, um…' I glanced at the half-eaten steak slice, 'brunch?'

He frowned at me.

'We're worried about our friend,' I continued. 'She's been missing since yesterday. We've texted but she's not answering, and she posted this weird video online.'

'Did you call?' he asked.

'Uh, well, yes, a few times. Thing is, I only live around the corner, and well, we found some of her stuff in the park.'

I held up the bag to show him. Superintendent Morris manoeuvred himself around the counter and pulled a flimsy piece of paper from under it.

'Fill in this form,' he said, pushing it towards me with a grunt.

'Oh, I already—' I started.

He tapped on the form with a noticeably bitten fingernail.

'The form, right, got it,' I sighed, reaching for the biro that was tied to the top of the desk with an old piece of string. 'So, do you have, like, a timescale on this? We're worried she might have been hurt, or something.'

'Or something?' He raised an eyebrow.

'Well, like I said, she made this video last night, and—'

'Just fill in the form, please,' he said.

I pushed the completed form back to him, and he picked it up, clicking his tongue as he gave it the most cursory of glances. 'You haven't filled in her full name.'

I hesitated. This was the tricky bit. 'Well, we don't *technically* know her full name. The thing is, you see, we only met her the other day.'

'I thought you said she was your friend?'

'Well, um, flatmate is more accurate. She just moved in.'

'Recent photograph?' he asked.

I pulled out my phone and showed him Esme's profile on ShowMe. 'This is her.'

He took a pair of spectacles from the pocket of his shirt and squinted at my screen.

'Right. And who was the last person to see her?'

I wondered if he already knew the answer to that, but I didn't dare accuse him. I was, after all, standing in a police station.

'In person? That would be me, I guess,' I said. 'We walked back from the pub together the night before last. No one has seen her since. Except online, of course.'

Superintendent Morris considered this for a moment.

'Look, I'm sorry,' I said. 'I know you probably just want to relax with your lovely pastry and your cup of coffee there. What is it with people in this town and pastries, by the way? I mean, quite frankly, who doesn't love a fresh cinnamon bun, but honestly—'

The Superintendent coughed loudly.

'Right, sorry,' I said. 'There must be something you can do to help our friend?'

'What is it that you would like us to do, exactly?' he asked. 'As far as I can tell, all that's happened here is a woman you met less than forty-eight hours ago simply hasn't texted you back. Is that about right?'

I took a deep breath. 'Whoever she is, I think she's in

trouble,' I said firmly. 'And I think, well, I think it might be something to do with the Crowhurst Killer.'

Morris suddenly swung round and looked directly at me. 'The who?'

'Peter Doyle.'

His eyes narrowed. 'Would you mind lowering your voice, please?' he asked.

I glanced around the reception area. We were literally the only people in there, and I really was not talking very loudly.

'Sorry,' I said, and then repeated in an exaggerated whisper, 'Peter Doyle.'

Morris's face stiffened. 'And what makes you think this has anything to do with that man?'

'Esme was doing a ShowMe about the murders here.'

'A ShowMe?'

'ShowMe… how can I describe it? It's like an app where you can share little videos of yourself. Like, doing your make-up or cooking or yoga poses. You're probably not a huge make-up guy, are you? Or yoga. I mean, not that you wouldn't be brilliant at it. Have you tried it? I'm sure you could do a fantastic downward dog if you wanted. Anyway, sometimes it's just a two-minute video of a cat sleeping. But, you can get news on there too, it's a bit like—'

'TikTok?' he asked.

'Right. Yes,' I sighed. 'Like TikTok. But wilder. Esme was making a sort of mini-documentary, filmed on her phone, about the murders in the Nineties here.'

'Right. I see,' he sighed. 'She's one of *those*.' He spat the word like he was referring to someone who voted Remain, rather than a harmless young woman.

Dylan, still leaning against the wall, gave me an 'I told you so' shrug.

'We haven't had one for years,' Morris said, 'but every so often, back in the day, we got some oddball coming in here claiming that they were the real killer, begging to confess everything. Sometimes they were convinced we had Peter Doyle locked up in the stationery cupboard somewhere. Or, worse, they want to ask me some questions for their bloody podcast. All that nonsense happened such a long time ago, I thought we'd seen the last of them.'

I wanted to tell him that 'nonsense' seems a funny way to refer to what technically amounted to a massacre, but then I remembered what Trevor said about smiling.

I leant closer to the counter and lowered my voice.

'Were you at the fayre, that night in 1996, Superintendent Morris?' I asked. I bared my teeth, and gave him, what I imagined, was my nicest possible smile.

Morris visibly recoiled, as if I was about to bite him. I relaxed my face and tried again. Where the hell was a clipboard when you needed one?

'I've lived in Crowhurst for nearly fifty years,' he said, proudly. 'And I've been to the Crawe Fayre almost every single one of them. But I wasn't there in 1996, no.'

'You weren't?' I asked. 'But I thought...'

'You thought what?' Morris lifted an eyebrow, almost daring me to contradict him.

I placed my hand on *The Gazette* front page in the pocket of my denim jacket. But at the last moment, I decided to leave it there.

'Uh, nothing. I just want to find my friend,' I said.

Morris put down his cup of coffee and met my eye. 'I'll just say this the once. If I find that you've been going around town, upsetting the good people of Crowhurst with questions about something that happened three decades ago, days before the most important day in our calendar, you will find out that we are not quite as welcoming as our reputation suggests. Do I make myself clear, Miss...' He glanced down at the form again. 'Miss Cornell?'

I nodded meekly and now it was his turn to force a smile.

'So, why don't you just leave this with us.' The Superintendent took the bag and placed it behind the desk. 'I've got your mobile number here. We'll, uh, send you a text if anyone comes in to collect it.'

'You're not going to look for her?' I asked, incredulous.

'Tell you what, if she still hasn't turned up by tomorrow, give us a call. Oh, actually, make that Monday. It's the fayre on Sunday, as I'm sure you know. Very busy day for us.'

Why, because of all the international giant vegetable thieves that descend on Crowhurst every harvest festival day? (Is what I felt like saying, but I figured I'd already pushed my luck far enough.)

With that, Morris turned around and started emptying multiple tiny packets of sugar into his coffee cup. I stayed where I was for a second. I knew I should stand my ground, refuse to leave until he actually got up off his steak-slice-fed arse and started pounding the streets, searching for Esme.

'The door is behind you,' he said, without looking up.

I turned around and shuffled out into the street, followed by Dylan. Even though it was still warm, there was a whiff of humidity in the air again, and the grey clouds were getting darker.

TWENTY-FIVE

TWELVE MONTHS AGO

Group Chat: The Deadbeats

Kirby
police useless, going to Fast Forward if u guys want a debrief

Seema
umm soz babe I have an appointment

Dave The Legend
oi oi got a root canal that needs filling have u?

Seema
pls shut up David

@davethelegend what about u? u coming?

Seema
unlikely, he's up on the roof again

u better not have taken Esme's mattress up there

Dave The Legend
calm down, when she eventually turns up, I promise I'll put it back

I swung Princess Elsa's plastic arm downwards, executing a perfect karate chop to Optimus Prime's head.

'Ha-ya!' I cried, sending the Transformer flying across the room.

Dylan and I had headed to Fast Forward to discuss what I was now calling 'The Situation', and Lily was playing a mammoth game of robots versus princesses on the counter. I couldn't resist getting involved and, of course, I had joined the team with the best hair. Dylan's mum would often bring Lily to work to play when she was on a shift, as Vinnie, her husband did long hours as a security guard at Crowhurst Business Park.

'No, that's wrong!' Lily squealed in delight.

'Is it? Is it wrong?' I teased, and started tickling her. 'Why is it wrong?'

'The robots are *friends* with the princesses!' Lily explained, picking Optimus back up.

'Oh,' I said. 'My mistake.'

'Say sorry,' Lily said.

I apologised to Optimus Prime in my best Elsa voice. Lily threw a muffin at my head.

'Lily!' Betty shouted from the kitchen. 'Don't make a mess, please. Dylan, can you take her to the bathroom and get her cleaned up? Vinnie's going to pick her up in an hour.'

While Dylan helped his sister, I nestled into our favourite battered settee in the middle of the café – in between the horror and the rom-com sections – with one of the sausage rolls that Trevor enjoyed so much. (When it came to the menu, Fast Forward was as resolutely old school as its decor, and Betty refused to serve any vegan options. Even the so-called veggie choices were full of tuna.) Still, the coffee was good, at least compared to the overpriced milky abominations I was used to in London's ubiquitous chain cafés.

I idly flicked through the DVD cases. I picked up one with the utterly delightful title of *Shrove Tuesday Bloodbath*. The woman on the cover was, for some unfathomable reason, dressed in a very short silk nightgown and had the tortured expression of someone who'd stepped on a piece of LEGO. A hooded figure, brandishing a large skillet, was seemingly threatening to bludgeon her to death, or flip her a pancake or two.

Video shops reminded me of when I was little, spending weekends with my dad. He'd rent a bunch of movies, hoping that I'd like at least one of them. Usually, I didn't, because he had no idea what would distract a sugar-high pre-teen for an afternoon, and I'd end up dragging him back to the store the next day to swap them for something else. You'd have thought he would've known better, because my dad pretends to be someone else for a living. You might have heard of him, actually. Most people would recognise him as the lead in the short-lived detective series *Necktie* that ran for three seasons in the early Nineties.

Necktie was a sort of stuffy, old-school police chief who had been coerced into running a new team of young, tech-savvy 'digital detectives' who all wore T-shirts and hoodies and called their new, technophobe boss 'Necktie'. It was the Nineties, the internet was new and people were all excited about the possibilities of owning a phone that wasn't roughly the size and weight of a large brick.

These days, Dad's career wasn't exactly primetime, but he'd occasionally pop up as a vicar or a lovable ex-con in an ITV Sunday-night drama, or on stage in a small-but-pivotal role for a touring theatre company. I wouldn't say he's quite national-treasure level, but well-known enough that I would get cries of 'oh, I just *love* him' whenever anyone found out he was my dad. And that's why I'm quite careful these days that no one does find out he's my dad.

Embarrassingly, I'd actually tried to follow in his footsteps, saving up to study acting when I was eighteen. But unfortunately, I got rejected for a grant, on account of supposedly having a rich dad, and had to drop out after the first year. I loved it while it lasted, though. I found speaking someone else's words easier than finding my own sometimes, and the handful of times we got to perform in front of an audience felt amazing. Not that I was any good, but there was something about the attention of strangers, watching and applauding our every move, that made me feel, I dunno, kind of invincible.

With a grimace, I shoved the DVD back on the shelf. There was something more than distasteful about the gory covers of terrible Eighties slasher movies. For a start, it was always a young woman hounded by a man with a phallic weapon (or in this case, a frying pan).

'Thought you'd prefer this one,' Dylan said from behind me.

I turned around to see him holding a battered copy of *13 Going on 30*.

'Give me a break,' I said, taking it off him.

'You don't like rom-coms?' he asked.

'And you do?' I scoffed.

'Love 'em. I'm actually quite romantic, deep down.'

'Sure you are,' I said. 'What's your favourite rom-com then?'

'*Friends with Benefits*,' he smiled.

'Sounds about right,' I said, rolling my eyes.

'What's yours?'

'Um, I dunno,' I pointed to the life-sized cardboard Vin Diesel beside us. '*The Fast and the Furious*?'

'I'm not sure that counts as a romantic comedy, Kirbs,' he said.

'Um, have you seen the way Paul Walker and Vin Diesel look at each other? And don't tell me it wasn't hilarious when they crashed that speedboat into a Boeing 747.'

DO NOT EVER TELL ANYONE but my actual favourite non-rom-com movie of all time was, in fact, Winnie The Pooh – and not even the proper Sixties one, either. No, my childhood fave was the 1997 direct-to-video 'classic' *Pooh's Grand Adventure*. It was the first film I remember watching with my dad, when I was about four. But if you thought I was going to admit that to Dylan Barnes, then you are more insane than Peter Doyle ever was.

At that moment, Betty brought over a tray of cappuccinos and effortlessly slid it onto the little round table in front of us. I could tell it took every ounce of her willpower not to ruffle Dylan's hair every time she walked past.

'You two look exhausted,' Betty said. 'Late night last night?'

'Uh, sort of,' I replied.

Betty gave me a suspicious look. I really liked her, but I don't think she'd ever quite forgiven me for my rather, hmm, let's say *forthright* review of her performance as Grizabella in the Crowhurst Dramatic Society's performance of *Cats* last autumn.

'Can I get you kids anything else?' she asked.

I loved the way she called us kids, even though we were pushing thirty. Betty was barely out of school when she had Dylan, so she was hardly a pensioner herself.

'Yeah, actually, you can,' I said. I laid the newspaper page on the table next to the coffees.

Her eyes immediately flicked to the photo of Jack Daw, and she noticeably shivered.

'Oh my, this takes me back,' she said.

'Did you ever meet Peter Doyle?' I asked her.

'Now you're asking,' she said. 'He was a couple of years older than my lot. We'd see him hanging around the school gates. Terrible what happened, absolutely tragic. Thank the Crow that Dylan's grandad took me camping on the Isle of Wight that summer.'

'Mum never stops talking about that holiday,' Dylan said. 'She's been trying to get Vinnie to take her back for years. Wants to relive her childhood.'

Betty gave into temptation and tousled his mop of hair. 'And this one will be coming with us, no arguments.'

I pointed at the photo of the fayre. 'Betty, what about these people? Do you recognise any of them? That's Superintendent Morris, isn't it?'

She picked up the newspaper and peered at it. 'Bob Morris, as I live and breathe,' she said, almost wistfully. 'Look at all that hair! He looks so young.'

I knew it. The Watsons were right. Morris had lied to me.

'What's all this about, anyway?' Betty asked. 'You seem awfully interested in the murders recently.'

'Uh, I'm doing a retrospective for *The Gazette*,' I said. 'It's the thirtieth anniversary, did you know?'

Her face twitched. 'Is anniversary the right word? Makes

it sound like a wedding or something. What happened was a tragedy.'

'Uh, yeah, of course. It'll be respectful. A tribute to the victims.'

Betty looked dubious. 'I'm not really into that sort of thing, to be honest with you. All a bit gratuitous, isn't it? Did you see that documentary they did on the dating-app murders on Netflix? Don't pay for it myself, I'm more of a *Strictly* girl really, but Tina from Book Club lent me her password. I say "lent"… I'm still using it five years later. Only to watch *Selling Sunset*, mind you. But, anyway, apparently, tourism in Eastbourne exploded after that documentary. I suppose we could do with a bit of that round here.'

She looked around the café, which was empty.

'You know this chap though,' she said, tapping the newspaper. 'Frank Garrett.'

She was pointing to a ruddy-faced man in an Oasis T-shirt wearing a crown of leaves and drinking out of a large stein.

'I have to see to Lily,' Betty said. 'But I'll catch you two at the fayre tomorrow. I'm in charge of the fortune-telling tent again this year. Should be a giggle. You should get yours done, Kirby. It's about time you sorted your future out.'

Before I could protest, she disappeared behind the counter and started fiddling with the coffee machine, leaving me staring at the newspaper, gobsmacked. Betty was right. How did we miss that?

Creepy Frank was at the fayre in '96. What a shocker.

TWENTY-SIX

TWELVE MONTHS AGO

I parked Foxy in the little country road that ran up to The Red Lion to drop Dylan off for work.

'You okay?' he asked, watching me stare blankly into the wing mirror.

'I keep thinking about the key,' I said. 'If Esme didn't get it from Max, then there's only one other person who could have given it to her.'

'Frank.' Dylan screwed his face up. 'You really want to bother Creepy Frank about this again? He's already told us he'd never heard of Esme.'

'What if he's lying?'

'You're beginning to sound like one of the Watsons,' Dylan said. 'What reason would Frank have to lie?'

'I can think of one reason.'

Dylan ran his hand over his face.

'Hang on a second, Kirby, what exactly are you saying?' Dylan asked. 'Surely you don't think—'

I turned to look him in the eye.

'He could be the person Esme met last night. We know he was at the fayre in 1996. And he's almost as obsessed with all this crow stuff as Dave is. He could totally know more about it than he's letting on. We don't call him Creepy Frank for nothing.'

'We call him Creepy Frank because you insist on giving everyone a nickname.'

'No, it's because he spends the entirety of his flat visits inspecting my chest rather than fixing the boiler.'

'Fair point,' Dylan said, grabbing his jacket and opening the passenger door. 'I have to go. Just do me a favour, will you? Don't go confronting Frank with that newspaper. You know what he's like. Let Superintendent Morris handle it.'

'Um, you mean the police officer who's also in this photo? Can we really trust him?' I asked. 'If you think Esme's not missing, then why are you so worried?'

'I'm not worried about Esme,' he said. 'I'm worried about you.'

'Okay, okay. I promise I'll leave Frank alone.'

Dylan got out of the car and I watched him walk into the pub. Once he was out of sight, I picked up my phone again and pressed dial on Frank's number.

He answered on the third ring.

'Hi, is that Mr Garrett?' I asked, lowering my voice an octave. 'I'm calling from *The Gazette*, I wondered if you had a few minutes—'

'Sorry, who is this?' he barked.

'Um, my name is Lois,' I said. 'I'm a reporter. We're running a really lovely piece on the history of the Crawe Fayre, and I just wanted to get a bit of background from you. I understand you're quite the regular?'

'Well, I'm not really the bloke to ask, to be honest with you. I really just handle the admin side these days. Storage, permits, that sort of thing. Is that of interest at all? Because I actually have a funny story about—'

'Were you there in 1996?' I interrupted, shifting into full journalist mode.

The line went quiet for a moment.

'1996?' Frank said, his voice faltering. 'Long time ago now. That was the year of the murders, wasn't it? Why are you asking about that?'

'You were there, weren't you? Thirty years ago? Did you see anything? Anything you could tell us about that night would be incredibly helpful.'

He paused again. 'A lot of people were there that night. Why are you asking me? What did you say your name was again?'

'Lois... uh, Lois Kent.'

'Is this some sort of joke?' Frank snapped.

'Shit,' I mouthed and quickly tried to jab the End Call button. But before I could, I heard something in the background. Another voice.

A female voice.

'Who's that?' I asked.

There was another pause, longer this time.

'That's my niece,' Frank said eventually. 'She's staying with me at the moment, not that it's any of your business. I have to go.'

'Hang on a second, that voice,' I started. 'It sounded like—'

But before I could finish, Frank hung up, leaving me staring at a black screen on my phone.

I *knew* that voice.

That was Esme.

TWENTY-SEVEN

TWELVE MONTHS AGO

Whacking Foxy into first, I pulled out and trundled down the high street, cursing the twenty-mile-per-hour speed limit.

Could it have been Frank who snatched Esme last night? What was that sick bastard doing with her down there in his grotty flat? As terrified as I was, I had to help her.

When I stopped at the traffic lights, I balanced my phone on the dashboard, opened ShowMe and started a live video.

'*Listen up, Watsons,*' I said, keeping my eyes on the road as I spoke. '*I think Esme has been a lot closer than we thought, all this time.*'

I paused for a second, wondering how far I should go. I tried to remember what Esme did in her videos, teasing the Watsons with little clues and details to pique their interest. I cleared my throat and carried on.

'*One of the people in* The Gazette *photo is our landlord, the guy who runs the fayre. He was there back in 1996. He told me he'd never heard of Esme, but I think he's lying. He's the only person who could have given her a key to our flat. And I think he knows exactly where she is.*'

The comments didn't take long to pop up.

TayTayLover:
go kirby! ur amazing gurl

Rambo69:
if Peter Doyle is alive, why bother coming back to that crappy little town? I'd be living it up in Hawaii

Shellfish_diet:
Perhaps Doyle never left? He could have been living in Crowhurst all along under a pseudonym. We have no idea what he would look like thirty years later.

Poirotsmustache:
ur saying this Frank guy *is* peter doyle??? why wait sooo long to take his revenge tho???

Shellfish_diet:
Perhaps ShowMeSherlock was getting too close to the truth?

Drakesboy:
has anyone considered that this could be an extraterrestrial abduction?

Specks of rain splashed off my windshield. Despite the fact that it was mid-afternoon, there was already a group of kids hanging around the bus stop on Courtney Road, hoods pulled low over their faces.

When I drove past them, ever-so-slightly breaking the speed limit, they shouted something unintelligible, but I managed to catch the words 'estate agent prick' as I parked up outside Stewart Heights.

The last thing I needed was random abuse from teenage boys. I was nervous enough already. Up until today, most of my reporting had been done on the phone, or by a unique process of googling and cut and pasting. Suddenly I was marching into police stations and confronting sinister landlords face to face. But I had no other choice. Frank had Esme in there, I knew it. And what if Shellfish_diet and the Watsons were right? What if Frank really was Peter Doyle, hiding in plain sight for all these years? Esme had unmasked him, and now he was making sure no one else found out the truth.

Fumbling with my keys, I rushed to unlock the door to the Stewart Heights lobby. When I finally got it open, I almost fell backwards into the bins.

There, standing in front of me, was a man-sized crow, beak wide open and black feathery wings spread wide.

'Caaaaw!' it screeched.

TWENTY-EIGHT

TWELVE MONTHS AGO

I stood there frozen to the spot as the crow loomed over me.

'Peter Doyle is gonna eat ya!' it cried gleefully, raising its wings aloft.

'No!' I shouted, shoving it with all my strength. It fell backwards, landing on the floor, then sat up.

I stood there, just staring at it for a second. The costume was basically a big cloak, covered with feathers made of cheap black cloth, hung over the shoulders. The head was a large black papier-mâché mask with a big grey cardboard beak sellotaped on, and two wild-looking red eyes stuck on the side.

'What did you do that for?' the crow whinged, its voice dampened by the layers of papier mâché covering his head.

I knelt down and peered into the beak to see Dave's pudgy face looking out at me.

'Jesus Christ, Dave, you scared the shit out of me,' I panted. 'Take that thing off, will you? Why are you wandering around down here with that on?'

Dave stood up and lifted the crow head off, revealing his

blond hair damp with sweat. 'I need to practise for the parade! There's much more room down here in the lobby.'

Under the cloak, he was wearing a pair of tight black leggings that left almost as little to the imagination as his infamous boxers. Finishing off the bizarre ensemble were a pair of chunky leather boots that gave him an extra two inches of height.

'It's gross,' I said. 'You realise someone murdered five people wearing this?'

'It's not the same one, obviously,' Dave said. 'Frank keeps that costume in storage now. They used to bring it out to display with the waxwork at the fayre. Not allowed to do that anymore. Disrespectful to the victims, apparently.'

'I don't have time for this,' I snapped, pushing past Dave and marching to the door of Flat One. 'I think Esme is in here.'

Dave popped the crow head under his arm and followed me.

'Uh, Kirby, you heard Frank this morning. He doesn't know anything about Esme.'

'Doesn't he?' I cried, my voice getting louder.

Suddenly Frank's door swung open, revealing him standing there, wearing a terrible too-tight beige polo-neck sweater and a face like thunder.

'What the hell is going on out here?' he barked.

Face to face with Frank, I suddenly felt tongue-tied. We stood there for a few seconds, looking at each other awkwardly. He glared over at Dave, who was sweating profusely all over his crow costume.

'David, you're not meant to let people see you wearing that

before the fayre. You know the rules. The identity of Jack Daw should be known to as few people in town as possible.'

Dave nodded sheepishly.

'The lobby isn't a playground,' Frank added, stepping back inside. 'Keep the noise down, will you?'

It was now or never.

'Wait, there's something I need to talk to you about,' I squeaked before he could shut the door.

'Is there something wrong with the flat?' Frank sighed. 'Have you broken something else? If this is about the toilet flush again? I told you, you just have to be more gentle with it...'

'It's about Esme,' I said firmly, with as much confidence as I could muster.

Frank stood steadfastly in the doorway, still looking at me blankly. I slipped my hand inside my jacket pocket and gripped my phone, ready to pull it out and start filming at any moment.

'Right. I already told you this morning, I've never heard of her.'

'See? And he's *still* never heard of her,' Dave said, placing a hand on my shoulder. 'Come on, Kirby, let's go back upstairs.'

'But she had a key, you see,' I said, ignoring him. 'And we've not seen her all day, and she's not replying to our messages. And I thought I heard something—'

'Heard something? What do you mean?' Frank asked. 'Was that you on the phone earlier?'

Before I could answer, we were interrupted by a voice, coming from inside the flat – the same voice I'd heard on the phone.

Esme's voice.

I stood on my tiptoes and tried to peer over Frank's shoulder. From what I could see, his flat looked a lot nicer than ours, all polished parquet floors and fancy designer wallpaper. I guessed this was what he was spending all our rent money on. Then I heard the voice again.

Frank went to close the door, but I placed my foot firmly in the hallway.

'That's Esme,' I said, as firmly as I could, even though my whole body was shaking. 'I can hear her. Let me in.'

I don't know what came over me, but I found myself pushing past Frank and forcing my way in. It was like something had burst inside me, sending a rush of red-hot adrenaline through my body.

'Kirby!' Dave yelled after me. 'Stop!'

'What do you think you're doing?' Frank cried as I strode down his hallway.

I wasn't listening to either of them, because I was desperately trying to figure out where the hell Esme's voice was coming from.

'Esme!' I shouted. 'It's Kirby! Are you here?'

The flat had a very similar layout to ours. I stuck my head into the kitchen, which was empty, save for some takeaway cartons. But I noticed something we didn't have in our kitchen – a small door at the back of the room. I marched over and pulled the handle, but it wouldn't open. Frank appeared behind me.

'What's in there?' I swung round, my heart hammering. 'Why is it locked?'

'You need to leave, right now,' Frank said.

'No!' I yelled. 'Esme is in here somewhere, I know it.'

I barged past him and opened the living room door. The

177

first thing I saw was a young girl sitting on the sofa, staring at her phone. But it wasn't Esme. This girl looked about fifteen, with a sullen expression and dirty blonde hair pulled back in a severe ponytail.

'Oh hey, hi,' I said. 'Sorry to bother you. I was looking for my friend.'

She looked up at me and scowled. 'Uncle Frank!' she yelled, turning her gaze back to her screen. She had that Crowhurst lilt to her voice, nothing like Esme's clipped London accent.

I heard Esme's voice again, and scanned the room, before realising it seemed to be coming from the girl's phone. I moved closer so I could see what she was watching, and I felt all the adrenaline drain from my body, like someone had stuck a pin in me.

She was on ShowMe, playing Esme's videos.

Shit.

Just then, Frank stomped into the lounge, his face red with rage.

'What the hell is this about?' he snapped. 'It's just me and my niece here. I don't know any Esme.'

'I'm sorry…' I stuttered. I wanted to move, but my whole body was frozen to the spot. Ideally, the ground would have opened up and swallowed me there and then. But in lieu of that, it would have been incredibly helpful if my legs would actually move.

'But this is the girl,' I said, pointing to his niece's phone. 'The one I've been telling you about. This is Esme. She turned up at the flat two days ago. Now she's missing, and no one's seen her since. I think something's happened to her.'

He stood there for a moment, hands on hips, glowering with rage.

'I don't care. You're lucky I don't evict the lot of you,' he seethed, before I could manage another half-assed apology. 'Or worse.'

'Please, just look at her, tell me if you've ever seen her before.'

He took the phone from his niece's hand, and she scowled at him.

'This is her?' Frank asked, turning the screen so I could see.

'Yes,' I said. 'Do you recognise her?'

He squinted at the screen, and snorted.

'Looks to me like your little mystery has already been solved,' Frank said.

He handed me the phone, and I stared at it, unable to quite comprehend what I was seeing. At the top of Esme's feed, there was a brand-new video, posted just an hour ago. It had been filmed pretty close up, and she was smiling at the camera. I pressed play.

'*Hi, Watsons! Taking a little social media break for my mental health*,' she said, and underneath the video there were the hashtags:

#vaycay #mentyb #seeyouintwoweeks

TWENTY-NINE

PRESENT DAY

I get in the car and drive, despite the fact that I can hardly hold the wheel, my body is shaking so much. When I'm a safe distance away from the dentist, I pull over, wind down the window and dry heave for a solid five minutes. Eventually, I calm down enough to re-read the messages from 'Esme'.

> Everyone in the group chat dies.

> I know your secret.

> You leave the group, you die.

It sounded absurd, but look at the facts: Esme – dead. Max – dead. And now, Seema – dead. There was only me, Dave and Dylan left on the chat. Someone was targeting us. So who was going to be next?

I quickly google Seema's name again, but nothing comes up. When I click on Surreywide.com, though, the top story is 'Police cordon off Crowhurst dental surgery after anonymous

999 call'. There's even a photo of the dentist's, draped in yellow tape, and I can see Morris's pug-face in the background.

Shit.

Maybe I should've stuck around to tell them what really happened – but what the hell could I tell them? That an undead influencer had risen from the grave to take revenge on her old flatmates? Somehow I don't think Morris was going to buy that one, especially after everything that went down a year ago.

I'd phoned Dylan and Dave over and over, but there was no response from either of them. Not knowing what else to do, I try the group chat again.

> Kirby
> @davethelegend @dylan where are you?

A few seconds later, I'm surprised and relieved when a new message pops up.

> Dave The Legend
> sorry no trains to crowhurst today, had to take the bus, just going past the Rec now.

Before I jam my foot on the pedal, I write back.

> @davethelegend stay there, I'm on my way

When I get to the Rec, minutes later, the place looks deserted. I park up right by the playing fields where they've been setting up for the fayre. The Ferris wheel and the helter-skelter are standing proud, and there's an array of tents dotted around already.

I text Dave again.

> @davethelegend I'm here, where are you?

> Dave The Legend
> by the arcade games

I wander over to the row of old-fashioned claw machines, and despite the horror of the past few hours, I can't help but feel a little tingle of… what? Nostalgia mixed with regret? Because this must be where Dylan won the cuddly Pokémon he gave me. That seems like a millennium ago now.

One cabinet is still full of the furry little yellow critters, probably exactly the same batch as back then, seeing as they were pretty much impossible to win.

I put my face up to the machine. It's one of those with the little joystick that lets you guide the grabber, and then you have to press the button to send it down into the pit of toys (where it spectacularly fails to pick up anything).

Then I spot something weird.

There's something else in there.

Everything else is a cuddly toy Pikachu, but there's another object in there that's definitely not furry. More, I dunno… *hairy*. It's obscured by all the toys, so I can't see it properly.

Even weirder, whatever it is, it's splattered in something red.

Like blood.

My heart starts thudding again. I fish out my phone.

> @davethelegend r u okay? I can't see you

No reply.

I have a horrible thought. Could Dave be the one doing all this, using Esme's phone to blackmail his old flatmates? He'd lied to us before. But this was a man who used a digestive biscuit as a coaster. I couldn't imagine he'd have the mental prowess to pull something like this off.

I peer in through the grubby Perspex of the cabinet, trying to make out what is in there. The machine says it's one pound for two goes, so I stick my hand in the pockets of my denim jacket, sweeping around the depths, past the old ChapSticks and hair pins, for any change. But there's nothing. Who the hell carries change these days? Then I see the palm-reading tent.

'Cross Madame Mystique's palm with silver and have your future told' the sign says. I poke my head inside and see the tent is empty, except for a little fold-out table covered with a purple cloth. Peeking out from underneath, is a jar full of coins.

I go over and grab it, but the lid must be superglued shut, because it won't budge. Eventually, I give up, take off my cardigan and wrap it round the jar. Then I chuck the thing on the ground, hard, and it smashes. I shake the broken glass and coins off my cardigan and begin sweeping through the debris. Avoiding any shards of glass, I pick out pound coins from the shrapnel and old buttons, and return to the claw machine, clutching a handful of golden coins. I remember that Dylan had told me the machine was programmed to give a prize one in ten times, so I'd need at least ten pound coins to be sure of winning. I managed to find seven.

The claw jolts into life when I stick the first quid in, and I ram the joystick forward, then hard to the left, before whacking the 'grab' button when it's above the object. Of course, I'm way out and it swings weakly against a Pikachu head instead.

After all those hours spent playing on my brothers' Game Boy, you'd have thought I'd be better at this.

On my next go, I nudge the joystick gently to get the claw exactly in line, and slam the grab button excitedly. The claw whirs down, opens its jaws, then closes them, somewhat pathetically, completely failing to get any traction on the item. I whack another coin in, and this time, it grabs whatever that thing is.

'Yes!' I cry, as the claw lifts it, agonisingly slowly, upwards.

I squint through the Perspex, and my stomach turns as the object is revealed in its entirety.

It's a hand. And it's definitely covered with blood.

I gag and try to hold back the vomit rising in my throat.

But the question is – *whose hand is it?*

Then, the claw suddenly decides to let go, sending the hand dropping with a thud on top of the Pikachus. Even though it's lying right at the top now, I can't make out any distinguishing features. I shove in another pound coin. And another, until I'm down to the seventh and final pound coin. Finally the claw grabs onto the hand, pulls it up and drops it into the chute.

Closing my eyes, I pull my sleeve over my hand and reach into the hole. Even through the cotton of my cardigan, it feels cold and damp, like a big lump of spam. I gingerly pull it out and squint open one eye. It's a real human hand alright, no doubt. And I'd recognise those disgusting nails anywhere.

It's Dave's hand.

THIRTY

TWELVE MONTHS AGO

Group Chat: The Deadbeats

> **Kirby**
> esme is okay thank god meet at the Lion for an emergency flat meeting NOW i need shots asap

> **Dave The Legend**
> down to clown baby

> **Seema**
> it's raining

> plllleeeeeasseee

> **Seema**
> fine i'll come but only if you guarantee we will not be drinking anymore of those gross shots

I was sitting with my head in my hands at our table at The Red Lion.

'I got *everything* wrong!' I moaned as Seema rubbed my back.

'Hey, it's totally on brand for you, sweetie,' she reassured me, gently pushing another shot of Cement Mixer into my field of vision.

Tonight's 'special' was one part Baileys, one part lime cordial (shake it up in your mouth until it curdles), and I'd been drinking them back-to-back since about six p.m., so my head was just a little fuzzy by this point. It didn't help that the only thing I'd eaten all day was a burnt sausage, half a croissant and a three-day-old satsuma I'd found in my glove compartment.

I'd explained everything to the others, and while there was some 'I told you so' eye-rolling, they had been sympathetic, and generous with the drinks. Appropriately, the storm had finally arrived, and The Lion was full of old boozers sheltering from the rain.

'This unbelievable story fell into my lap, and I just didn't question it. I should've known it was all too good to be true. Now I've pissed off half the town, riled up all the Watsons, made a fool of myself in the police station, and to top it all off, I'm probably going to get us all evicted. I am a terrible journalist and an even worse human.'

'Oh, hunny, that's not true. You're a good person,' Seema said.

I looked up expectantly, waiting for her to finish her sentence.

'And, um, you try really hard at journalism,' she added.

'Don't beat yourself up about it Kirbs,' Dylan said. He'd just finished his shift in the kitchen, and was still in his whites. 'You were just trying to help. Wherever Esme is, she's safe, and that's all that matters now.'

I winced, remembering how he'd rolled his eyes when Esme claimed she was helping people.

He was right, of course; Esme was okay, and that was the most important thing. I mean, I still thought the whole 'menty b' thing was weird, but that's Gen Z for you, right? I wasn't supposed to understand what went on in their heads.

Dave came back from the bar clutching six packets of crisps, which he proudly splayed on the table, like it was 2000 BC and he'd just hunted the tribe's deer for the evening.

Seema popped a crisp into her mouth. 'Ugh, are these all roast chicken flavour, Dave?'

'Don't blame me, blame the chef.'

'Er, I don't handmake the crisps, Dave,' Dylan said.

'Yeah, no shit. You don't handmake *anything* here. It was the only flavour they had left, sorry.'

'That's cos no one in their right mind likes roast chicken flavour,' Seema said.

'Ooh, shall we rank the top-five best crisp flavours?' Dave asked excitedly.

'Uh guys, sorry to interrupt this scholarly debate, but, just so you know, it's kinda not helping with the whole, "told the whole world a serial killer was back from the dead thing".'

'Sorry,' Seema said. 'But, you know, look on the bright side, you got loads of followers on ShowMe now.'

I put my head back in my hands and groaned. 'God, I'll have to delete my account, otherwise the Watsons will probably hunt me down and chase me up Staker Point.'

'Well, at least you'll get your step count up.' Seema patted my back again.

I checked my watch.

'Seven thousand and two steps,' I sighed. 'So close. The irony is, I think this is the best I've ever done.'

'You know you can trick those things,' Dave said, without taking his eyes off the crisps. 'Just shake your wrist, like this, and the watch thinks you're walking.'

Dave mimed the action, furiously shaking his hand in a suggestive manner.

'Oh, so *that's* how you manage to rack up fifty thousand "steps" a day, David?' Seema said.

Dave scowled at her.

'What's the point of cheating your steps?' Dylan asked. 'You'd only be lying to yourself.'

'You're right. It's pointless. It's over,' I said. 'I might as well give up the whole adulting thing. Never gonna happen.'

'I know a way you can get another fifty in,' Dave said, pointing to the bar.

'Fine,' I sighed, getting up.

Minutes later, I returned with a tray of fresh pints and a bottle of red. I figured Cement Mixers followed by wine would be an excellent combination, and would definitely cause me no problems whatsoever later on. Besides, my life was a mess anyway, so I might as well go down in style.

'So, are we all coming to watch me at the fayre tomorrow?' Dave asked.

Dave had spent the day rehearsing in his costume (which was still extremely tight around the middle apparently, despite his low-calorie hot chocolates), and he'd not stopped whinging about how hard it was to see while wearing it. The only way to see out was through the beak, so we weren't to worry if he ignored us at the fayre, because he probably wouldn't be able to see us. Either that, or he would just be blind drunk.

'Seriously?' I said. 'After everything, the last thing I want to do is watch half the town dance around a maypole, worshipping their mighty crow.'

'Thorny Crow,' Dave corrected me.

'Whatever. From what I've learnt about Peter Doyle, I cannot believe the town is still carrying on with any of that Crow bullshit.'

'Hey,' Dave said. 'It's a tradition that's been going on for hundreds of years.'

'So has *Fast & Furious*, but no one would mind if that ended,' I said.

'This is Crowhurst! We're not going to stop celebrating our history just because of some psycho,' Dave said proudly.

If you cut Dave down the middle, it would say Crowhurst all the way through, like a stick of seaside rock. I didn't think it was possible to be patriotic about a town, but he managed it.

'Uh, sorry,' I said. 'Just thought it might come off as, I dunno, slightly distasteful, due to the fact that the guy stabbed five kids to death thirty years ago?'

'Sweetie, have you taken a look at the world recently? This whole planet is distasteful,' Seema said, filling my wine glass to the brim. 'Humans gonna human.'

'Well, I think it's gross. And another thing, don't you think it's just a tiny bit weird that Esme didn't stick around to go to the fayre? That was the whole point of her trip, right? Why would she turn up here for one day, then suddenly decide to go on holiday? All those videos about the Crowhurst Killer, she was so sure she had *something*. I don't think she'd just drop it all to go for a bloody spa weekend.'

'That generation get a headache and suddenly they need two weeks off to focus on their mental health,' Dave said.

'That's not fair, Dave,' Seema said. 'We have no idea what was going on with Esme. She did seem kind of sad to me. Like a piece of her was missing somehow.'

'With respect,' Dave said. 'You're a dentist, not a doctor.'

'I'm not even a dentist, babe,' Seema moaned. 'Yet. And I never will be if I keep coming to the pub instead of revising.'

'Or keep watching *The Kardashians* when you should be revising,' Dylan said.

'Or keep shagging Hot Dentist when you should be revising,' I added.

Seema ignored us and reached for the wine bottle.

'Oh, hang on a second, have you guys ever done it in the dentist's chair?' Dave asked her.

Seema sipped her wine and said nothing. Dave's jaw dropped as his eyes lit up with unbridled glee.

'You have!' he cried. 'You've shagged him in the chair! Jeeze, Seema, I've had my wisdom teeth out in that chair! That cannot be hygienic.'

Seema had confided in me once that she would often pop into Crowhurst dental surgery after HD's final appointment of the day, and not only that, she often asked him to keep his blue scrubs and gloves on. Seema leant in close and lowered her voice.

'You know, the first time we did it on the chair, the earth moved. Like, literally.'

'Oh please,' Dave scoffed. 'You've been watching too much *Bridgerton*.'

'I'm serious! We saw the telephone lines shaking outside the window.'

'Was it a Tuesday?' I asked.

'Um, yeah, I think it was actually. How do you know that?' Seema said.

'That's the day we print *The Gazette*,' I explained. 'The vibrations from the printing press shake the telephone poles in the business park, and it makes the lines all over town wobble.'

Dave started snorting into his beer, but before Seema could pour the whole pint over his head, Dylan tapped on his wine glass to get our attention. 'Okay, so now we've established that Hot Dentist is not, in fact, the world's greatest lover, and Esme is safely tucked up in her parents' mansion, googling the next serial killer she's going to make up some bollocks about, I have something I'd like to announce.'

We all turned to look at him expectantly.

'Mum and Vinnie have agreed to let me take over the Fast Forward lease,' he smiled. 'And they're going to invest their savings in The Rookery. It's going to be a real family business.'

'No way!' I jumped up and threw my arms around him, squeezing a little too tightly and almost knocking him off his stool. 'That's amazing!'

I immediately released my grip when I realised what I was doing.

'Um, thanks, Kirbs,' he said, and I felt my cheeks blush the colour of my Echo Falls.

'Sorry, that's the Cement Mixers talking,' I mumbled. 'I mean, hugging. Can a drink hug? Never mind. You know what I mean. But I am super happy for you, Dyl.'

'Me too,' Seema added. 'Can't wait for all the free meals we're gonna get.'

'Yeah, well done, mate,' Dave said, slapping him on the back. 'You're gonna have to actually learn to cook now though, no more microwave meals.'

'I'll do my best,' Dylan laughed. 'It does mean I'll probably have to move out of the flat at some point. Go back to Mum's for a while to save some money.'

'About time we got rid of you,' Dave said.

'Yeah, the place will be a lot tidier without you,' Seema teased.

I looked round the table at my friends, pouring wine, laughing and joking with each other. I should have been buzzing, so how come I had a horrible feeling in the pit of my stomach?

I would miss Dylan, for sure, but it wasn't only that. As much as I wanted to believe Esme had just randomly decided to give up chasing Peter Doyle, it didn't quite add up. Sure, maybe it was a side-effect of drinking six Cement Mixers in the space of forty-five minutes, but I couldn't shake the feeling that something was rotten in the state of Crowhurst.

'Wait,' I said. My head was woozy, and the more I watched my friends enjoying themselves, the more it felt like we were letting Esme down. 'There's still a few things that I don't understand. Like, we still have no idea where Esme got a key to our flat. And where the hell did she go that first night after the pub? Her mattress wasn't even inflated!'

Seema and Dave exchanged a quick glance, then studied their drinks very closely.

Dylan put a hand on my shoulder. 'Kirby, you don't have to play detective anymore. It's over, she's fine. Don't waste any more of your life worrying about it. Come on, let's get another drink and I'll let you beat me at the quiz machine.'

'No,' I slurred. 'Trevor always told me, a good journalist trusts their instincts, then backs them up with proper research. Well, my instincts are telling me something isn't right.'

Dylan ran a hand over his face and blew out his cheeks. 'No offence, Kirbs, but your instincts haven't exactly been bang on so far. If Esme is in any trouble, it's a job for the police. It could be dangerous, you know.'

'Dangerous? So you *do* think there's something suss going on?'

'No.' He shook his head. 'I think you're going to get yourself fired. You told me your editor said no more videos. Wherever Esme is, she obviously doesn't want to be found.'

'Well, I need to know for certain that she's okay,' I said. 'She's still not answering messages or picking up her phone. I can't let her down. I could make another ShowMe, ask the Watsons to—'

Dylan interrupted me by putting his pint glass down hard on the table. 'Kirby, I just told you the best news of my life, and you're still going on about ShowMe. It's time to stop now. You're always saying you want to do something with your life, but whenever you have the chance to make a sensible decision, you run the other way.'

I shot up straight, like someone had dropped an ice-cube down my back. 'That is not true. You're the one who said you only lose if you stop trying. Well, this is me trying.'

Dylan shook his head. 'Are you trying to help Esme, or are you trying to get more likes and follows on that app? Ever since she arrived, you've been obsessed with that thing, how many views you've got, how many comments. It's worse than the step count every five minutes! But at least that was good for your heart. This is unhealthy, Kirby. You have to let it go.'

'Wow, don't hold back, Dylan, tell me what you really think.'

I saw Dave and Seema look at each other awkwardly. In fact, the whole pub seemed to go a bit quiet.

'Come on, guys,' Seema pleaded. 'We've all had a bit to drink.'

'What I really think?' Dylan said. 'Since when have you been interested in that?'

'Hey, don't be a wanker, mate,' Dave said. 'It's been a long day.'

'I couldn't care less about followers,' I snapped. 'I'm not some twenty-year-old chasing likes. I was trying to actually do something good for a change.'

'And what good did you do, Kirby?'

'Dyl, that's not fair, I—'

'I'll tell you what "good" you've done. We almost got evicted this afternoon,' Dylan continued. 'You upset my mum dredging all that crap up from the past. And let's not forget that we came this close to spending the night in the police station. I am opening a new business in three months, and unlike you, I can't just run away if things don't work out. Crowhurst isn't just a nice little holiday for me, Kirby. My whole life is here. So if you're going to keep doing this, I'm sorry, you'll have to do it without me.'

That hit me like a three-ton truck, and I felt tears prick my eyes. Without saying another word, I pushed back my chair, picked up the half-finished bottle of wine, and walked out into the rain.

THIRTY-ONE

TWELVE MONTHS AGO

The rain was actually doing something useful for once: cooling me the fuck down. Where the hell did Dylan get off, telling me what I could and could not do? All my life, I'd had people telling me I wasn't good enough, that I wasn't ready, that it was time to grow up. Now I'd finally found something I *was* good at, and men were still lining up to tell me to sit down and shut up.

I was stomping down the dark country road where I'd parked Foxy earlier, when I heard a voice from behind me.

'Kirby, wait!'

'Nope,' I yelled, not bothering to look back.

'Come on, please,' Dylan pleaded. 'Hear me out.'

I turned around suddenly and he stopped in his tracks.

'No, you hear *me* out,' I said. 'My whole life, people – actually not people – *men*, men have been telling me to be quiet, to shut up, to give up. I didn't think you'd be one of them.'

'That's not true, Kirby, I just...'

I reached the car, yanked open the driver's door and chucked the bottle of wine on the passenger seat.

'What are you doing?' Dylan shouted. 'You're way over the limit.'

I ignored him, slammed the door shut and flicked the lock. I got the squeegee out of the glove compartment and waved it at him menacingly. Dylan sighed and tapped his knuckles on the glass of the window. I wound it down halfway and he leant on the roof of the car to speak through the gap.

'You can't sit in the front,' he said calmly. 'It counts as being in charge of a vehicle.'

I wound the window back up, then scrambled over the front seat and into the back. I gave him a 'happy now?' face, swung my feet up and folded my arms.

Dylan coolly opened the back door.

'Can I come in?' he asked.

I silently cursed myself for forgetting to lock it. He sat down beside me and closed the door.

'Come to tell me I'm a fame-hungry influencer again?' I asked. 'Or just a coward who runs away the moment things don't go my way?'

'No,' he said calmly. 'I just wanted to make sure you didn't try and drive back home.'

When I remained silent, he opened the door to get out again. 'Okay, well, fine, I'll leave you alone now. We'll wait for you in the pub.'

'Wait, you don't get off that easy,' I said to him, yanking on the sleeve of his whites. 'What gives you the right to treat me like a child?'

'Because you're acting like a child!' he said.

'Do. Not. Call. Me. A. Child.'

'I didn't say you *were* a child, I said you were *acting* like one.'

'Jesus, who's acting like a child now?' I huffed.

'Okay, look, I'm sorry I went off on one back there. It's only because I care.'

'You care? Why?' I asked. I unfolded my arms and turned to face him. 'You're moving out soon. We probably won't see each other much anymore anyway.'

His lips tightened and he breathed out sharply through his nose. 'Why do I care? You're seriously asking me that?'

'Yes, Dylan, I am really asking you that. We're just flatmates. We've not even known each other that long. I'll probably get fired and be back in London by Christmas. So why do you give a shit what I do? You have your TRLs to keep you busy.'

He shook his head and looked directly at me. 'You know what your problem is, Kirby Cornell? You can't see what's right in front of your eyes.'

A tingle ran through me. Did that mean what I thought it did?

'And what exactly am I supposed to be looking at?' I asked.

'Come on, isn't it obvious? You really haven't noticed? I like you, Kirby.'

'Give over. You flirt with everyone,' I mumbled.

'Not the way I do with you!' he said. His face was getting closer to mine now. 'You just don't see it, I don't know why! Every time I pay you a compliment, you play it down. And every time I flirt with you, you just laugh at me, or get annoyed. I don't know what else I have to do to make you see that—'

Before I knew what I was even doing, I kissed him. The tannin of red wine mingled with my cherry lip salve, creating an intoxicating cocktail I couldn't resist. Or maybe I was just drunk. Yes, very possibly I was just drunk. But as Dave said, it had been a very long day.

'Wow, um, okay,' he said, leaning back.

'Sorry,' I said, suddenly feeling embarrassed. 'I don't know where that came from. It was the only way I could think of to shut you up for a second.'

He opened his mouth in mock indignation. 'Wait, me? You're telling *me* to stop talking?' he laughed. 'That's rich coming from—'

'Don't,' I said. 'Otherwise I'll do it again.'

Dylan raised both of his conventional eyebrows.

'Kirby Cornell, you can shut me up anytime you like,' he said, a grin spreading across his face.

'Here,' I said, handing him the wine bottle. 'This'll keep you quiet.'

He put it to his lips and tipped his head back.

'So does that mean you forgive me?' he asked, wiping his mouth.

'Alright, so maybe a tiny part of me did want Esme to be missing. Finding her was going to be my big comeback,' I told him. 'I needed a win to prove to everybody that I could do this. But I should've just shut up and done what Trevor told me to.'

Outside, there was a crack of lightning that lit up the sky, and we heard the pings of hard raindrops ricochet off the roof of the car.

'Doesn't sound like a passing shower.' Dylan knocked on the ceiling. 'You sure this thing is waterproof?'

'Guess we're stuck here for a while,' I said, taking the wine bottle back.

Maybe it was something about the sound of the rain pattering against the windows or the way the moonlight illuminated his face as Dylan looked at me, or the fact that the car heater had packed up sometime around 2017, but I felt the urge to move closer to him. I grabbed Dylan's coat, laid it over our laps like a blanket, and we sat there in silence for a bit, just listening to the rain.

Eventually, an idea occurred to me. I got out my phone and leant into him.

'Smile,' I said, quickly snapping a pic of the two of us.

'Woah, give me some warning next time, my hair's a mess!' He laughed, brushing his fringe back. 'Since when have you been into selfies?'

'I'm starting to get used to being on camera,' I told him.

'Right...' Dylan said slowly, letting his hand brush my thigh. 'So this "big comeback" of yours – come back from what exactly? Why are you so desperate to prove yourself to the great and good of bloody Crowhurst, of all places?'

I took a breath.

'The truth is, I didn't leave my job at NewsBites,' I said. 'I was fired.'

'Fired? Why?'

'Every single idea I pitched for the website was rejected. Eventually my editor took me aside and told me to try writing about something personal that mattered to me. Something *true*. So I suggested a first-person piece about my relationship with my dad.'

'Alright,' Dylan said. 'That doesn't sound so bad.'

I paused and listened to the patter of the rain against the windshield.

'My dad is Jason Dangerfield,' I said.

Dylan tilted his head at me. 'The actor?'

'Yep, the semi-national treasure, star of *Necktie* and *Celebrity Parkour Challenge*.'

While Dad had been on TV a lot when I was little, his later work had been mostly theatre and the odd reality show. But while his star had faded from his Nineties heyday, re-runs of *Necktie* and a ubiquitous advert for toilet paper meant he was still a recognisable face.

'"Braver, stronger, smarter"? That's your dad?' he asked, incredulous. 'My mum used to have a massive crush on him. Still does, I think.'

'Well, she's got terrible taste. He left me and my mum when I was seven, so I can't say he was the most hands-on of fathers. And you have no idea how often I had that fricking phrase repeated to me. Every school trip, every college party, every meeting-the-boyfriend's-parents dinner.'

The *Necktie* catchphrase probably would've died a death before the millennium but for the series of commercials Dad did about fifteen years ago for Lucky Buns toilet tissue, who incorporated 'Braver, stronger, smarter' as their slogan, and had Dad repeating it with a wink as he disappeared behind a bathroom door with a large roll under his arm. You can imagine the wonders that did for my social life.

'So, what happened with the article?' Dylan asked.

I took another deep breath and tried to explain. 'It was meant to be this thoughtful, nuanced piece about having a famous parent. I called it "In everybody's front room but mine", because he was constantly on the telly when I was growing up, but I barely saw him in person. At the time, I thought it was because he was away filming, but later, I found out he was having affairs. I was actually stupidly pleased with the article when I finished it. I thought it was the best thing I'd ever written. Heartfelt, honest, but funny, too. And my editor agreed, but with one addition. He went and put a stupid clickbait headline on it.'

'Uh oh,' Dylan said. 'What was it?'

'"I'll never forgive my famous dad for destroying our family."'

'Sheesh.' Dylan ran a hand through his hair.

'Of course, it got shared everywhere. Dad was just about to sign a production deal for a new show with Netflix, apparently. *His* big comeback. But after my article went viral, they backed off.'

'Was he furious? What did he say?'

I turned to the window, watching the droplets race each other down the glass.

'That was the worst thing. Nothing. Just a stern letter from his lawyers to my boss. Needless to say, I didn't pass my probation.'

'They fired you for that?'

'Well, um, not just that,' I said. 'The comments on the story were horrible. At first, I just ignored them, but pretty soon my phone was full of notifications every time I turned it on. People tracked me down on social media. I say "people", what I mean is toxic *Necktie* fans. Told me I was a useless bitch who wasn't worthy of being my dad's daughter and couldn't write for shit. Some of them said they weren't surprised he didn't stick around, that I was probably the reason he left. Then I made the mistake of replying. "Talking back". And that just made it worse. I called each and every one of them a prick, and, of course, they posted my comments all over social media, as if I'd proved their point. My editor went nuts.'

'I'm sorry, Kirbs, that must have been awful.' Dylan put his hand on mine, and our fingers interlaced.

'The thing is, Dyl, I think, deep down, I wanted it to happen. I wanted Dad to notice me. As a kid, I always had this stupid fantasy that if I behaved myself and worked really hard at school, then my dad would ask me to come and live with him and my brothers. It never happened of course. So I guess this time I tried a different way to get his attention. But it backfired, big time. I made an idiot of myself. And him.'

Dylan squeezed my fingers between his, just gently, but enough to give me butterflies.

'That's why I use my nickname now,' I went on. 'And my mum's second name, instead of Clare Dangerfield. I didn't want people googling me and finding out who I was. I wanted a fresh start. No one here knows I got fired, and if Trevor found out I'd lied on my CV, I'd be out on my arse.'

I rested my head against the cold glass of the window. 'Some fresh start this turned out to be.'

'I get it,' Dylan said. 'I never knew my dad – my real dad, I mean – but when I was a kid I liked to imagine he was like Willy Wonka, owner of a secret chocolate factory somewhere. And one day, he'd turn up, out of the blue, and ask me to run the factory with him.'

'You never talk about your dad,' I say. 'What happened?'

'He died before I was born. Lung cancer, apparently. It was just me and Mum for years, and she was pretty miserable. Depression, I think, even though I didn't realise it until much later.'

I put my hand on his and squeezed. I noticed little raised bumps on his fingers – scars, I guessed, from all the sharp knives he used in the pub kitchen.

'No grandparents?' I asked.

'They pretty much disowned Mum when she got pregnant with me at seventeen. But then, Mum met Vince,' Dylan continued. 'And they had Lily, and things got a lot better. Hard, of course, because Lily needed a lot of extra care at first, which was expensive. But for the first time I can remember, Mum is actually happy now, which means I can do my own thing, you know?'

'Chocolate factory?' I ask.

'Nah, these days, I'll settle for The Rookery. Maybe I'll create a signature dish that people would come from miles away just to try.'

'Like the hamster in that movie?'

'What?'

'You know, the hamster who lives in the chef's hat?'

Dylan thought for a moment. 'Are you talking about *Ratatouille*?'

I shrugged. 'I just remember there was this little chef hamster that lived in this guy's hat. In France. Maybe he was a mouse? Anyway, he made a really, really good—'

'Ratatouille?'

He started laughing, and before I knew it, I was giggling uncontrollably too. It was like a tap had been turned, and all the stress from the past couple of days was pouring out.

'Kirby Cornell,' he said, trying to hold back his laughter. 'One thing is for sure, you are most definitely an idiot.'

'Woah, thanks a lot!' I whacked him with the squeegee.

'So, have you thought of a nickname for me yet?' he asked.

'Hmm.' I thought for a second. 'You know, I think I still need to do a bit more research.'

'Maybe this will help,' he said, curling his hand around my waist.

I leant into him again, and he kissed me back, hard, and my hand found its way under his damp chef's whites.

'You sure?' he asked, looking down as I ran my fingers across his stomach.

'Hmm, I dunno, you *did* call me an idiot,' I said, moving my hand up to his chest.

'Okay, what if I told you you're also incredibly perceptive, very hot, and I really like your car?'

'Okay, now I'm sure,' I smiled, kissing him again.

His hands ran through my hair as I loosened his belt. When he kissed my neck, I lay back on the seats, pulling my top off and wrapping my legs around him. The smell of rain on his skin and the sound of the storm gathering force, together with the sweet buzz of the wine was overwhelming, and everything that had happened over the last two days evaporated from my mind.

But then, without warning, a high-pitched beeping filled the Mini, breaking the spell.

'What the hell is that?' Dylan said.

'I don't know…' I said, sitting up. Suddenly, it dawned on me. It was coming from my wrist. 'Shit, it's my stupid watch!'

'Oh, don't tell me,' he groaned.

'Yes!' I cried triumphantly, looking at the display. 'Ten thousand steps!'

'Congratulations. And all it took was a little strenuous activity.'

'Not *that* strenuous,' I said, throwing him a look. 'Not yet, anyway.'

'Can you please make it stop?' he asked.

'What do you want me to do, snog it?' I started jabbing at

204

the screen, trying to get it to stop its overly enthusiastic song of congratulations.

Dylan took my wrist, unclipped the strap in one smooth motion and chucked the watch over his shoulder.

'Now, where were we before we were so rudely interrupted?' he asked, kissing my neck again.

Approximately seventeen minutes later, Dylan and I were lying on the back seat, our half-naked bodies tangled like Tetris pieces.

'I cannot believe we just had sex in a Foxtons Mini,' he said. 'I mean, we have a flat with perfectly good beds, but we've ended up in the back seat of your car.'

I tilted my head at him.

'Aw, it's kind of romantic, like we're teenagers running away from our disapproving parents.'

'Romantic? I don't remember this bit in *The Fast and the Furious*,' Dylan smiled.

'It's in the director's cut,' I said. 'You need to check out the DVD extras.'

I wound the window down to clear the condensation and let the night air cool my face. Along with the warm, fat drops of rain, the sounds of the fayre being set up in the distance leaked into the car. Dylan leant back, stretching his toned arms above his head, and I nestled into his chest.

My eyelids grew heavy, and I let Dylan's gentle heartbeat lull me to sleep. But just as I was drifting off, something caught my eye. There was a small tattoo on his shoulder that I hadn't noticed before. Maybe it was the dim light, or the fact that the alcohol and lack of food was finally catching up with me, but I swear it looked like a black bird.

Or a tiny little crow.

THIRTY-TWO

PRESENT DAY

I jump back in shock, dropping the cold, bloody hand on the grass. I stare at it for a second, unable to take in what I'm looking at. Lying there, its five bloated digits limp and ashen, there's no question it's real. I want to be sick. Actually, I think I am going to be sick.

Steadying myself on the claw machine, I dry retch. As there's little in my stomach besides peanuts and wine, nothing comes. I pull out my phone to call the police, but there's a message on the group chat.

> **Dave The Legend**
> ereigjhnpppp

Hands shaking, I tap out a reply.

> **Kirby**
> what? where are you? r u okay?

> **Dave The Legend**
> Apologies, it's awfully difficult to type with one hand.

I barely have time to take a breath before another message pops up.

> **Dave The Legend**
> I'm in the hay maze. Help me.

I look over at the hay-bale maze behind the playground. The bales are stacked up about six feet high, much taller than last year. In broad daylight, the maze had looked completely harmless. I mean, how scary could a pile of hay possibly be? But now, with the sun beginning to set, going in there seemed foolish at best. But what choice do I have? The challenge was to find your way to the middle, so maybe that's where Dave is.

If he's still alive.

Because I have the horrible feeling that I'm not chatting to Dave anymore.

I step inside the maze, stray wires of hay brushing against my face. I get to the end of one passage, turn left, then right, then left again, meeting one dead end after another.

Story of my life.

Before long, I'm totally lost and beginning to panic. But just as I'm starting to wonder if I might have to spend the rest of my life here, my phone buzzes again.

Dave The Legend has left the chat.

My stomach whirls, and I wonder if those airline peanuts are finally going to make a reappearance. I know what that means. But by now, I can't remember the way back to the exit, let alone the middle. I'm stuck. But there is one thing I can do.

I call Esme's number.

After a few seconds, a soft ringing drifts over the hay bales. It sounds like it's just a few metres away. I follow the noise, and moments later, turn a corner and find myself in the centre of the maze. And there, to my horror, is Jack Daw.

The crow has its back turned to me, but there is no mistaking the cheap costume – the black feathers, the grotesque cardboard beak protruding from the papier-mâché head. As I inch closer, I see it's bent over something, and it takes me a moment to register what it is.

A body.

Dave's body? It's too dark to see.

I can't help but let out a stifled gasp. The crow stands up slowly and swivels round to face me. I freeze, rooted to the spot. It lifts the trowel in its hand and takes a step towards me. I try to peer inside the beak to see who it is, but in the fading light, all I can see is blackness.

'Who are you?' I stutter.

It cocks its head and then brings up a single feathery finger to its beak, making a 'shhh' action.

Fear engulfs me, and I turn and run, taking the first path I can see, only to slam headfirst straight into a bale of hay. It's another dead end.

It feels like the walls of hay are closing in on me, and I can't breathe. My pulse is racing so fast I don't know what's going to explode first, my heart or my Fitbit. I spin round, spitting straw from my mouth, and see the monstrous figure of Jack Daw, walking slowly towards me. There's no need for it to rush, I'm trapped. My back against the bale, all I can do is watch it get closer, its wings dragging behind in the dirt.

In the distance, I can hear sirens. The police must have tracked my car here. They'll never get here in time though.

I'll be dead before they can find their way through this stupid maze.

I'm trapped.

I can't go forward, I can't go back. Then it hits me – there's only one direction I *can* go. I turn around and jump, grabbing the top of the bale. Then I ram my Converse into the hay to get a foothold. And, with one great effort, I hoist myself up and clamber up onto the bale. I take one last look at Jack Daw, who's just standing there, tilting its head at me, like this is all a game. Then I jump down the other side.

Finally out of the maze, I lean back against the hay wall, panting, trying to catch my breath for a second. My head's spinning, and it's all I can do to stop myself from passing out. As my vision begins to blur for a second, I wonder if I should just close my eyes and let it wash over me. But the next thing I know, I'm wide awake, like someone has thrown ice-cold water in my face.

'Don't move,' I hear a gruff voice shout.

I look up and see Superintendent Morris, his face sweaty, sleeves rolled up like doughnuts around his arms. At first I feel a wave of relief. Then – terror.

The sirens sounded way off, so how did he get here so fast? *Unless he was already...*

But I don't have time to think.

I have to run.

Before Morris can reach me, I make a dash for Foxy, jump in and slam the accelerator down. The wheels spin as I speed off, spitting a cloud of dust and hay in my wake and leaving Morris standing in the middle of the Rec, slack-jawed and stupefied.

THIRTY-THREE

TWELVE MONTHS AGO

The next thing I knew, harsh beams of daylight were shining directly into my face. I sat up immediately, confused as to my whereabouts. I saw Dylan, still fast asleep with his head against the window and the memories of last night began to seep back into my consciousness. I studied his face for a second, tracing the outline of his chin with my eyes, admiring the light coating of dark stubble across his jawline.

Then my gaze rested back to his crow tattoo. What was that all about? Dylan always made out like Crowhurst's grisly history was best left in the past, so why would he get a tattoo of their horrible mascot?

While last night the car had felt hot as hell, now I was shivering with cold. I pulled Dylan's shearling jacket on and then poked him gently with the squeegee in his ribs until his eyes fluttered open.

'What? Where are we?' he mumbled, taking in his surroundings before realisation crossed his face and he smiled. 'Oh, hi there.'

'Morning,' I said.

He sat up, yawned and reached for his T-shirt. I stopped him before he could put it on.

'So, this is, um, cute?' I said, rubbing the tattoo on his shoulder gently with my finger.

'Oh that?' he said. 'That's the mark of the crow. It's the weirdest thing, everyone in Crowhurst is born with it somewhere on their body. Must be something in the water.'

I gave him an unimpressed look. 'Too soon.'

'Alright, alright,' he laughed. 'You want the true story? This was actually my first ever tattoo. I hate this thing. Got it when I was fifteen. Me and Dave came back from the fayre steaming drunk. We were both meant to get one, and of course, he chickened out after he saw me scream the place down. The tat parlour on Sampson Street did it. That guy should probably be arrested. Mum went absolutely spare when she saw it.'

'I bet she did,' I said, remembering how she'd shuddered when I showed her the photo of Jack Daw. I scrambled through my clothes until I found my phone. I knew I was going to have to make some sort of cringeworthy apology video today, but that could wait, at least until I'd sorted my sex hair out. I flipped the camera on myself so I could use the phone as a mirror and started trying to flatten out the mad red mane.

Looking at myself on the screen, I immediately noticed something was missing.

'My watch!' I said, my hand instinctively going to my wrist. It was gone.

I stuck my head under the driver seat while Dylan fished around under his clothes.

'Here it is,' he said, pulling it out of the gap between the seats. He gently took my arm and very sexily slipped the watch onto my wrist.

That's when it hit me. I *always* wore this watch. I didn't wear much jewellery or anything, but I only took that damn thing off for two things – a shower or, well, you remember the other one.

'You okay, Kirby? Your heart rate just started going crazy,' Dylan said, looking at my Fitbit screen.

I grabbed my phone and loaded ShowMe. As I played Esme's vaycay video again, I could feel the pieces of the puzzle shifting in my brain, like tectonic plates aligning. I paused it when she came close to the camera and zoomed in. I took a screenshot, then flipped to my camera roll, and zoomed in again.

'What are you doing?' Dylan asked.

'This is how the Watsons do it. If I adjust the brightness by 20 per cent... there,' I said, pointing to the screen. It was beginning to pixelate, but it was definitely there. 'Look at her neck, you see it?'

Dylan shrugged. 'What?'

I clasped his face with both my hands.

'I was right,' I said. 'Esme is in danger. This video is a fake.'

THIRTY-FOUR

TWELVE MONTHS AGO

Group Chat: The Deadbeats

> Kirby
> meet outside the flat NOW

Dave The Legend
are you having a laugh? its pissing it down. Where r u guys anyway? Is Dylan with you?

Seema
maaaate I just washed my hair

> Dylan is with me, see you there in 5

Dave The Legend
Dylan u dirty dog!

Seema
wooooooooooooooo! Kirbs u go gurl

> zip it and get ur arses outside, its about Esme

I scrambled over the seats and jammed the key in the ignition. Then I found the out-of-hours phone number for the council on my phone (which wasn't hard, because it was constantly at the top of my recent calls list).

'What are you doing?' Dylan asked, wiping sleep from his eyes.

'Trusting my instincts, then backing them up with research,' I told him.

I put my phone on the dashboard and turned on speaker-mode while I pulled on my trainers.

'Oh hello, so sorry to bother you. I'm a resident on Courtney Road,' I said when someone eventually picked up, doing my best impression of an elderly woman. 'Could you be a dear and tell me what's happening with the roadworks here?'

I heard the guy on the end of the line tap away at his keyboard for a bit.

'Hold for a second, please, I'll have to call the contractors and find out.'

While the hold music played, I jammed my foot on the accelerator and started driving back to Courtney Road.

'We know exactly what's happening with the roadworks. They're being filled in,' Dylan said. 'You've been on at the council for months to restart them.'

I shot him my best shut-up-for-a-second-or-I'll-kill-you stare.

'Hello? Are you still there?' the guy from the council said. 'Scheduled to be finished later today, actually.'

'Yes dear, I am still here, yes. Now, about these roadworks. Thing is, they're far too noisy. I want to register a noise complaint.'

'It's just one more day,' he said. 'You'll have to be patient and—'

'Sorry to interrupt, but that's not acceptable,' I said. 'Haven't you read the legislation, young man?'

Dylan leant over from the back seat and mouthed 'What?' at me, like I'd finally lost my mind. I shoved him back.

'I have it right here, in section... um, thirty-two of the county council regulations,' I continued. 'It says that if there is noise louder than twenty-seven decibels, then you can't continue with the work.'

I swore I could hear him groan on the other end of the line.

'Uh, I don't currently have that document in front of me. But, madam, if we pause the work now, it's just going to take longer to finish,' the council man said, exasperated. 'And that means more noise in the long run.'

I wasn't having that. 'As a resident, I want my complaint escalated to the highest level please. The noise is, uh, really affecting my... erm, hyper...' I leant over my shoulder. 'What's that noise thing Trevor has?' I whispered to Dylan. 'Hyper-something?'

'No idea,' he said. 'He's your boss. I've never met the guy.'

'Hyperacusis, that's it,' I said, and then more loudly into the speaker. 'Hyperacusis.'

'What's that?' the council man asked.

'Google it, isn't that what you young people do these days?' I told him as we turned into the high street.

I heard him tapping away at his computer for a moment.

'Oh right,' he read aloud. '"A hearing disorder where sounds others perceive as normal seem uncomfortably and often unbearably loud."'

'That's right. It's a very serious medical condition,' I said.

'Incredibly painful. Any loud noise is like someone jamming an ice-pick into my—'

'Yes, yes, okay, I get the picture. One moment.' The man sighed. He took my name and address, and I heard him fire off a few emails. 'While a complaint is being processed, all work on the site will be paused until we can send out someone with a sound meter to check the levels.'

He hung up just as I pulled into the Stewart Heights parking bay. After a few minutes, we saw the road workers begin loading their equipment into their van, and getting ready to leave.

'What the hell, Kirbs?' Dylan leant forward, resting his arms between the two front seats. 'You've been moaning about those roadworks since you moved here.'

I yanked the hand brake up, unclipped my seat belt and turned around to face him.

'Something bad has happened to Esme,' I said. 'And now I just need to get the proof.'

'Where from?'

I pointed to the huge hole in the road.

'Down there, of course.'

THIRTY-FIVE

TWELVE MONTHS AGO

By now, the rain was full-on chucking it down again, so much so that it was difficult to see where we were stepping. I had to be super careful not to fall in the massive hole in the road. Again.

'What are we doing here, Kirby? We're going to get arrested!' Dylan yelled.

'Uh, I don't think we need to worry about that. We've seen just how proactive the police are in this town,' I told him. 'But if you're really worried, just stand back there, that way you'll have plausible deniability when the FBI start jumping out of helicopters and waving their badges.'

We were standing around the roadworks outside Stewart Heights. The workers had gone, and the coast was clear – for now. Dave had his cagoule hood pulled so tightly around his face that it looked like he might lose all blood flow to his head any minute. Seema had refused to come out, having just washed her hair, but she had promised to keep watch from the window. To be honest, right now, I couldn't blame her. I had no idea if we were going to find what I was looking for, or how much trouble we were going to get in.

I looked down into the hole, which was rapidly filling with muddy rainwater. It was deep and dark down there, and I couldn't see a thing. There was nothing else for it, I was going to have to go in.

'Dave, take my phone for a sec, start filming.'

Dave dutifully did what he was told and pressed record.

'*Alright, some of you may recall my previous video here,*' I said, pointing behind me, '*which, yes, ended with me falling arse backwards in that hole over there. If you haven't seen it, go and check it out, it's actually more important than I realised at the time. Well, I'm going back down there. But this time, it's to prove Esme is in grave danger.*'

Brushing the wet hair from my face, I ducked under the barrier. I took back my phone, lay down on the ground and shined the torch into the roadworks. I could make out the big concrete sewage pipes, and just near them, something metallic, catching the light of my torch.

Bingo.

I dangled my arms into the hole, but it was too deep. I couldn't quite reach it.

'Kirby,' Dylan said, for the fifth time that morning, 'this is crazy. You're going to hurt yourself.'

'Just shush and hold my legs, will you?'

I balanced my phone on the edge so the torch was illuminating as much of the blackness as possible.

'Dave, come here and give us a hand,' Dylan yelled over the rain.

Dave peered up and down the road before joining him. He took one of my legs and Dylan took the other, and slowly, they lowered me down. It was totally gross down there, full of dank brown water and bits of debris. It felt a bit like I was being dipped into a giant bowl of Dave's Coco Pops.

'Just a bit further, I can almost reach it!' I shouted back.

They shifted me down another couple of inches, and my fingers hit mud. I plunged my hands down into the shallow water and splashed around until I felt something hard and cold, and grabbed onto it.

'Got it!' I yelled. 'Pull me up!'

I clung on to the chain as hard as I could as they hauled me back. With the last of my strength, I heaved myself onto the pavement, and rolled onto my back, exhausted. Dylan took my hand and helped me stand up and brush myself down.

The three of us stood there, looking at Esme's necklace.

'Now do you believe me?' I panted, the adrenaline still pumping through me. 'How can Esme be wearing *this* necklace in her latest video, when it's been at the bottom of this hole since Thursday?'

A fizz of elation surged through me. I'd finally proved I could do this. I grabbed my phone, hit the camera icon and started filming myself.

'Hey, Watsons,' I said, wiping the mud from my face. 'Look what we found.'

I turned the phone round to film the object. The heavy rain was washing off the dirt, and the light of the street lamp illuminated the gold of the chain.

Just as I clicked upload, my phone chirped with an alert from the group chat.

> Seema
> um, guys, r u seeing what I'm seeing.

Kirby
yes! It's Esme's necklace!

Seema
no look behind u

I looked round, only to be blinded by the blues lights of a police car.

THIRTY-SIX

TWELVE MONTHS AGO

Group Chat: The Deadbeats

> **Seema**
> ummm guys no biggie but there's a police car driving up the street

> they have the siren on

> and the lights

> maybe they're going somewhere else?

> nope.

> they're not

> GUYS

I stood there in the pouring rain, soaked to my skin and clutching Esme's broken necklace.

Two, very pissed off, uniformed police officers stood in front of me: the middle-aged man with a patchy grey beard was, of course, Superintendent Morris. Behind him, the constable from the station attempted to shelter them both with an umbrella that was too small for the job.

Morris flashed an ID card at us, as if the police car behind them wasn't identification enough. Dave gave a sheepish little wave, and Dylan looked like he wanted to disappear off the face of the earth.

I was probably in big trouble, but I didn't care.

'She's not on vacation,' I said, wiping the wet hair out of my face.

'I'm sorry?' Morris raised a thick eyebrow. His glasses were misted with condensation, and he looked very unhappy to be away from his warm office at the police station.

'Esme. Our flatmate,' I said. 'She's missing. Remember, I filled in one of your forms. This necklace proves it.'

Morris looked at me blankly. I realised I was panting.

'Okay, listen. She was wearing this the night she arrived in Crowhurst two days ago,' I said, holding up the necklace. 'But I broke it off when I fell into the roadworks. But in her latest video, she's wearing it. But she *can't* be wearing it, can she? Because it's been six feet underground this whole time. It's an old video. It must be! So that means someone *else* posted it to make it look like she's fine, so we'd stop looking. Someone took her.'

I paused for breath.

'I think Peter Doyle took her.'

Morris looked at me like I was a school kid who'd asked to use the bathroom for the sixth time that day.

'This area was cordoned off, was it not? Have you been filming here?'

'You don't understand, I had to. This proves she's—'

'Let me stop you there, Ms Cornell,' Morris said. 'Esme Goodwin has been declared officially missing.'

Another crash of thunder rumbled overhead, and Morris looked up at the sky anxiously. At that moment, Seema came running out of the entrance to Stewart Heights, her hair wrapped in a towel and her coat over her head.

'What's going on?' she asked. 'Kirby, you're absolutely filthy.'

She pulled the towel from her head and put it around my shoulders. I took her hand and gave it a squeeze.

'It seems your little internet campaign worked,' Morris explained. 'Our phones have been jammed with callers. All of them have been following your videos. Some of them managed to track down Esme's parents, and this morning we had a call from her mother. She confirmed that she's not heard from her daughter in three days.'

I stood there speechless for a moment. I couldn't believe it. My ShowMe videos had worked.

'That's... well, that's great,' I stuttered. 'Well, not great. But, I mean, it means you're going to look for her now, right?'

'That's what we're doing right now,' the constable said. 'We're not here about the trespassing, Ms Cornell, we're here to speak to you.'

'What? Why? What do you mean?' I panted.

'You said that's Esme's necklace?' Morris asked, ignoring all three of my questions. 'Would you like to tell me exactly what you are doing with it?'

'I just told you, we found it, down there.' I pointed to the hole behind me. 'It came off when Esme pushed me in the roadworks. You can check her ShowMe video.'

'We're very aware of the video,' Morris said. 'It not only

shows you and Esme in a physical altercation, but you can be clearly heard insulting her. And, it's also been brought to our attention that shortly after it was filmed, you posted another video online. One in which you claim Esme Goodwin was taken by a mysterious figure.'

'That's right, because you wouldn't listen and—'

'And in *that* video, you have what appears to be blood over your T-shirt.'

I froze. For the first time since we got here, I felt the cold. 'You can't be serious,' I gasped. 'That wasn't blood, that was curry sauce! Who told you that was blood?'

'Like I said, you have some very astute followers.'

'The Watsons? Oh, you have got to be kidding me,' I cried. 'They'd see Jesus in a piece of burnt toast! You can't listen to every wild theory they come out with!'

I couldn't believe it. The Watsons were supposed to be on *my* side. Now they were accusing me of what… murder?

'Even I think this is crazy,' Dave said. He came up beside me and put his arm around my shoulders.

'You've got this all wrong,' Seema said. 'Kirby is the one trying to find Esme.'

'All the same, under the circumstances, we think it would be best if she came with us.'

I stood there, covered in dirt, dripping with freezing cold rainwater, and stared at Morris's angry little face.

'You're arresting me?'

'We are not arresting you, Ms Cornell. But we would appreciate it if you accompanied myself and Constable Pascal back to the station.'

My whole body started shaking. 'I've already given you a statement,' I stammered. 'I've told you everything I know.'

'Let me be clear,' Morris said. 'You were the last person to see Esme Goodwin. If you choose not to come with us now, we may have no other option than to place you under arrest.'

'But we all saw her live video yesterday,' Seema said.

'A video which apparently, and rather conveniently, has completely disappeared,' Morris said.

Constable Pascal opened the door of the police car and smiled ominously, as if she was inviting me in for a nice warm cup of cyanide.

I looked around at my friends, but there was nothing anyone could say or do. I was standing in front of the police holding a very-possibly-dead woman's necklace. Morris was right. I was the last person to see Esme, and, as the live video was gone, no one could prove otherwise.

Seema stood there shivering while Dave shrugged and gave me a 'what can I do?' face. Dylan glared at him angrily.

Resigned to my fate, I started walking slowly towards the police car, my soggy Converse squelching with each heavy step. But before I could reach it, Dylan stepped forward in front of me.

'Wait,' he said.

Everyone, including me, turned to stare at him. What the hell was he doing?

'Kirby wasn't the last person to see Esme,' Dylan says. 'I was.'

THIRTY-SEVEN

I slam my foot on the accelerator and drive away from the Rec as fast as possible, leaving Morris in my dust.

My hands are cold and clammy on the steering wheel. Dave is dead. I cannot believe Dave The Legend is *dead*.

And who the hell was in that crow costume?

When I reckon I'm a safe enough distance away, I pull into a side street and lie on the back seat, staring at my Fitbit and waiting for my heartbeat to slow below one hundred BPM.

I try calling Dylan again, but there's no answer. A horrible thought crosses my mind.

Is it him? Is he the one doing this?

I mean, it's not like it would be the first time he'd done something terrible…

No. What was I thinking? Even after what went down with Esme, Dylan could never be capable of something like this… could he?

I check Surreywide.com for any reports on Seema, and my heart sinks when I see the top story.

**POLICE FIND BODY AT LOCAL DENTIST SURGERY.
DISTINCTIVE YELLOW AND GREEN CAR SEEN
DRIVING FROM SCENE.**

Shit.

It is only going to be a matter of time before the police catch up with me again. With its garish paint job and giant Foxtons logo, this stupid car might as well have a big flashing 'ARREST ME' sign on the roof. Quickly, I google 'Foxtons estate agent Crowhurst' and call the number.

'Good evening,' I say, when a very young-sounding man answers. I try to make my voice sound as posh as possible, putting those acting classes to good use. 'I'd like to arrange some viewings. ASAP. I really need to see...' I look at the phone and scan the website for local properties. 'Um, 16 Griffin Drive. And 213 Scully Street. Oh, and also 12 Buckland Avenue.'

'And you want to see all these immediately?' the man replies. 'You do realise it's past seven p.m.?'

I poke my head up and take a furtive peek out of the car window. I swear I can hear sirens in the distance.

'Are you saying you're not interested? I can give Acorn Homes a call if you prefer? I'm sure their agents would absolutely love the commission. I, um, represent an extremely wealthy local family. I can't repeat the name for confidentiality reasons, I'm sure you'll understand. I believe you've heard of Burnley FC?'

'Oh, you don't mean...'

'Yes, I do.' *Crap. What was that footballer's name?*

'Dennis King?' the estate agent says.

'Don't say it out loud, please!' I say. 'He'd prefer this kept confidential. He wants to buy at least six more properties in the area, one for each of his children. But it's very urgent, so we'll need to do the viewings simultaneously. They'll meet you at the properties.'

'Right, well, there's only three of us in the office right now, but we'll send out our agents straight away.'

'What about the Norbridge branch?'

'Um, okay, yes, we'll get them on it too,' he replies.

'Good,' I say, hanging up. All those green and yellow Minis driving around town should hold up Morris for a while.

But in the meantime, I needed to get as far away from here as possible.

THIRTY-EIGHT

TWELVE MONTHS AGO

Group Chat: The Deadbeats

> **Dave The Legend**
> @kirby pick up your phone, they're keeping dylan in for questioning

> **Seema**
> u coming home? u okay?

> **Kirby**
> sorry, i need to go to work

> **Seema**
> on a Sunday babe?

I parked up about two hundred yards from Crowhurst Business Park. After the roadworks debacle, Dave and Seema had gone back to the flat, while Dylan went with the police to the station. I'd made a stop-off at the McDonald's on the A34 for some hash browns and a banana milkshake, just to calm me down, and settle my raging hangover.

Turns out, spending the night on the back seat of a Mini after a night on the Cement Mixers, then jumping in a muddy hole in the middle of a thunderstorm wasn't conducive to feeling fresh and funky the next morning. Who knew?

According to my work emails, the police were holding a press conference this afternoon, just before the fayre started, due to the increased press interest around Esme. The hashtag had really taken off, and more and more people online were wondering if her disappearance was related to the murders thirty years ago.

I sat in the car for a while, wondering what the hell to do. All I knew was that Esme was out there somewhere, and instead of looking for her, the police were wasting time talking to Dylan.

I thought about that night we all went to The Lion. After we had our burgers, Esme popped to the Booze and Biscuits shop on the corner to buy a vape refill. I must have been asleep on the sofa by the time she came in. *If* she came in. That deflated mattress was still playing on my mind.

Why had Dylan told the police he was the last one to see Esme?

I could only think of two plausible explanations: 1) he had done something terrible to Esme or 2) the reason she didn't sleep in her bedroom that night was because she spent it in his.

Even though the thought of it made me want to throw up, I prayed it was option two. As painful as it was, I'd rather accept I was just another one of his TRLs than dare to believe he could've hurt anyone…

If I could prove Peter was still alive, and that he could actually be back, then I could clear Dylan's name and show Trevor I really was a decent journalist, all in one go.

I needed to find the witness, the person Esme went to meet at The Rec two nights ago. Whoever it was, they knew the truth about what really happened to Doyle.

I still had the newspaper front page from Esme's bag, although it was pretty soggy by now. I couldn't make out half the faces in the photo. But I knew where I could find another, complete edition from August 1996.

Every back issue of *The Gazette* was stored in the Surreywide building somewhere. Hundreds of the bloody things. And if I could dig out a complete copy of this issue, I could find out what's in the rest of the article, and maybe that could help me find out who the witness was.

I knew Trevor wouldn't be there on a Sunday, so I would be free to search through the archives without a bollocking or having to make him constant cups of tea. Only problem was, I wasn't sure where he stored them. I sucked up the last of my milkshake and pulled my work pass out of the glove compartment.

The office felt weird with no one in it. I didn't think I'd ever been in there without Trevor breathing down my neck (not literally obvs, he keeps a respectful distance from all his employees). But something else had changed since Friday: a large whiteboard was standing next to Trevor's desk. On it, he'd ranked all the current news stories on Surreywide.com in order of popularity.

Wow, looks like he's really taking this whole pivot to digital thing seriously, I thought.

I spent a few minutes looking in cupboards and rifling through the filing cabinets, but there was no sign of the newspaper archives. I was about to give up when the office door swung open and a familiar voice echoed across the room.

'Cornell, what on earth are you doing here on a Sunday?'

Oh crap. Trevor.

'Um, would you believe "overtime"?'

He let out an exasperated sigh, which, if you spoke fluent Whatever Trevor as I did, roughly translated as 'I was not born yesterday, Cornell'.

Ten minutes later, Trevor and I were sitting at his desk. He'd made the teas while I tried to explain (and by explain, I mean lie) to him why I'd broken in here on a Sunday (his words, I mean, I literally had a key to the door). It turned out Vinnie the security guard had texted him as soon as he saw the lights go on in the office, and of course, Trevor had driven straight here. It had taken him three cups of stronger-than-usual tea and more sausage rolls than I could count, but he'd just about calmed down about missing the FA Cup quarter final replay on the telly.

'There's a police press conference today,' I said. 'The missing girl, Esme Goodwin, she was, well, is, my flatmate. The one I told you about. This could go national, Trevor. *The Gazette* should be all over this. I could go down there and—'

'Do you really think you're ready for that sort of thing?' he asked. 'You have no experience in a pressured environment like that. And besides, there's really not much point.'

Trevor tapped the whiteboard behind him with a wipeable marker.

'What is that?' I asked.

'This,' Trevor said, 'is called the "hit list". All the news stories on Surreywide.com and how many hits they've got so far. It's so the bigwigs at Surreywide HQ can determine what people are clicking on, and make more of it.'

My heart sank.

'So it's happening? We're being assimilated?'

'I'm afraid so. And you haven't heard the best part yet,' he sighed. 'The board are incentivising their reporters to get the top-ranking story. They're offering a £10 M&S voucher for whoever writes the most-read story of the month.'

'That's ridiculous,' I cried. 'Crowhurst doesn't even have a Marks and Spencers!'

I scanned the list. The top-ranking story, with 7,212 hits, was '22 Celebrities Who Don't Look Alike', closely followed by 'What Your Favourite Pasta Shape Says About You' with 5,047.

I was hit by the horrible realisation that this whiteboard didn't just display a list of mind-numbingly vacuous articles, it was a terrifying vision of my future: competing for the mere prospect of a gastro meal deal that I would, with any luck, one day have the honour of placing in the office microwave. All thanks to the mighty benevolence of the Surreywide board members.

The rest of my career, if I even still had one, was going to be spent trawling the internet for some inane tweet that a celebrity had posted about their equally inane new workout routine, and then somehow squeezing five hundred even inaner words out of it. (And, yes, inaner is a word. I was a trained journalist, you know, even if the whole town seemed to have forgotten that fact.)

'Half of these don't even count as news, let alone local news,' I said. 'They're clickbait.'

'Digital is a numbers game, as you well know. They need hits, simple as that. And what do hits mean?'

'Um, prizes?' I offered.

'Advertisers.' Trevor popped a sausage roll in his mouth and chewed loudly.

'But none of these articles have anything to do with Crowhurst,' I said.

He nodded sadly. 'Exactly. And that's why a local paper is the lifeblood of its community, Cornell. Without it, people don't know what's going on in the place they live. And if they don't know, they don't care. *The Gazette* is finished, and, as far as I'm concerned, so is Crowhurst. It's over, Cornell.'

I looked at Trevor, slumped in his chair in front of the whiteboard, a half-eaten sausage roll in one hand. I swear, if he sighed one more time, he would completely deflate.

'You needn't worry,' he said, not even summoning the energy to look at me. 'You're young, you can find a new job. Your whole career is ahead of you. It's me who's on the scrap heap.'

'I dunno,' I said. 'I might well be joining you.'

I brushed my hair back around my ears.

'Go on.' Trevor closed his eyes and exhaled, clearly bracing himself for another verbal onslaught.

'It's like this. I was fired from my last job. I wrote this stupid online article that went viral, and I tried to argue with the trolls in the comments. Got the website into all sorts of legal trouble. I thought if I told the truth, no one would ever hire me again. So—'

'Kirby, I—'

'No, please, for once just let me get this out. I need to tell you this, because—'

'I know,' Trevor interrupted.

My jaw dropped. 'What do you mean, you know?'

'I know you lied on your CV. I have been in the journalism

game for quite a while. And despite what you might think, I do know how to use Google.'

'And you went ahead and gave me the job anyway?'

'Kirby, I'm well aware my generation is on the way out. My methods are antiquated, out of date. I'm yesterday's man. I knew someday I'd have to pass on the baton. And as much as it went against my better judgement, I knew I needed to take a risk on someone like you, someone not afraid to shake things up. I always hoped you'd take over as editor of *The Gazette* one day, and finally bring it into the 21st century. But I waited too long, played it too safe, and now it looks like you'll never have that chance.'

I span his wheelie chair round so he was facing me. 'Well then, if we're going to go out, let's go out with a bang.'

'What are you talking about?'

'The Peter Doyle story I told you about, well, I followed my lead up.'

Trevor began taking an intake of breath, preparing for one of his big sighs, but I carried on regardless.

'I know you said no more ShowMes, but, well, I'm sorry, I didn't listen. And you know what, I'm glad I didn't. The whole reason the police are holding a press conference at all is because of my videos, and I think…'

I fished in my pocket for the newspaper I'd found in Esme's bag.

'I think whoever this witness was, Esme was looking for them on the night she went missing. I think she found out what really happened in 1996.'

Trevor narrowed his eyes, but for once, no big sigh emerged. 'What are you saying, Cornell?'

Now it was my turn to take a deep breath.

'Peter Doyle is alive.'

Trevor didn't say a word; instead, he picked up the front page and held it up to the light.

'There have been all sorts of conspiracy theories about Peter Doyle over the years. I've heard them all. Still alive, back from the dead, fathered a secret child. Some people said he was pushed off the cliff by a scorned lover. And you know what, this newspaper has printed none of them. Do you know why? Because it's town tittle-tattle, and here at *The Gazette*, we deal in facts. And the police said he jumped.'

I wanted to tell him that his facts weren't selling a lot of newspapers, but I thought that would go down about as well as a cup of cold sick.

'All this,' he added, almost wistfully, 'is old news.'

'Not anymore,' I said. 'Esme is officially a missing person. The police are looking for her. Someone has done something to her, I'd swear my life on it. The FindEsme hashtag has gone crazy. My last video had 12,000 views, that's nearly twice as many as the top story on your whiteboard there. This is what people in Crowhurst are going to be talking about, Trevor. Not potholes or broken parking meters. If the board wants hits, let's give them hits. Let's show them that people still want to read about this town. By tomorrow, every other newspaper and website will be running a story about Esme. But they don't have what we have.'

I pointed at the front page of *The Gazette* from Esme's bag.

'A soggy old newspaper?' Trevor said.

'This could prove the police have been lying for thirty years. You said you wanted me to shake things up around here, well, it's not too late. Just help me find another copy of this. Whoever Esme was looking for is in this photo, and

I think they know the truth about what happened to Peter Doyle.'

Trevor spun his swivel chair round to look at his whiteboard and sipped his tea thoughtfully. Then he turned back and met my eye.

'Okay Cornell,' he said, throwing the last of his sausage roll in the waste paper bin. 'Follow me.'

THIRTY-NINE

TWELVE MONTHS AGO

Trevor led me down the stairs to the basement, where the giant printing presses dominated a room the size of a tennis court. The monstrous green metal machines were quiet – as the paper only printed on a Tuesday evening – but they were still pretty intimidating. Like a relic from another age, the old-fashioned offset printing press consisted of two huge cylinders, and a massive reel of newspaper ready to be dragged through the giant winders at high speed. Then, at the end, there was a sharp blade that cuts the paper into individual pages.

A little metal staircase went up to a platform next to the giant cylinders. There, on a small control panel was the very exciting button that started – and stopped – the presses.

'Have you ever done it?' I asked.

'Done what?'

'Yelled "stop the presses!" and slammed that button?'

'No, Cornell. *The Gazette* has a fine tradition of getting it right. On time, every time.'

'You must have wanted to, though? Just once?'

'Well, I just hope I never have to,' he said, but I swear I saw the tiniest of smiles cross his face at the thought.

I'd never been down there before, but I always knew when the paper was being printed, because, as Seema had found out, the vibrations from the presses reverberated through Crowhurst Business Park, making the telegraph poles wobble, and you could see the telephone lines shake all across Crowhurst.

Usually this room was off limits, because the presses could be pretty dangerous (apparently someone from the *Manchester Evening News* fell in one once and lost a leg). I wondered what would happen to this place once Surreywide took over. They'll probably knock it down and turn it into a multi-storey car park (the absolute last thing Crowhurst needed).

'I can only usually come down here with earplugs *and* ear defenders on,' Trevor chuckled. 'But it's a wonderful sight when they're rolling. I used to sit here and just watch. There's nothing like it really, especially when it's your by-line on the front page.'

Of course, I wouldn't know what it felt like to get a front-page by-line, but I decided now was not the best time to mention that.

'Do you know why they called it "hot off the presses"?' Trevor continued. 'Because the paper was literally warm to the touch when this old girl spat it out.'

I was about to mime throwing up, because that sounded completely gross, but when I glanced over at Trevor, he was gazing at the printing press like it was his favourite aunt, so I nodded respectfully instead.

We walked past the machinery to a large metal door at the back of the room. Trevor pulled a bunch of keys from his pocket and unlocked it, and I was immediately hit with the musty smell of decades-old paper.

'And here's our equivalent of the internet,' he said. Piles of boxes, filled with dusty old newspapers, lined the room, stacked almost to the ceiling. 'These go back about fifty years, and the Nineties issues are over... here.'

He motioned to two towering pillars of papers towards the back.

'So you'd have to search through all these if you wanted to check something?' I asked.

I looked at my phone, which held every bit of information in the universe within six inches, and back at the mountains of newspapers.

'Yes,' Trevor said. 'No Google back when I started. The best we had was a floppy disc. Big London papers digitised everything, but we never had fancy equipment like that. No, here we just piled 'em up high. The whole history of the town is here, in this room.'

'Okay, okay,' I said, holding up my hand. 'I get it. Local papers good, internet bad.'

Thankfully, *The Gazette* was only a weekly paper, so I managed to find the editions from 1996 pretty quickly. I started to pull out copies, and soon, I was sitting in a sea of newspapers, scattered across the office floor, my fingers black with newsprint.

There were around ten articles about Peter before the murders. Among them, I found a few colour photos of him, and, although unshaven and clearly not a regular at the barbers, he didn't look like a psychopathic murderer. But then again, what is a psychopathic murderer meant to look like anyway? He was even kind of handsome, in a rough and ready sort of way, with a brooding, almost dangerous, look in his piercing blue eyes.

Some of the reporting on Peter sailed pretty close to the wind. *The Gazette* really had it in for the guy, even before the murders. I knew from my training that suggesting someone's guilt could land a reporter in contempt of court. From the look of these articles, Peter Doyle had been condemned before he ever picked up a knife. They don't hold back: his Polish ancestry, the implication he was living here illegally, and a few derogatory comments about his dishevelled appearance thrown in for good measure.

I held up one of the articles, which showed a confused-looking Peter Doyle, clutching a half-empty bottle of vodka. The headline said: 'Local menace terrorises amateur dramatics club with profane outburst'. According to the article, all he did was shout 'bollocks!' at their performance of *The Pirates of Penzance*. And having sat through a number of the club's more recent shows, I could sympathise.

I remembered what Dylan had said about every town having their own bogeyman, and it looked like Crowhurst had decided early on it would be Peter Doyle. After reading the articles, it was no surprise that he killed himself before he could be caught. I don't think he'd have stood a chance in front of a jury of his peers.

'This is Peter here?' I pointed to the photo.

Trevor gathered up a bunch of the newspapers I'd discarded and made a makeshift stool. He sat down, flattening his trousers out with his palms, like he was about to tell a child a bedtime story. But I had a feeling this one wouldn't put me to sleep.

'That's right,' Trevor said. 'I was only twenty-six myself, still a junior reporter back then. We did a few stories on Doyle. He was the local ne'er-do-well. People said he came over here from Poland without the proper documentation, so he lived in a run-down caravan down by the river, doing odd jobs. Constantly in trouble with the police, though. Selling pot to the local teenagers, shoplifting – minor misdemeanours like that. But in Crowhurst, that was enough to make him public enemy number one.'

'The local bad boy?'

'You could call him that, yes. That's probably why the Parish Council let him be Jack Daw that year. Frank used to hire Doyle to put up the tents and take them all down again after it was over, which meant he knew where everything was, how all the rides worked. That year, Doyle said he would waive his fee if he could play Jack Daw. If you play the crow, everyone in town is supposed to buy you a pint afterwards, so he probably thought it was an easy gig for a free night on the slosh. And in their grand wisdom, the council thought that giving him some responsibility might sort him out a bit.'

'Boy, did they get that wrong,' I said.

'In those days, we were allowed to throw stones at the crow. They were only supposed to be pebbles, but some of the kids decided to chuck big rocks at him. Terrible behaviour, but like I said, Peter wasn't exactly popular. A bunch of them went up to Staker Point every year afterwards, drinking, lighting bonfires, getting wasted on God knows what. Started launching fireworks at Peter's caravan while he was in there sleeping off the cider. So he butchered all of them with the ceremonial trowel, then chucked himself off Staker Point. Still drunk out of his head, no doubt. The police found the blood-stained crow costume in his caravan the next day.'

My stomach turned. 'Why did he do it?'

'These days, Peter would probably have been diagnosed

with one of those neuro conditions that all you young people seem to have. But back then, he was just the local crazy. The whole town hated him, so I guess he finally snapped. He was a pretty volatile person. Gave poor Bob Morris a black eye down The Red Lion once.'

'Wait, was Morris on the force back then?'

'Bob? Thirty years ago? He would've just been a constable, I suppose. Not senior enough to work on a homicide case like this. He was probably on the search team though. They needed every man available for that. The police eventually pulled up a body from the River Muse, but it took them a few days to organise a search party and a winch. When it rains around here, the river overflows, and there had been a storm that week. The body was pretty badly beat up, decomposed and pecked apart by the buzzards down there.'

'Peter?' I asked.

Trevor shrugged. 'Doyle didn't have any family, and he sure as billy-o didn't have any friends in this town. I doubt the police had any of his DNA on file either. It wasn't like today, when you can scoop it off a half-eaten sandwich or a dirty tea towel. But it didn't matter. They were looking for a body, and they found a body. Stands to reason it was Peter Doyle. At least, it benefited the police to think that. And the town. If people thought that he was still out there... well, that would not have been good for tourism.'

'So the police, who are the only people who claim to have spoken to this witness, have a really good reason to lie about it,' I said.

As Trevor talked, I'd kept looking for the August 15th issue, the one that matched the front page in Esme's bag. But it was the only edition that wasn't there.

'Esme must have taken it,' I said.

'Not possible,' said Trevor. 'This room is locked at all times, and Surreywide has Vinnie on call twenty-four-seven. He's the only person with a key.'

Trevor rifled through the pile of papers and pulled out the editions from a week before and a week after 15 August.

'Very odd,' he said. 'It should be right here. These papers are not meant to be removed from the archive.'

I looked at the edition of *The Gazette* that followed the murders. On the front page was a photo of several police officers at the top of a rocky cliff, cordoned off with police tape. It must have been taken when they found the body.

'Is this where Peter's caravan was?' I asked.

'Yes, up on Staker Point, through the woods behind the Rec,' Trevor said. 'You can see it there in the corner of the photo.'

I flicked through the paper to a double-page spread of photos from the fayre in the middle. And there, in full colour, was an attractive young woman, laughing as Jack Daw strode through the Rec, wings aloft.

'Gosh, that photo is heartbreaking,' Trevor said. 'Everyone is so happy, no way of knowing the horror that was going to hit them just hours later. Goodness, Betty looks so young there.'

'Wait, did you say Betty? It can't be. She told me she wasn't even in the country.'

The woman in the photo couldn't have been more than a teenager, but she had Betty's soft brown curls and sharp blue eyes.

'She was a real beauty back then,' Trevor was looking over my shoulder. 'Every boy in Crowhurst had a crush on her.'

She was gorgeous, it was true. But there was something even more surprising about the photo.

Betty was heavily pregnant.

FORTY

Crowhurst police station was too small for a press conference, so Superintendent Morris had taken over the Community Centre.

Of course there was no air con, so it was hot and sticky as hell in there. After the storm, the weather had cleared, and it was another bright, sunny afternoon in Crowhurst. Half the town had turned up, but most of them had been told to wait outside.

According to Trevor, this hall was where the police had held the first press conference after the murders back in the Nineties. After that, the media presence got big enough that they started holding them up the road in Norbridge.

I snuck in the back, just before proceedings were about to begin. Trevor had eventually agreed to let me cover it for *The Gazette*'s final issue. So far, Esme's disappearance hadn't made many national headlines, but thanks to the ShowMe trend, there had been enough rumbles to force Morris's hand. There were even a couple of journalists from London up at the front. The story was growing, and people wanted answers.

A flimsy table had been set up at the end of the hall, and

there was a man in a tie clutching a Sky News foam-covered microphone. The rest of us were sitting behind in lines of plastic chairs, waiting for something to happen. Nervous chatter filled the room.

Eventually, the familiar form of Superintendent Morris stepped out and everyone went quiet. He looked visibly greyer than when I'd seen him earlier, if that was even possible. With the pace of an elderly sloth, he pulled out the chair at the centre of the table, sat down, adjusted his glasses and shuffled the papers in front of him.

He was followed by an attractive woman wearing what looked like a designer suit. She didn't look much older than me, but I assumed from the dark hair and flawless skin, that it must be Esme's mum. Even with rubbed, red eyes and just the faintest touch of make-up, she looked beautiful. Seeing her, clearly distraught and desperate, made me want to find Esme even more. I couldn't help but think of my own mum, and wonder how she'd react if something happened to me.

Morris leant into the mic, and a sharp screech of feedback reverberated around the hall.

'Good afternoon, everybody. Thank you for coming. It was necessary to organise this conference in a short amount of time, so I hope you'll forgive the, um, somewhat rushed arrangements. We were hoping to keep this investigation internal for the time being, but because of the interest from certain, uh, online activities, we've decided to hold this conference.'

Morris looked around the room nervously.

'Esme Goodwin, twenty-one years old, was last seen leaving Stewart Heights on Courtney Road on Friday 15 August at 10:24 a.m.'

He held up a photo of Esme that I recognised from her social media. A few cameras flashed and there was some murmuring from the crowd.

10:24? That was at least ten hours after I'd seen her. What new information had Dylan told them?

Morris continued speaking. 'And now I'd like to introduce Charlotte Goodwin, Esme's mother, who we've asked to say a few words.'

He shifted his chair backwards and motioned for her to speak.

'I just want to say,' Esme's mum said between sobs, 'that if you can see this, Esme, wherever you are, we miss you and we just want you to come home. Please. Please, come home.'

Her sobs broke into dry heaves as she turned away from the mic. Morris looked at her, uncomfortably, and I remembered what Esme said about her mother: a wolf in Gucci clothing.

'We are consulting with the National Crime Agency,' Morris continued. 'While we remain open-minded concerning the circumstances of Esme's disappearance, there is currently no evidence to indicate a third-party involvement. She does not appear on any CCTV footage recovered from the area. We will continue to pursue all lines of inquiry to ascertain why she went missing. We will continue to search extensively, and we're appealing for anyone who might have seen Ms Goodwin after her last sighting to come forward. I'll now take a limited number of questions.'

There were a few more mumbles from the crowd before one person stood up.

'Thank you, Superintendent. Veronica Lewis, BBC Radio Surrey. How confident are you and your team that you'll find Esme alive?'

Morris's eyes narrowed. He clearly didn't appreciate the tone of the question.

'Our working hypothesis is that Ms Goodwin may have been the victim of an accident somewhere between her flat and the train station,' he said. 'The route from her building to the station goes past the River Muse, which has a strong undercurrent, especially after a storm.'

Veronica sat down, seemingly satisfied with that, and a young guy in an ill-fitting suit stood up.

'Robert Stroud, *Sussex Tribune*. Is it true that Esme's necklace was found in the roadworks on Courtney Road?'

'That's correct. A member of the public found some of Esme's belongings, but we believe these items were lost before she went missing.'

'What about the videos about Esme on the ShowMe app?' Robert asked. 'Has the FindEsme hashtag influenced your investigation at all?'

'No,' Morris replied, barely hiding the annoyance in his voice. 'But actually, thank you for bringing the social media up. It's vital that we're able to conduct our investigation without... interference... from enthusiastic members of the public. There are very defined protocols we have to follow, and any, uh, unofficial efforts to assist us can, in fact, hamper our work. If anyone does have any information about Esme, again, I'd ask them to go through the proper channels.'

Morris began to collect his papers and stand up, and I felt a sudden panic surge through me. It was now or never. I stuck my hand up, and Superintendent Morris's face went pale. Trying his hardest to ignore my hand waving at him, he looked desperately around the room for a question from anybody else.

'And if there are no further questions, that concludes today's press conference,' he said. 'Thank you all for attending.'

'Uh, hi,' I shouted from the back, before anyone else had a chance to interrupt. 'Kirby Cornell, from *The Crowhurst Gazette*.'

I saw Morris's eyes widen when he heard my name.

'If you believe there's no third-party involvement,' I started, 'then who posted an old video on Esme's ShowMe feed? Do you think it's—'

Morris audibly exhaled, his lapel mic sending the sigh echoing around the hall. 'We believe Esme herself posted that video. We're a small-sized force here, but we are currently investigating and reviewing all evidence *objectively*.'

Now, maybe I was being paranoid again, but it sounded like he put a hell of a lot of emphasis on the word objectively there, while eyeballing me.

'I would reiterate, at this stage, there is no evidence of any third-party involvement – and nothing in our inquiries has changed this position.'

'Excuse me, Superintendent Morris, but you didn't let me finish my question,' I said. 'You've seen my footage on ShowMe. Do you think it's possible Peter Doyle is still alive?'

I held up my phone and started filming. This was it. Finally I felt like I was doing something worthwhile. Speaking truth to power. Making a difference. Eat your heart out, Lois Lane.

There was some hushed chatter from the room and Morris's face reddened.

'Peter Doyle's body was retrieved from Staker Point thirty years ago.'

'The body was never formally identified,' I said.

'We have a witness statement that corroborates the order of events.'

'I think that witness is lying,' I said.

The hall erupted. Esme's mum looked shocked and confused. Morris glanced around, as if hoping someone off-stage would help him.

'I've taken all the questions that I'm willing to answer this morning,' he mumbled. 'We'll keep the press informed of any further developments when and if they occur.'

With that, he stood up and started removing the mic from his lapel. There was another short, sharp blast of feedback as he walked off into a backroom.

The crowd began to shuffle out, leaving me sitting there like a lemon. Eventually I got up and wandered towards the table at the end of the hall. I poked my head round the door of the backroom. There was Morris, a polystyrene cup of tea in one hand and a phone in the other. He appeared to be having a very heated conversation with someone.

Suddenly, there was a tap on my shoulder. I turned around to see Charlotte Goodwin, and I froze. Up close, she looked so much like Esme, they could've been sisters.

'Oh, hi,' I mumbled, bracing myself for a (probably well deserved) slap.

'I just wanted to say thank you,' she said, her cut-glass accent breaking my stupor.

'What?'

'Thank you for everything you've done to help the search for my daughter,' she said, wiping a tear from her eye. 'I'm sorry. I just miss her so much. We were *very* close.'

Not knowing what to say, I nodded meekly.

'I have to go and speak to Esme's father now,' she went on.

'But please keep doing what you're doing. God knows the police here have been absolutely useless.'

She rolled her jade eyes towards Morris, gently touched my shoulder, and left as silently as she had arrived, leaving me standing there, dumbfounded. I thought back to Esme's video with the sweater, and the happiness in that woman's face when she returned it. That was exactly how Charlotte Goodwin had looked at me.

When Morris saw Esme's mum leave, he put his phone down and sighed. 'The press conference is over, Ms Cornell.'

'Is it? Because you didn't answer my question,' I said. Fuelled by Charlotte Goodwin's words, I felt more confident than ever before.

'I wasn't aware that you were a crime reporter. Aren't roadworks more your speed?'

'Well, everyone's a crime reporter now, right?' I said, as I waved my phone at him.

Morris's expression stiffened and I lowered my phone.

'You're in danger of upsetting this investigation,' he growled.

'Upsetting it? I'm the one that started it! If it wasn't for my FindEsme hashtag, you wouldn't even be looking for her,' I cried.

'And maybe if you and your friends had told us the truth in the first place, we would have found her by now,' Morris replied.

He meant Dylan.

'What happened with Dylan Barnes?'

'You know I can't tell you that.'

'Off the record,' I said, feeling like a proper journalist. I made a show of putting my phone in my jacket pocket.

'All I can tell you is he's not a person of interest,' Morris said. 'He's been released without charge.'

Even though I was still furious with Dylan for lying to me, I'd never felt so relieved.

'We believe Esme's disappearance is a tragic, but isolated, accident,' Morris continued.

Tragic? Why did he use that word? Did that mean he thought she was dead?

'But what about Peter Doyle? Did he really fall, or is it possible he's back, and Esme Goodwin is his next victim?'

Morris took off his glasses and cleaned them on the sleeve of his shirt. 'That,' he said very carefully, 'is nonsense.'

'Is it? Or maybe it's in your interest that Esme doesn't turn up? Since she might be able to prove that you let Peter Doyle get away?'

His face turned red again. He did *not* enjoy that question.

'Unless you want to find yourself spending the night in the holding cell, I would advise you to go home. That is, of course, unless you think that an evening at Crowhurst Police Station would make a good video on your app there?' His voice was getting louder, more aggressive with every word. 'You people have got some nerve. Do you really care about victims, or do you just care about how many views you get on your videos? I've seen what kids like you are getting up to online, messing around on crime scenes and ruining important evidence – not to mention intruding on grieving families.'

'Esme's mum seemed to disagree with you,' I said.

Morris's voice dropped an octave. 'I did a little internet research of my own, Ms Cornell,' he said. 'Or should I say Ms Dangerfield.'

A sliver of ice-cold anxiety ran through me when he said that name.

'So what?' I asked, trying to sound as confident as possible. 'That's not a secret.'

'No, it certainly is not. Not after that article you wrote. Very… informative, I must say. I was actually quite the fan of *Necktie* back in the day. Braver, stronger, smarter – isn't that what he used to say? Met him once, actually. Very nice chap. Didn't deserve the slating you gave him, that's for sure. Came all the way down here to hand out prizes at the raffle, years ago. His fame was fading a little by then, mind you. I wonder if he's aware that his daughter is trying to play detective too? Maybe I should give him a little phone call and tell him what you've been up to.'

'I'm a twenty-nine-year-old woman, Superintendent,' I said, as convincingly as I could. 'You think threatening to call my parents scares me?'

Full disclosure: it did scare me, very much so. I'd done enough damage to my dad's reputation already. I was sure Morris was bluffing. As if my dad ever came to this crummy little town. But the last thing in the world I could handle was another letter from his lawyers. I had to pull out the big guns.

'If anyone here is keeping secrets, it's you. You didn't tell me the truth back at the station, did you?' I said. 'You were there that night thirty years ago.' I fished out the front page of *The Gazette* from my pocket and placed it on the table in front of him. 'This is you at the fayre in 1996, isn't it? Did you see what happened to Peter Doyle?'

'I thought I told you to go home,' Morris said, not even looking at the newspaper.

'My followers have confirmed this is you. They're already

coming up with all sorts of theories about why you lied about it. But fine, if you don't want to set the record straight, that's up to you. I'll just make a new video and—'

He pinched the bridge of his nose and sighed in resignation.

'Fine. It's not something I particularly like to talk about, especially with the murder tourists who come in the station asking questions. Do you know how many weirdos we used to get badgering us after the murders? It's easier just to say I wasn't there,' he said. 'I was only a youngster myself at the time – twenty-two – just got the job on the force. I didn't see what happened to Peter, but I was one of the first on the scene at Staker Point the morning after the murders. Talk about in at the deep end. I'd never seen a dead body before, and then, suddenly, I'd seen six of them in a week. There was no family to identify Doyle, no conclusive DNA match. But, Ms Cornell, please listen to me. The chances that the body wasn't Peter Doyle are a million to one. And besides, his girlfriend saw him jump, and two days later, we found a body. We didn't need DNA to tell us what we already knew.'

'But, just to be clear, the body was never formally identified?'

'Off the record?' he asked.

'Off the record,' I replied.

'No, the body was never formally identified. Now, please, go home.'

With that he stood up and stared at me silently, until I turned around and walked out.

But what Morris didn't know, was I'd left my ShowMe recording live in my pocket the whole time.

FORTY-ONE

I feel like Foxy might explode at any second.

I'm jamming the accelerator down, and she's just about pushing fifty mph, pretty much the fastest she's ever gone. And it's taking every last ounce of power she has to make it to the top of Staker Point.

I don't know why I've come here. Maybe some deep part of me wants to pay tribute to Esme. It's the weekend of the fayre, so this is the anniversary of her death, after all. But the truth is, I think I might want to join her.

My phone is blowing up with alerts. With one hand on the steering wheel, I grab my phone and check Surreywide.com again. As well as reporting that a body has been found at the dental surgery, there's now a grainy photo of me taken from the CCTV, with a request to call if anyone has any information about 'this woman'.

Police have apparently cordoned off the Rec too, so that means they've probably found Dave's hand by now. It won't take them long to find my fingerprints all over the claw machine.

In short, I am well and truly fucked.

Esme, Max, Seema, Dave. All dead. Wherever Dylan is, at least he hasn't 'left the chat' yet. But surely it's only a matter of time. I should just keep going and drive right off Staker Point.

I'm worthless. I always was. Better to end it now before the police catch up with me. Or, worse, whoever hurt the others finds me.

As the car reaches the peak of the cliff, I see the moon rising ahead of me, huge and shining like a mirror ball. I push my foot down harder on the accelerator, even though it makes no difference – she's flat out as it is.

It'd be so easy to keep going. In a few seconds, all of this would just go away.

At the last moment, I see a figure in front of me, silhouetted in my headlights.

I scream, slamming on the brake and yanking the steering wheel hard. Foxy skids to a halt just before reaching the edge, spraying earth and stones over and into the river far below.

I peer through the windscreen, my heart pounding my chest like it's Tyson Fury in the final round. I flick the headlights off, and see a young girl in a sunset jacket, shielding her eyes with her arm.

It can't be... it literally *cannot* be.

But it is.

It's Esme.

FORTY-TWO

TWELVE MONTHS AGO

Imagine the worst village fete in history crossed with... In fact, don't bother crossing it with anything, just go ahead and keep imagining the worst village fete in history, because that pretty much sums up exactly what the Crawe Fayre is.

The Rec was dotted with canvas tents and faded bunting stretched as far as the eye could see. Over by the playground there was a big bucket for apple bobbing, and on the other side there was the world's least difficult maze, constructed from what looks like about twenty hay bales, stacked on top of each other, not quite high enough that an averagely tall person couldn't easily see over.

Rows of tables were piled high with gigantic pumpkins, marrows and squashes, while food stalls offered an array of fried treats. Thankfully the Grillennium Falcon was nowhere to be seen, but there were plenty of hot dogs, sweet peanuts and toffee apples for sale at unreasonable prices. And if you wanted to get completely wasted, there was hot cider, cold cider, mixed berry cider and even a dubious-looking home-brew called Scrumpy Max, which was probably highly illegal.

I bought a drink and wandered around the field. I assumed that Dave was in one of the tents, preparing for his big performance, or 'getting into character' as he put it, like he was Crowhurst's answer to Daniel Day-Lewis. Although I think the extent of Dave's method acting amounted to downing three pints and then attempting to squeeze himself into that stupid crow costume.

There were even some old-school rides, complete with garish approximations of celebrities daubed on the sides. A wonky-looking Brad Pitt circa 1997 stared out from the dodgems, while a lopsided Will Smith and someone who I *think* was meant to be Britney Spears (but looks more like a furious Bratz doll) adorned the funhouse. It was a weird vibe. Medieval paganism meets twentieth-century fairground, with ghost trains and waltzers rubbing shoulders with corn dollies and face-painting stalls. There were rows of ancient arcade games, including those terrible claw machines that are so wobbly it is almost impossible to win a prize.

My phone had about six voicemails from Superintendent Morris. He was, understandably, furious about my latest ShowMe video. I didn't care. Peter Doyle might never have jumped off Staker Point. And that meant he could be back. But one person knew for certain. Morris said Peter had a girlfriend who saw what happened, and although I didn't want to believe it, I thought I knew who that might be. She was here at the fayre somewhere, I was sure of it.

Draining the last of my cider, I slumped against the back of a hot-dog van and stared at the ghost train. It was covered with the same luminous generic slack-jawed zombies as every other ghost train I'd seen in my life. Everyone seemed to be giving me the cold shoulder. I didn't know whether they'd seen my videos and thought I was stirring up trouble, or they wanted to mind their own business. Maybe they just wanted to enjoy the one day of the year when the town did something fun, and not be harassed by a mad conspiracy theorist.

But I wasn't mad. A young woman really was missing, and here they all were, bobbing for apples and carving spoons out of tree branches. It was all a bit creepy, and I felt like they were about two cans of Strongbow away from a group orgy on the bouncy castle. Sometimes it felt like Crowhurst actually *wanted* Peter Doyle to come back. Like this whole thing was some sort of devil worship or dark-arts ritual. And I was not here for it. Not while there was a twenty-one-year-old woman missing. At least I hoped she was only missing, and not…

There was a small group of teenagers over by the helter-skelter. Almost all of them had their phones out, filming everything. One was sweeping his phone over the Rec, another was trying to film himself recreating what he imagined Esme's last movements would've been.

I tapped one of them on the shoulder. She was blonde and wearing a knee-length floral summer dress. When she turned around, I recognised her immediately.

'Hey, you're Frank Garrett's niece, right?' I asked.

Her eyes widened when she saw me.

'Oh my God, you're Kirby, aren't you? From upstairs? My uncle really hates your guts,' she laughed.

'That's me,' I said. To be fair, after barging into his home and accusing him of kidnap, I couldn't really blame Frank for crossing me off his Christmas-card list.

'Are you still looking for Esme?' she asked. 'I've been

watching your videos. They're so, like, unrehearsed and natural. You have a real off-the-cuff vibe going on.'

'Uh, thanks, I guess,' I mumbled. 'Does your uncle know you're here?'

'Of course. Uncle Frank runs this whole thing, never shuts up about it,' she said. 'He made me carry all the old fayre crap out of his basement and help him set up. He says all this ShowMe stuff is great for publicity. The fayre is busier than ever this year.'

'Right, but I'm more worried about Esme to be honest.'

'Oh for sure, *love* ShowMeSherlock. Total girl boss. That's why we're here. We're addicted to her videos.' She motioned to her friends behind her. 'Although, I'd really like to start my own investigations one day, just like you and Esme.'

Suddenly I had the feeling that I'd invited a bus load of sheep to a party of wolves. If Peter Doyle was looking for some new victims, he could really take his pick here.

'The fayre *is* sick, though. I made a great video of me and Tyler bobbing for apples over there. It's hilarious, you should do one. I'm already getting some great engagement on it, look.' She held her phone up so I could see the abundance of little red hearts on the video.

Before I could say anything else, I noticed the crowd parting, craning their necks to look at something. I stood on my tip-toes to see a figure dressed in jet black walking towards us. It was Jack Daw, the Thorny Crow himself. I had to admit, there was something quite chilling about the way he lurched across the Rec. I mean, sure, the costume wasn't exactly straight out of Jim Henson's Creature Shop. You could tell it had been worn and re-worn many times over the years. But you'd never know it was Dave under there, covered in feathers and twigs and a cheap-looking homemade crow mask, complete with large grey cardboard beak.

'Hey, Dave, over here!' I shouted.

He turned towards me and put up a big feathery finger to his beak, as if to say 'shhhh'. I'd forgotten, he wasn't allowed to talk. One of the Rules of the Crow, apparently. The parade would be starting soon, which meant I was running out of time.

While everyone was distracted, I made my way through the crowds until I found Madame Mystique's palm-reading tent. I poked my head through the canvas opening to see Betty, dressed in a long purple shawl and a head scarf, sitting behind a little wooden fold-out table. There was a single candle burning beside her, which seemed a little risky, considering the tent was probably thirty years old and insanely flammable.

'Betty,' I gasped. 'Thank God. I need to speak to you.'

'I think you mean "Madame Mystique",' she said, in a silly voice. 'And if you want to speak to me, you'll have to cross my palm with silver first, my love.'

There was a jar beside her, half full of pound coins and fifty-pence pieces.

'Sorry, I don't have time for that. I think you might be in danger.'

She looked startled. 'What are you talking about?'

'Peter Doyle,' I said. 'I think he's back.'

'Oh, Kirby,' she said, her face relaxing. 'You're not still on about that ridiculous nonsense, are you?'

'It's not nonsense, I think he hurt Esme, or took her, or—'

'Kirby, you need to calm down,' Betty said. 'I think you've had too much cider. You didn't touch any of that Scrumpy

Max, did you? That stuff will make you see things. Or make you go blind, one of the two…'

'Betty, I know,' I said firmly.

Her expression changed, just for a second, before she regained her composure.

'Know what, love?'

'I know you were there that night, thirty years ago,' I said.

The lights of the ghost train next to us flickered across the thin fabric of the tent. I couldn't read her expression. She was either furious or stunned. Or both.

I pulled *The Gazette* front page from my back pocket. 'You were here at the fayre thirty years ago. Heavily pregnant. Were you the witness Esme was looking for before she disappeared?'

'What are you accusing me of, Clare?' she asked, her voice not wavering.

'I just need to know, Betty.'

She took off her head scarf and motioned to the table in front of her.

'Sit down here for a second, will you? Someone might come in. At least let's make it look like I'm telling your fortune.'

I did as I was told and Betty took my hands in hers.

'Esme sent me a message on Facebook. She said she knew I was the last person to see Peter Doyle alive. She wanted to meet. I said no, of course, but then she told me she knew something… something about Dylan.'

My heart skipped a beat. 'She blackmailed you?' I asked.

'We met on the Rec, and I told her the truth about that night, on the condition she would keep everything secret.'

'And you trusted her?'

'I had no choice.' She looked down at my hands and gently

traced the lines of my palms. 'I needed to protect Dylan. But I never touched that girl, I swear. After we talked, she walked off, and I never heard from her again.'

Betty had the same ocean-blue eyes as Dylan, and the more I stared into them, the more I believed what she was saying was true. Like her son, Betty didn't lie unless she had to. I took my hands away from hers and looked her in the eye.

'I need to know – did Peter really jump?'

Betty looked at me for a moment. 'Sometimes a little white lie can protect the people you love, you know?'

I nodded.

'The truth is, Peter didn't jump,' she said.

'Oh, Betty,' I started. 'No one could blame you if you—'

'No,' she stops me. 'That's not what happened. When the word spread through town that something terrible had happened up on Staker Point, I ran to find Peter as fast as I could. I'd been to that caravan so many times, I knew the way off by heart, even in the dark. When I found him, he was drunk. I asked him outright if he did it, if he'd hurt those kids. He swore he'd been in his caravan the whole time.'

'Did you believe him?' I asked.

'I… I wanted to. I really loved him. And he was the father of my baby. Our baby.'

My jaw dropped and I instinctively covered my mouth with my hand.

'You mean…?'

Betty nodded.

'I couldn't turn him in,' she continued. 'So I told him to run. I told him that I'd tell everyone that he jumped, so they wouldn't come looking for him. I told him that the only way to protect our child was to run away and never, ever come back. And then I walked home. Leaving Peter standing alone on that cliff edge that night was the hardest thing I've ever had to do. But I did it for my son. When the police found the body a week later, I was shocked. But I guessed that Peter really had thrown himself off. Probably wracked with guilt. But please, Kirby, you can't ever tell Dylan.'

I felt dizzy, like the world was spinning. Peter Doyle was Dylan's father, and he didn't know. He could never know. *It would kill him.*

'Of course,' I stammered. 'I won't say a thing, I promise. But, Betty, that body the police found – I don't think it was Peter.'

Betty met my eyes, and didn't blink.

'Part of me would dearly love to believe that. But, Kirby, this is why the past is best left alone. No good can come of meddling in this, trust me. Now, if you'll excuse me,' she said sadly, retying her head scarf, 'I have customers waiting, and the parade is about to begin.'

'You're not safe here,' I told her.

She shook her head. 'Kirby, the whole town is here. This is the safest place I can be.'

I shuffled out of the tent, past the queue of two people waiting, and sat down, defeated, on the grass. No one had seen Peter actually fall. And no one could be 100 per cent sure whose body the police fished out of the River Muse.

Had Esme been right all along? Was it Peter Doyle that took her that night, to stop anyone finding out the truth?

That he was alive.

Peter Doyle was alive.

My heart was racing. If Peter was here, and taking revenge on everyone that had wronged him, then the whole town was in danger. I had to tell Trevor. We had to warn them.

'Cornell,' he said when he picked up my call. I could barely hear him over the sound of the music.

'Where are you?' I shouted, sticking one finger in my ear.

'What?'

'Where are you?' I repeated.

'I'm at the fayre, of course, over by the cider stand,' he said.

'Which cider stand? There's about twenty of them!' I cried. 'Listen to me. I was right. Peter Doyle is alive, and I think he's back. We're all in danger, the whole town—'

'Sorry, Cornell, I can't hear a thing with my earplugs in. Give me a second, will you? I'll just find somewhere quieter.'

I waited for a second, but then I heard another voice. Trevor was talking to someone else.

'Oh,' I heard him say. 'Yes, I know she's been impulsive, but I think she might really be on to something. Right. Right. Well, yes, that does sound unethical. I did not authorise that, no. I actually have her on the line right now, let me—'

Before I could hear another word, there was an audible gasp on the other end of the line, and I heard the soft thud of a phone falling on grass.

'Trevor? Trevor?' I yelled.

All around me I could hear music blaring from the cheap PA system, mixed with the raucous laughing and chatter of the crowds. I span around, scanning the field for the cider tent. But everything was a blur of flashing lights and bunting.

'Trevor?' I spluttered again into my phone.

But the line was dead.

FORTY-THREE

I started to shake. But before I could even begin to process what had just happened, the classic-rock music blaring from the tannoy speakers suddenly stopped. It was replaced by a haunting traditional folk song, and the crowd whooped their approval.

I watched as everyone gathered in the centre of the field. Traditionally, when the sun began to set, it was time for the Jack Daw to begin his walk through the fayre. Groups of children squealed in delight as a woman passed out handfuls of grapes. Some of them were now wearing leaf crowns, for Christ's sake. I could make out Betty, at the front of the crowd, in her long, purple flowy shawl. Frank was there too, mouth agape in rapture, and even Morris was pushing his way to the front, wide-eyed. Honestly, it felt like they were one Wicker Man away from a human sacrifice.

Then Jack Daw appeared, waddling through the crowd in his cheap-ass crow costume. Grapes began to fly through the air as he cawed in mock distress. He was flanked by two other guys, whose sole job seemed to be to hold his wings – which appeared to be made of balsa wood and fake feathers – aloft.

He held up the trowel, stabbing the air triumphantly and goading the crowd, which roared in rapturous delight.

A cold trickle of fear sobered me up for a second. I was joking about the human sacrifice… *I mean, they wouldn't, would they?*

I steadied myself against the hot-dog van and gave myself a mental slap across the face. I had to pull myself together. What was I thinking? Too much cider, too much ShowMe and too much bloody Crowhurst. But the thumping of the drums did seem to be getting louder and louder. What the hell was in that scrumpy?

But then, as I squinted, the lights and music swimming in front of my eyes, I realised something about the person dressed as the crow.

Dave was a big lad, nearly six foot tall. This crow seemed at least half a foot shorter than that. And his physique, well, this crow was lean, svelte almost. I was far more familiar with Dave's beer belly than I should have been – God knows he wasn't shy about showing it off down The Red Lion every time Tottenham scored a goal.

But this Jack Daw was short and wiry. Just like the crow in the photo in *The Gazette*, in fact.

It's Peter. Oh my God, it's Peter… He'd got Trevor and now he was coming for the rest of the town.

My head was swimming, but I knew I had to do something. I launched headfirst into one of the revellers in the crowd. 'Sorry!' I yelled, pushing several of them out of my way.

But then I felt something sharp poking into my ribs, and I

looked up to find myself staring straight into the shiny glass eyes of Mr Jack Daw himself.

I froze for a moment. The drumming stopped and everyone in the crowd went quiet. The crow continued to stare at me blankly without saying a word.

'I know who you are,' I stuttered.

With that, Jack Daw opened up his big cardboard beak and let out a long, creepy 'caaaaaw'.

'Alright, that's enough,' I said, somehow gathering a bravery I didn't know I possessed.

I turned around to the crowd. 'It's Peter!' I shouted. 'It's Peter Doyle. You're all in danger.'

I reached up and grabbed the crow mask, pulling it off his head with one swoop.

'Hey!' he cried, trying to wrestle the mask off me. 'You can't do that to the Thorny Crow!'

I yanked it off him, and immediately stepped back in shock. The man looking back at me had a greasy ponytail and a goatee. He couldn't have been much older than me.

It was not Peter Doyle.

'Who the fuck are you?' I spluttered.

'Gordon Dillberry,' he said, almost apologetically.

'Gordon fucking Dillberry?' I cried. 'But I thought you ate a dodgy kebab and had to stay home?'

'Are you kidding? I'd never pass up an opportunity like this. The Thorny Crow is the noblest honour that can be bestowed—'

'So where's Dave?' I interrupted.

He shrugged. Suddenly, something small and hard hit my forehead and bounced off onto the ground. I looked down to see a *fricking grape*. I spun round to see the whole crowd staring at me. Somebody had shut off the music, and instead they were all chanting at me.

'*Who's exposed the Thorny Crow? Who's exposed the Thorny Crow? Who's exposed the Thorny Crow?*'

Oh my God, I didn't have time for this *Midsommar* bullshit. I pushed Gordon Dillberry out of the way and tried to make my way through the crowd. But they kept chanting at me.

'You don't understand,' I tried to yell. 'He's here, Peter Doyle is here somewhere.'

But my voice was drowned out by the chanting, and the drumming had started again.

Now I was really scared. *Because if Gordon Dillberry was in the Jack Daw costume, then where the hell was Dave?*

FORTY-FOUR

TWELVE MONTHS AGO

Group Chat: The Deadbeats

> Kirby
> dave where are you

> where the fuck are any of you???

> I'm serious guys dave is missing. I need help

I found myself breaking into a trot, with no idea where I was going. If this was a movie, I'd probably run into a hall of mirrors, and find myself chased by a hundred wobbly reflections. But I ended up near the dodgem cars, which seemed way more appropriate to my life.

Then I saw someone, on their own, at the edge of the Rec, just behind the swings. The rest of the revellers were all watching the end of Jack Daw's parade. So who was this, and why were they so keen to get away?

I recognised the swaggering figure immediately.

Dave.

Part of me was relieved he was okay, and not stabbed to death with a trowel somewhere. But this was supposed to be his big night. Where was he going, and why hadn't he been the one wearing his beloved crow costume?

I was about to call out to him, but before I could open my mouth, he began walking into the woods behind the playground.

Where the hell was he going?

He hadn't seen me, so if I was fast, I could follow him and find out exactly what he was up to. I crossed the Rec and made my way through the trees. But the woodland quickly became darker and thicker the further I went, and I quickly lost sight of him. Even illuminated by the orange glow of a hazy mid-August sunset, the woods felt gloomy. Claustrophobic almost.

Then, suddenly, I saw Dave up ahead. He was talking on his phone, and I could see now that he was holding a bulky plastic bag in his other hand. I pressed myself up against the nearest tree and tried to listen.

'Yeah, she's here, but she's all over the place. She won't be a problem,' he was saying.

Was he talking about me? Who the hell was he talking to?

His voice became muffled as he walked further into the woods. 'And if she is, I'll deal with her...'

Keeping my head low, I tried to creep slowly behind him, using the undergrowth for cover. But as I steadied myself on a fallen log, I caught sight of my wrist.

'9,997!' my watch face flashed with delight, indicating I had, by some miracle, almost reached my daily goal. I knew if I took three more steps, the watch would start to play its insanely loud, high-pitched beepy song of congratulations.

Shit! This is why exercise is a terrible idea, people.

I quickly clasped my hand over the watch before it hit 10,000, slipping it off my wrist and ducking down. Eventually, I found the off button and stuck the damn thing in my jacket pocket. But when I poked my head up, Dave was gone. With no choice but to continue trekking towards the summit, I kept going. After about ten minutes of steep incline, the trees began to thin out, and I came to the top of Staker Point – a five-hundred-foot-high cliff towering over the River Muse.

There, just at the edge of the clearing, was a run-down, decrepit-looking mobile home. I felt a horrible nausea creeping through me. Even covered with moss and weeds, I recognised it from the photo in *The Gazette*.

Peter Doyle's caravan.

Suddenly, my thoughts were interrupted by a sharp cracking noise. I instinctively ducked behind a tree. After a second, I peered out to see Dave making his way through the trees towards the caravan. He started fiddling with the padlock that was attached to the door.

I watched him disappear inside, the door closing behind him. As the adrenaline began to subside, I suddenly felt very scared indeed. What the hell was Dave doing in Peter Doyle's old caravan? There was only one way to find out…

Hands shaking, I stuck a location pin in the group chat and tapped out a message.

> Kirby
> found Dave. Get here quick

Then I stepped out from behind the tree and made my way to the caravan door. I placed my ear against it, trying to hear what was going on in there.

Silence.

273

With a deep breath, I pushed the door open. Inside the caravan it was pitch black. Flicking on my phone torch, I held it up and shone it around.

'Hey!' Dave cried, the light blinding him for a second.

I squinted at him as he held a hand up to shield his eyes. In the other hand, he was still clutching the plastic bag.

'What the hell, Dave? What are you doing up here?'

I grabbed the bag off him and shone my torch inside. It was full of sandwiches.

I recoiled, filled with confusion. Was he coming up here for a fricking picnic?

'Kirby, wait, I can explain,' Dave stuttered. 'It's not what you think…'

Suddenly, there was a polite cough from the back of the caravan, and I swung my torch away from Dave.

Someone else was there, sitting on the bed. A plume of smoke obscured their face, but I smelt the unmistakable scent of Strawberry Ice.

No. It couldn't be.

My torch light illuminated their face, and my jaw dropped.

'Oh, hi Kirby,' Esme said, nonchalantly taking a puff on her vape pen. 'Miss me?'

FORTY-FIVE

TWELVE MONTHS AGO

'Esme!' I almost screamed. 'Are you okay? Did he hurt you?'

I rushed over, patting her arms and body, checking for injuries like a frantic mum whose kid had just fallen off their tricycle. When I realised she was fine, physically at least, I took her head in my hands, and almost kissed her forehead.

'It's alright,' I told her. 'The others are on their way, you're safe now. Everything's going to be okay.'

But she just sat there, staring at me like I was crazy.

'Um, yeah, thank you, Kirby,' Esme said, gently removing my hands from her face. 'I know.'

'But... but, has he been keeping you here?'

My first thought was that Dave had kidnapped her, locked her in Peter Doyle's caravan and was keeping her alive with Pret sandwiches. But something didn't quite add up. She looked... well, totally unbothered. Which was great, and totally on brand for her, but I had been expecting something a tad more dramatic.

Esme was wearing a completely different outfit to when I last saw her in her live video, and her hair looked freshly washed. I swear she even had a coat of fake tan on. Dave had obviously been bringing her more than just sandwiches.

'What exactly is going on here?' I demanded.

'I can explain—' Dave began.

'Stand down, Legend. I'll handle this.' Esme took my hand and pulled me back to face her. 'Kirby, you deserve a proper explanation for all of this. Actually, you deserve a lot more than that. You've totally excelled yourself. Better than I could've imagined.'

'What are you talking about?' I asked. The evening suddenly didn't feel so warm anymore.

'You need to understand three things. One, no one kidnapped me. Two, Peter Doyle is long dead. And three, there's no Crowhurst Killer. At least, there hasn't been one for thirty years.'

I could see where this was going, and I didn't like it. Not one little bit.

'You faked it,' I stuttered. 'You faked your own disappearance.'

'Now you're getting it,' Esme said.

The world was starting to spin again. 'But why?' I asked. 'Why would you do something like that?'

Esme looked at me like I was a child asking why they couldn't have chocolate for dinner. 'Um, have you seen my follower count lately? Through the fricking roof, girl.'

I shook my head in disbelief. 'You did all this, just to boost your follower count?'

'You should be pleased,' Esme said. 'Your account has blown up too.'

My blood was boiling now. Fear and confusion had been usurped by pure, molten anger.

'I could not give less of a shit about that,' I said.

Esme shrugged, a trademark movement of hers I had *not* missed. I started pacing around the caravan, my legs working as hard as my brain.

'Please do not tell me you faked all this for likes on a stupid app?'

'Well, not just that,' Esme said. 'It's also been very financially rewarding. You wouldn't believe what some people would pay for a collab like this.'

'What do you mean, collab? This is a fricking promotional partnership?'

'Well, sort of. I figured my ShowMe engagement would go wild if everyone thought I'd been kidnapped – or worse – by one of the killers I was investigating. After all, these days it's the victim that gets all the attention, right?'

After I'd done three laps, I finally leant against the side of the caravan, speechless.

'Okay, listen,' Esme said. 'The plan was pretty simple – come down here, make a few videos about the so-called Crowhurst Killer, and then "mysteriously" go missing, just for a bit.'

'But we saw you get snatched on the street.'

'Did you?' Esme asked. 'Or is that just what you thought you saw? We set it all up, and since then, I've been hiding out up here. Dave has been bringing me supplies, keeping look-out, and making sure you kept on the right track, of course.'

Dave raised his hand and smiled at me sheepishly.

'Unfortunately, that meant I had to pretend that I was going to be Jack Daw this year, so no one would wonder where I was tonight,' Dave said. 'And slip Gordon Dillberry twenty quid to go along with it.'

'So that explains the bag full of sandwiches,' I said quietly, the pieces falling into place.

'I had to get the bus all the way to Norbridge for those,' Dave added, unhelpfully.

'Well, I couldn't very well eat any of Betty's sausage rolls and steak slices, could I?' Esme said. 'Jesus, hasn't that woman heard of tofu?'

I clenched my teeth, half out of fury, and half so I didn't lose my shit and bite someone.

'But what about your "mental health break" video? Who posted that?'

'I did, of course,' she said. 'One of my old outtakes. We had to make it look like someone was trying to cover my disappearance up. That's where you came in, Kirby – my own little ShowMeSherlock.'

'You've been watching my videos?'

'Of course. They're a bit rough and ready, but that kind of unprofessional style does really well on ShowMe these days. You spread the word, got everyone talking about me. You even noticed my necklace. And did such a good job of galvanising the Watsons. Those guys can be a little... well, you know.'

My head still whirling, I stumbled out of the caravan, desperate for some fresh air. The night sky was clear up here, and the moon was high, illuminating Esme as she stepped out onto the edge of the cliff behind me.

'Come on Kirby, don't leave just yet. We're almost done, and you've played your part perfectly so far. Thanks to your performance at the press conference, I'm the top story on the MailOnline, the number one trend on all apps. All thanks to Kirby Cornell, "world's best journalist".'

She clapped her hands together in mock applause, and my stomach curdled. I'd been nothing but a sock-puppet, a fool made to dance to Esme's sick little tune.

'Really,' Esme continued. 'I'm genuinely impressed. In fact, you were a bit too good, if anything. You weren't meant to find me. Not yet anyway.'

'You set me up,' I said quietly, as the whole charade began to dawn on me. 'That night after the pub when you got me to download ShowMe. It was all leading to this?'

'Well, I lit the spark, you might say. I wasn't sure you'd go for it, but you did me proud. And, well, if it hadn't been you, it wouldn't have been long before one of my Watsons started sniffing around.'

'I can't believe this.'

'Kirby, chill.' She sighed dramatically. 'There's no victim here. Only winners. Look at the attention we've drummed up for this dry little town. It's exactly what they needed.'

'No victim? What about your mum? She's been out of her mind with worry. Or how about the families of Peter Doyle's victims, did you think about how this might affect them?'

'Did you?' she asked, pointedly.

I didn't have an answer for that.

'You needn't worry about my mother. It's not like she ever gave a shit about me before this happened. That Oscar-worthy display at the press conference? Jesus, Meryl Streep would've been proud. When I saw that online, I almost threw up. The bitch didn't even realise I was missing until it was trending.'

The moonlight caught Esme's cheekbone for a split second, reflecting what, if I didn't know better, looked like a single tear.

'And now what? I mean, what was your plan exactly?' I said. 'To live in this shitty caravan for the rest of your life, with Dave bringing you a veggie baguette every morning? Or do you waltz back into town, fully made-up, ready for your *Daily Mail* exclusive?'

'I'll tell you what we're going to do now,' Esme said. 'You are going to turn around, Kirby, go back to town, and forget you ever came up here. We planned to keep this going until the climax of the fayre. We have a big finale worked out. I'm going to run out of the woods, having escaped the clutches of Peter Doyle. You were supposed to be down there to film it all. But thanks to you, all those journalists will be there to see the whole thing. The traction is going to be in-*sane*.'

I shook my head. 'Forget it. I'm not lying for you, Esme.' I took my phone out and pressed the ShowMe icon. 'You want a video? I'll make one right now, and tell everyone what you've done.'

A faint smile crossed Esme's face.

'No you won't,' she said. 'Look behind you. Here come the cavalry.'

FORTY-SIX

I get out of the car and walk towards the woman, my heart pounding. But as I get closer, I can see she's not Esme. Sure, she has the same jet-black bangs, and even that damned baguette bag. But, close up, I can see she's younger, with a rounder face.

It's definitely not Esme.

'Are you crazy?' she says. She's got a Crowhurst lilt in her voice, a world away from Esme's clipped London accent. 'There's a cliff edge right here! I thought you were going to go straight over! I had to run out in front of you to get you to stop.'

'Uh, yeah, shit.' I peer over the edge into the pitch blackness below. 'It's so dark, I guess I didn't see it. Um, thanks, I guess.'

'You here for the anniversary too?' she asks.

'Excuse me?' I say.

She takes a step closer to me and squints at my face.

'Oh sorry, I thought you were a ShowMeSherlock. But I can see you're a bit old for that, no offence.'

'A ShowMeSherlock?' I say. 'What do you mean? She's dead. Esme Goodwin is dead.'

'Yeah, no shit. That's why I'm here. Esme was the original, but there's hundreds of us now. We're all ShowMeSherlocks. Call it a tribute, if you like. A lot of Esme's followers were really inspired by her work. She really did some great things. Rest in power, right?'

'You're a fan?' I ask. More than a fan, I'm guessing. With those leggings and her bag, she looks like she's gone totally *Single White Female*.

'The Watsons didn't want her death to mean nothing, you know? So we took up the mantle. We investigate cold cases, track down missing people, that sort of thing. Just like she did.'

'Right,' I mumble, trying to take in what she's saying. 'And you're up on Staker Point in the middle of the night because…?'

She shrugs and turns back towards the cliff edge. 'Same reason as you, I'm guessing. This is where she fell, right? One year ago, almost to the day. I was looking for Peter Doyle's old caravan up here, but I couldn't find it. I swear this is the right place.'

'But why?' I ask.

'I'm looking into the most intriguing case of all: what really happened on the night Esme Goodwin died.'

'Oh shit,' I say under my breath.

This was the last thing I needed. Hell, this was the last thing the world needed. A bunch of teenage wannabe detectives with plastic spades, clumsily trying to dig up the past like it was damp sand. A past that should stay buried.

'What did you say?' She leans in closer, and then steps back in surprise. 'Oh my God. You're Kirby Cornell, aren't you? You're the one who found Esme? You barged into my uncle's flat. And we met at the fayre. You probably don't remember, do you? It was the night Esme died.'

I think back to that horrible night. A lot of the fayre is a blur now, but I could swear the Watson I met there was blonde.

'Really? You're Frank's niece?' I ask. I peer at her more closely. I know it's been a year, but she looks totally different. 'But your hair, your clothes. You look just like…'

'Her?' she smiles. 'Thanks. So, are you making an anniversary tribute video too?'

'No,' I say. 'I don't really do that anymore.'

'Yeah, we noticed you'd disappeared. How come?'

'Uh, well, I, um, retired,' I mutter.

'Shame, a Kirby Cornell comeback would be lit AF. Hey, we could do a collab! Uncle Frank is away for the summer, and he said I could film in Esme's old room before they knock the whole building down. Apparently he's got the original Jack Daw costume from 1996 down in the basement. We could go try it on. Imagine how many views we'd get for that!'

She waves a bunch of keys at me.

'What do you mean, knock Stewart Heights down?' I say. 'I thought they had new tenants in there?'

'Nah, Uncle Frank says he's cleared the whole place out. Apparently the housing market has gone to shit, so he's selling it off.'

'Oh, right,' I say, the gears in my brain starting to turn as I absorb this information. 'I'll give it a miss, thanks.'

'Suit yourself.' She slips the keys back in the bag around her shoulder.

Part of me never wants to see that flat again, but it's hard not to feel a twinge of nostalgia for the place where I had so many happy times. My mind flashes back to some of those drunken nights, pissing ourselves at Dave's terrible jokes, watching endless YouTube playlists of old Beyoncé videos and trying to convince Dylan to cook for us at one in the morning.

I snap out of my thoughts to see the girl has her phone pointed right at my face.

'Are you filming me?' I cover my face with my hand.

'*This is wild*,' she says, but I can tell she's not talking to me, she's talking into her phone. '*I'm here with* the *Kirby Cornell! She's really here, Sherlocks, in the very spot where Esme died one year ago! Major exclusive!*'

'Hold up a second,' I march up to her and push her arm down. 'Can you stop recording, please?'

'Hey, back off,' she says, her expression suddenly flipping from genial to downright vicious. 'Don't touch me. I can film where I like, it's a free country.'

If only she knew the truth, that half a mile away from here, someone was dressed as a crow, butchering my friends one by one. Now that would make one hell of an anniversary video.

'I'll give you something to film in a minute,' I snap.

'Would you mind saying that again, on camera this time, please?' she asks, in a weirdly polite tone.

'Uh, no,' I say, turning away. 'I won't.'

She points the phone at me again anyway. 'What do you think about the theory going around that you did it?'

I stop dead in my tracks. 'Did what? What the hell are you talking about?'

An almost undetectable smile crosses the girl's face. 'Some people think you murdered Esme, right here, a year ago.

There's *loads* of videos about it. Did you see the one with Esme's mum?'

Her words run through me like an electric eel in an ice bath. Charlotte Goodwin. My nightmares were haunted by Esme's mum almost as much as they were by Esme herself. I never had the guts to contact her after what happened. I was always terrified she'd take one look at me and see the truth.

'Here, I'll show you,' the girl says, and before I can stop her, she's searching for a video on her phone. She sticks it in front of my face and the screen fills with Charlotte Goodwin's beautiful, angular features. She's being interviewed by an off-screen presenter, but there's a familiar Surreywide.com watermark on the video.

'Clare Cornell?' Charlotte says. She gazes off into the middle distance. The look in her eyes reminds me of those soldiers in the movies, haunted by awful PTSD from witnessing their whole squad die horrifically. It's the same look I catch in the mirror sometimes. 'You're asking me about the woman who found my daughter and put it all over the internet? Well, I hope her and her friends had fun playing detective. That was the hardest part of all this, seeing that video shared across the whole world.'

There's a bitterness in her voice that makes my skin feel raw, like someone's scraped a blunt razor over my knuckles. But when she stops and looks directly at the camera, it's like she's staring directly into my soul. 'Are you watching this somewhere, Clare? I wonder, did you ever stop to think about how that felt for me?'

A lump the size of a grapefruit forms in my throat.

'I am so, so sorry,' I say to the screen. I know she can't hear me, and I know she probably never will. But I say it anyway. 'I never should have made any of those videos.'

I look up at Frank's niece, hot tears pricking my eyes.

'Oh, that's *perfect*,' she coos. 'Don't move. Let me get this reaction on camera. The lighting is great here, with the moon behind us.'

She points her phone at me again, and I feel a heat rising up my chest and into my mouth. I've had enough of this.

'Listen to me. Esme was a real person who died. She's not a character from a reality show. And neither am I. No one wants to see ShowMe videos of me. Or any of this crap, for that matter. Why don't you go and find something worthwhile to do?'

She laughs. A mean, incredulous snort that only serves to make me angrier.

'Remind me,' she says, her voice all sweetness and light. 'Am I talking to the same Kirby Cornell that barged into my lounge, demanding answers? The Kirby Cornell who recorded police officers without their permission?'

I can feel my temper rising. She's standing so, so close to the edge of the cliff. All it would take would be a tiny, little push...

No.

She's just trying to get a reaction, trying to make me do something stupid on camera. Something I'd regret.

'So come on, tell me.' The girl walks up to me and holds her camera right in front of my face. 'Did you do it? Did you kill Esme Goodwin? My followers *reaaally* want to know.'

I take a deep breath.

'Tell you what, you want a confession?' I say, brushing my

hair behind my ears. 'Go ahead, start recording. I'll give you your exclusive.'

I lean towards her, close enough that we're almost touching, her silly baguette bag pressing up against me. It takes everything I have to keep my voice calm.

I clear my throat, and look directly into her camera. Then I say it, as clearly as I can.

'I'm guilty as hell.'

FORTY-SEVEN

TWELVE MONTHS AGO

'Kirby!' I heard a shout from behind me.

To my relief, I turned to see Seema and Dylan, making their way up the hill.

'We got your pin,' Dylan panted, reaching the clearing. 'What the hell is going on?'

I look at his face in the moonlight, trying desperately to read his expression.

'Did you know?' I cried, ignoring his question.

'Did I know what? What are you talking about?'

'Just tell me, did you know?' I asked again.

The wind whipped around my legs, blowing a few fallen leaves over the edge of the cliff and into the night sky.

'Kirby, we just got here, I have no idea what you're talking about.'

'Esme's here,' I yelled, pointing behind me. 'She was never missing. Her and Dave, they made the whole thing up.' I looked to Seema. 'You really didn't know anything about this?'

'Not me, darl, I swear,' she said, wiping the sweat from her brow.

Behind us, Esme and Dave stood together on the cliff edge, silhouetted by the moon.

'Mate, is this true? How could you?' Dylan said. 'After everything I did…'

Dave hung his head. 'I've been following Esme on ShowMe for months. I loved her videos – they always went so much deeper than the mainstream media. We started DMing each other, and she suggested coming to stay with us. But she wanted everything kept on the downlow. She said her mum had cut her off, and she needed somewhere to stay for free. I knew Frank would freak out, so we pretended Max had sub-let her the room. When she told me the real plan, well, I thought it couldn't hurt anyone…'

'It was you who gave her the key to the flat,' Dylan said. 'I ought to level you.'

Dave's expression darkened. 'You guys never listened to me, you always shot down everything I said. Well, Esme was different. She treated me like an adult, not an overgrown man-child.'

'I risked everything to protect you,' Dylan said.

'What do you mean, risked everything?' I asked.

Dylan turned to face me. 'Esme didn't spend the night in my room, she spent it in Dave's,' he explained. 'I saw her coming out of his room that morning. He begged me not to tell anyone. He said he didn't want you and Seema to take the piss. At the time, it didn't seem a big deal. Even after Esme disappeared, I never for one second thought Dave had anything to do with it. I believed him when he told me he just got amazingly lucky that night. But now we know why he really wanted it kept quiet.'

I stood there, slack-jawed, struggling to take this all in. Dylan never slept with Esme.

'But why did you tell the police you were the last one to see her?' I asked.

'The police were going to drag you off, Kirbs, and probably charge you. Dave wasn't stepping up, so I had to do something. I told the police the truth, that I saw Esme leave, but I kept my promise to Dave and didn't tell them he slept with her. I thought that would make him a prime suspect, and I never believed he would be capable of hurting anyone.'

I was floored. Dylan had risked everything to protect his friends – his reputation, all that money he'd sunk into the restaurant. Part of me wanted to hug him, the other part wanted to push Dave off the cliff.

'When you did that, I felt terrible,' Dave said. 'But, I swear, I never wanted to hurt anyone. Esme said it was a victimless crime.'

Dylan's eyes burnt blue in the moonlight. 'Me and you are done, mate,' he said, and the lack of emotion in his voice only made it sound more devastating.

We were interrupted by a polite cough from Esme's direction. 'As moving as this little reunion is,' she said, stepping towards me, 'don't you think you're being a little hypocritical, Kirby? I mean, you did your fair share of lying yourself.'

We stared at each other for a moment, and I felt a fury building inside me. I really was a ducking idiot. But I still had a chance to make this right.

'I didn't want to lie to anyone! You set me up,' I said, holding up my phone. 'I'll tell the whole world the truth. All your little Watsons will know you're nothing but a fraud.'

Esme's face stiffened. 'Think about it. If you do that, what good will it do? You'll just look like a gullible idiot who led the whole town on a wild goose chase. Or should I say crow chase? Not cool, Kirby. Not cool.'

'I could not give less of a shit,' I said.

'Well, maybe you'll give a shit about this,' Esme said. 'I did stumble upon one juicy detail during my investigation.'

My blood froze. 'We've had enough of your lies, Esme,' I said, trying to sound tough. But inside I was shaking. I knew exactly where she was going with this. And I couldn't let her do it. It would destroy Dylan and everything he'd worked for. I'd die before I let that happen.

'Peter Doyle had a girlfriend in town,' Esme continued. 'Did you know that? And it turns out she still lives here. So, if you're really going to tell everyone my secret, I guess I'll have to reveal that to my followers instead.'

'So what?' Dylan said. 'Who cares about that?'

'I think you'll care, Dylan,' Esme said, 'when I tell you her name was Betty Barnes.'

FORTY-EIGHT

Dylan stood there, not moving a muscle. But I could tell that inside he was erupting.

'Esme,' I yelled. 'Don't. Don't do this. Please.'

'It's either this or you walk away and forget you ever saw me,' she spat.

I went to say something else but the wind caught in my throat.

'Betty Barnes was pregnant when Peter Doyle died,' Esme went on. 'And that child is living in Crowhurst today. Should be about, what, thirty years old by now?'

I turned to look at Dylan. Even in the dark, I could see the blood draining from his face.

'Shut up,' he said. 'Shut up now.'

'No one knew who the father was, or at least, no one was supposed to know. She was only seventeen. Fell in love with the local bad boy. You can understand that, right, Kirby? Poor Betty didn't know what Peter was capable of though. She had no idea what he was... or who he would become. But she found out. And then she pushed him off, right about here, wasn't it? I mean, I know she told everyone he "jumped", but come on! No one really believes that. So I guess that means both your parents are killers.'

I saw Dylan's face stiffen. 'It's not true. You're a liar, and no one is going to believe this.'

'I think you *know* it's true,' Esme replied. 'You've always known, haven't you?'

Esme held up her phone as a cold wind blew across the cliff. She tapped the screen and started recording. Her expression suddenly transformed, her sardonic tone disappeared.

'*Hey, Watsons! I'm here to tell you the real secret about Peter Doyle. He has a child, living right here in Crowhurst—*'

Dylan turned to me. 'This can't come out, Kirby. If people knew that about my mum, they'd hate her.'

'Esme, stop,' I said firmly. 'Dylan's family doesn't deserve this.'

'Calm down, it's not live,' she said, still pointing the phone at me. 'But it could be.'

I stepped towards her, and she shuffled backwards, dangerously close to the edge of the cliff.

'Delete that video,' I said. 'You don't need to do this. We'll go back to town, tell everyone the truth about the kidnap. There's still time to make this right.'

'Are you kidding? I spent years building up my profile, I'm not about to throw all that away.'

'Fine,' I snapped, making a grab for her phone. 'I'll do it for you.'

She pushed me back, waving the phone in the air.

'Careful, Kirby, remember what happened at the roadworks. You don't want to fall arse backwards off Staker Point.'

I tried to grab the phone again, but this time Esme took hold of my arm and pulled me closer to her.

'I was trying to help you,' she hissed. Her breath was stale, and close up, I could see the bags under her eyes from sleeping in a freezing caravan for two nights.

'Oh yeah, I forgot,' I spat. 'You're all about helping people, aren't you?'

'You wanted a big story, right? Well this is it. The secret son of the Crowhurst Killer. Maybe he'll give you an exclusive interview?'

The ground under my feet started to slip. A couple of small rocks tumbled off the edge, bouncing off the cliff and into the water somewhere far below.

'Let me go,' I cried. 'We're going to fall.'

I could see Dave and Seema standing there, frozen to the spot.

Suddenly, Dylan lunged at Esme.

'Give me that!' he snarled, grabbing at her phone, and Esme released me.

'Like father, like son, hmm?' she said.

Released, I stepped back, away from the edge. Seema threw her arms around me and squeezed tightly. We watched in horror as Dylan and Esme wrestled for the phone.

Esme got a firm hold on it, but as she did, she lost her footing.

'Get off me,' she yelled at Dylan as she shoved him in the chest.

He put his hand up to defend himself, but knocked her backwards. Esme's hands flew up, and her legs came out from underneath her.

'Dylan, no!' I screamed.

I watched in horror as Dylan tried to catch her, but he was too late.

'Oh fuck!' Seema gasped.

Esme's mouth stretched wide open in shock, her glass-green eyes bulging with a mix of fear and confusion, her face pale even under the copious layers of fake tan. As she fell, her phone flew out of her hand. She grasped for it as it flipped in the air, like it was in slow motion.

Her hand connected with the phone, and for a split second, I saw the faintest trace of a smile as her fingers clasped around it.

Then she went over the edge. We heard a scream, which got gradually quieter as she fell.

And then, eventually, there was a horrible, dull thud.

FORTY-NINE

TWELVE MONTHS AGO

Dylan was rooted to the spot, frozen, like time had stopped. Dave had his head in his hands. I rushed to the edge and looked down.

There, just visible on the rocks below, we could see Esme's crumpled body, limbs at terrible angles, her eyes open and a trickle of dark red blood running from her head.

Dylan dropped to his knees. 'What did I do?' he mumbled into the ground.

'She'll be okay, won't she? Please, tell me she's going to be okay,' Dave said, breathlessly. 'We can save her. Seema, they taught you first aid at dental school or wherever you went, didn't they? You can go down there, you can help her, right?'

He took hold of Seema's shoulders and shook her.

'Help her for fuck's sake!'

Seema broke away from his grasp and looked over the edge.

'The issue isn't with her receding gums,' Seema snapped. 'She's dead, Dave. She never should've been up here in the first place.'

There was no route down, and even if there was, there was

no way anyone could have survived that fall. At the bottom of Staker Point, the River Muse crashed its way through to Norbridge and beyond. If you slipped climbing down, it would sweep you away to certain death.

'Fuck fuck fuck fuck,' Dylan repeated to himself, curled up into a ball on the grass.

'I cannot deal with this,' Dave mumbled.

I didn't know if I could deal with this either. But I took a deep breath and tried to gather myself. I pulled Seema and Dave aside.

'Listen to me. It was an accident,' I told them. 'But we need to call 999, now.'

'Kirby's right,' Seema said.

'No, she isn't,' Dave said, quietly but very firmly.

Dylan had stood up now, and all the blood had drained from his face. 'I killed her,' he said softly. 'If you call the police, I'll go to jail.'

Dave went over and put an arm round him, but Dylan's eyes remained fixed on me.

'This isn't going to look like an accident,' Dylan said. 'Especially if anyone finds the video on her phone. She recorded the whole thing. They'll say I'm just like my father.' He paused for a moment, and then, almost inaudibly whispered, 'Maybe I am just like my father.'

His hands went to his mouth, and I could see he was beginning to go into shock. My heart went out to him, it really did. But we had to do the right thing.

'I'm sorry,' I said, reaching for my phone. 'There is no other option here.'

'What are you doing?' Dylan looked up at me, the fear in his eyes momentarily replaced by simmering rage.

'I'm calling the police, obviously. And the ambulance, the fire brigade, whoever else they've got.'

Dave put his hand on mine, very gently at first, but then, when I resisted, more firmly.

'You can't… Kirby, listen to me. Think about what this will do to Mum. First Peter, and now her son. Think about Lily. All the money they invested. They'll lose everything.'

My hands were shaking as I tapped out three nines on my phone.

Seema and Dave looked at each other.

'Kirby, just wait a second, will you?' Dave said. 'I mean, what exactly are you going to say?'

I couldn't believe what I was hearing.

'Seriously? You're worried about getting into trouble now, Dave? You should've thought of that before you started this whole mess. Esme's dead. I'm going to tell them the truth.'

Dylan's face was whiter than the moon. 'The truth? They'll never believe that,' he said. 'You don't understand. It'll look like I'm the one who kidnapped her, kept her here, and then I killed her. I did kill her… I, oh God.' He crumpled, a broken man.

'Esme might still be alive down there. We have to help her,' I said. 'We can't just walk away.'

Seema looked over the edge and shook her head. 'I'm telling you, there's no way she survived that,' she said.

I ran a hand over my face and lowered my phone. 'There are people looking for her. Her mother, the Watsons… there's no scenario where we get away with covering this up. We have to tell the police.'

'We will,' Dave placed a hand on each of my shoulders. I'd

never seen him act so seriously. 'I promise you, we will tell them, Kirby. But we need to get our story straight first.'

'What do you mean, get our story straight? There's only one story here.'

Dave paced up and down for a second, thinking out loud. 'Okay… so what if Esme came up here to make a video about Peter Doyle? It makes sense that she'd be looking for clues at the old caravan. She could easily have slipped while making a ShowMe. That could happen, right? Then, Kirby, you came up here looking for her. You discover the body. You solve the mystery.'

'Why would anyone believe that?'

'Everyone has believed you so far,' Dave said. 'All those thousands of followers, hanging on your every word. You're the one controlling the narrative of this whole thing. You can make a video, showing everyone where you found Esme.'

'I'm not going along with this,' I said. 'I'm going to tell the truth.'

'Think about what would happen if you did that,' Dave said. 'They'll say you were helping Esme fake the whole thing. We'll all go to jail.'

My blood goes cold. 'But, that's not—'

'That's what it will look like,' Dave said. 'The whole town will blame you. They'll say you and Esme concocted this together and dragged us all into it. There's a bunch of journalists from all over the country down there right now, ready to feast on this. Our lives will be ruined. Dylan's life will be ruined. He took the blame for me back at the roadworks. I betrayed him then, I won't do it again.'

I could feel myself start to shake again. I thought about my dad seeing this on TV. His only daughter, a liar and a fraud.

'He's right,' Seema put a hand on my shoulder. 'It's going to look pretty bad for all of us. Especially you. Look, Kirby, we can't help Esme now. We'll take Dylan back down, make sure no one sees us. Give us five minutes, then call 999, tell them you've found Esme's body.'

'We'll vote on it,' Dylan said. It was the first time he'd spoken for a couple of minutes, and his voice was cold and serious now.

Dylan had risked everything for me. He'd stepped up when I was in trouble with the police. He was the one who'd tried to get me to stop all this ShowMe nonsense. Didn't I owe him this?

'And if we do it, we have to swear on it,' Dave said. 'Swear we'll never tell anybody.'

He looked over to Dylan, who nodded. Seema followed suit.

They held out their fists, and slowly, one by one, raised their thumbs. First Dylan, then Dave, then Seema.

It was me who'd fallen for Esme's lies, me who'd sent the whole town into a frenzy. This was all my fault. So, with a heavy heart, I stuck out my hand and lifted my thumb too.

I stood there, dumbfounded as Dave and Seema led Dylan down the hill and into the woods.

After waiting a few minutes, I dialled 999. It felt like an out-of-body experience, like someone else was controlling my movements. I told the operator that I'd found a body off Staker Point and hung up.

I tapped out a message on the group chat, the final one I ever planned to send. As far as I was concerned, the Deadbeats were over.

> Kirby
>
> Dylan, you need to know. Your mum never believed Peter Doyle killed those people. She said he was innocent. And Esme was wrong, Betty didn't push him. But she never saw him jump either, she told him to run away and never come back. But he didn't want to leave you.

Then I opened ShowMe, turned the camera on myself, and started filming.

'*Hey…*' my voice cracked immediately. '*I'm at, uh, I'm at the top of Staker Point. And… and I've just called the police. They'll be here any second. I hope. But… I'm so, so sorry to report that I've found a body, and I think it's Esme's.*'

FIFTY

I leave Frank's niece standing at Staker Point, staring at me like I just slapped her, and get back in Foxy.

I meet my reflection in the rear-view mirror for a second, wipe away my smudged eyeliner, and then look down at my hand.

Slowly, I uncurl my fingers to reveal a bunch of keys.

She shouldn't have let me get so close.

If her uncle had been keeping the old Jack Daw costume in his basement, then I had to wonder what else he had down there. Dylan was still in the group chat, which meant he was still alive. And if Frank was the one doing this, then maybe he had Dylan back at Stewart Heights.

I drive to Courtney Road with my headlights off the whole way. When I arrive, I check Surreywide.com again.

FORMER CROWHURST RESIDENT NAMED AS SUSPECT AFTER BODY FOUND

Clare Cornell-Dangerfield, the journalist who discovered the body of social-media influencer Esme Goodwin last year, after her tragic fall from Staker Point, has been named as the person seen in CCTV footage outside Crowhurst dental surgery today.

Friends dead, tick. Accused of multiple homicide, tick. On the run, tick. Well, congrats, Clare. I didn't think you could top last year's knock-out success, but you've smashed it.

It's only a matter of time before Morris catches up with me. Maybe if I can reach him first, I can convince him I'm no killer and buy myself some time to find Dylan. Luckily, thanks to all those angry voicemails from last summer, I have his number.

'Superintendent? It's me, Clare Cornell,' I say when he picks up. 'Just listen to me. I didn't hurt anyone.'

'Just tell me exactly where you are,' he says, surprisingly calm. 'And we can have a nice, friendly chat about it at the police station.'

I know what that means. I can't risk wasting any more time, especially being interrogated by a smug Superintendent Morris. Not while there is a killer on the loose. And not while Dylan is still alive somewhere. At least, I hope he is.

'You have to trust me,' I say. 'Someone is targeting me and my old flatmates. They have the Jack Daw costume.'

Morris can barely contain his incredulity.

'Trust you?' he blusters, losing his cool. 'After that bloody stunt you pulled at the press conference? Why should I believe a word you say? You made a mockery of me and the entire force, not to mention your profession. Now tell me where you are, Ms Cornell, and I promise you we'll get to the bottom of this.'

I grip my phone with frustration, but try to not to lose my

temper. I need to get him onside. But he was right, I'd blown what little credibility I had.

'I shouldn't have recorded you,' I admit. 'But to be fair to me, I was right, wasn't I? That body wasn't Peter. He never jumped.'

'Didn't he?' Morris says. 'Maybe you need to actually check your facts for once, like every good journalist should.'

What was that supposed to mean? I glance at my Fitbit. We've been talking for almost a minute already. In the movies, the hero always knows exactly how long it takes the police to trace a call. I have no fricking idea. But I figure it must be getting close. I hang up and quickly google 'Peter Doyle' and 'body'. Predictably, a Surreywide.com story is the first hit. It's from just a few months ago.

PETER DOYLE'S BODY OFFICIALLY IDENTIFIED AFTER OVER THIRTY YEARS

A member of the public has come forward with new evidence that finally put to rest a conspiracy theory that had been growing online since last year. Thanks to the DNA of a previously unknown relative, who has asked to remain anonymous, remains from the body found in the River Muse in 1996 have now been officially identified as local resident Peter Doyle. Surrey Police have now closed the case known as 'The Crowhurst Killer'. Superintendent Robert Morris said: 'This proves what we always knew to be true, but it's reassuring for the people of Crowhurst to finally be able to extinguish the ridiculous rumours and speculation from last summer.'

Peter Doyle only had a single living blood relative. And that was the one and only Dylan Barnes.

FIFTY-ONE

The lights are off in Frank's flat when I get to Stewart Heights, so I let myself in.

Even as I creep through the gloomy hallway, I can't stop thinking about that Surreywide article. Dylan had risked everything to keep his father's identity a secret, so why would he willingly go to the police for a DNA test? Even if his name wasn't released to the public, Morris would have to know he was Peter Doyle's son. And if there's one thing I'm certain of, it's that Superintendent Morris cannot be trusted.

In the kitchen, I go straight to the small, wooden door in the corner, the one that Frank was so keen I didn't open last summer. Now I think I know why. I find the key on the bunch that fits, and open the door to see a small staircase going down into almost pitch darkness.

Some might say that it's even more stupid to go into a dark basement than to run into a hay maze, but if Dylan is down there, I don't have a choice. I feel around for a light switch, and grab hold of a pull cord on the inside of the door. When I yank on it, a grubby little lightbulb in the middle of the basement briefly flickers to life, and then makes a little 'pop' sound before fading to darkness.

Guess it's my phone torch then. I pull out my phone, take a gulp and venture down the stairs. As my eyes adjust, I can see the basement is full of dusty cardboard boxes, overspilling with junk. There's a big cupboard marked 'fayre prizes' and a pile of plastic chairs stacked against the wall. But there's no sign of Dylan.

There's a worktop at the back, with bits of machine parts and tools.

I run my finger across it, and notice there's no layer of dust, like the one that lightly covers the boxes. I pick up one of the old saws, and, although it's hard to see in the dim light of my phone, it looks like there's something wet on the blade. I dab my finger on it and hold it close to my torch.

It's red.

I drop the saw and step backwards. That's when I notice something squidgy under my foot, and I shine my phone torch down to see a big, dead rat.

Gross.

On closer inspection, it appears to be *half* a dead rat. I don't know whether it's been chewed to bits by some larger, scarier animal, or someone's sawn it in half. But, to be perfectly honest with you, right now I do not want to know.

I suddenly have the terrible feeling that I am not alone down here.

There's a long, protracted creaking from behind me. I swing my torch around the room, and in the darkness of the corner, I see something that almost makes me drop my phone. It looks like a figure, standing rigidly still, watching my every move. I want to scream but my entire body is paralysed. It takes an enormous effort just to raise my arm and shine the light into the corner.

And that's when I find myself face to face with Peter Doyle.

FIFTY-TWO

Okay, so, I really didn't expect Peter Doyle to have chewing gum stuck all over his face.

To say the waxwork has seen better days is an understatement. I gingerly stick out a finger and poke his nose, partly to reassure myself that he is actually made of wax, and not just standing very, very, still.

When he doesn't move, I feel a bit braver. I get right up in his grill and look him straight in his glassy eyes.

'What are you doing down here?' I ask him.

Dave and Dylan weren't kidding when they said he looked like a very hungover Michael McIntyre. Although, the more I look at him, the more I'm seeing Jason Statham in a wig. He's thickset, with piercing blue eyes, and whoever made him has painted a light shading of stubble sloppily across his chin.

I notice there are some more cardboard boxes stacked behind him, so I shift Peter to one side and take a look. I guess Frank put this stuff into storage once all the attention from the murders died down.

Sat on the floor, and using my torch, I rifle through the

contents. It's all the bits and pieces from the old Peter Doyle exhibit, including a stack of *Gazette* articles.

One of them immediately catches my eye. The headline reads: 'Crawe Fayre welcomes *Necktie* star', and underneath there's a photo of a dashing-looking man with a shock of red hair. Morris had been telling the truth, Dad really did visit Crowhurst. The date on the paper is August 2018.

Jason Dangerfield, star of ITV's classic drama *Necktie* was a surprise VIP guest at the Crawe Fayre yesterday, taking on an entirely new role: chief judge for the giant marrow competition! But the actor, who runs his own production company, wasn't just in town to enjoy the festivities. He's researching a possible big budget series based on the events of the 1996 fayre. Asked whether he would be playing the psychopathic murderer Peter Doyle himself, Dangerfield replied: 'You'll have to wait and see! He's certainly a character that fascinates me. What drives a man to do that? As an actor, finding that dark place deep within us is the challenge. But what's really important to me is that we tell this horrific story accurately, and with respect to the families of the victims.' As for reprising his most famous role, the star simply said: 'Over my dead body.'

Jesus. Thank *God* that series never happened. But I can't believe Dad was in Crowhurst. Out of all the crappy places in the whole wide world, we'd both ended up here. Was that too much of a coincidence? I had to wonder if this Peter Doyle show was the project that got cancelled after my NewsBites article went viral.

Also in the box, is a framed copy of *The Gazette* from

1996, the same front page that Esme had in her bag, with the headline 'Exclusive! Witness saw Peter Doyle jump'. It feels so weird to see it again. I unclip the frame, take it out and stick it in my pocket. But when I go to close the box, I notice a Post-it note stuck on the lid. It looks like it lists all the items from the exhibit.

Waxwork of the murderer Peter Doyle, holding the murder weapon in his right hand
The original Thorny Crow costume from 1996
Original photographs showing the Crawe Fayre in 1996.
Peter Doyle can be seen as Jack Daw, the Thorny Crow
Front pages from The Crowhurst Gazette *after the bodies were discovered*

I quickly rummage through the rest of the stuff in the box and realise something horrible.

The crow costume is missing. And so is the ceremonial trowel.

Suddenly, my thoughts are broken by a noise from upstairs that sounds like the front door closing. I stand completely still, looking up at the basement door for any movement. I swear I can hear footsteps above me. Shit. I left the front door unlocked. Did Frank's niece follow me back here?

I peer upwards, and see a shadow pass the door. I duck behind a stack of junk and press myself against it, my hands shaking. I take a second to compose myself, then lean out from behind the boxes. It looks like the coast is clear. But do I make a run for it now, or just wait it out in the dark?

I sense my chance, and, as lightly as I can, I dash towards

the stairs. I'm about to reach for the first step, when I hear a footstep above me. Any moment now, whoever it is, is about to come down.

Quickly, I run back and head for the cupboard in the corner. I jump inside and shut the doors behind me. I push the door open, just a millimetre, and look out. It's a tiny gap, but if I squint, I can see through.

I stand there in the dark for a moment and listen for footsteps on the stairs. I hear them getting louder and louder as whoever it is comes down the hallway. I try to press my body as far back into the cupboard as possible. But as I squeeze further in, something soft brushes my leg.

Oh shit.

Please, please, please, do not tell me that is the rest of that fricking rat.

With huge trepidation, I bend down slowly – not taking my eyes off the gap in the door – and with one hand, reach down to feel what it is. I breathe a sigh of relief when my hand hits synthetic fluff. It's not a dead animal. But when I pick it up and look at it closely, my jaw drops. As my eyes become accustomed to the darkness, I can see what it is.

A cuddly Pikachu. What the hell is that doing in here?

Suddenly there's a noise, and my attention goes back to the gap in the door. I look out to see a dark, hulking figure enter the room, and I freeze with fear. I daren't switch on my phone torch, but I peer out as best I can. I watch as the figure moves methodically through the room, looking under the worktop and behind the boxes. He must know someone is here. It's only a matter of time before he reaches the cupboard, and me.

My heart is thumping so loudly, I swear he's gonna hear it.

I push myself back and realise there's not just one Pikachu, but about a hundred of the bloody things. This must be the storage cupboard for the cheap-ass claw-machine prizes.

Well, I'll say one thing. This is not how I thought I would meet my end. Troweled to death in a cupboard full of fluffy Pokémon.

I almost fall into them and have to stick out a hand to steady myself. But when I do, I knock the cupboard door, and the hinge lets out a long, horrible squeak. I freeze. The figure looks up, surprised, and spins around. Then he swivels to face the cupboard.

He's looking straight at me, and I can now see he's wearing the crow costume.

He starts to walk towards me until he's just metres from the cupboard. I stand as still as I can, trying not to make even the slightest noise.

He takes a step closer. Any second now he's going to open the doors and see me, clutching my phone and a stuffed cuddly toy. And I'm dead.

It's now or never.

I wait until he's as close as possible, take a deep breath and kick the cupboard door open with all my strength. The door hits him, and he leaps back in surprise as a hundred Pikachus pour out. I don't give him time to say anything, I just run for it. He makes a grab for me as I try to dart across the room, but I duck and swerve to the left. As I do, my ankle turns under my foot and I fall, hard. I scrabble to my feet, but it's too late. He's on me.

That ghastly, cheap-looking cardboard beak is bearing down on me. He lifts the trowel up, ready to bring it down into my neck.

I lift my arms in front of my face in a vain effort to stop him. But this is it, there's no escape. He's going to murder me. I'm going to be stabbed to death with a trowel by a Peter Doyle-wannabe in a crappy bird costume. And there's nothing I can do about it. I look around for anything I can grab, anything I can use to hold him off. Anything that isn't filled with fricking fluff and sawdust.

But there's nothing.

This is it.

As his beak bears down on me, the tip scratches against my face, and I turn away. That's when I remember what Dave told me about the mask. The only place he could see out of was the beak…

I grab the nearest Pikachu, and with my other hand take hold of the top of the beak and pull it open. Then, with all my strength, I shove the toy down his beak and ram my knee between his legs.

Then I run, as fast as I can, the hell out of there.

FIFTY-THREE

I run out into the lobby, but when I get to the front door of the building, it's dead-locked. Panicking, I scramble through my pockets for the keys. But they're not there.

Shit, I must have dropped them when the crow caught me.

There's nowhere else to go but the stairs. When I get up to the fourth floor, my heart skips a beat: the door to our old flat is ajar. I push it open, and flick the light switch by the coat hooks, as I had done a thousand times before, but the hallway fails to illuminate.

I slam the door behind me, and it locks. I lean against it, catching my breath for a second before I look around. There's a dank, musty smell, but to be fair, there always was. Even though the place has been almost completely cleaned out, I feel like I've jumped back in time. The lounge is bare, but if I squint, I can still see the Deadbeats there, squeezed on the sofa, arguing over the remote.

When I poke my head into the kitchen, I notice something sticking out from under the (now unplugged and, sadly, empty) fridge. I bend down to pick it up, and I can't help but let a smile cross my lips for a second. It's the Polaroid photo of the Deadbeats. It must have fallen under here when Frank took off all our fridge magnets. I brush the dust off it with my hand and see something that sends an ice-cold pang of fear running through me.

Everyone in the photo has a hole through their faces, like someone has forced a biro through their heads. Max, Seema, Dave, me and...

Wait, not all of them. All except one.

Dylan.

I start shaking again. Someone is picking us off, one by one. But why is Dylan the only one not punctured?

Does that mean he is still alive? Or does that mean...

Before I have time to finish my thought, there's a knock on the door. And then, the metallic clunk of a key sliding into the lock. The sound as it turns is almost guttural.

Everything seems to go in slow motion. I need to move, *now*.

I barge into the box room, looking desperately for something I can use as a weapon. The rest of the flat is bare, but there are piles of boxes in here. Frank must be storing anything of value from the flats here while he clears out the building. Sitting on top of them is something I never thought I'd be so glad to see again – Dave's old bong. God knows why Frank wanted to keep this, I mean, it is probably an antique but I can't see it fetching much on eBay. But it reminds me how, when Dave got stressed out, he climbed up on the roof. And, well, I sure as hell was stressed now.

I shut the bedroom door behind me and push the boxes up against it. The exercise bike is still here too, so I shove that behind the door, and then slide the small window at the back of the room open. Hitching myself up onto the window sill, I reach up and try to grab the gutter above me, but I can't quite get to it.

On tiptoes, I stretch my fingers out, and they just brush the plastic of the gutter. I glance over my shoulder and see the ground below.

A long way below.

There's nothing else for it. I steady myself against the rough brick of the wall and jump upwards. I grab onto the gutter and it creaks, like it's going to snap any second. Quickly, I heave myself up onto the flat roof of the building. I lie there for a second, just panting. Then I lift my heel and kick the gutter, over and over until it falls to the ground. That should stop anyone else climbing up here if they do break through my barricade.

There's no way up. Or down.

So, now what?

The police won't help me, there's a murderous crow below trying to slit my throat, and I'm stuck on a roof in the middle of nowhere. If Dylan is alive, then Jack Daw is coming for him, and here I am, stranded and powerless to save him.

Jammed behind the metal ventilation pipe, is the inflatable mattress that Dave used to bring up here. I pull it out, it's half deflated, but it's still more comfy than the asphalt. I sit on it and look out over the town.

Down below, I catch sight of headlights shining through the darkness. A car leaves the parking bay and drives off down Courtney Road. Whoever was in that costume, it looks like they've left. For the moment, I'm safe.

As the adrenaline subsides from my body, and my heart rate finally begins to slow, I feel my eyelids grow heavy, like I've been unplugged. Every part of me wants to lie here and let sleep just wash over me. But I can't. I need to stay awake and figure out who was in that Jack Daw costume, how they got hold of Esme's phone and why they would want to hurt a bunch of deadbeats like us.

The police could have found the phone with Esme's body, I guess, which would mean that Morris and Pascal have it. But after they concluded it was death by misadventure, then all Esme's personal effects would have been returned to her family.

Her mum.

Sat on the half-inflated mattress, I search ShowMe for 'Charlotte Goodwin'. Hundreds of users have shared the interview that Frank's niece showed me.

I replay it over and over, like a penance, wondering how Charlotte must be feeling today, the anniversary of her daughter's death. Before I know it, tears are streaming down my face.

I remember the way Esme talked about her mum, her barely concealed resentment, and how she died without ever having the chance to reconcile with her. What would Charlotte have given to talk to her daughter one last time?

If I'm going to die up here, on this stupid roof, the least I can do is say goodbye to my mum.

I haven't spoken to her for months. Only the odd text and email, or a short phone call, where I'd pretend to be getting on the tube to avoid any meaningful conversation. To be honest, it had been like that ever since I'd left for theatre college. As a kid, I'd always resented her for not letting me live with Dad. Of course, when I grew up, I knew she'd absolutely done the right thing. But deep down, I could never really shift that feeling that I'd been denied a different life. A better life.

Scrolling through my contacts, I find 'Mum' and my finger hovers over the dial button for a second. I know once I press call, I'll have to go through with it. I don't know what the hell I'm going to say, but it doesn't really matter. I just need to hear her voice.

'Clare?' She picks up after the second ring, her voice bright, cheery almost. Like she's been sat by the phone, waiting to speak to me, even though our conversations never really extend beyond the mundane.

'Hi, Mum,' I say, my own voice hoarse from crying.

'I haven't heard from you for so long,' she says. 'Everything okay? Are you back from hols? Where are you? It sounds windy there!'

'Uh, yeah, I'm back,' I say, squinting at the Crowhurst skyline. The tears blur with the blinking lights of town in the distance, making kaleidoscopes in my eyes. Although I'm sure it's the prettiest it's ever looked, I've never hated the town more than I do at this moment.

'I don't know why anyone would take a holiday from London, mind you,' she goes on. 'There must be a million things to do there—'

'Mum, I have to tell you something,' I interrupt.

'What is it?' she asks immediately, her tone nose diving from chipper to anxious in an instant.

'I'm not in London,' I say.

'What do you mean, love? Did your flight get cancelled or something?'

'No,' I say. 'I haven't been in London for years.'

There's a pause.

'What are you talking about?'

'I got fired from my job at NewsBites, Mum. Remember

that story that I wrote about me and Dad? Well, it, um went a little bit viral.'

'Oh. Well, that's supposed to be good, isn't it?'

'Not really. The comments were horrible. They said I only got the job because of Dad in the first place. And the worst thing is, I think they were right, Mum. I'm terrible at this. That's why I had to come here, to Crowhurst. It's the only place I could find a job.'

'Crow what? Where on earth is that?'

'It's this crappy little town in the middle of nowhere,' I say. 'I got a job on the local paper here. It was the only place that would hire me.'

'Why didn't you just tell me?'

I can feel the tears coming again. 'I was ashamed,' I say. 'I thought everyone would think I was a failure.'

I can hear her exhale through the phone. 'Oh, Clare. Is that what you were worried about? I could never be ashamed of you. No matter what you do, I'll always love you. I loved you when you were born, I love you now, I'll love you until I die.'

'Thanks, Mum,' I sniffle. 'I know I never say it, but I love you too.'

'I know you do, Clare. And you can always tell me the truth,' she says. 'You know that, don't you? You can tell me anything. I'm your mother, for goodness' sake. I would never judge you. Why don't you come home, love? Whatever's happened, we can sort it out.'

'I will,' I say. 'I'm going to come home. There are just a few things I need to do here first.'

'Clare, are you okay?' She doesn't try to hide the concern in her voice.

Now it's my turn to pause.

'I'm in a bit of trouble,' I say eventually. 'I've messed everything up, Mum. I don't know what I'm doing. To be honest with you, I don't think I've ever known what I'm doing. And I feel like I'm running out of time to make things right.'

I'm full-on crying now.

'What's happened? You can tell me.'

'I wouldn't even know where to start,' I tell her. 'I'm trying to fix it, but I don't know if I can. I'm stuck.'

'Listen to me, Clare. Are you listening? I need to remind you of something.'

I nod, still sobbing.

'Are you nodding over the phone again?' she asks.

'Oh, sorry, yes,' I say.

'Remember, you're braver, stronger and smarter than you think you are.'

I wipe the tears from my eyes and start laughing.

'Mum, please don't tell me you're quoting *Necktie* at me?'

'No, you silly goose. It's from that Winnie the Pooh movie you were obsessed with. You and I watched it together over and over when you were little, and I used to repeat that phrase back to you at bedtime as you were falling asleep. That's where your dad nicked the idea for his silly catchphrase. Managed to completely lose all its meaning though, didn't he? It's not about getting stronger, it's about realising how strong you already are.'

All my life, people had been telling me that I wasn't good enough – be braver, be stronger, be smarter.

'I'd forgotten,' I say.

'Well, something must have sunk in, because look at the things you've done. When we didn't get the grant for you to go to college, you saved up all the money yourself. Then you went off to London to be a journalist, not knowing a soul. And now, you've gone to this Crow place and carried all this on your shoulders. You've always been resourceful, Clare, deep down. You just needed a little push.'

'Thanks, Mum,' I say. 'I think I know what I have to do now.'

'Just promise me, once you're done, you'll come home, you hear me? I love you.'

'I love you,' I say back, and hang up.

I look down at the inflatable mattress, and give my bum a little wiggle. Okay, it's a bit saggy, but with a few strong puffs, I reckon I can get this old thing bouncy enough. Because Mum is right, I can be resourceful when I need to be. But this time I don't need anyone to give me a push.

Because I'm going to jump.

FIFTY-FOUR

Holding the mattress high above my head, I step as close to the edge of the roof as I dare, then lob it into the air. It lands directly below me in the shrubbery by the parking bay. At least if I miss it, I'll land in the bed of weeds and probably only break both of my legs, rather than my spine.

What was it that Mum said? You're braver than you believe? Well, it's time to put that to the test.

I kneel down, grab onto the edge and hang off, legs dangling. I close my eyes so I'm not tempted to look down, and count to five before letting go.

The fall is over in seconds, and I land with a soft thud on the mattress, which squeaks loudly when all ten stone of me crashes down on it. But I survive, spine fully intact. I yelp in pain as soon as I stand up though, and when I try to run over to Foxy, my ankle immediately turns over. I have to hop the rest of the way.

Once safely inside, I pull the newspaper page out of my pocket and trace my finger across the front-page photo. This version is clean, and I can see everyone's face clearly.

Peter Doyle, in his horrible cheap crow outfit

Frank, the creepy landlord with a basement full of crow paraphernalia

Bob Morris, the man who tried to cover up Peter's missing body

Betty, the teenage crush of a serial killer

What am I missing?

If I'm really smarter than I think I am, then I should be able to figure this out.

What about the Watsons? Esme had half a million followers. They were all wannabe Sherlocks, maybe one of them analysed all my videos and figured out what really happened to their hero? For all I know, that's what Frank's niece had done.

I put the newspaper on the passenger seat and search for her ShowMe feed. Sure enough, there's my big, silly face, admitting my guilt to the world. The video already has thousands of views and comments. After I stomp off, Frank's niece turns the camera on herself as she treks down from Staker Point. I stare at her face as she waffles on about her big exclusive. If I was a Watson, I'd study her expressions, looking for signs that she was lying, or trying to hide something. As she reaches the Rec, I turn the volume down, and try to focus on her body language. There's something off about the video. But it's not her, it's what's going on *behind* her.

The earth is moving.

But that's impossible...

It's barely noticeable, but I swear the telephone lines behind her are shaking. I can't help but think back to that night in the pub, teasing Seema about shagging Hot Dentist. The earth moved that night too. That only happens when the printing press is running. But that press hasn't been in action since *The Gazette* folded nearly a year ago, right after Esme died.

Thank you, Seema.

I look over at the paper on the seat beside me and think about what Esme said, that someone on this front page knew everything about the Crowhurst Killer. I'd always assumed she meant Betty. But now I wonder… was Esme a better detective than even she realised? Because there's someone else on this front page that I never noticed before. It must have been smudged on Esme's edition.

I almost laugh. I was missing what was right in front of me. Again.

Foxy starts on the second try, and I speed off, checking my rear view as I go. My ankle is pulsating so much, it feels like it's going to burst. Every time I press the clutch, a shooting pain runs through my whole body like there's a bloody great spike on the pedal.

But luckily I don't have to drive far, because I have a pretty good idea where Jack Daw is.

Ten minutes later, I pull into Crowhurst Business Park, and as soon as I get out, I feel the dull thud of vibrations underfoot. I was right. Someone has started the presses.

Delving inside my glove compartment, I'm thrilled to find my work pass (under a pile of KitKat wrappers and an old Foxtons brochure I never got around to throwing out). I hobble inside, and down the flight of stairs to the printing press, the vibrations getting stronger as I approach the door. As it swings open, it lets out a haunting, ominous creak, leaving me face to feathery face with Jack Daw.

Behind him, the cylinders spin, sending reels of paper zooming through them. I've never seen the presses on before, and there's a constant loud hum and clatter as it spits out and chops up copies at the end. Someone is actually printing new issues of *The Gazette*. Jack Daw stands there, just in front of the metal staircase that leads up to the cylinders, seemingly rooted to the spot. When he starts shaking and grunting, I realise something is wrong. Whoever is under those feathers, they can't – or won't – move.

Gingerly, I walk over to Jack Daw, place my hands on either side of the papier mâché head and lift it off.

And there, underneath, is Dylan Barnes.

FIFTY-FIVE

A little thinner in the face, with shorter hair, but it's Dylan, and he's alive. Oh, and one other new addition to his look – he has a large strip of tape over his mouth.

With one big yank, I pull it off and he grimaces in pain.

'What are you doing here?' I ask. 'And why are you dressed like this? What the hell is going on, Dylan?'

'Kirby, move…' he just has the chance to say before he suddenly shoulder barges me. My ankle gives out and I fall to the floor. I look up to see a man rushing towards us holding the sharpened trowel.

It's Trevor.

Before I can open my mouth, Trevor lifts the trowel high and drives it deep into Dylan's stomach. A strangled gasp ejects from his lips as his body goes limp and he falls to the floor.

'No!' I scream.

I scramble backwards on my bum towards the metal staircase as a small trickle of bright red blood slowly makes its way towards my feet. I can feel myself beginning to hyperventilate.

'Trevor,' I say, trying to stop my voice from shaking. 'What the fuck?'

'Sorry?' he says. He walks straight past me, and up the staircase. When he reaches the control panel, he presses the button and the presses gradually whirr to a halt. The vibrations fade and the room falls eerily silent. Only then does he reach to his ears and pull out two yellow foam earplugs.

'That's better,' he says, walking back down and picking up the crow head. 'Now, where were we?'

'You… you killed him,' I cry.

'Of course I did,' Trevor says calmly. 'I saved you, Cornell. He's the Crowhurst Killer.'

'He's not,' I stutter. 'He can't be.'

Trevor looks down at Dylan's bleeding body and tilts his head.

'Excuse me for disagreeing, but from where I'm standing, he looks very much like the Crowhurst Killer, don't you think? I mean, he's dressed as Jack Daw, the Thorny Crow and everything! And I'm fairly sure he killed all your friends, didn't he? Everyone in the group chat?'

'Not quite everybody,' I say.

'Ah yes,' Trevor says. 'There is just one more member of the Deadbeats who is a little bit too alive.'

Trevor turns to look at me, and there's a glint in his eye that makes my skin prickle. I try to stand up, but I can't put any weight on my ankle.

'Going somewhere?' Trevor asks, and a horrible realisation floods through me.

'It was you, wasn't it? You killed them, not Dylan. You killed them all.'

Trevor raises a bushy eyebrow and turns to face me. 'That's

a bit rich, coming from you, isn't it? You're accusing *me* of murder, after everything you and your friends did?'

'We didn't kill anybody,' I say.

'Oh, didn't you?' Trevor says. 'I've seen the video.'

He moves towards me, and I shuffle backwards onto the first step.

'You're the one who's been messaging us from Esme's phone, aren't you?' I say.

'You mean this phone?'

He pulls an iPhone out of the pocket of his jacket and waves it at me, mockingly. I recognise the neon case immediately. It's Esme's.

'Esme was recording when she fell, you know? Poor thing was still clutching onto her phone when they found her at the bottom of Staker Point. The police had to prise it out of her death grip, apparently. She must have really, really liked this thing.'

'Where did you get it?' I stammer.

'It wasn't hard to lift from her mother's house. She let me look through a box of Esme's things during our interview. Even had her old keyring in there.'

Of course. It was Trevor who was interviewing Charlotte Goodwin in the Surreywide video. I'd been so focused on her answers, I'd missed who was asking the questions.

'But why?' I ask. 'Why go to all this trouble to bring the Deadbeats back to Crowhurst? We're just a bunch of nobodies.'

'The small matter of your little group chat,' he says. 'Once I got the phone from Charlotte's mother, I discovered all your inane little chats. But among the guff, there was rather too much incriminating evidence on there, you see. I can't risk the truth about Peter coming out. I've deleted the messages from Esme's phone, of course, but they are on all of your phones too.'

He's right. Esme's text was still on the group chat:

Crowhurst Killer is a lie.

And there was the final message I'd written to Dylan: *Peter Doyle is innocent. He didn't jump. Betty let him go.*

'Pretending to be Esme was the perfect way to lure you all back here,' Trevor goes on. 'But now, if you'll excuse me, I do need to finish the job.'

'Your by-line,' I say, 'it was your by-line, right there on the front page Esme had in her bag. You wrote that story in *The Gazette*. I was looking for someone in the photo. But your name was there, right under it in black and white. *You're* the one who knows everything about the Crowhurst Killer. Peter Doyle never killed anyone, did he? It was you.'

Trevor's nostrils flare. 'Oh, still blabbering on about Peter Doyle, are we? Didn't you see the news? Peter is very, very dead. As dead as your friend Esme, in fact. Funny, isn't it? How they both met their ends in a very similar way.'

He takes another step towards me, holding the trowel in one hand, and using the other to steady himself against the railings. I shuffle backwards as a sick grin spreads across his face. 'You know, I thought I was too old to put that tatty costume back on, but it still fits, even thirty years later.'

'I don't understand, Trevor,' I stutter. 'You were like a mentor to me.'

'That's the problem with getting to this age, Cornell.

Everyone expects you to be a father figure. But in reality, I'm just old. I decided I'm not quite ready to pass the baton over to the next generation yet, though. I still have a few more exclusives in me, don't you think?'

I feel for my phone in my pocket. It's still there, but God knows how much battery per cent I have left.

'Why did you do it, Trevor? All those years ago, why did you kill those kids and frame Peter?'

I shift my bum up another step. Trevor moves slowly towards me, pointing the sharpened trowel towards my throat.

'For Crowhurst of course,' he says, as the light glints off the trowel and into my face. 'We were once the shiniest apple in England's orchard, but by the Nineties, we were a joke. The Crawe Fayre was a joke. Even the Thorny Crow was a joke. *The Gazette* was dying because nothing ever happened in this boring little town. London was full of terrorists. Yorkshire had their own ripper. Lord, even Norbridge had a kiddy fiddler or two. But Crowhurst had nothing. So I came up with an idea to make us a little more notorious.'

'You killed five teenagers to bring in more tourists?' I ask.

'No one was going to miss those stupid kids anyway. They were nobodies too, just like you and your friends. I paid them a fiver each to throw rocks at Peter at the fayre. Then, when he went back to his caravan to get drunk, I put on the costume and climbed up to Staker Point. They thought it was Peter, and one of the little bastards launched a firework at my head. Thank God I had the Jack Daw mask on. The bang really buggered up my hearing though. Never been the same after that.'

'So you framed Peter for the murders? You're a fricking psychopath.'

'Glad to see you've lost none of your linguistic prowess, Cornell,' Trevor says. 'Peter got what he deserved. He was a disgrace to Crowhurst. A filthy immigrant, impregnating our women, selling drugs to our school kids.'

'Was he? Or was that just what you wrote in the paper?'

'Didn't I tell you, Cornell, that a story is only as trustworthy as the person telling it?' Trevor says. 'I planted the costume in Peter's caravan while he was fast asleep, drunk out of his head. It just so happened that's when sweet Betty came a-calling. I hid in the caravan and heard their whole sad little exchange. After Betty left, I had a lovely chat with Peter. He was babbling about Betty and how she wanted him to run away. He said he'd never leave his unborn son. He said he'd fight to prove he was innocent. Well, I'm sorry, but there was no way in heaven I could let him do that. So I took him up to the cliff for another beer, tried my best to calm him down. But he just wouldn't stop talking. So I gave him a little push.'

I think about Dylan. He'd spent a year thinking his dad was the worst piece of shit in the universe. And Betty, poor Betty, who'd done everything she could to try and save the man she loved.

'The following year, the fayre was more popular than ever,' Trevor continues. 'Full of tourists, spending money in our shops. Eating at our cafés. Sales of *The Gazette* went through the roof! I even got promoted for my exclusive story about the witness. It turned out, all Crowhurst needed was a bogeyman. In a strange way, Peter Doyle brought us all together. The only problem was, it didn't last. The fame ran out, as fame often does. By the time you arrived in Crowhurst, we were back to being a joke. The town began to crumble again, and I was forced to sell *The Gazette* to those idiots at Surreywide. No one remembered Peter Doyle. The internet had arrived, and there were a thousand other psychopathic murderers to read about at the touch of a button. Our only chance was the TV series.'

'TV series?'

'I would have thought you'd know all about it. After all, it was your father who was set to be the star. A six-part Netflix series based on the murders, with none other than Jason Dangerfield playing Peter Doyle! I was even helping him with his research. It was just what we needed to propel Crowhurst back into the national consciousness. But your silly little clickbait article put paid to all that, didn't it? And you realise, Cornell, that this is all your fault. Because if you hadn't got your father cancelled, then Esme would still be alive.'

FIFTY-SIX

By now, I'd crawled backwards all the way up the metal staircase and onto the raised platform. Trevor has followed me up. I press myself against the railings, my head next to the giant cylinders. There's nowhere left to go.

'Esme's death was an accident,' I stuttered. 'What the hell has that got to do with my dad?'

'I'd never have been forced to, how do they say it, "collab" with her if you hadn't so carelessly destroyed your father's career.'

Of course. Esme had told me that night on Staker Point that she was working with someone. I'd always thought she meant Dave, but he was just her lapdog. Trevor was her co-conspirator.

'After the TV series fell through, I needed a new plan. So I decided to take the board's advice and "pivot to digital".' Trevor smiles. 'Just not in the way they wanted. I set myself up as a Watson and fed Esme enough titbits about the murders to pique her interest. I'd seen from her videos how inept she was, how she'd follow up dead ends and come up with ridiculous theories without ever coming close to the truth. I gave her the

334

tip-off about Betty and slipped her that newspaper front page from the archives.'

'Wait,' I gasp. 'You were a Watson?'

'Shellfish diet!' he smiles. 'If you can't beat 'em, join 'em, isn't that right? Don't say you didn't notice my excellent grammar.'

Suddenly it all made sense. Whenever I started to give up on Esme, Shellfish-bloody-diet had been the one nudging me back on track. He'd been manipulating me the whole time.

'Once Esme took the bait, I offered her a rather nice sum of money to fake her disappearance,' Trevor goes on. 'She jumped at the chance to be the star of the show, of course. All we needed was a gullible reporter to get the story out to the masses. Sensationalise it for the internet. Turn it into clickbait. And that's where you came in, Cornell. It would've worked a treat, too, except you had to go and find her too soon. You and your friends ruined everything. "Stupid influencer falls off cliff" hardly compares to "Crowhurst Killer returns!" does it? And now look what's happened to our town.'

'What do you mean?' I ask.

'Haven't you seen the high street? Shops closed. Flats knocked down. What did I tell you about local papers? They're the lifeblood of a town. Since *The Gazette* folded, the community died. We need Peter Doyle more than ever. But now, thanks to your friend here, we have one last glorious opportunity to resurrect him.'

Trevor motions behind him with the trowel.

'The son of Peter Doyle! Crowhurst Killer Junior! Isn't that just beautiful? The son of the notorious serial killer takes his horrific revenge on his flatmates, the only witnesses of his murder of Esme Goodwin. The police will find your bodies here, along with him in the Jack Daw costume. And me, the only survivor.'

While Trevor is droning on, I scan the room, looking for any means of escape. But I've hit a dead end. Trevor is blocking my way down, and the giant machinery behind me means I am trapped on the platform.

'You're insane,' I say. 'No one will believe you.'

'No? But, Cornell, haven't you seen the paper? People believe everything they read.'

'What are you talking about?' I ask.

'Tomorrow's paper, I mean.'

He reaches into the back pocket of his corduroys and pulls out a rolled-up, freshly printed, copy of *The Gazette*.

'Hot off the press,' he smiles. 'Still warm.'

He uncurls it to reveal the front page. My jaw drops as I read the headline.

CROWHURST KILLER'S REVENGE

'Isn't it glorious?' Trevor says. 'The first issue for over a year! And a major world exclusive as well. We've even scooped the internet on this one.'

'You've got no proof Dylan did any of this,' I stutter.

'Oh really?' Trevor looks back at Dylan's body at the bottom of the steps. 'He's dressed as Jack Daw, just like his dad. And if that's not enough, wait until I leak the footage on Esme's phone. After that, no one will doubt that Dylan Barnes has followed in his father's footsteps. And the community will come together once more, united by a common enemy. Someone to hate. Someone to blame all their problems on. After this, Crowhurst will be more infamous than ever! The

Crawe Fayre will be our Halloween, and the whole world will know Jack Daw!'

I reach into my pocket for my phone.

'I'll kill you before you can make a call,' Trevor snarls. 'You've nowhere left to run, Cornell.'

He takes another step towards me. This is it. This time there are no Pikachus to save me, no hay bales to jump over. I'm dead.

FIFTY-SEVEN

PRESENT DAY

'Here, you don't have to kill me, just take it.' I hold my phone up to Trevor.

He snatches it and studies it for a second, his thumb scrolling through my group chats.

'There we go, all the evidence deleted,' he says, almost jovially. 'There's just one more thing I should do...' Then he turns the phone to me so I can see the screen. It's the Deadbeats chat.

Kirby Cornell has left the chat.

Tossing the phone behind him, he gives me one of his big sighs, paired with a pitiful look.

'I think you know what that means. I'm sorry, Cornell. It'll be a lot quieter around Crowhurst without you.'

Quieter.

When he says that, something clicks. Trevor is not wearing his earplugs...

If I can make a loud enough noise, maybe I can hurt him. And there's one easy way to make a loud noise: screaming, which is something I happen to have got pretty good at over the last couple of days. But before I can even take another breath, Trevor clamps his greasy palm over my mouth.

'Finally found a way to shut you up,' he hisses as I struggle under his grip.

'Ugggmmmm,' I grunt, trying to whack him around the head, but he holds me at arm's length before I can get a decent blow in. I'm done for. Then, behind him, I see a miracle. Dylan has pulled himself up.

He's alive.

My heart soars for a second, before I see he's badly injured. He's clutching his stomach, moving agonisingly slowly as he makes his way towards us. Blood is still pouring out of him. If Trevor turns around and sees him, it won't take much to finish him off.

But if I can reach the button to start the presses, the noise will be loud enough to distract him, maybe long enough for Dylan to reach us. I stretch out as far as I can, and my fingertips just brush the button. I wave my hand frantically, trying to slap it, but it's just millimetres out of reach.

As I swing my arm again, I notice every time I do, the step count on my Fitbit goes up by one, and my mind momentarily flashes back to laughing at Dave in The Lion, shaking his wrist, showing us how he gets his steps up.

Of course... that's it! Oh, Dave, I've never been so grateful for you being such a wanker.

I've done 9,895 steps today (all that running away from the crow has actually done me a favour) but I need more... and fast.

I start shaking my hand, as hard and vigorously as I can, and Trevor stares at me in utter confusion.

9,910

9,911

9,912

It's going too slowly!

9,963

9,964

9,965

Trevor's expression hardens, like he's finally had enough of my nonsense, and he lifts the trowel high, ready to plunge it into my chest.

'You said you wanted me to shake things up,' I think, curling my fingers and waggling even faster. 'Well this one's for Dave.'

Then, finally, out of nowhere, the watch starts its horrible, excruciatingly loud beeping, and Trevor's face contorts in pain. He releases his grip from my mouth and puts his hands over his ears.

'Dylan, now!' I shout.

Dylan rushes towards us and up the stairs. Still dressed in the black feathers, he's like a lumbering injured bear, using all of its final energy for one last attack. He charges at Trevor, rugby-tackling him around the waist. It all happens in a blur. Trevor comes down hard, the trowel spinning out of his hand.

'He was going to... he was going to...' Dylan stops talking and falls to his knees. The harsh strip lighting behind him casts his shadow towards me, almost touching my toes, and the trowel lies between us, glinting like a talisman.

I turn to look at Trevor's crumpled body for a moment, and then, we hear him gasp and his eyes flick open. He starts to get to his feet, his eyes shooting to the trowel. Before he can move another muscle, I lift my good foot and kick him hard in the chest, sending him flying over the edge of the railing and down onto the printing press.

Guess I really am stronger than I thought.

Quick as a flash I slam my fist down on the button, and the presses grunt into life, sending the rolls of paper thundering through the mills, splashed red with blood.

'New record!' my watch announces proudly as it ticks up one more step.

FIFTY-EIGHT

I kneel down next to Dylan. His eyelids flutter, and he looks like he's falling in and out of consciousness.

'Come on, Dyl.' I slap him lightly round the cheek. 'You're not done yet, you gotta get up.'

'I'm not going anywhere,' Dylan croaks.

With one last effort, he pulls himself off the ground, but keels over again just as quickly. I sit him up and lean him against the railings.

'Just hold on.' I scramble around for my phone. 'I'm calling an ambulance. You'll be okay.'

He shakes his head slowly.

'How did you end up here?' I ask him. 'I've been calling and texting you all week.'

He rummages in his jeans pocket for a second and then pulls out a brick-shaped black Nokia phone, like the one my mum used to have when I was a kid.

'I don't think this thing can get WhatsApp.'

I look at him, confused.

He smiles, and I think he's going to laugh, but instead, he just coughs up a pool of thick, viscous blood.

'Got rid of my phone. Bought a shitty old Nokia off eBay. Didn't want anything to do with the group chat or ShowMe or any of that. Mum freaked out after you found Esme. I paid them back the money and they sold up. Moved down to Fareham, and I went with them. Saw you on the news, got the first train back to Crowhurst. Turned up at Flat Four, and that bastard there was waiting for me. Tied me up, locked me in the boot of his car. Brought me here and dressed me in this stupid costume.'

So that's why Fast Forward was boarded up.

'But I saw the DNA story on Surreywide.com,' I say. 'It really was Peter Doyle's body after all.'

'I was sick of living a lie… living in fear that someone else would find out who my dad was. Finally got up the courage to talk to Mum about it all. I had to know for sure, so we went to Morris, told him Peter was my dad, and they were able to match my DNA to the body they pulled from the river.'

He turns to look at me, his eyes aching with pain. I take his hands in mine and try to haul him up.

'Kirby, it's no good, I can't… There's something you need to do… You still got ShowMe on here?'

I nod.

'Start recording,' he says.

'Really?' I pant. 'You want to preserve *this* moment for all of posterity?'

'You have to show everyone what really happened here. We can't let that be the story.' He nods his head towards the stack of freshly printed newspapers.

I lift my phone, but something stops me as I go to load up ShowMe.

'I can't do it,' I tell him.

'You can, Kirby, you have to.'

'No,' I say. 'A story is only as trustworthy as the person telling it. I lied to this town, I lied to Morris. Hell, I lied to everybody in the country. They won't trust me, and I can't blame them. But they'll trust you, Dyl. It's got to be you.'

He goes to protest, but he can see in my face, I'm not in the mood to argue.

'Okay,' he grunts. 'Start recording.'

I point the phone at him, and press record. Dylan focuses his attention on the camera.

'It was Trevor Phillips,' he coughs. 'Trevor was the Crowhurst Killer, not Peter. He killed those people thirty years ago, and he killed my friends tonight.'

I go to lower my phone, but Dylan holds up his hand.

'Wait,' he stutters. 'Keep recording. There's something else. We need to tell everyone what really happened that day on Staker Point, okay? Like you always said we should. Esme Goodwin faked her disappearance. But we found her hiding in the old caravan up there. Kirby wanted to tell the truth, but Esme knew… she knew that my dad was Peter Doyle. She was going to broadcast it to everyone. I tried to stop her, and… she fell. I pushed her. I didn't mean for her to fall, but I should never… It was my fault. I'm sorry…'

I stop the recording, because his eyes have closed.

'Dylan?' I place my hand on his face. I think I'm crying, but it might be the sweat dripping from my forehead into my eyes. 'Dylan? Hey, wake up. Please. Please.'

He doesn't reply.

'Come on,' I beg, shaking his shoulder, but he remains horribly still. I really am crying now. 'You know, I finally came up with a nickname for you. Don't you want to know it? Don't you…'

I trail off. It's too late.

He's gone.

Wiping my tears with my sleeve, I stand up and close the ShowMe app. I won't be needing it. Instead, I find 'Morris' in my contacts, and send him the video.

EPILOGUE

Dear Ms Cornell,

Hopefully this is the correct email for you.

Further to our previous email, we are keen to move forward with the development of *As The Crow Lies* as a multi-part documentary and have potential interest from several major streaming services, including Netflix and Amazon, with Apple also expressing interest.

We've also secured interviews with Charlotte Goodwin, Robert Morris and Frank Garrett, and filming permissions at various locations around Crowhurst. We hope to begin production later this year.

Once again, we would very much like to have you on board with this exciting project, both as a contributor and consultant. Please see the attached document for remuneration details, which I hope will be to your satisfaction.

Regards,
Mark Draper,
Nightlite Productions Ltd

I'm walking down Crowhurst high street when the email pops into my inbox. It's actually the fifth email I've got from Mark and his crew at Nightlite Productions, offering me, it's fair to say, quite a lot of money for a consultant role on their new documentary – a dream gig as a proper, national journalist. So far, I haven't replied to a single one. I'll never forget the Deadbeats, but I'm not sure this is the way I want to honour their memory.

Of course, all the national papers picked up the story, and ironically enough, Crowhurst is more famous than it ever was. The last three months have been filled with endless police interviews and many, many hysterical phone calls to my mother. Not to mention funerals.

I've just put down the deposit and first month's rent on the world's tiniest studio flat, just outside London, but not far from Mum. And I've got a new job, working at a theatre. I'm even going to start doing acting classes there in the evening. I don't know how that's going to work out, but I do know that, this time, I will definitely be trying my best (and yes, don't worry, I will always, always be a hot mess).

As for ShowMe, you won't be shocked to hear I've deleted my account. Likes and follows are great, but I'm going to try and get my validation from a different source from now on: me. Winnie the Pooh was right – I just have to believe in myself a little bit.

Eventually, I pass the intersection with Courtney Road, and without thinking, I walk down towards Stewart Heights, or what's left of it. It's the first time I've been back since that night. I feel like part of me needs to see it, not that there's much to actually see, as it's covered with scaffolding and safety barriers. It's being turned into a Pret A Manger, apparently, and I've heard the residents of Courtney Street are absolutely thrilled.

I continue walking until I get to Crowhurst station, where I'm just in time for the once-a-day train to London. Once I've found the quiet carriage, and settled down with my coffee, I open the email from Nightlite and tap out a reply.

Clare Cornell is out of the office. She has limited access to emails but will reply when she returns.

It's true, there are three sides to every story, but I don't think anyone really needs to hear any more of mine.

I press send on the email, and my phone makes that satisfying little whishy sound. But as I'm about to stuff it back in my bag, it beeps again, this time with a WhatsApp notification.

You've been added to 'Fiona's Hen Do Spectacular'

136 Group Members

I smile, click on the options tab, select 'disable notifications' and stick my phone back in my pocket. Then I turn, rest my head on the cool glass of the train window, and watch the countryside rush by.

ACKNOWLEDGEMENTS

Thank you for reading this book, I hope you liked it.

I would also like to thank:

Danielle, I couldn't have done it without you.

My amazing agent, James Wills.

My fantastic editor, Peyton Stableford.

Rachel Richardson, Victoria Sautter, Annie Ku, Helena Maybery and everyone at Watson, Little.

Polly Grice, Zoe Giles and everyone at Head of Zeus.

James Melia, Sophie Normil, Lucy Nalen and everyone at Gallery Books.

Sue Gibbs and everyone at Heyday.

My family – Linda, Kenneth, Ewan, Ben, Laura, Uxue, Alex and Amaia.

My friends – Becks Dawkins, Laura Bassett, Elliot Stubbs, Dan Markson, Sian Drinkwater, Dean Weston, Amber Harwood, Nick Harding, Tom Scully, Russell Winborn and Alex Buckland.

Everyone on the group chats – The Sherlocks, The Dudes, The Crumpets, Workaholics Anonymous, Katfans, Sitcoms, Movies Please Darleengs, Chilton Family, Twisters 2 on 20, Bob Esponja, Rocketvan Dweebs, Spookie Doughnuts, Will Luke Delete This?, Freedom Croissants and Chilton Brothers.

Early readers – Helen Wright, Rosie Mullender, Lucy Rainer and Vicki Laycock.

And Britney Spears, Chris Morgan, David Blackmore, Kirby (RIP total legend), Bucky, Binx, Prue, Orange Scraggles, Evil Prue, Coco and Sheba.

L.M. Chilton has left the chat.

Read on for a preview
of the debut thriller from

L.M. CHILTON

DON'T
SWIPE
RIGHT

ONE

I've done some bad things.

I don't mean your everyday, run-of-the-mill misdemeanours. Listen, I'll freely admit I've got at least two more credit cards than I need, a mild crisp addiction and I really, really need to work on my core. No, I'm talking about the *truly* awful things, the ones you'd like to bury so deep that you can pretend they never actually happened.

Rough estimate, I'd say I'd done, maybe fourteen things, total, that Mary Berry would raise a concerned eyebrow at. But out of all of them, I'd say the *second* worst thing I'd ever done was currently unfolding right in front of me: my best friend's hen do, a.k.a. the hen do from hell (I say hell, but I was pretty sure even the devil had never been forced to drink Bellinis out of penis-shaped straws at 8.30 p.m. in Cameo's on a Thursday evening).

And, plot twist, as maid of honour, it was totally my own fault. My excellent plans for karaoke and Chinese food had been deemed 'untraditional' by Sarah's old school-mates, as if dressing in T-shirts emblazoned with the badly photoshopped face of the groom was what Henry VIII had envisioned when he invented hen dos (I'm assuming he had something to do with it along the line). So, this was what I'd come up with instead, and it was currently dying on its arse.

'Everyone! Time for Mr and Mrs!' shouted Amy (I was pretty sure her name was Amy, but it could equally well have been Helen or Anne. Or Daisy).

The six of us were sitting awkwardly around an overly shiny table in one of the U-shaped booths that surrounded Cameo's (currently very empty) light-up dance floor. It was too early to be busy, and we pretty much had the place to ourselves, save for a couple of businessmen at the bar, who looked about two vodka and Red Bulls away from wrapping their ties around their heads and attempting the haka.

'So... question one, what is Richard's shoe size?' Amy/ Helen/Anne/Daisy asked.

I closed my eyes and sank into the faux-leather, hoping it would envelop me.

'Fuck knows,' Sarah slurred as she fiddled with the Bride-to-be sash that hung around her shoulders, her face turning a ripe shade of beetroot. 'Ask me something dirtier!'

'Okay, umm...' Amy (probably) said, frantically looking down the list of questions for something suitably risqué before giving up. 'Err, what's his favourite position in bed?'

I couldn't take any more of this. As the group groaned in unison into their Bellinis, I pulled myself out of my seat and took slow steps backwards into the clouds of dry ice that billowed up from the dance floor. Guided by the neon lights that spelled out 'Create your own adventure' across the wall, I made my way to the sanctuary of the bathrooms, praying someone had dug an escape tunnel behind the condom machine.

Once there, I found an empty stall, nudged the toilet seat closed with my foot and sat down. As the thumping bass of the generic house music faded to a dull thud, I pulled my phone out and opened Connector, the dating app *du jour* that was either: a) thwarting any chance I had of a sensible post-break-up recovery, or b) providing a useful distraction from my increasingly dubious life choices, depending on who you listened to.

After a good ten minutes of swiping through the endless stream of almost identical men looking far too fresh after climbing Machu Picchu, I was interrupted by the sound of the bathroom door swinging open. Seconds later, I heard Sarah's voice echoing off the tiles.

'Gwen! Are you hiding in here? You're going to miss Pin the Cock on the Groom!'

'Shit,' I mouthed, quickly stuffing the phone back in my bag and poking my head out from the stall to see Sarah standing in the middle of the bathroom holding two plastic champagne flutes.

'Ah, there you are,' she said, handing one to me. 'Please tell me you've not been sat in there playing on dating apps again?'

'No, just reading the graffiti,' I lied.

Sarah looked at me the same way people look at a really cute puppy that's peed on the floor.

'I know what this is about,' she said, shaking her head and smiling sadly. 'I was worried all this might be a bit much for you. It's only been a couple of months since, well, you know. You don't have to stay if you don't want to…'

'What, and miss sticking a cardboard penis on a picture of your naked fiancé? No way! I mean, I'd only be doing the exact same thing at home anyway.'

'Gwen,' Sarah sighed. 'You can drop the act with me. It's okay to be upset about Noah, you don't have to—'

'I keep telling you, it's fine, I'm fine, really, everything is *fine*,' I said.

Usually, I found that if I repeated the word fine often enough, I could at least convince myself that everything would be, well, you know, fine.

'Okay, well, good, I guess,' she said. 'Come on then, I need you out there, I'm getting totally mullered at Mr and Mrs.'

'I'm not surprised,' I said, hopping up onto the bank of sinks so I was at her eye level. Sarah was a good three inches taller than me, even without the block heels. 'Sar, are you really sure about all this?'

'The hen night?' Sarah said. 'No, not really, it's awful, but you said Flares wouldn't let us in again after you—'

'No, no, not the hen. I mean, are you sure about *this*.' I pointed to her neon-pink bride-to-be sash. 'The wedding, Richard...'

'Oh for God's sake, not this again.' She rolled her eyes. 'I know you and Richard aren't exactly BFFs, but you don't know him that well yet—'

'Do you?' I interrupted.

After some bad experiences with dodgy boyfriends at uni, Sarah had mastered the art of spotting red flags, immediately jettisoning any man who showed even the slightest indication of being a tosspot. That's why I'd been surprised when she fell for Richard so quickly. While there was nothing intrinsically wrong with him, beyond his obvious good looks and trust fund, there was nothing very right with him either. I guessed that's what she liked about him – he was completely average. Their romance had snowballed since meeting (in real life, just like our grandparents used to!) at a work conference last summer. Shortly afterwards, Richard had surprised her during a hike up some random hill with a ring secreted in one of the many, many pockets boasted by his favourite cagoule.

And now, six months later, Sarah was about to move out of our shared flat, leaving me to face the horrors of singledom without her. And that was absolutely fine. I was totally, totally okay with it and anyone who suggested otherwise didn't know me very well *at all*.

'We may not have been together long, but I do know he's one of the good ones,' Sarah said. 'And God knows there's not many of those around. So I would love it if you two at least tried to get along.'

I looked down at my scruffy Converse. As I opened my mouth to say something, a telltale beep rang out from the depths of my bag, cutting me off. Sarah's eyes swivelled towards it like a trained sniper.

'I knew it!' she cried as I reached for my phone. 'You *have* been swiping! Can you leave that thing alone for just one evening? This is supposed to be the best night of my life!'

'Um, isn't that the wedding night?'

'No, that's the second best. The best night,' she said slowly, taking my wrist and pulling it gently from my bag, 'is dancing 'til two a.m. with your closest friend in Eastbourne's second worst club and getting pissed on champagne.'

'Hun, this is not champagne,' I said, waving my plastic flute at her.

'Whatever.' Sarah released my wrist. 'It's the end of an era, right? Sar and Gwen, one last night on the town before I move out. That's just as important to me as the big day.'

'Well then, you really should straighten your tiara, mate, it's all wonky.'

As Sarah turned back towards the bathroom mirror to fix her tiara, I stole the chance to reach into my bag again. That familiar beep only meant one thing: I had a new Connector message, and I was insanely curious to see who it was. But just as my fingers curled around my phone, I heard Sarah exhale loudly, like the air being let out of a tyre.

'For Christ's sake, Gwen, have you forgotten how mirrors work? I can see you!' she snapped. 'Give me that thing!'

'Fine!' I sighed, holding the phone out for her between my thumb and forefinger. 'It's your wedding photos that will look asymmetrical if I don't find a plus-one before next week.'

The wedding was, predictably, on Valentine's Day.

'If it's going to be a dickhead off this thing,' she said, putting down her glass and plucking the phone from my hand, 'I'd rather you didn't bring anyone.'

'Hey, come on, they're not all bad,' I cried.

'Really? What about that guy last week who used hand sanitiser instead of deodorant?'

'Well, at least he was resourceful,' I offered. 'And at least I'm trying to get back out there. It's not easy, you know. We can't all magically bump into the love of our lives in a conference centre in Milton Keynes.'

'The problem isn't *you*,' Sarah said. 'The problem is, this app is chock-full of absolute bellends.'

As if to prove it, she began poking at the screen with her index finger, like a grandmother trying to choose a chocolate biscuit from a selection box.

'See what I mean? They all look like serial killers,' she said.

'Woah, woah, slow down!' I cried as she abstractly swiped left and right through about twenty profiles. 'You're missing some real potential there!'

Suddenly the phone beeped again.

'Oh look, it says you got a match.' Sarah sighed.

'Gimme that!' I squealed, snatching the phone from her.

I scanned the app frantically, terrified to see who she'd accidentally matched me with. But the image on the screen was surprisingly pleasant. Dirty blond with dark eyebrows, 'Parker, 34, Data Analyst from Eastbourne' had an almost feminine face that made him quite striking.

'Likes going out and staying in, travelling, movies and roasts on a Sunday,' I read out loud.

'And, oh, works in fucking IT, obviously,' Sarah said, looking over my shoulder.

'Well, nobody's perfect.' I shrugged. 'Look, it says here he has a good sense of humour, doesn't take himself too seriously and, as you can see from the excellent selection of photos, he really enjoys laughing in various pubs with two to three different mates.'

'Is there an "unmatch" option?' Sarah said, miming sticking a finger down her throat.

'Well, I could block him, but…'

'Good, and when that's done, turn that thing off and come back to the table.'

When she saw me wavering, her face softened for a second, and she placed her hand on my shoulder.

'You promised to lay off the dating, remember, at least 'til after the wedding. All these silly boys won't replace Noah, you know?'

I bristled. My ex was the last person I wanted to think about right now. I sighed and put my phone face down on the sink.

'Oh, and listen, don't hate me, but Richard's on his way,' Sarah added matter-of-factly.

I flung my head back and groaned dramatically. If there was one thing that could make this night even lamer than it already was, it was Richard.

'Are you fricking kidding me, Sar?' I whined. 'Is that even allowed? What happened to this being a traditional hen night?'

'Oh come on, Gwen, I think it stopped being traditional the second Daisy inhaled the willy-shaped helium balloon.'

'Dammit, I knew her name was Daisy!' I hissed to myself.

'Don't stress, he won't cramp our style,' Sarah continued. 'He can just sit quietly in the corner until we finish the games.'

'Great, can it be the other corner?'

'Gwen! Be nice. It's the twenty-first century, everyone is having a "Sten Do" now. And it's a good chance for him to meet the girls before the wedding. Please try, just for me, okay?'

I folded my arms sulkily. 'Fine. Just gimme a minute to freshen up, will you?'

'You're not going to message that Parker guy, are you?' Sarah said, looking at me suspiciously.

'Definitely 100 per cent not,' I said.

'Smart,' she said, checking her tiara one more time before turning to leave.

'Hey, Sar, wait a sec,' I called out.

'Yeah?' she said, looking back over her shoulder.

'Twelve,' I said.

'What?'

'Richard's shoe size,' I said. 'It's twelve.'

'Shit, of course,' Sarah said. 'Thanks! How do you even know that?'

'Cos I wrote the quiz, you idiot,' I told her. 'Now get out of here.'

And with that, she blew me a kiss and walked out, leaving me sitting on the bank of sinks staring at my distorted reflection in the stainless-steel tap. I might have been stranded in singledom, but I desperately wanted Sarah to have the wedding of her dreams and never, ever have to navigate her way through the minefield of flotsam on a dumb dating app to find a halfway decent human being to share her life with. Deep down though, something about this particular 'happily ever after' didn't feel so, well, *happy*.

I hopped down from the sinks in an attempt to shake the feeling off. As I went to stuff my phone back in my bag, I caught a glimpse of Parker's profile, still open on the screen. I paused, my finger hovering over his face. With my other hand, I grabbed my glass and downed the last of the warm prosecco.

'Fuck it,' I thought, as I typed out a message.

Gwen: wyd? currently stuck at the hen do from hell, fancy giving me an excuse to get out of here?

ABOUT THE AUTHOR

L.M. CHILTON is a journalist with fifteen years' experience working on TV shows for the BBC, ITV and Channel 4 in the UK, as well as writing columns for magazines such as *Cosmopolitan* and *Glamour*, and reporting for national newspapers across the world, everywhere from Doncaster to Delhi. He lives in London, procrastinating. *Don't Swipe Right*, his debut novel, was published by Head of Zeus in 2023.